Blessings of Mossy Creek

A collective novel featuring the voices of

Sandra Chastain, Virginia Ellis,
Debra Dixon and Martha Shields

with

Susan Goggins, Lillian Richey, Gayle Trent,
Rita Herron, Karen White, Berta Platas,
Martha Kirkland, Chloe Mitchell and Missy Tippens

Smyrna, Georgia

BelleBooks, Inc.

ISBN 0-9673035-5-9

Blessings of Mossy Creek

Published by:
BelleBooks, Inc. · P.O. Box 67 · Smyrna, GA 30081
We at BelleBooks enjoy hearing from readers. You can contact us at the address above or at BelleBooks@BelleBooks.com

Visit our website— **www.BelleBooks.com**

First Edition June 2004

10 9 8 7 6 5 4 3 2 1

Cover art: Laura Austin & Cindy Chadwick
Cover design: Martha Shields
Mossy Creek map: Dino Fritz

Mossy Creek Hometown Series

"Delightful."   — Georgia Former First Lady Marie Barnes

"Mitford meets Mayberry in the first book of this innovative and warmhearted new series from BelleBooks."
    — *The Cleveland Daily Banner, Cleveland, Tennessee*

"MOSSY CREEK is as much fun as a cousin reunion; like sipping ice cold lemonade on a hot summer's afternoon. Hire me a moving van, it's the kind of town where everyone wishes they could live."
    — Debbie Macomber, *NYT bestselling author*

"A fast, funny, and folksy read. Enjoy!"
    — Lois Battle, *acclaimed author of Storyville,*
    Bed and Breakfast, and
    The Florabama Ladies Sewing Club And Auxiliary

"SUMMER IN MOSSY CREEK takes you to a land that time has not forgotten, but has embraced."
    — Jackie K Cooper, *WMAC-AM, Macon, Georgia*

"Colorfully and cleverly portrayed. A wholesome story."
    — Harriet Klausner, *Amazon.com's top reviewer*

"The characters and kinships of MOSSY CREEK are quirky, hilarious and all too human. This story reads like a delicious, meringue-covered slice of home. I couldn't get enough."
    — Pamela Morsi, *USA Today bestselling author*

"I want to live in Mossy Creek."
    — Astrid Kinn, *Romance Reviews Today*

"These southern belle authors have done it again, even better this time."
    — Bob Spear, *Heartland Reviews*

"The stories that make up the Mossy Creek anthologies should be savored—they make readers hunger for more."
    — Jill M. Smith, *Romantic Times Magazine*

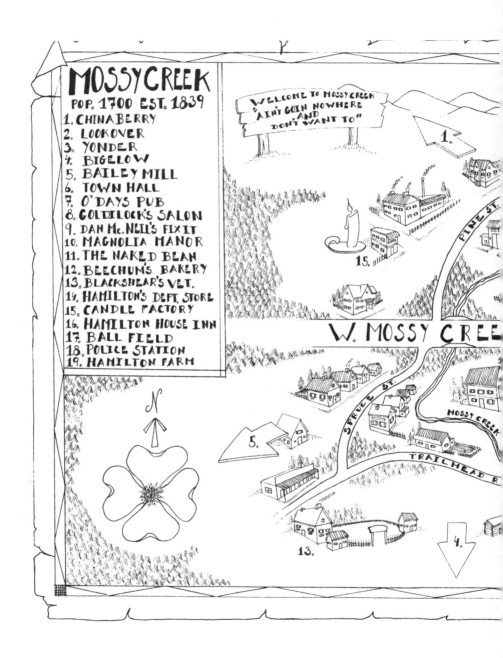

MOSSY CREEK
POP. 1700 EST. 1839

1. CHINABERRY
2. LOOKOVER
3. YONDER
4. BIGELOW
5. BAILEY MILL
6. TOWN HALL
7. O'DAYS PUB
8. GOLDILOCK'S SALON
9. DAN Mc.NEIL'S FIXIT
10. MAGNOLIA MANOR
11. THE NAKED BEAN
12. BEECHUM'S BAKERY
13. BLACKSHEAR'S VET.
14. HAMILTON'S DEPT. STORE
15. CANDLE FACTORY
16. HAMILTON HOUSE INN
17. BALL FIELD
18. POLICE STATION
19. HAMILTON FARM

WELCOME TO MOSSY CREEK
"AIN'T GOIN NOWHERE
— AND
DON'T WANT TO"

W. MOSSY CREE

PINE ST.

MOSSY CREEK

SPRUCE ST.

TRAILHEAD R

N

Blessings of Mossy Creek

Odd Places & Beautiful Spaces
A Guide to the Towns & Attractions of the South

Mossy Creek, Georgia

Don't miss this quirky, historic Southern village on your drive through the Appalachian mountains! Located in a breathtaking valley two hours north of Atlanta, the town (1,700 residents, established 1839) is completely encircled by its lovely namesake creek. Picturesque bridges span the creek around the turn-of-the-century town square like charms on a bracelet. Be sure to arrive via the scenic route along South Bigelow Road, the main two-lane from Bigelow, Mossy Creek's big-sister city, hometown of Georgia governor Ham Bigelow. (Don't be surprised if you overhear "Creekites" in heated debate about Ham, who's the nephew of longtime Mossy Creek mayor Ida Walker.) You'll know when you reach the Mossy Creek town limits — just look for the charming, whitewashed grain silo by the road at Mayor Walker's farm. Painted with the town's pioneer motto — *Ain't goin' nowhere, and don't want to* — the silo makes a great photo opportunity, and the motto perfectly sums up the stubborn (but not unfriendly) free spirits you'll find everywhere in what the chamber of commerce calls "Greater Mossy Creek," which includes the outlying mountain communities of Bailey Mill, Over, Yonder, and Chinaberry.

Lodging, Dining, And Attractions: Shop and eat to your heart's delight around the town's shady square. Don't miss *Mama's All You Can Eat Café*, *Beechum's Bakery* (be sure to say hello to Bob, the "flying" Chihuahua), *The Naked Bean* coffee shop, *O'Day's Pub*, the *Bubba Rice Diner*, *Hamilton's Department Store* (featuring the origami napkin work of local beauty queen Josie McClure), *Hamilton House Inn*, the *I Probably Got It* store, *Moonheart's Natural Living*, and *Mossy Creek Books And What-Nots*. Drop by town hall for a look at the notorious Ten-Cent Gypsy (a carnival booth at the heart of a dramatic Creekite mystery) and stop by the town jail for an update on local shenanigans courtesy of Officer Sandy Crane, who calls herself "the gal in front of the man behind the badge," Mossy Creek Police Chief Amos Royden (recently featured in *Georgia Today Magazine* as the sexiest bachelor police chief in the state). And don't forget to pop into the newspaper offices of the *Mossy Creek Gazette*, where you can get the latest event news from Katie Bell, local gossip columnist *extraordinaire*.

As Katie Bell likes to say, "In Mossy Creek, I can't make up better stories than the truth."

A Who's Who of Mossy Creek

Ida Hamilton Walker — Mayor. Devoted to her town. Menopausal. Gorgeous. Trouble.

Amos Royden — Ida's much-younger police chief. Trying hard not to be irresistible.

Katie Bell — Gossip columnist and town sleuth. Watch out!

Sue Ora Salter Bigelow — Newspaper publisher. Fighting the Salter romance curse.

Jasmine Beleau — Fashion consultant. Her secret past is a shocker.

Josie McClure — Failed beauty queen. Budding interior designer. Talent: origami napkin folding.

Harry Rutherford — Josie's mountain man and fiance. PhD and local version of Bigfoot.

Hamilton Bigelow — Governor of Georgia. Ida's nephew. A typical politician. 'Nuff said?

Win Allen — aka Chef Bubba Rice — The *Emeril* of Mossy Creek.

Ingrid Beechum — Baker. Doting surrogate grandma. Owns Bob, the famous "flying" Chihuahua.

Hank and Casey Blackshear — Run the veterinary clinic. Most inspirational local love story.

Sandy Crane — Amos's scrappy dispatcher. If Dolly Parton and Barney Fife had a daughter. . .

Ed Brady — Farmer. Santa. The toughest, sweetest old man in town.

Rainey Cecil — Owns Goldilocks Hair, Nail and Tanning Salon. Bringing big hair to a whole new generation.

Michael Conners — Sexy Chicago Yankee whose Irish pub lures dart-tourney sharks.

Tag Garner — Ex pro-footballer turned sculptor. Good natured when bitten by old ladies.

Maggie Hart — Herbalist. Tag's main squeeze. Daughter of old lady who bit him.

Millicent Hart — See above. Town kleptomaniac. Sorry she bit Tag. Sort of.

Del Jackson — Hunky retired lieutenant colonel. Owns Ida's heart. For now. See Amos.

Bert Lyman — The voice of Mossy Creek. Owner, manager, DJ of WMOS Radio.

Opal Suggs — Retired teacher who adopts needy kids. Talks to her sisters' ghosts who foretell NASCAR winners.

Dwight Truman — Chamber president. Insurance tycoon. Ida's nemesis, along with Ham Bigelow. Weasel.

Swee Purla — Evil interior design maven. Makes even Martha Stewart look wimpy.

Lady Victoria Salter Stanhope
The Cliffs
Seaward Road
St. Ives, Cornwall, TR3 7PJ
United Kingdom

Hey, Vick!

Hope things are good along the white
cliffs of Dover. Over here, across the
ocean, we're finally done with summer
and resting up before the holidays.
Some of the local churches have come
to me with an idea to publish
inspirational stories in the *Gazette*
each week -- you know, to get us all
in the spirit of Thanksgiving,
Christmas, Hanukkah, and Kwanzaa. When
it comes to inspiration, Creekites are
eager to share. I'll send you some of
my columns and the stories people tell
me. I plan to publish them in the
paper under the title *Blessings Of
Mossy Creek*. That sounds so much
better than *More Juicy Gossip in Mossy
Creek*, doesn't it? As usual, I expect
to do some snooping and report more
than people intend to admit. We have a
lot of little dramas going on around

here this fall. I'm not leaving *them*
out of the mix.

You'll like the story I'm including
with this note. I should have
mentioned it over the summer -- it
took place back in June -- but there
was so much going on that I just never
got around to telling you. I'm also
including the article I ran in my Bell
Ringer column afterwards. I know you
love wedding stories, so enjoy!

Blessings and good gossip
to you and yours,
Katie

P.S. I can't believe I almost forgot
to tell you! I've been nominated for a
newspaper award! I'm off to New York!
Watch out, Big Apple!

In Mossy Creek, a wedding is a community affair.

🐾🐾🐾🐾🐾🐾🐾🐾🐾🐾🐾🐾🐾🐾🐾🐾🐾🐾🐾🐾🐾🐾🐾🐾🐾🐾🐾🐾🐾🐾🐾🐾🐾🐾🐾

Harry's Unexpected Blessing
Chapter 1

"Count your blessings!"

Reverend Hollingsworth's benediction was bellowed more than said, and I found myself reeling at the impact. He'd caught me by surprise again. The small, mild-mannered preacher — small, at least, when compared to my six-foot-eight-inch, two-hundred-seventy-pound frame — had another personality when he climbed into the pulpit. Reverend Hollingsworth — "got the Spirit," as Josie's mother, LuLynn McClure, put it, but not when he talked about the damnation side of religion. No, when he spoke about the fires of hell, Reverend Hollingsworth's countenance turned dark and woeful. Only when he spoke on the joys of God's love did excitement overwhelm him. His voice shook with emotion, and he pounded his fist and Bible on the pulpit. Then he climbed down and greeted everyone at the front door with a smile and voice as soft as an angel.

He was an interesting dichotomy.

I'd never taken much stock in organized religion. The God of my science resided in the flora and fauna of the North Georgia mountains where I did my research. But ever since Josie said "yes" to my proposal of marriage, she'd been coaxing me to the hundred-year-old oak pews of the Mossy Creek Presbyterian Church. And I have to say that, so far, I didn't mind all that much. The experience had proven at worst a little dull, but sometimes most entertaining.

"How many blessings do *you* have?"

The Reverend pointed his bony finger directly at me, it seemed, though I was halfway back and on the very edge of the sanctuary, right under the stained glass window depicting the Apostle John. I knew better than to think I'd been singled out, of course, but for some reason that phrase bored into my consciousness like a black beetle bores into the bark of a red-gum.

Blessings? Me?

There was a time in my life when I would've laughed in anyone's face who talked to me about blessings. A house fire six years ago left me half broken and badly burned across my chest and face. I spent an excruciating year in several hospitals specializing in burn trauma and skin grafts, then spent three even more painful years watching people's reactions to my monster face. Two years ago I built a cabin on Mount Colchik, north of Mossy Creek, and like the monster I was, retreated to my den to conduct my research. My work was the only blessing I had in those dark days. My research was not only conducive to my hiding from the world, it required it.

My Ph.D. in environmental biology had earned me a grant from the Environmental Protection Agency to study the effect of acid rain on the indigenous hardwood trees of the Appalachian Mountains. So I lived like a hermit for two years, sending down to the world the data I collected.

Though I lived high above the world, I existed far below it . . . in a kind of hell. I was at the lowest point in my life, and felt singularly *un*blessed.

Until sunshine walked onto my mountain.

Remembering that day, I slid my arm along the back of the pew, easing Josie against me. She gave me a serenely loving smile and shifted a little closer. A fresh wave of her subtle scent caught me. Mountain laurel. She'd extracted the oil herself from the small white flower that blooms in the early spring, a technique she'd learned from some long-ago Martha Stewart show.

I played idly with a strand of her chestnut brown hair that had escaped the tortoiseshell clip trying to confine it. Thick and straight, Josie's hair reached halfway down her back. She'd threatened to shorten it last summer to a more professional cut to go with her new decorating career, but kept it long when I asked her to. LuLynn called Josie's hair her one beauty, but Josie's mother was wrong. Josie's beauty went deeper than hair or skin. She glowed with beauty that came from her soul.

My wife-to-be was as natural, as unique and as hardy as the mountain laurel that grew on the rocky slopes that had surrounded her all of her life. I knew how I'd lived without her . . . in darkness. And I was certain I never wanted to be without her light again.

Blessings? Josie was *Blessing Incarnate* . . . the only blessing that mattered.

I held her small hand as we stood for the invitation song. After the final *amen*, the congregation meandered toward the door, everyone stopping to talk to everyone else. Except me, of course. Oh, a few of the men shook my hand and mumbled things like, "Nice to see you." But I was a newcomer to Mossy Creek and though I'd been accepted by most of the townspeople, it was a surface acceptance. To be fair, I still had my research to conduct, so I wasn't in town all that much. To use one of Josie's decorating metaphors, I wasn't a pleat in the fabric of the town. I was more like an oddly colored button that hadn't been sewn on yet. Since I still caught a few *what-a-freak* stares now and then, I knew the general citizenry hadn't quite decided if I matched well enough to go to the trouble of threading the needle.

It didn't matter to me, of course, except that it mattered to Josie. Having grown up here, she was woven into the fabric that was Mossy Creek. Though she'd only realized that when she became recognized for her decorating skills, which were now in great demand. That made her happy, so I was happy to stand behind her as she chatted her way out of the church.

Suddenly a heavy hand fell on my shoulder. I glanced around to find Mac Campbell, one of Mossy Creek's best-known lawyers. At six-foot-four, he was also one of the few men in town who came remotely close to matching me in size, with the possible exception of the police chief, Amos Royden, who reached the six-four mark in cowboy boots. Both men could look me in the eye without straining their necks too badly. Mac also had as much education as I did, and I enjoyed talking with him. So I turned with genuine pleasure.

As I did, he grabbed my hand and shook firmly. "How'd the wind treat you, Harry?"

I squeezed his hand in return. A spring storm had blown through several weeks before with straight-line winds of hurricane strength. Mossy Creek hadn't sustained much damage, nestled as it was in a valley, but the wind felled some of the oldest and mightiest trees all over the surrounding mountains, especially toward the top. I'd spent a week clearing a path to my cabin on Mount Colchik, then another cleaning debris off of it and from around it. This was the first time I'd been to town since.

"Lady Luck was sitting on top of my cabin," I said. "A hemlock and an elm were both heading toward my roof, but it looked like they canceled each other out. When I got there, their top branches were enmeshed, holding each other up." I folded my fingers together and spread my elbows over Josie's head to demonstrate.

She glanced up, then turned from her conversation with

Jayne Reynolds, visiting this morning from the Mt. Gilead Methodist Church. Jayne smiled at me, but nestled in her arms, her baby boy, Matthew, stared at me as if he might cry. Josie nodded. "You should've been there, Mac. I've never seen anything like it."

"Well, I'll be . . ." Mac rubbed his chin. "You start cutting on one, they'd both come crashing on your roof. How'd you get them down?"

"I threw a rope around one, then Josie and I pulled them down toward the back."

"Both at the same time . . ." Mac nodded. "Of course. It was the only way. You should've called. I could've helped."

"Mac, that's so sweet!" Josie peered up at me, one eyebrow raised. "I told you to call someone."

Mac's words had taken me aback, but I shrugged them away. Easy to make promises after the fact. "*Someone* is rather vague, Josie." Then, deciding to show her just how much his promises were worth, I turned to Mac. "I'm going to be cutting them up for firewood and lumber. You can help me with that."

"Hey! I can help, too."

The voice came from below, and we all glanced down to find Clay Atwood, the boy whom Mac and his wife, Patty, were in the process of adopting. At nine he was small for his age. From what I'd heard of his early years, that was probably from not having an adequate diet. From what I'd seen since Patty and Mac had taken him in, Clay had a good heart despite the abusive father Chief Royden had taken him away from.

Josie spoke first. "Of course you can help, Clay." She ruffled his brown hair. "But you have to leave Dog at home, I'm afraid."

Mac and Patty had inherited a mutt named *Dog* along with Clay. The boy raised disbelieving eyes to his future father. "But Dog could —"

"Josie's right," Mac placed large hands on the boy's thin shoulders. "Dog has to stay home with Maddie and Butler. They're his canine buddies."

"It's not that we don't love Dog." Josie sat back down on the pew so she was at Clay's level. "But he might wander off to go exploring, and he'd probably get lost."

And eaten by a bear, I thought, but held my tongue. I thought children should grow up aware of the dangers of the mountains, but Josie had gently scolded me more than once for forcing reality on children. I had to admit I tended to go into far more graphic, scientific explanations of those dangers than a child could comprehend and, as Josie told me, I had to practice restraint for our own future children.

The possibility of me fathering a little girl just like her mother made me smile. More blessings to come.

"Awwright," Clay agreed reluctantly, making me realize that daydreams had caused me to miss more explanations of why his dog couldn't help clear the trees. Not that I would need to remember the exchange. It wasn't as if Clay and his father would actually be helping me. After all, Mac was just making polite conversation.

"Josie!" LuLynn called from the last pew in the church. "Remember I've got a hen in the oven."

"All right, Mama. We're coming." Josie gave Clay a brief kiss, then rose to shake Mac's hand. "We appreciate your offer to help, Mac." She glanced around him. "Where's Patty?"

He pointed down toward the church basement. "She's at a meeting to plan this summer's Vacation Bible School."

Josie nodded, looking around. "Jayne's disappeared. She must've taken Matthew outside. Tell Patty hello. Y'all are coming to the wedding, aren't you?"

"Are you kidding? It's the event of the year."

Josie waved goodbye as she headed for her mother. "Hope you're not allergic to roses, Mac!"

Once Josie was out of earshot, Mac glanced at me. I

shrugged. "Josie's second favorite flower, since laurel fin-ishes blooming too soon for a June wedding. LuLynn had Mrs. Townsend order twenty dozen white roses from Atlanta."

Mac paused. "Eugenia Townsend? LuLynn ordered flow-ers from Mossy Creek Flowers and Gifts?"

I didn't like the amazed look on his face. "Josie insisted on buying as much as possible of all that wedding parapher-nalia in Mossy Creek. Something wrong with Eugenia at Mossy Creek Flowers and Gifts?"

"No, no," Mac said quickly. "I'm sure Eugenia's fine... now. Haven't heard her mention any problems in a long time. It happened over twenty years ago, after all."

"What happened over —"

"Harold!" LuLynn called. She always insisted on using my formal Christian name. "Do you *like* dried-out chicken?"

Dried-out chicken was less important to me than the possibility that something might occur to make Josie's wed-ding day less than perfect. "Mac, what happened over twenty years ago?"

"Harold!!!"

"Nothing that amounts to a hen's feather," Mac assured me. "Eugenia wouldn't deliberately sabotage an order as lucrative as this one must be. Besides the money, the town would never forgive her. No. Everything's fine. I'm sure."

I didn't like the word *sabotage*. "Mac —"

"Harold, we're leaving." LuLynn crossed her arms over her chest. Josie had already escaped outside. "Do you want to *walk* the five miles to Bailey Mill?"

Despite her pretensions and predilection toward snob-bery, I liked my soon-to-be mother-in-law. I didn't want to make her mad at me six days before I was going to marry her daughter.

I backed toward the church door, but kept my gaze locked into Mac's. "About Eugenia Townsend. You're sure?"

Mac nodded and waved me on. "The worst Eugenia would do is overcharge LuLynn, but that will only make LuLynn think she's getting the best."

Since that was true, I allowed myself to be mollified. I'd heard from more than one source that nobody in town, except Katie Bell, the official queen of gossip, knew more than Mac about Creekites' business. Not that he was a busybody. He represented nearly all of them in legal matters.

"Call me after your honeymoon about cutting up those trees," Mac said. "I'm serious."

I waved an acknowledgement — it's always better not to let people know you expect the least of them — and walked out of the church. I blinked as I hit spring sunshine and felt my hand grabbed in a firm shake.

By now I knew the steel of that grip. "Reverend Hollingsworth. Enjoyed the sermon."

"Why, thank you, Dr. Rutherford." He always seemed immensely pleased to be complimented, making you feel as if you were special because you're the only one who'd noticed. "I enjoyed writing that one."

"And delivering it," I couldn't help adding.

He smiled softly. "Yes. I do love a good, rousing topic."

"Harold!"

"I'm coming, *LuLynn*!" I knew she didn't like me calling her by her first name in public, especially at church, but since she was thirty-eight — only five years older than me — I couldn't bring myself to call her *Mother*. I nodded to the Reverend. "See you at the rehearsal on Friday."

"Harold, where is Josie?" LuLynn called. "Isn't she with you?"

"I thought she was out here with you."

I glanced toward the emptying parking lot, but didn't spot my beloved. Scanning the churchyard, I finally caught a glimpse of her dark red dress under the spreading branches of a white oak that had been there as long as the church. She and Eleanor Abercrombie were bent over the roses growing on the picket fence that lined the bank of the east branch of Mossy Creek.

With a fond smile, I made my way over. Josie had grown up tending roses with her Grandma McClure. Since her grandmother was now deceased, Josie never lost an opportunity to milk advice from those with more experience. Eleanor was a charter member of the Mossy Creek Garden Club.

"*Tsk, tsk.*" The older woman shook her head over a rose branch trying to reach the lowest limb of the oak. "This isn't the way to train a climbing rose. It'll never get sun up there." She pulled at the thorny limb as I approached and coaxed it down along the fence. "There, there. That's it, sweetie. Join your sisters."

Josie helped by pulling it between two boards of the fence. "Why aren't there any blooms?"

"The prom at Bigelow High last night, dearie. Teenagers cleaned out every rose on every unguarded bush in the county. I doubt there's a single rose left in Mossy Creek *or* Bigelow." Mrs. Abercrombie winked as she straightened. "'Cept in private gardens like mine, of course."

"Yours are too valuable to decorate a high school gymnasium." Josie smiled at me absently and sucked on a finger she'd obviously pricked.

Mrs. Abercrombie patted several branches on the climbing rosebush and tsked again. "Look at these yellow leaves. These bushes need some work. Delia Mitchell's been taking care of them for the church. She covets the Bigelow County Rose Trophy, but doesn't want to do what it takes to win it. You can't grow roses and sit on your duff all day."

"No, ma'am. I know," Josie said.

"Roses are like young'uns." Mrs. Abercrombie included

me in her admonition as I took Josie's hand and smoothed a drop of blood off her finger. "You might as well learn the truth now, you both about to get hitched, and all." She nodded sagely. "They're like children . . . you got to tend them constantly, or they'll go wild on you."

"No need to worry about that, Mrs. Abercrombie," I said. "Josie's in her rose garden every day, rain or shine, cold snap or heat wave."

"I was taught by one of the best," Josie insisted.

"You were that," Mrs. Abercrombie agreed. "Your Grandma Gladys McClure won the county fair's rose contest eighteen years running, God rest her soul." Mrs. Abercrombie peered toward the parking lot. "And your mama's about to have a conniption over in her *Coupe DeVille.* You'd best get."

Josie gave Mrs. Abercrombie a hug. "I'll try to make it over to your house sometime this week. I'd like to see your Silver Passions while they're peaking." Then she turned to me and slipped her arm through mine as we walked toward LuLynn's Cadillac. "Mrs. Abercrombie always wins the rose competition in the Bigelow County Garden Contest, which is next Saturday afternoon, after the wedding. This year, she has a silver rose that's —"

"Josie McClure," LuLynn yelled, "you going to starve that husband of yours before you even get your apron strings tied around him?"

Josie winced. "She doesn't mean that."

I squeezed her arm. "I know. Don't worry about it."

LuLynn was a dichotomy, too. A homecoming queen whose crowning moment had been snatched away from her over twenty years ago by the bizarre incident that burned down Mossy Creek High during halftime of the big game with Bigelow High, LuLynn helped manage her husband's cattle farm but now was a die-hard fan of Martha Stewart, never caring that the home decorating guru's crown was a bit tarnished. LuLynn had thrown herself into Josie's wedding plans with a vengeance, determined that this wedding would be the envy of every mother of a marriageable-aged daughter in Bigelow County.

Josie was no pushover, though, and had definite ideas about how her wedding should be. So there'd been more than one argument between the bride and the mother-of-the-bride that would've brought down the rafters of any church. Since I'd never heard Josie raise her voice to another living creature, I dragged her up to my cabin on Mount Colchik every time she and her mother verged on new warfare.

But for the moment, peace reigned. Josie and LuLynn discussed Mrs. Abercrombie's roses as Josie's mostly-silent father, John McClure, drove us to the McClure farm in the Bailey Mill community. There we would feast on LuLynn's roasted chicken at Josie's last Sunday dinner as a single woman.

Josie sighed wistfully. "I wish I could grow roses as wonderful as Eleanor Abercrombie's. I would build my bouquet around a single Silver Passion."

"Wouldn't that be stunning." LuLynn was practically salivating. "Oh, well." She reached into the backseat to pat Josie's knee. "You'll have a Silver Passion rose one day. You've got your Grandma Gladys's touch." It was the kindest thing I'd ever heard LuLynn say to her daughter.

I lifted Josie's hand to my lips. "I'll see if I can buy some of them from Mrs. Abercrombie."

The car suddenly went silent. Even the engine seemed to hesitate. Then the entire McClure clan erupted in laughter.

I let it subside to an audible level before I asked, "Not a good idea?"

With a final giggle, Josie placed a kiss on my cheek. "My dear, sweet, naive Harry. You can't buy even *one* of Mrs. Abercrombie's Silver Passions. They're priceless."

The biologist in me begged to differ. "No plant is priceless. Any gardener worth her salt would've made grafts so she can grow more."

"Not by next Sunday," LuLynn said.

"What's next —" Then I remembered. "Some contest, right?"

"Not just *some* contest," Josie said. "The Bigelow County Garden Contest."

"Only the biggest floral competition in the county," LuLynn said. "The rivalry between the Bigelow Garden Club and the Mossy Creek Garden Club is famous. Why, it's been featured in *Southern Living*."

The gospel according to *Southern Living*. LuLynn considered it a supplemental text to her real bible, *Martha Stewart Living*.

"It's especially exciting this year," Josie said. "Geraldine Matthews is Bigelow's biggest threat this year. She has some gorgeous bushes. Why, her Martha Washingtons are as wide as a plate! But Mrs. Abercrombie has developed her Silver Passions for years. They simply take your breath away. I'm certain she'll keep the rose trophy in Mossy Creek. Everyone else in Mossy Creek thinks so, too."

"Of course they do." Then I had to ask, knowing it was a sore subject. "What does everyone in Bigelow think?"

"They —"

"The rose growers down in Bigelow can kiss Eleanor Abercrombie's manure spreader."

John McClure's comments were always succinct, typically colorful, and rare enough that we all stared at him in surprise. Although Bailey Mills was an outlying community from Mossy Creek, its inhabitants considered themselves staunch Creekites and so were dyed-in-the-wool Bigelow despisers.

Josie broke the silence with another giggle. "In other words, we don't care what people in Bigelow think."

"Unless this contest is fixed, Eleanor will win," LuLynn added with absolute certainty. "She always does."

Josie sighed. "So you see, Harry, no amount of money will buy one of Mrs. Abercrombie's roses. I'll have to make do with a white rose from the florists in Atlanta." She smiled and slipped her hand into mine. "But that's okay. I'm getting *you* — the best prize of all. The flowers in the church won't matter."

❦ ❦ ❦

I didn't believe Josie's statement for a single second, because everything else about our wedding was a matter of monumental importance — down to the shade of pink Josie should wear on her fingernails. I had to drag Josie away from her mother several times during the next few days, though she wouldn't let me take her all the way to the cabin. Too many details left to be taken care of.

Thursday was an especially trying day, so I drove Josie into town to visit Eleanor. Mrs. Abercrombie's garden was filled with roses of all hues. Some of them were truly breathtaking, but their real magic was making Josie forget all about the wedding for several hours.

Mrs. Abercrombie's roses reminded me of Mac Campbell's startled face when I mentioned Mossy Creek Flowers and Gifts and his comment about Eugenia Townsend having some reason to exact revenge on Josie because of some nebulous something between Eugenia and LuLynn over twenty years ago. His words nagged at me. I didn't want to tell Josie my suspicions. She would again be disappointed in me for not trusting the people of Mossy Creek to look out for each other.

Surely Josie or LuLynn had checked with Eugenia about their flower order. The thing was, in my field of empirical research I'd learned to leave nothing to chance. I had to check on my own.

I knew something was wrong before the door of Mossy Creek Flowers and Gifts closed behind me early on Friday afternoon. The first clue was the stillness. A flower shop should have been singing with activity with a wedding the next day. This one was as quiet as a church on Monday morning.

The second clue was the sudden pallor on the face of the young woman behind the counter. Josie had introduced us at some Mossy Creek function or other so I knew her reaction was more than could be attributed to the first sight of my scarred face.

Three strides took me to the counter. "Good afternoon. Muriel, isn't it?"

She swallowed. Hard. "Ye... Yes, Dr. Rutherford."

"Call me Harry, please." My tight smile didn't bring color back to Muriel's cheeks. "I came to check on the flowers my fiancée ordered for our wedding tomorrow."

"Flowers?"

"This is a flower shop, isn't it? The only one in Mossy Creek?"

"Ummm... yes. It is." She was stalling.

"Three months ago, my fiancée and her mother ordered flowers for our wedding tomorrow. Twenty dozen white roses, I believe it was."

Muriel dragged her gaze from mine and glanced at the computer sitting to her right.

"Right. Yes. I remember."

"Funny, I don't see a single white rose around the shop.

26

Have they already been delivered to the church?"

I barely heard her soft, "No."

My voice was almost as quiet. "What are you saying, Muriel? The flowers aren't ready yet?"

She backed up a step. "They were never even ordered."

I closed my eyes to better control the rage flowing through me and saw the image of Josie's tear-stained face as she walked down an aisle unadorned with flowers. No way could I let that happen.

I opened my eyes and let my gaze bore into Muriel's. "Eugenia Townsend did this deliberately, didn't she? Because of something that happened between her and LuLynn McClure over twenty years ago."

"I don't know! I was only two-years-old then."

"What was it?" I demanded. "What happened back then?"

"I don't know, exactly. I've only heard things."

"What have you heard?"

"I'll lose my job if I..." She trailed off and sighed. "It was the year that Mossy Creek High School burned down. LuLynn McClure... although she wasn't a McClure yet... was about to be crowned homecoming queen. Mrs. Townsend was first runner-up."

"That's all? Are you saying my bride won't have flowers in the church on her wedding day because LuLynn beat out Mrs. Townsend in some stupid popularity contest two decades ago?"

"Mrs. Townsend claims Mrs. McClure only won the crown because she'd been . . . because she was pregnant by the captain of the football team. Didn't matter that she married him a few months later."

That was the first time I'd heard that gossip, but since Josie had just turned twenty, the math was right. It was no excuse for Eugenia's revenge now, however. "Where is Mrs.

Townsend? I need to have a few words with her."

Muriel shook her head. "You can't. She went to visit her sister up in Chattanooga for the weekend."

"And left you behind to deal with the mess she *deliberately* made."

Muriel's brown eyes teared up. "Tell Josie I'm sorry. I didn't know until this morning, just before Mrs. Townsend left."

I turned and stared blindly out a window at the town square. People walked around as if nothing had happened, as if tomorrow wouldn't be the blackest day of the year.

What was I going to do?

I turned to Muriel. "You can order flowers, can't you?"

"Mrs. Townsend does all the wholesale ordering for the shop..." Her gaze cut to the computer. "But I know where she orders them from."

"Get on the phone. Please. I can't let this happen to Josie."

"I... white roses are a specialty item. We get them from warehouses down in Atlanta. It could take several days."

"Surely they can arrange for overnight delivery. If not, I'll drive down there myself and pick them up."

Muriel stepped over to the keyboard. "I'll ask."

By six o'clock that evening, we'd talked to every floral warehouse in a two hundred mile radius. No one could promise us even a dozen white roses before Monday. It was a weekend in June, the month of weddings, and they were all ordered out.

Every floral avenue exhausted, I staggered back onto the sidewalk. The bright spring sun shed no light on my dark dilemma.

Where could I possibly get white roses in the next eighteen hours?

I wandered around the town square, desperate for a

solution. Shop owners nodded to me as they waved away their last customers or rolled up the sidewalks. Most shops in Mossy Creek closed at 6 p.m., with the exception of the theater and café. Anna Rose Lavender and Beau Belmont were auditioning locals for the summer musical season.

I'd never felt so alone, even at the top of Mount Colchik. Although...

Why was I surprised? Every one of us was alone, ultimately. No matter how much Josie talked about Creekites standing by each other through thick and thin, the people of Mossy Creek weren't any different from people in big cities. Everyone looked out for themselves.

My gaze fell on a bed of begonias at the corner of cross pathways leading to the bandstand in the middle of the square. I'd seen Eleanor Abercrombie and her husband, Zeke, tending the bed earlier in the week, their backs curved by years of bending over flowers.

In my desperation, I was sorely tempted to steal them. But I couldn't, not even for Josie's wedding. Begonias wouldn't do, anyway. They were a shy little flower. Eleanor Abercrombie was famous for her roses. Why couldn't she have planted some on the square?

Suddenly I straightened, my head swinging west. The Abercrombies might not grow roses on the square, but I knew where they did. Eleanor Abercrombie thought the world of Josie. Surely she wouldn't let Josie's wedding be ruined, even to win the Bigelow County Garden Contest.

I headed toward Spruce Street, praying to the God I didn't believe in that Josie was wrong... that Mrs. Abercrombie's Silver Passions *could* be purchased. I would offer my entire bank account to find out.

I never got the chance. Mrs. Abercrombie wasn't home. I banged on both her front and back doors, but the only answer was silence.

Standing on the bottom step leading up to her back porch, I glanced around at the wealth adorning her backyard. Rose bushes lined the whitewashed wooden fence, laden with blossoms in nearly every hue of the rainbow.

Where had Mrs. Abercrombie gone? And would she be gone long enough for me to do the unthinkable —

"Hey! You there!"

I turned to see Mrs. Abercrombie's next-door neighbor, Clevine Wallace, making her way slowly around the side of the house. Mrs. Wallace was eighty if she was a day, with arthritis so bad she walked with two canes.

"What are you up to, young man?"

"Good evening, Mrs. Wallace. Do you perhaps know where Mrs. Abercrombie is, and what time she'll be home?"

"Who's that?" Mrs. Wallace came several steps closer, then paused to push her glasses up on her nose. "Why, you're the young man Josie McClure's gonna get married to tomorry, ain't you?"

"Harold Rutherford, ma'am. About Mrs. Abercrombie..."

Mrs. Wallace shook her head. "Eleanor and Zeke won't be home until tomorry morning. Had an emergency with their daughter, Nancy, over in Yonder."

"Tomorrow? What about the garden contest?"

"Oh, they'll be back for that, don't you fret. Eleanor'll rush home tomorry just in time to do some last minute trimming, I expect. She's got to beat Geraldine Matthews, ya know."

I explained what had happened. "As you can see, it's imperative I talk to Mrs. Abercrombie. Do you have a phone number for her daughter?"

Mrs. Wallace shook her head. "That's a gawl-dern shame, that's what it is. Imagine Eugenia acting like that. Holdin' a grudge for twenty years. Even by Creekite standards, that's something. Why, nobody in town'll give her any business now."

"A phone number?"

Mrs. Wallace peered at me closely. "You ain't thinking you're gonna get Eleanor's roses, are ya?"

"I'm desperate. Josie is going to be heartbroken when she finds out that she won't have any flowers for her wedding. Not even a bouquet."

Mrs. Wallace shook her head. "Eleanor might cut you some on Sunday, after the contest, but not before."

"Sunday's too late, and she has hundreds of flowers. How many does she need for the contest?"

"Every single one. The judging's on the entire garden, not just one flower."

"What about other rose bushes in Mossy Creek? Surely the other ladies in the Mossy Creek Garden Club can spare some roses from their gardens."

Mrs. Wallace's face brightened, then fell. "That's true, son, but most of 'em donated their roses to the high school prom last Saturday. You might find a few buds, but that's about all."

I glanced at my watch. I had an hour before I had to be at the rehearsal. "Please give me the phone number of Eleanor's daughter, Mrs. Wallace. I can't give up."

"I could, I reckon, but it won't do you no good. Eleanor, Nancy, and Zeke are all heading to Nancy's in-laws, 'cause Nancy's mother-in-law's sick. Eleanor and Zeke got to take care of the grandkids while Nancy takes care of her mother-in-law."

I felt hope recede. Still, I had to try. "Please. Maybe I can catch them before they leave Nancy's house in Yonder."

Mrs. Wallace pursed her lips all the way back to her house next door. She looked up Eleanor's daughter's number in her address book and let me call from her phone.

She was right. There was no answer. I left a plaintive

message, begging Mrs. Abercrombie to call me as soon as she could. But in my heart, I knew it would do no good.

Back on the sidewalk, I paused in the fading sunlight for one last look at Mrs. Abercrombie's roses. I could come back late that night and steal them, but that would be despicable. Plus the whole town would know who did it. Even if Mrs. Wallace didn't tell, people would recognize the flowers. It would be just as hard on Josie to have her husband in jail as to face a church with no flowers.

No flowers. Josie was going to be devastated. From what I'd seen, her idol, Martha Stewart's, entire decorating premise centered around flowers. Sure, we could use other kinds of flowers in the wedding, but Josie had her heart set on roses.

I wanted to rail at every rose-stripped Creekite garden I passed on the way back to my truck. How could all those rose bushes let Josie down like this?

That night at the rehearsal, I put off telling Josie as long as possible. There was nothing she could do about it, anyway. I'd tried everything short of...

Short of scouring the mountains for old farmstead roses that had gone wild. Of course. Why hadn't I thought about that sooner? Hardy, old-fashioned roses that had survived on their own weren't as showy as the modern hybrids, but at least they were roses.

I spent the entire night wandering the dark mountains in search of roses, without even a sliver of a moon to help. I knew where several bushes were from my years wandering the mountains, and I found a few more after the sun came up.

The wedding was slated to start at one, so I was forced to start back down the mountain with my sack full of roses just after ten. My arms, face and back were covered with gashes. Wild roses don't give up their beauty willingly.

Exhausted from stress, the sleepless night and exercise, I thought I was imagining things when I heard voices. When I rounded the next bend, I stopped dead. Two women were walking just ahead carrying sacks laden with wild roses.

I shook my head. Was I hallucinating? "Hello there."

They smiled and greeted me. I'd met them before, but not at Josie's church. Mossy Creek Garden Club members. Peggy Caldwell and Mimsy Allen. Only Mimsy was a true Creekite. Peggy had moved to Mossy Creek just a couple of years ago.

"Shouldn't you be at home taking a shower and getting dressed?" Peggy asked.

"I'm going now, but first I have to take these roses by the church. You see, Eugenia Townsend at Mossy Creek Flowers and Gifts didn't —"

"Didn't order Josie's flowers," Mimsy finished. "We know."

"You do?"

"The whole town knows," Peggy said. "What do you think we're doing up here on a Saturday morning?"

I was stunned. "You came all the way up here to pick roses for Josie?"

"Of course we did." Mimsy sniffed as if insulted. "You don't think we'd let Josie get married without roses, do you? Why, Eleanor's grooming her as a future member of the Mossy Creek Garden Club."

"I..." I could hardly believe it. "Thank you."

"Are you headed down to town, now?" Mimsy asked.

"Yes. I need to get these to the church so I can pick up my tux."

Mimsy grabbed Peggy's sack, poured her flowers into it then handed it to me. "Take your sack and ours down to Ed Brady's truck, will you? We've got a few more bushes to strip."

"You mean . . . Mr. Brady's here? Are there any others?"

"Well of course," Mimsy said. "Half the town. The other half's at the church, arranging the flowers we're shipping in by special delivery, courtesy of some connections Mayor Walker has with an out-of-state grower. But don't worry. *We'll* make it to the church on time. Just see that *you* do."

My astonishment must've been plain, because Peggy placed a warm hand on my arm. "Don't you understand? You're not alone up here, Dr. Rutherford. Creekites care about each other, and take care of each other. I had a hard time grasping that fact, too, when I first came to town. But you're a Creekite now. Might as well get used to it."

"I . . . I can't thank you enough."

"You got that right," Mimsy chirped. She pushed me on down the trail. "So get on down the mountain with your load. Put your sacks in the back of Ed's truck. He'll see they get to the church. You go get a hot shower. You look like you need one."

❦❦❦

By noon, I was at the church. I walked in and stopped dead in my tracks. There were probably thirty people scattered about the sanctuary, arranging roses on the altar, in vases along the pulpit, on the ends of pews.

I walked down the aisle in wonder. As I passed, the workers greeted me casually, as if this kind of thing happened every day. Halfway down, I realized that the roses arranged in cascades across the pulpit were special.

"You look right handsome in your tux, young man."

I turned to face Eleanor Abercrombie. "Your roses."

She nodded. "That's right."

I couldn't believe it. "The contest..."

"Happens every year. Josie will get married only *once*." Her pale blue eyes narrowed. "You see to that."

"How much do I owe —"

34

"Don't insult me, young man."

I took her hands in mine. "Thank you for doing this for Josie. It means so much… to both of us."

"*You're* most welcome, Harry Rutherford. From the bottom of all of our hearts. And just so you know, I didn't do this for Josie. Well, all right, I did it because I love her, but I also did it to uphold the town's honor." Her sun-weathered face beamed up at me. "Don't judge Mossy Creek because of Eugenia Townsend. Just because one bush has root rot doesn't mean the whole garden needs digging up."

I kissed her cheek. "I can't thank you enough."

"No need to." She pulled back and reached down into a pew. "Like I said, you're handsome in your tux, but it needs one more thing."

She straightened and pinned one of her Silver Passions on my lapel. "This isn't the best one. I used that in Josie's bouquet."

"Mrs. Abercrombie, are you sure you want to pin one of your prize roses on me? I have to confess. . .yesterday I thought about stealing them."

She chortled. "Why, I'm flattered." Then she patted my chest. "They're exactly where I want them to be. You're one of us now. When you need help, all you have to do is ask."

All I had to do was ask, and a whole town would come to my rescue. Even though I'd earned a second masters degree in quantum mathematics, I couldn't begin to count those kinds of blessings. They were infinite.

Mossy Creek Gazette

VOLUME IV, NO. 1   **MOSSY CREEK, GEORGIA**

The Bell Ringer

McClure-Rutherford Wedding Filled with Surprises

by Katie Bell

The wedding of Josie McClure and Dr. Harold (Harry) Rutherford took place on Saturday afternoon in the sanctuary of the Mossy Creek Presbyterian Church amid a sea of roses and silver candles.

Josie's father, John McClure, gave the bride away.

The bride wore a white satin off-the-shoulder gown embroidered with seed pearls and a matching white, pearl-encrusted cap trailing a wedding veil loaned by the matron of honor, Jayne Reynolds. Josie's mother wore a pink knee-length dress.

The groom and the father of the bride wore black tuxedos.

The reception, a gift from Win Allen, aka Chef Bubba Rice, was held in the Sunday School rooms in the church basement. Chef Bubba provided the traditional refreshments which included his special punch, finger sandwiches, cheese straws, fresh fruit dips, nuts and wedding cookies. The groom's cake was appropriately shaped as a chocolate log, a tribute to Harry's profession as a professor of environmental botany. The wedding cake was four tiers high and decorated with wild roses, whose scent filled the hall. Since the groom's nickname is *Bigfoot*, Chef Bubba also provided a size twenty-two chocolate shoe, filled with marzipan roses. Harry laughed and said that it was the first time anyone had ever made a tribute to the size of his feet.

Joe Biddly's string quartet surprised the happy couple at the reception. Joe serenaded Harry and Josie with two, shall we say, *untraditional* choices of music: *Are You Ready To Go Now*, originally recorded by *The Chuck Wagon Gang* — I think — and *There's Gonna Be a Hot Time in the Old Town Tonight.* I think it's fair to say those songs were truly unexpected by the wedding couple and everyone else in attendance.

"The Voice Of The Creek"

Good morning, Mossy Creek! This is Bert Lyman, WMOS FM, bringing you, as we in journalism like to say, 'all the news that's fit to print and some that isn't.' Even if this is radio.

First, our own Katie Bell is still out of town at the newspaper awards luncheon in New York. I'm finding it hard to believe that the gossip columnist from our little *Mossy Creek Gazette* was nominated for a major award. Others might think being a finalist in the *Quaint Weekly Newspaper Columnist* category is a put-down, but Katie will be the first to tell you that she'd rather be quaint than overlooked, as if anybody could ever overlook Katie.

We'd like to overlook the weather today. We've had a week of rain. Sagan Salter, that would be *Doctor* Salter, our anthropologist and resident Cherokee cultural expert, says it's the *wog*; that's the animal responsible for punishing those who aren't true to their past. The wog is calling the rain spirits to deliver the Cherokees back to the land beneath where they lived before they came to the surface and became 'the people.'

At any rate, the rain is behaving peculiarly. It drowns the mountains and farmland to the north of Mossy Creek but skips over the farms between Mossy Creek and Bigelow to the south. Chief Royden rescued a couple of hikers (we're on the Appalachian Trail, you know) who nearly got washed away by Mossy Creek yesterday. But the leaves are changing beautifully and the roadside stands are full of bright red Sweet Hope apples from the orchards up at Bailey Mill, so tourists are heading our way like pilgrims on a sacred march. They know our reputation for hospitality. There was a time when apples and moonshine were Mossy Creek's number one exports.

The Bereavement Report would normally be omitted this morning, for the only passing we have to report is that of Willis, Officer Sandy Crane's mascot at the police station. To all of us who knew him, that old gray tomcat was a lot more human than most folks. He was the only animal in Mossy Creek on speaking terms with Bob, Ingrid Beechum's Chihuahua. You could set your watch by Willis heading for O' Day's Pub every afternoon. He knew exactly when it was time for Sandy to drop by for a tonic water and a few minutes of *Oprah* on the bar TV. Willis never missed his lap time. If Oprah had asked Willis if life was working for him, all she'd have gotten was a satisfied purr. A cat doesn't need many blessings to be happy.

Since we're talking about passing over, Ezekiel Straley, owner of the Mossy Creek Funeral Parlor, says his chapel is open to any of our autumn guests who might like to tour the facility and burial grounds with the thought of joining us in eternity.

I'm pleased to report that the gossip about trouble between Ezekiel and Argelia Rodriguez, our local dance instructor, has been highly exaggerated. Chief Royden has been called in twice to intervene, but I don't have any other details. At least none I can report without getting in hot water with Katie Bell. She's been working this story for months. So she'll fill you in when she gets back from New York City.

In Mossy Creek, we never say you can't make
a silk purse out of a sow's ear.

❦❦❦❦❦❦❦❦❦❦❦❦❦❦❦❦❦❦❦❦❦❦❦❦❦❦❦❦❦❦❦❦❦❦❦

The Wisteria Tango

Chapter 2

"Turn that music down! Do you hear me, Ms. Rodriguez? Turn it down! The Emersons can't send their mama to Jesus with that infernal piano tinkling away!"

A fist punctuated each angry yell, thudding against my ballet studio's plate glass window.

I ignored it and continued to count for my little ballerinas. "*Un, deux, trois, quatre.*"

"Twinkle, Twinkle, Little Star" played on at the same reasonable volume.

The girls, knees bent in a second position *plié*, began their ascent, glancing nervously towards the window that dominated the front of the building.

"Turn it down!" my tormentor shouted. "Argelia Rodriguez, can you hear me?"

"My goodness," one of the mothers said, loud enough for me to hear from across the room. "It's so unlike him."

The other mothers' heads bobbed in agreement.

"He buried my granny," another said.

I ignored the chatter, just as I ignored the Neanderthal banging on my window.

"Girls, pay attention." I clapped out the beat, and the children's eyes returned to the front. "Fourth position."

Little pink leather-slippered feet slid on the polished

wood of my lovely dance floor. I moved to the black stereo system that flanked the wall opposite the window and cranked the music up a notch.

An agonized howl rose outside. "Turn it down, dammit! Or I'm calling Chief Royden!"

The mothers filling the seats that lined the wall by the door looked at each other. Like me, they probably had thought to call the chief of police, too, but not now. No one made a move toward the phone. Besides, everyone knew my troublemaker wouldn't dare come inside.

A wild-eyed face pressed closer to the glass. Ezekial Straley, my mortal enemy. His tightly knotted tie was askew, and his short, blond hair stood on end.

He finally noticed the mommies and smiled weakly, then glared at me. The little girls quit pretending to dance and clustered together.

"Don't worry, kids. He won't come in," I said, putting my arms around them protectively.

With an extra-evil squint of his eyes, he stomped out of sight. Moments later, his car, a black-finned land yacht, raised a rooster tail of dust as he gunned the engine uphill, back to the funeral home.

I finished the class and sent the girls home, anxiously apologizing to each mother as she left, wringing my hands the entire time.

I needed them. Their daughters could choose from any number of ballet classes down in Bigelow, and if Zeke Straley continued his war, they would desert me.

They had Bigelow, but I was stuck. Committed to Mossy Creek by virtue of seventy-five thousand dollars, my entire life's savings. I had renovated a former gas station into a charming and functional dance studio and home I called Wisteria Cottage. I'd named it the first moment I saw the old gas station, draped in fragrant, light purple blooms, like grape bunches all over. The name carried all my hopes for graceful, tranquil living.

Of course, later I conceded I was an ignorant Yankee as I cursed and hacked at that same wisteria with a machete after discovering it was hoisting my roof into the treetops.

Still, the new paint was dry, the piano was tuned, and the floors gleamed. My business was thriving. And Mossy Creek's gentleman mortician was determined to end it.

I went out on the porch, a glass of water in hand, and stared up at the white-columned funeral home on the hill. A few autumn leaves drifted down on the long row of cars lining the sweeping driveway. The grieving Emerson family, no doubt.

Sandy Crane pulled her pick-up truck into one of my parking spaces. She came by for aerobics class every morning before work. "I wonder why he hasn't called the chief on you again?" she called as she slammed her truck door closed and hoisted her workout bag.

Other ears in the parking lot turned to me like military radar. My aerobics class was arriving in force.

"Just a matter of time, I guess." I didn't share the window-pounding story. They'd all hear about it soon enough. Gossip traveled through Mossy Creek faster than a rhythmic *tarantela*.

"I wouldn't worry. Amos thinks Zeke's weird," Jayne Reynolds said as she walked up the steps with Matthew bouncing on one leotard-clad hip. Her coffee shop, *The Naked Bean*, was our after-aerobics hang-out place.

That cheered me up. If the chief thought Zeke was strange, maybe he wouldn't pay attention to his complaint when he made it.

Jayne looked great, glowing from the success of her business and motherhood.

Who would guess that a feud between her and Ingrid

Beechum had almost wrecked the coffee shop less than two years ago? *I need a dose of that serenity*, I thought, trailing in after my students.

Conversation buzzed around us as Sandy, Jayne, and the other students speculated about the inevitable showdown between *the mortician and the ballerina*, as Zeke and I were now known. Scared as I was, I wasn't as tense about it as I would have been six months ago. Moving to Mossy Creek had done wonders for my attitude. My New York state of mind had been mostly purged.

The transformation had taken some time. What I called *aggressive self-preservation* had been misunderstood by Creekites, at first, as pure crankiness. Rainey Cecil, at Goldilocks Salon, told me bluntly that I needed a perm *and* an enema. That had hurt, but it started my change into a real resident of Mossy Creek. I was still cranky, but at least I wasn't a cranky *Yankee*. I wrapped my crankiness in a *I'll whup your ass* kind of attitude that was pure Creekite. Now, I fit in.

"Ezekial hates noise," Ingrid Beechum said. "Even the faintest sound of your music from across the street. It's why he built the funeral home on two acres up on the hill off the square. *No noise*. Until you came along." She was on the floor, stretching and touching her toes with her fingertips. She smiled at her ability to touch her toes and then at Jayne's baby. Not bad for a fifty-five-year-old surrogate grandmother. Little Matthew smiled back.

"No noise," the other women echoed, grinning.

"So I've heard," I said dryly.

❦❦❦

Straley wasn't exactly a stud. When he wasn't screaming, mouth open so wide I could inspect his dental history, he looked a little like a blond-haired *Mr. Bean*, the British comedy character, only taller. As my aerobics class finished their cool-down I glanced out the window and saw him standing in the parking lot. I was glad he didn't appear to have a gun. I strode to the door. "What now?"

"Ms. Rodriguez," he said softly, his voice deep and a little raspy, probably from his screaming fit. "I'm sorry about the scene earlier. We were conducting a funeral, and I wanted to be sure you knew."

I stepped off my stoop and stalked over to him. "You let me know, all right. Your clients are beyond being bothered by a few wisps of music that escape from my studio, Mr. Straley, but mine are only eight-years-old. You scared them." I tried to keep my voice down, honest.

"The music needs to be lower, Ms. Rodriguez, for the sake of the grieving families."

He didn't see the New Yorker in me rising, but Jayne must have. She hurried outside, dabbing her face with a towel. "I never see you at The Naked Bean anymore, Zeke. You ought to drop by. Have a complimentary latte."

"I'll try to find the time," he said politely. He turned back to me. "I have another matter I must discuss with you, Ms. Rodriguez." The rest of my aerobics class wandered outside to lend moral support. He frowned at the cluster of stern faces that sidled up behind me. "In, er, *private*."

A collective sigh of disappointment rose around us, the sound of my students' deflated hopes, followed by the unsettled murmur of implacable curiosity. I wouldn't put it past these tough Southern flowers to pump their fists and yell, "Fight, fight!" As little as I wanted to get personal with Mr. Bean, it would be better to have this discussion in private.

"Sure," I answered him. "Want to come inside?"

He seemed surprised. "Now?"

I nodded, staring him in the eye.

He looked at the posse of women behind me, and a

panicky look crept over his face. "Alone?"

"Just give me a minute to shut down the studio. I'll wait for you in my apartment, Mr. Straley." I turned to my sweaty, beady-eyed back-up group. "I'll be fine. See you later, ladies."

Not a single, cheerful, positive thought went through my mind as I stepped inside my tiny suite off the studio. Truth was, I was scared to death that he'd ruin my business. I'd invested every penny I owned in the studio. I waited, sitting on the sofa, knees knocking, until I realized he wasn't coming in. I walked back outside. The parking lot was empty.

Footsteps crunched on the pebble walkway from around the side. Mr. Straley appeared, staring curiously at the flowerbeds and window boxes, like a tourist in a museum.

"Appraising the property?" I leaned against my celery-green Beetle.

His smile was spare, as if he rationed them out. "You seem to have invested a lot in the place. I didn't get a chance to look at it earlier."

"Let's get this over with, Mr. Straley. What did you need to speak to me about?"

"Noise, as usual," he said softly, looking up the hill towards the red brick funeral home, with its white-columned portico, as if someone up there could hear him.

"I don't play my music loudly," I said, perplexed. "Why do you keep coming down here yelling like an excited frat boy?"

He seemed offended by my analogy. "I come down because there are hurt people up there, emotionally drained and facing more of the same. The least you could do is show a little respect for what they have to go through."

"It's not that loud," I insisted. "I'll prove it." I dashed back in the studio and stood with my arms crossed until he followed me. Then I pushed the play button on the sound system. Throbbing techno music filled the room, the kind of kinetic throbbing that used to make my Aunt Flavia complain because she said her pacemaker tried to keep up with the beat.

I grabbed him by the sleeve of his suit and tugged him into my apartment, then closed the door. "See, no noise. Not even in my own apartment — ten feet from the studio."

"Not here. But up there on the hill —" he signaled with his chin " — up there it sounds like a discotheque."

Like he'd ever been in one. Hah. "That's impossible."

"Really, it does. It must have to do with the bowl-shaped hollow your cottage sits in, and my property on the ridge. It's a natural amphitheater."

I crossed my arms again, looked bored, then went to my apartment's front door and held it open. "Thank you, Mr. Straley."

"If we can't talk this out, Ms. Rodriguez, I'll take the next step." His fists were clenched.

I gulped. The next step was probably an attorney. "You do what you have to do."

"I will. This conversation was a mistake." He marched outside to his big, ugly car. I followed him to the front stoop. He halted and looked at me. "I'm sorry about scaring those children."

I arched a brow. "Then leave me *and* them alone."

He ducked into his car and left.

Coward.

❦ ❦ ❦

My afternoon ballet class brought a little good news, business-wise: Several of the mothers asked for a weekend adult class. I made up a flyer announcing the new class as soon as the kids left, printed three copies, and headed towards town to post it.

Sandy caught up with me as I came out of Mossy Creek Books and What-Nots. The owner, Pearl Quinlan, not only let me post a notice on her bulletin board, she signed up for the class. I was smiling.

Sandy hitched up the khaki pants of her officer's uniform, hunched her compact little shoulders under a khaki windbreaker with Mossy Creek Police Department emblazoned on the back in big neon letters, and scrubbed a sturdy hand through her mop of curly blonde hair. She looked like Shirley Temple on patrol. But her frown said she was on official business.

"*Hon*, what did you do to Zeke Straley the other night? He's filed a formal complaint against you."

I froze. "What kind of complaint?" In my mind, I saw my lovely studio boarded up and covered in vines, weeds choking the garden, as a triumphant Ezekial Straley drove a funeral cortege past the sagging, empty, doorway. Something sharp twisted in my heart. I mourned my loss already.

"He says you're breaking the noise ordinance. Says he's not goin' to back down this time. The chief confabbed with Mayor Walker but neither one of 'em can decide whether the ordinance applies to a dance studio, so the mayor's gettin' the city attorney to offer an opinion."

"Who's the city attorney?"

"Mac Campbell." She frowned. "He's Zeke's personal lawyer, too."

I was toast.

❧❧❧

Zeke's black-finned Cadillac was parked in front of my studio when I returned. I jumped out of my Volkswagen, ready to give the mortician a black eye.

He held up his soft white hands, warding me off.

I glared at him. "Afraid of a little ballerina, Mr. Straley?

I heard you went to Chief Royden. I heard you filed a complaint." My fists clenched.

He smiled sourly. "I did, but that's not why I came by."

"Signing up for a class?"

He blushed. *Red as Santa's underwear*, as Sandy would say.

"I need to learn to dance." He cleared his throat and grimaced. He pulled a starched handkerchief from an inside pocket of his suit coat and dabbed at his pale brow.

I was too astounded to even hoot with disbelief.

"The National Funeral Directors' conference is in Orlando this year," he went on, "and the theme is *Caribbean*. I just found out there's going to be a *tango* contest." His voice lowered, as if he were saying a dirty word.

"The tango is from Argentina, not the islands."

He shrugged.

"Doesn't matter. I *have* to tango." He surveyed the road behind me, his eyes swiveling back and forth like a creepy ventriloquist's dummy. He didn't want to be seen with me. "Morticians can be very competitive, Ms. Rodriguez. You can be sure when we sponsor a contest, it's a fierce battle for supremacy."

"I had no idea," I murmured, my head swimming with visions of super-hero funeral directors. *Straley in spandex*. I closed my eyes at that one. When I opened them, he was gazing at me grimly. I arched a brow. "You need a partner for the competition?"

"No. The convention organizers will provide professional dancers for the attendees to dance with. Don't worry, Ms. Rodriquez. I'm not asking you to risk your virtue by going on a road trip with me. Just teach me to tango."

I chewed my tongue. So what if he was weirder than your average Elvis sighter? I'm from New York. I can handle *weird*, especially now that I knew he was in a bind. I had him at my mercy. "So you'll drop the complaint against me?"

He sighed. "Yes."

"All right. Let's go inside and talk."

His remaining blush drained away. "No. Not alone. Not now." He stared at Wisteria Cottage as if it were a massage parlor and he couldn't be caught there. "I have only three weeks, Ms. Rodriguez. Can you teach me in your spare time?"

Three weeks to learn the tango for a competition? I stifled a laugh and started to tell him no, but when I opened my mouth, the little word got stuck in my teeth. "Sure," I heard myself say. "I can teach you."

"I keep odd hours. Do you think you can fit me in at unusual times? It depends on my, er, workload."

I glanced up at the funeral home. Workload? *Yuck.* "Of course. Not a problem. Can you start next week?"

"Why not tonight?"

I thought fast. "Because I have to work out a lesson plan."

He bought it. "Of course. Thank you. You're a sport, Ms. Rodriguez. I'll go by the police station right now and withdraw my complaint."

My heart filled with hope. "Call me Argie."

"Thank you, Argie. Call me Zeke. I'll do my best to be a good student." He shook my hand firmly. "This means a lot to me."

I smiled. "I assume you want these lessons to be kept a secret?"

"Absolutely."

"All right."

He exhaled and looked relieved. Then he climbed into his big, black shark-finned car and rolled smoothly up his driveway and around to the back of the funeral home.

My business was saved.

Except I only had one week to learn how to tango.

🐞🐞🐞

Three days later, Jamie Green, postman extraordinaire, dropped a box off at my door, along with the usual bills and junk mail.

"Pearl Quinlan could have ordered this for you, you know," he said, tapping the box's Internet bookstore logo.

And have the entire town know I had ordered *A Beginner's Guide to the Tango*? Not in this lifetime. "Thanks, Jamie, I'll call her about the next one."

I used a kitchen knife to tear the package open, then eagerly tipped it to allow the DVD box to fall into my waiting hand.

It caught, then slid slowly out. I screamed. Lurid pink and yellow letters spelled out, *Secrets of the Polka Masters*. My scream brought Jamie Green running back onto the porch.

"What's wrong, Argie?"

I stared at the horror nestled in brown paper wrapping on my breakfast table. "Nothing, Jamie. Just a bug."

"Want me to kill it for you? It's the wisteria. Bugs love it, even in the fall when it's not blooming."

Great. "Thanks, Jamie. I'll handle it. Just startled me, that's all."

He left, and I shelved the tape. Maybe I could offer polka classes. Jamie was right. I should have called Pearl. I picked up the cell phone and punched her number, the imagined taste of crow filling my mouth.

🐞🐞🐞

Weird Zeke had opened the door to a part of me I didn't know, and wasn't sure I wanted to know. I wanted to learn to tango, but who could teach the teacher? With a name like *Rodriquez*, I was expected to know the dance instinctively.

But in fact, before opening my studio, I'd been a career ballerina. From age five, when I first entered *Miss Louise's Ballet School* on Amsterdam Avenue in New York, *ballet* had been my life. I'd spent ten years in agreeable servitude to the New York City Ballet, where all my roles had been classical.

Without any free time, I had socialized very little, and my Aunt Flavia, who raised me after my mother died, was an elderly recluse. I never knew my father, or anything about his Cuban heritage, much less the heritage of other Hispanics.

So now I called Maria Echeverria, a friend who lived an hour's drive southeast of Mossy Creek, in the small city of Gainesville. Gainesville calls itself the poultry capital of the south, and it makes a good run at the title. The majority of the poultry plants' workers are Hispanic, and Maria, a coordinator for Catholic Services, helps them through the baffling world of government agencies, from driver's licenses to registering for kindergarten.

She was amused by my request. "You want to find a tango dancer? In a chicken plant?"

"Don't chicken processors dance on their days off?"

"The tango is from Argentina. Most of my clients are from Central America."

"I'm desperate, Maria. Get the word out, okay?"

She laughed again. "Why don't you just go to Atlanta? They teach classes there."

"That's a four-hour round-trip drive. I can't get away from my studio that long."

She clucked her tongue. My *Tia* Flavia used to do that, and it drove me crazy. She called the crackling sound *friendo huevos*. Frying eggs. "You are too impatient, Argelia. If you

50

want to teach Latin dances, you need to learn from an expert."

"Why can't a local chicken plucker be an expert?"

A deep sigh was my answer. "I'll look," she said. "But don't expect any miracles."

She sounded as optimistic as I did.

Jayne showed up that evening with her toddler on one hip and a thermos of good coffee in her free hand. "Oh what a *tangoed* web we weave," she intoned from my apartment steps.

"Pearl *promised* not to tell anyone," I said, holding the screen door for her. "When my CD came in, she even hid it under the counter."

"I'm not anyone. I'm your best friend, and Pearl knows that." She looked at me kindly. "And I'm here to help."

I sighed. "Thanks, but I'm afraid it'll take more than good coffee."

"Not coffee. *Dancing.*"

I stared at her. "What?"

"I know how to tango. My husband and I learned it in a dance class on our honeymoon cruise. We fell in love with Latin dances. We used to dress up and go to the Latin nightclubs in Atlanta. He was an incredible dancer." Pain shadowed her eyes briefly, remembering the husband who'd died less than two years ago, while she was pregnant with Matthew. Despite our friendship, there were things I didn't know about her. This topped the list. "You. . .tango? Really?"

"Yep. And I'm pretty good at it, if I do say so myself." She put Matthew down on a blanket and shooed my curious cat, Rudy, away from his exuberant reach.

I finally recovered from shock. I grabbed her by the shoulders. "If you can help me, you will be my hero *forever.*"

Jayne grinned. "Let's get to work."

I picked up the stereo's remote control and hit *play.*

The new CD probably had a groove in it from overuse, already. But after a moment, the rhythmic beat of its music filled the studio.

"Okay," Jayne said. "First thing is, we face each other."

We played the music softly — I didn't want Zeke to hear wisps of tango music up at the funeral home — and glided barefoot across the polished wood of the dance floor, watching our reflections in the mirrors and the darkened glass of the large picture window. After a few jokes about who ought to lead, we settled down to business.

Jayne was no professional, but she knew the moves, and I was a quick learner. Three hours later I was a tango expert. After Jayne and Matthew left I reached for the phone.

"Mossy Creek Funeral Home," Zeke answered.

"Whenever you're ready to dance, Zeke Straley, I'm ready to teach you."

There was a pause. I muffled a nervous sigh. Had he changed his mind?

"All right. Thank you," he said, and hung up.

I stared at the phone in my hand. That was it? After all the work I'd done, I expected a little excitement on his part; but then, he didn't know about my quest for lessons, and God willing, he never would.

Content, I went to bed feeling like Goldilocks in the three bears' house — everything was *just right*. As I drifted to sleep, the thought that Goldilocks was an intruder who was chased away never crossed my mind.

🌼🌼🌼

A pounding at my back door woke me up. I shoved off the covers and looked at my bedside clock. Three a.m. I struggled into my big black robe, an old opera costume piece abandoned at my New York apartment long ago by a friend.

Zeke stood outside, shifting impatiently from foot to

foot. I pulled the door open. I had promised to teach him on his schedule, but it never occurred to me it would be before dawn.

"I apologize for the hour, Argie. Is this a bad time?"

I gaped at him, then finally managed to shake my head. I stepped aside to allow him room to enter. He smelled like lemon household cleaner and drugstore aftershave, a combination I could have gone my entire life without inhaling, especially when I thought of the scent it might be covering.

I slept with my long, dark hair in two sleek braids to keep it from tangling. Since I always wore my hair up during the day, Straley had never seen its length before. I caught him glancing at my hair repeatedly. Nervous, I schlepped over to the stereo in my faded bedroom slippers and pushed the green button on its front. The sexy rhythms of the tango filled the studio.

I glimpsed my reflection in the mirrored wall opposite the *barre* and almost cried out. I looked like a cross between *Pippi Longstocking* and the *Wicked Witch of the West. Serves him right*, I thought, and abandoned the idea of changing clothes.

At least I could see *him* in the mirror, too. I was starting to think that maybe he was a vampire. On second thought, that would have been great. He would sleep while I conducted my classes, and I could keep him away with garlic. Garlic was cheap.

I started on the basics and was dismayed to find that he was a good dancer. I needed extra Jayne classes, and quickly, or he would catch up with me. We spent the rest of the night practicing the basic but intricate footwork characteristic of the tango. It was like playing *Twister* to music.

"No, Zeke, I put my foot between yours as you step back, then you step back in and support me as I move my foot out and put the other one behind you." We tried it in slow motion. *Perfect.* Zeke's hand splayed out against the small of my back, surprisingly confident and strong. After three hours of dancing I trusted him to hold me when I leaned back.

We tried it again. My foot stepped between his, I leaned back, his foot slid forward, and mine started to move back. He held me all the way to the floor, where we landed in a heap.

He scrambled to his feet and pulled me up. "I'm sorry. I guess I shouldn't have moved my foot."

"That's okay," I said, rubbing a sore hip. "I'll just have a little bruise." Outside, the sky had lightened. "How about some coffee?"

He smiled. "How about tea? I brought some gourmet selections from The Naked Bean."

Startled, I realized I'd never seen him smile before. I smiled back. Maybe this would work. It was worth getting up in the middle of the night, even getting tossed to the floor, if it would make him like me and not harass my classes anymore.

We sat on a bench on the porch with our steaming cups of tea and listened to the birds wake up as the sun rose. I told him about the tango's history, and he listened attentively, then set his empty cup down and looked at me.

"You're a good teacher, Argie," he said solemnly. "I figured you were, since you've attracted so many students."

I shrugged. "I'm the only game in town," I said lightly. "Outside of Bigelow."

He nodded, considering my words. His eyes slid over my dramatic black robe and his expression changed. "Say, do you always dress like that at night?"

I looked down at the billows of black pooling around the bench. "It's my bathrobe."

"My bathrobe is blue velour."

Too much information. I curved my lips a little. "Give me some warning next time, and I'll wear jeans."

His brows rose. "My schedule is erratic."

I shrugged again. "I'll work with you, Zeke. I have a full day today, though."

He nodded and after an awkward handshake, got into his car and drove back up the hill.

I rinsed out the cups and went to bed. I had four hours until my morning aerobics class, which the students had now nicknamed *The Mossy Creek Estrogen Brigade*, showed up.

When they did, I had circles under my eyes from the dance marathon the night before.

The class bulged, and I don't mean their comfy posteriors. There were so many new people that it was difficult to maneuver. I felt like yesterday's salad, wilted and limp, but mentally I felt great as I counted heads. If I could keep Zeke happy and my classes growing, I would have it made.

The ladies did fine, even the new ones who didn't know the routines. I was too busy considering the logistics of splitting the class in two to pay them much attention as they left. They didn't seem to mind. With few exceptions, they whispered and chuckled among themselves, Maybe I was paranoid, but I kept wondering if they suspected me and Zeke.

At six, Jayne showed up with Matthew again. Poor little guy must have had an earache or some such mystical ailment. He cried the whole time we danced. I gritted my teeth against the headache that formed between my eyes. It grew worse when we cranked the volume up to hear better, and pounded my temples when Zeke called, threatening to sic Chief Royden on us if we didn't turn the music down.

"People are trying to grieve up here," he said.

I was so mad I nearly threw my cell phone at a wall.

"Don't let him get to you," Jayne said.

"He already has."

At midnight, Zeke had the nerve to show up. "I apologize for losing my temper earlier," he said. I wanted to slam the door in his face, but one slammed door would lead to others, as my Aunt Flavia said, and I didn't want more trouble. "Shut up and dance," I ordered.

As it turned out, his pager went off only minutes after his arrival. He asked to use my phone, and in a polite tone, too, no doubt learned at mortician's school. I thrust it at him. "Here."

As he listened he pulled a little pad and a pencil from his pocket and started to write. "Sure, Chief. No problem." He seemed to be the Boy Scout of the mortician's world, always prepared. "Yes, Chief, I'm getting the details." He wrote faster. "Two males? Do you know approximate weights of the bodies? Oh." He licked the end of his pencil. "*Pieces of bodies.* Got it." He thumbed off his phone and gazed at me, frowning.

"I'm sorry. That was Chief Royden. There's been a bad wreck on the road to Bigelow. Bikers. Racing. Not local men. Can I come back before dawn? I can bring something for breakfast."

I bit my lip, trying not to think about the grisly details of the bikers' accident. It suddenly dawned on me that Zeke's job required a doctor's cool detachment but a minister's compassion.

"I'll be waiting," I told him.

🐾🐾🐾

It was two in the morning before he came back. I put the teapot on while we warmed up with familiar steps. He didn't offer any gory details about the wreck, and I didn't ask for any. He looked exhausted, though. I felt sorry for him. "You're getting pretty good at the tango, Zeke."

"It feels natural now." He turned me sharply and danced

me back a few steps before turning again.

The kettle whistled, and we retreated to the kitchen for tea.

"I'd get used to keeping vampire hours if I could sleep all day," I said.

"I never get used to night work," he said. "People seem to pass on mostly at night, but no matter how late I work, I can't ignore my daytime duties."

I nodded. "You're passionate about the funeral business. Like I am with my classes. No matter how tired I am, I still have to teach, and I have paperwork to do. It's worth it, though. I feel as if I'm keeping the art of ballet alive by sharing it with children."

He got a strange look on his face.

I froze. "Did I say something wrong?"

"No. I just realized that you feel the same way about your work as I do about mine."

"Pardon me if I don't share your enthusiasm for funeral homes."

"People die every day, Argie. It's part of life, but an overwhelming part for the family. Even if it's an expected death, after a long illness, there's so much to do, and everyone expects the arrangements to be done quickly. My job is to take the burden away from the family, as much of it as they'll let me. I give comfort, and the relatives are assured that their loved one's remains are handled with dignity."

That was more than he'd said to me the entire time I'd known him. "You've found a purpose for your life."

"And so have you."

"Yes, and that's why I love it so much. Why did you go into the funeral business?"

"When I was little, my father died in Vietnam. I was only six and only vaguely remembered him, but when I was a teenager, and my grandfather died, I was at his bedside, holding his hand.

"Dying isn't pretty, and I wondered for the first time what it was like for my dad, alone in a jungle on the other side of the world. I wanted him to be clean, with his hands folded on his chest, like my gramps. I wanted the family around him to say goodbye before we put him in the ground. Mom said they shipped what they found back, and there was a memorial service. The memorial service meant so much to her. I never forgot that."

I couldn't think of anything to say, so I squeezed his hand.

He squeezed back. "Your turn, Argie. What made the ballerina into a teacher? Why aren't you still dancing?"

He had touched on a wound that was barely scabbed over, but I wanted to match his candor. He deserved it. "When I was with the New York City Ballet, I knew that my career wouldn't last as long as I'd hoped. It hurt when I realized that my leaps weren't as high, my feet ached longer after rehearsals, and I started losing roles to fifteen-year-old girls. I knew that I was slowing down, so I quit before they fired me. I moved to Mossy Creek." The pain must have shown on my face. He squeezed my hand again.

"It's okay," he said. "You're home now."

"Does this mean you're going to stop harassing me?"

He shook his head. "I can't let you ruin my business. You can move somewhere else in town — there're lots of places. Nicer ones."

"None like Wisteria Cottage."

"Romantic nonsense. This was Moe Bradley's Pure Oil station. It's ancient."

"Now it's *my* Wisteria Cottage." I pulled my hand out from under his and crossed my arms over my chest.

He laughed. "Let's dance. We'll figure out some compromise. Dance. It's nearly breakfast time."

Despite myself, I softened. "I've got cinnamon rolls in

the fridge, ready to bake."

The music started, and he pulled me into his arms again. "Move, Argie." He was not talking about dancing.

"I'll dance, but I won't move."

He dropped the subject, proving he could be smart.

Before he left, he shook my hand. "I've never talked like this with anyone," he said.

"That's what friends are for," I answered, and darned if I didn't mean it.

🌿🌿🌿

The ballet moms were nervous at the next day's class. Straley didn't come to bang on the window, so I thought maybe something had happened in town to concern them. But no one mentioned anything.

Straley knocked on my door as the class let out, and I nervously let him in, causing raised brows and arched looks among the moms.

"You're the best," he said. "I forgot to give this to you last night." He put a wad of money in my hand and closed my fist over it. "I can't stay now, but I'll see you tomorrow."

I was too exhausted to argue and too relieved that he hadn't come to make a scene. I shoved the bills into a stoneware pot by the stereo and returned to my class.

I didn't see him again until the next day, when he showed up in the middle of my three o'clock class, ready to dance. "Have you lost your mind?" I almost shouted.

"Time's running out. I've got to practice."

I tangoed with him in the kitchen, out of sight of the girls who pirouetted in the next room. Our dancing had improved. We performed the basic tango steps smoothly, allowing us to work on the complicated footwork and turns.

I glanced at my watch. Ten minutes had gone by. "Good grief." I pushed the kitchen door open and skidded to a halt on the polished wood. "All right girls, let's dip now. I mean, *plié*."

I got through class, barely. I hadn't just bitten off more than I could chew; I was choking on it. I collapsed on the sofa beside the moms, who gaped at me. Maybe I was losing my mind. I wondered if I could teach dance at a nice rest home, when they sent me there.

The ballet class was unusually subdued, which suited me fine. Something was definitely going on, though. Whenever I left the room, I could hear furious whispering from the studio. I wondered if I should ask Zeke to listen from his hilltop and tell me what the moms said. Apparently, he could hear the grass grow from up there.

❦❦❦

The cool afternoon sunlight slanted across the notepad in my lap, gilding my plan for adult ballet class. This moment alone in my tiny backyard garden was a guilty pleasure carved from my busy schedule. With a cup of tea at my side, stray breezes tickling my face, and Rudy pouncing on imaginary mice in the autumn leaves, it was absolutely therapeutic.

The past few days had been hectic and surreal.

"Do you have a moment?"

Straley. There was no escape. No one had ever told me the gas station was haunted by the mortician on the hill. I sighed and nodded, removing my feet from the other garden chair so that he could sit down.

He was jacketless, white shirtsleeves rolled up despite the cool air. His dress pants still looked fresh from the cleaners, though. He sat down, his face creased with worry.

"What's wrong, Zeke?"

He sighed. "I've heard things that concern me, Argie."

I put the pad down, wary. "Oh yeah? Like what?"

"Stupid gossip, that's all. But gossip can hurt. If Katie Bell ever picks up on it —"

"What are the gossips saying?"

"That I'm spending the night with you and paying you for it." Sweat glazed his forehead.

I was on my feet and didn't remember standing. "What?" I wanted to hit him. Then the humor of the situation got to me. I sat down again, laughing.

Zeke, who had cringed a little when I jumped up and shouted, stared at me, astonished.

"The hooker ballerina and the lovesick mortician," I hooted.

He looked a little hurt, and then his expression lightened, and he began to laugh, too. "The horny undertaker and the tango call girl."

"*Sex, ballet, and funeral parlors* — film at eleven."

Our howls gradually subsided to occasional giggles and snorts.

"Isn't it weird how things that aren't funny can make you laugh when you're tense?" He leaned back in his chair and looked up into the canopy of oaks.

"Scared about the dance competition at the morticians' convention?"

"Not anymore," he said. "I'll look like I know what I'm doing, at least. I hate to look foolish, and I want to participate in everything."

"I know what you mean. I auditioned for some big roles and won because I wasn't afraid to try."

He looked over at me, slouched in the chair and comfortably rumpled. "You're not afraid now, are you? With all the talk and all. You're. . .treating me like a friend. Most people keep their distance from me. They think I'm creepy, I guess. I don't know anyone who would have done what you're doing for me."

Touched, I only smiled, afraid to say anything that might ruin the moment.

He gazed into space, lost in thought. "Argie," he said after a long moment. "Did you know the wisteria vines have lifted your roof almost off on this corner? I don't know why you like that noxious weed. It's like encouraging kudzu."

I sighed and stood up.

"Where you headed?"

"To get my machete. Want to help?"

"Wish I could," he said. "I have to get back and finish a corpse."

And I had touched his hand. *Eeew.*

"Argie, can I ask a favor? Do you mind if I bring someone to our class tonight?"

"A girlfriend? Just teasing." I rooted around in the tool bin next to the house and pulled out the machete, new but already nicked from use.

"No," he said seriously. "Joe Murdock. He's the funeral director in Bigelow. He wants to compete in the tango competition, too, and he needs dance help, and I told him you could give him some pointers."

"If I teach Joe, will you stop pestering me to close my studio?"

"No, but I'll help you find a lovely new location for it."

I held up the machete. He paled and left.

I sagged. How had I come to this? Argie Rodriguez, tango instructor to the funeral directors of Bigelow County.

🐾🐾🐾

Zeke and Joe appeared at nine p.m., just as my spaghetti was ready. Joe turned out to be small and balding, with a tough beer belly and thick arms and shoulders. Despite his mortician's uniform of dark suit, white shirt and blah tie, he looked ready for a fistfight.

He looked at me, chin raised. "Is something wrong, Ms. Rodriguez?"

I felt myself turn red. He'd caught me staring. "You don't look like a funeral director."

A spark of humor lit his eyes. "It throws people. My customers never complain, though." He and Zeke traded grins.

Funeral parlor humor. I made a mental note to raise the fee for midnight dance lessons.

I taught Joe the basics, but he was no Zeke Straley. Zeke immediately grasped new steps and performed them with grace. He seemed pleased when Joe stepped on my feet or collided with me, moving forward when he was supposed to move back.

Joe smiled through his mistakes, and when Rudy appeared, fur ruffled, to see why I was yelping in pain, Joe made such a fuss over him that he won the old kitty as a friend for life.

Afterwards, Joe said that he'd never had so much fun.

"Most women are kind of weird about my line of work," he said. "Sometimes they try to treat me as if I'm clergy, but that brings on a different kind of weirdness."

I understand their dilemma, I thought. *Who wants to think, when a man caresses her, that his hands have been in a corpse's stomach?*

I staggered into bed at three a.m., thinking that maybe there would be some mention of me in the mortician's association newsletter.

The next morning Jayne told me I needed to rest, and Sandy suggested cucumber slices for the bags under my eyes. She also asked me if I could use a little extra money, and offered to give me the phone number of a friend who needed a little light housework done.

I didn't know what to say, except thank you, and no. I

was touched that they were worried about me. It gave me the warm feeling of being part of the community. On the other hand, it made me realize that I wasn't the only person aware of my sense of impending doom regarding Zeke Straley.

I had more offers for part time jobs. The resthome needed helpers in the cafeteria. The elementary school could use some temporary help with a new shipment of books. O'Day's needed a waitress. My smile felt pasted on by the end of the week.

It didn't help things that two mothers canceled their little girls' ballet classes. Both had legitimate reasons, or so it seemed, but the timing seemed suspicious, and one was seen entering the studio in Bigelow.

I called Jayne to report the rumors about me and Straley.

"Oh, that's nothing," Jayne said smoothly. "People are always wondering if I'm sleeping with someone. So far, the gossip has me grinding coffee beans with at least ten different Creekite bachelors. The age spectrum ranges from young Nail Delgado to old Ed Brady. Hey, I've got customers. I'll talk to you later."

I hung up, baffled. In New York City there are too many people for one person to get so much attention. The folks of Mossy Creek must have nothing better to do.

Late that night Zeke showed up with Joe again.

"What can we do to make things better?" Joe asked earnestly. He had heard the gossip all the way in Bigelow. His eyes gleamed brighter than his bare scalp.

That was it. I started to cry. "You want to help. All of the people offering me part-time jobs want to help," I said between sobs. I was burbling like a toddler. "If everyone quit being so damned helpful, I'd be able to get something done."

"What do you want done?" Zeke asked. He kept lifting and dropping his arms like a helpless scarecrow in a stiff wind. "I dropped my complaint about the noise. I'm learning how to dance. I think we've even become friends, right?"

I sobbed louder, taking in big gulps of air. My nose was stopped up so I breathed through my mouth. I probably looked awful, too. I do not cry pretty.

Zeke turned to Joe, alarm on his face. "I think she's lost it. What do we do?"

"Flour and plaster absorb lots of liquids," Joe suggested. "If we dust her, her tears might dry."

I stopped crying, distracted by the thought of the sorts of things Joe might have to dust with plaster on any given work day.

"We can't dust her with plaster," Zeke quipped. "She's alive. The stuff will eat her skin."

Feeling queasy, I slipped over to the stereo and turned the now-familiar tango music on, carefully avoiding looking into the mirrored wall. I'd had enough stress for one day.

"Let's dance, guys," I said. All I'd ever wanted to do was run my own dance studio in a quiet little town. When the music librarian for the ballet had pointed out a travel magazine story about the notoriously colorful little Southern village with the motto, *Ain't going nowhere — and don't want to*, it had piqued my interest.

One visit and I knew Mossy Creek was where I wanted to live. So here I was, stuck, my bridges burned behind me. Ahead of me, too, it seemed. I wasn't going *nowhere.*

Straley shook my hand gently as he left. "Don't worry, Argie. Things have a way of working out," he said. "I wouldn't fret about the gossip, and we've only got two more days until the convention. Things will get back to normal. You'll see."

"Thanks, Zeke," I said, not believing him. He hadn't said he'd stop pressuring me to move my studio.

Two more kids dropped out the next day. I called Zeke

and left a message on his answering machine, but he didn't call back.

On Thursday, the day before he was supposed to leave for the morticians' convention in Orlando, Zeke appeared in the middle of the afternoon ballet class, tapping on the big glass window. The moms all turned around, then looked from me to him, wide-eyed.

I told the girls to continue their barre exercises, and stepped outside. "Go around to the back room," I said to Zeke. "Put on some headphones and practice your moves. I'll join you as soon as I can."

"Headphones?" He snapped his fingers. "That's the solution! Get all the kids to wear headphones, and then you won't have to play the music so loud."

"It's not loud," I answered, closing the door.

A few minutes later, I sneaked into the back room. "I'm granting you five minutes while my students take a break."

He gave me a thumbs up, then put his arms out. Since he was wearing the headphones, I danced a couple of steps to music only he could hear. Slight pressure on my right hand signaled me that he was about to dip me, and I let him lower me almost to the floor. It was perfectly done. He would be the star of the morticians' conference. I left him to practice and ran back to finish leading the *barre* exercises.

Jayne dropped by. "Watch out, the women of Mossy Creek are on their way."

"What?"

"They were at my shop, discussing your problem with Zeke and how you need money, and that your students were dropping out and you were doing extreme things to make ends meet. They've decided to straighten you out. I think they're planning an intervention."

"Intervention?" I whispered. "Isn't that what they do to confront alcoholics and drug users?"

"Something like that."

"Oh, my God." I looked out the window. A big blue Cadillac was nosing into a parking spot, the driver visible only as two gnarled hands and a wisp of blue hair. Adele Clearwater. A leading meddler in the Mossy Creek social scene. She and Jayne had clashed during the Ingrid-Jayne feud. "They're here."

I thought of Zeke dancing in my back room. There was no way he could hear my warning with his headphones on. Joe was supposed to stop by, too.

Jayne made herself comfortable on the sofa. Matthew chortled and smiled and promptly became the center of attention among Jayne's fellow mothers.

I gave Jayne a *what the heck is happening here?* look.

She grinned back.

Ingrid Beechum came in and promptly took Matthew in her arms, followed by Adele, Pearl Quinlan and her cronies and other Creekite mavens. I turned off the music and led the girls in stretches. For a couple of minutes, the silence was interrupted only by my instructions and the murmur of the women who were now crowding the walls of my studio.

A loud voice came from the other side of my bedroom door.

"Hey, you stepped on my toe!"

Everyone froze. It was a man's voice.

"That's Joe Murdock's voice in there," Pearl said loudly. "He's from Bigelow."

All eyes turned to me.

"Class over, girls," I said brightly. "Don't forget to stretch every day." I was anxious to get the little girls and their mothers out before the showdown began.

There was a gasp from behind me. I whirled. Pearl and Ingrid walked over to the other side of the studio and opened the door, catching Zeke dipping Joe, whose bald head almost scraped the floor. The two men looked up, shocked, and Zeke dropped Joe, who lay there, looking at the crowd, upside down.

"I'm okay," he said.

A woman screamed. Chaos took over as the little girls and women rushed to look.

"Hysteria in the wisteria." Jayne laughed. "I can see Katie Bell's headline for The Bell Ringer column next week."

I felt like a toy boat in a rushing stream. The situation was out of my control.

Zeke unplugged his headphones from the back room's CD player, and the tango music swelled to fill the room. He stepped over Joe. The crowd parted as he came to me.

"Let's show them, Argie," he whispered.

"What about your reputation?"

"About as shot as yours," he said. "Let's show them what a great teacher you are."

"This won't put the gossip to rest."

"Oh? Trust me. I'm good at putting things to rest. A professional, in fact." His eyes twinkled.

We danced, faces serious, putting all of our concentration on the sexy, sinuous dance. The women crowded in, watching. As we turned, I saw that Joe was dancing with Jayne, who was coaching him on where to put his feet.

"Hey, Argie, I want to learn to do that," Pearl said.

"Me, too. You've been holding out on us." That was Ingrid.

Soon the entire crowd was clamoring to learn the tango, the rumba, and the merengue. I found myself promising to start a weekly Latin dance class. Jayne rolled her eyes and I grinned, knowing I could count on her for some more midnight lessons.

A small, plump, dark-haired lady in a suit plowed through the group, closely followed by a short man who looked Hispanic. He was dressed like a laborer in his Sunday best: hair slicked back, crisp, glaring white collared shirt and stiff new blue jeans with a big silver buckle on the belt.

"Hi, Maria," I called as Zeke and I executed a neat figure eight formation with intertwined steps.

Maria watched us, eyebrows raised. "I found you a tango teacher, but I see it's too late. This is Flaviberto Cespedes."

I shook hands with him. "Muchisimo gusto," I said.

Senor Cespedes seemed a little frightened by the sudden surge of women who surrounded him, demanding classes.

I slipped outside, evading the congratulatory hugs and slaps on the back. I left Zeke to face the gossip alone, but I could see he was grinning, enjoying the praise. The tango CD segued into a wild Dominican merengue beat. I watched through the front window as little Flaviberto showed the women how to boogie, Latin style. He and Ingrid were face-to-bosom, hips gyrating. Her grin was incandescent. The rest of the women waited their turn. The little girls from my ballet class were dancing with each other. It looked like a crazy party.

Zeke stepped outside, grinning at me. "Quite a guy, that Flaviberto," Zeke said, We sat down on the bench.

"I'll have to put him on the payroll," I said. "His chicken plucking days are over."

The sun was setting, and the cool autumn air smelled wonderful. I leaned back against a trellis and smiled, enjoying the peaceful moment.

"We certainly gave this town something to talk about," Zeke said.

"You bet. I hope this doesn't mean the end of our friendship?" I'd kind of gotten used to him.

"Heck no, we're neighbors. Besides, who else will drink tea with me at three in the morning?"

I shuddered. "I was hoping I'd get some sleep now."

He laughed.

"Hey, as long as we're buddies, you won't complain about my music or try to make me move?"

He sighed dramatically. "Just keep the music down. It's loud on the hill."

"I doubt that. It's a good hundred yards from my front door to yours." This was old ground.

"I think I figured out why the sound carries so well. Want to hear my theory?"

I glared at him. "Is it the ridge and natural-acoustics nonsense again?"

He held up his hands in mock surrender, then lifted one finger higher to point. "I think the noise is coming from your roof." He pointed at the corner nearest us, where the wisteria vines were twining in and out of the soffit. "I can go in your attic and lay down lots of insulation to soundproof it."

I considered his idea. "It makes sense. Okay, let's try it. I'll get rid of the wisteria, too."

"You'll never get rid of the wisteria," he said. "Don't you know it's like kudzu? Once you plant it, that's it. If you stay still long enough, it'll wrap around you."

I glared at the gnarled green invader working on my roof, then a thought hit me. "It's like me, isn't it?"

"The wisteria?"

"Yeah," I said, warming to my idea. "Once planted it won't give up — just like me. Watch out, Zeke Straley."

He laughed. "Truce?"

"Truce." We linked our pinkie fingers to seal our friendship. Behind us, inside my studio, the music changed back to a tango. He got up, bowed, and offered his hand. I stood and accepted it.

As the sun dropped, turning us into silhouettes, Zeke and I danced under the bare, promising vines of the wisteria, sweet symbol of my tenacity.

Lady Victoria Salter Stanhope
The Cliffs
Seaward Road
St. Ives, Cornwall, TR3 7PJ
United Kingdom

Dear Vick:

I *hated* being out of town during the Zeke/Argie fracas. I just got home from New York. With humility I can say that little old me won in the *quaint* columnist category. Not bad for a writer from a town of only 1,700 people. I could barely believe it last spring when Sue Ora sent in my nomination. I mean, yes, as publisher of the *Gazette*, she's expected to be proud of her staff. And since she's married to a Bigelow, she's used to taking risks. But still, I was shocked and thrilled that she thought I had a chance at a national award.

I should have known I'd win. But I have to give Sue Ora a lot of credit for letting me and the rest of the staff write pretty much what our subscribers want to read, even if it

is *quaint*, local, and very, very
personal. We don't print any national
news and very little state news. We
barely even mention our own county
seat, Bigelow, if we can avoid it.
After all, there's always so much
happening right here in Mossy Creek.
Who has time to cover the rest of the
world? Have to dash now. I'm on the
trail of a mysterious night rider who
roams our hills on a Harley.

Your inquiring, award-winning reporter
Katie Bell

Who might like to visit New York
again, but there's no place like Mossy
Creek.

P.S. What happened to your recipe for
scones? I'm getting requests from our
readers.

Lady Victoria Salter Stanhope

The Cliffs, Seaward Road
St. Ives, Cornwall, TR3 7PJ
United Kingdom

My dear Katie:

Congratulations! I believe you'd find St. Ives to be quaint enough to win newspaper awards, too! Our little house was considered by my husband's ancestors to be their regal cottage by the sea. I won't argue with Stanhope family history, but I have learned that it also housed fishing boats and smugglers. Somehow I can't see the Stanhopes as fishermen.
We could live in London where the Stanhope Investment firm is located, but we prefer to stay here. My husband goes into the city twice a week but conducts the rest of his business by computer. Oh, by the way — I've found a connection to one of the original children from the marriage of Isabella Salter and Richard Stanhope in Mossy Creek. It seems their son, Salter Stanhope, immigrated to Australia about 1880 to look for gold. Apparently he didn't find any because he seems to have kept going.

As for my scone recipe, I've written it on the other side of this letter.

By the way, I'm investing in my neighbor's antique shop, so if you want any real English pieces, let me know.

Vicki

Victoria's Recipe for English Scones

1 lb. self-rising flour

1 tsp. salt

4 oz. butter

2 oz. sugar

1 cup half and half

Set oven for 450 degrees.

In a mixing bowl, sift flour and salt. Rub in butter until mixture resembles fine bread crumbs. Then add sugar and mix with the half and half until it becomes a soft dough. Turn out on a lightly floured surface and knead quickly. Then roll out to 1/2" thick. Cut into triangular sections.

Place scones on greased baking sheet and brush tops with beaten egg or milk. Bake (this is a hot oven) for 8-10 minutes. Cool on a wire rack. When they are cold, split and serve with preserves and clotted cream.

You probably can't get authentic clotted cream in Mossy Creek, but you might try making your own with this recipe a friend shared with me.

Clotted Cream

1/2 pt. whipping cream (already whipped)

1 tablespoon sour cream

Mix together thoroughly and spread on top of preserves on the split scone.

In Mossy Creek, people expect generosity,
but they know that sacrifice deserves reward.

🌱🌱🌱🌱🌱🌱🌱🌱🌱🌱🌱🌱🌱🌱🌱🌱🌱🌱🌱🌱🌱🌱🌱🌱🌱🌱🌱🌱🌱🌱🌱🌱🌱🌱🌱🌱

Rewards

Chapter 3

Dear Katie Bell:

This past summer I worked really hard, read a lot of books, and learned some important things. I *guess* you could call 'em blessings. Mainly I learned how great a place Mossy Creek is to grow up. And I learned who I am and where I belong. My full name is John Wesley McCready, and I am nine years old. My mom is the secretary at Mount Gilead Methodist Church, and my dad works at the bank.

While I was out of school this summer, I did some odd jobs around town to earn the money to get my mom a nice birthday present. My mom says Mossy Creek is about the only town left where you can let a kid roam around on his own for the summer and not worry. Still, I had to check in with her at the church and my dad at the bank a few times every day. But other than that, I was pretty much on my own. My grandpa used to take care of me on summer vacations, but he passed away this spring. I sure do miss him.

My odd jobs were easy, but it was harder than usual to stay out of trouble. Everything I did seemed to go wrong.

Before my grandpa died, I used to visit him most days at the Magnolia Manor nursing home. He liked it when I read books to him that he read as a boy, like *Robinson Crusoe*, *Treasure Island*, and *Huckleberry Finn*. Sometimes I would

75

climb up next to Grandpa and we'd pretend that his hospital bed was a raft and we were Huck and Jim going down the Mississippi. Grandpa liked that, but the nurses said I was jumping on the bed and being too "boisterous." One of them told my mom on me.

I tried to help Grandpa all I could before he died. When he got really sick and they had to feed him through a tube, I helped swab out his mouth with foam rubber swabs, and then I got clean ones and let him suck ice water off of them. The nurses all said I was real brave then. I started to read *Harry Potter* to Grandpa, but he died before Harry even got to Hogwart's.

I still visit Grandpa, only now I visit him in the cemetery behind Mt. Gilead Methodist Church. He's buried beside Grandma in the shade of a willow tree whose branches come all the way to the ground. Our family plot is surrounded by a little concrete wall a couple of feet high. Sometimes I like to pretend that the walled-off plot is the ship in *Treasure Island* and that I'm Jim Hawkins.

One day the cemetery caretaker called my dad and told him that I was stepping on graves. My dad talked to me that night and told me that was disrespectful. We like to respect the dead here in the South. That's why people pull their cars to the side of the road when a funeral procession goes by, even if the policemen don't make them.

My friend Little Ida Walker thinks it's spooky and gross that I know where my dead body is going to be buried when I die, but I don't think so at all. I know the exact spot I'll be put to rest, and I like to lie in the grass there just a few feet from Grandma and Grandpa and watch the clouds go by.

I figure being buried in a place that you love is kind of like being planted like the tomato seedlings I planted for Miss Lorna Bingham back in the early summer. Sort of natural-like. All the McCreadys, and my mom's family, the Hardys, are buried there in that cemetery, so I won't be alone. It's nice to know you have a place to belong, even after you're dead.

I made a lot of friends among the old people at the nursing home, and so after Grandpa died I went back there to see them and do little chores for them. They tried to pay me, but I figured they needed their money for the snack machine in the lounge.

Anyway, here's how I got in trouble. When we came back from a vacation down in Florida I brought a box of saltwater taffy to the home and gave some to all my old friends. What I didn't think about was that almost all of them have false teeth.

The taffy was pulling out their plates right and left before I realized what was happening. They like to have never got the taffy out of their dentures, and one of the nurses got mad at me. But the old people said it was the thought that counted. Old people look funny when they talk without their teeth, and Mr. Jaybird Johnson made some funny faces that scared one of the nurses but made me and him laugh and laugh. Then that mean nurse talked to my mom again and she told me I couldn't go back to the home until I learned to behave.

Right after I got in trouble at the nursing home, my mom suggested that I help Miss Bingham plant her vegetable and flower gardens. Miss Bingham has diabetes and is in a wheelchair so she can't do her planting by herself. She can only hoe a little. When Mom suggests something, that means you pretty much have to do it. She said, "I think you need to help an elderly person this summer so that you'll think twice about aggravating them, like you did at the home." So because of the taffy trouble, I couldn't play Little League baseball for Coach Looney. Instead I had to work for Miss Bingham for free.

She can't hear too good, but that's probably just as well, because she's always a lot more interested in talking than listening. She told me how to plant her tomato seedlings even though I already knew since I helped Grandma and Grandpa plant theirs for as far back as I can remember. She told me to be careful with the roots because without roots the plants couldn't stand. "Plant 'em deep," she'd say as I dug the holes. "Water 'em good," she'd say as I carried water from the spigot at the back steps to the garden in an old bucket.

"People are like plants," she said one day. "Without roots you have nothing to stand on. Roots help you understand who you are and where you came from. With your roots in good Mossy Creek soil and some careful tending, like these tomato plants, you'll grow up just fine."

"I don't know, Miss Bingham," I said. "Sometimes I think that I won't stay in Mossy Creek when I grow up, no matter what the town motto on the sign says. This town is so small, every time I do the littlest thing wrong, somebody calls my mom and rats me out. I'm thinking that a bigger town might be better for me."

Miss Bingham shook her head. "Let me tell you a story that happened to me when I was a girl. My daddy gave me some beans to plant in several rows he had just plowed in the field. I planted and planted, covering the beans up with a hoe as I went. But directly I got tired of planting beans, so I dumped the rest of them in a ditch and covered them over with dirt and went on to the house.

"But do you know what happened? Later on, those beans sprouted up all in a cluster, and my daddy knew what I did and gave me a whipping with a switch. Now the moral of that story, son, is that you reap what you sow. If you're a good boy, good things will happen to you. Understand?"

"Yes ma'am," I said. But I wasn't sure I believed her.

Later on in the summer, I went back to Miss Bingham's to help her string and break beans and shell peas because she has arthritis and can't do it very well on her own. The lady that stays with her cooked up a pot of beans and peas with fatback, a pone of cornbread with cracklin's, a squash casserole and some fresh sliced tomatoes. We had a big feast and I ate so much and drank so much buttermilk that I thought I was going to pop.

Miss Bingham said it did her heart good to see a growing boy eat a hearty, home-cooked, home-grown meal at her table again.

Miss Bingham insisted on paying me to do all this work for her, but since she doesn't have much money, I sneaked the dollars back into her change purse when she fell asleep in her wheelchair. Sometimes when I'm passing by this fall, I see her asleep in her little garden. I usually just adjust her bonnet so she won't get too much sun and go along my way. She likes her naps.

I read a lot this summer, including all the *Harry Potter* books, and some adventure books like *White Fang* and *The Adventures of Tom Sawyer*. Like I said before, I think it's fun to pretend that I'm in those books. Little Ida and Timmy Williams and me sometimes go over to the square and climb up the base of General Hamilton's statue and pretend that we're in the crow's nest of the *Pequod* looking out for Moby Dick. We play *Heidi* and *Little Women* with Little Ida sometimes. Those are girls' books, but we don't mind.

On Wednesday mornings this summer, I went to the library and read to the little kids for story time. Sometimes I acted out the stories as I went along, which they really seemed to enjoy. And then I picked out books to read for myself.

I did most of my summer reading at night. In the daytime, I worked. Mrs. Beechum paid me a little to sweep the floor at the bakery every day and take Bob the Chihuahua for a walk so he wouldn't pee on the customers' legs when he got nervous, which was pretty much all the time. Since that hawk flew off with him he's been real nervous, even for a Chihuahua.

It was trying to take care of Bob that got me in trouble again.

Bob has a bad habit of nipping at customers. Folks don't usually like it when they come in to buy fresh bread and get peed on or bitten into. This summer Mrs. Beechum said, "A Chihuahua with personal issues can just take the joy right out of the bread-buying experience." I decided to break Bob of his bad habit, and I thought Mrs. Beechum would be grateful, but she wasn't. In fact, when she saw what I'd done, she told me not to come back in the shop again.

And all I did was bite him back. I figured that a dose of his own medicine might make him straighten up and fly right. No joke intended. One morning Bob seemed to get overly excited by my sweeping — he was trying to chase the broom around — and nipped me on the heel. So I got down on my all fours and bit him. Not hard enough to draw blood or anything. Just hard enough to make a point. I don't know who was more upset — Bob or Mrs. Beechum. Bob's eyes, which already looked like they wanted to pop out of his fuzzy head, got even bigger than usual. And so did Mrs. Beechum's, for that matter.

I like Miss Jayne Reynold's cat, Emma, better than Bob or even the pet ferret over at Miz Quinlan's bookstore. Emma likes to rub noses with me, and when I hold her she purrs like a motorboat. This summer Miss Jayne let me bus the tables after the morning rush at her coffee shop and sometimes I gave Emma a little piece of doughnut off people's plates. For a cat, she really liked doughnuts.

In fact, she decided she liked them so much she jumped

up on a table and knocked off a whole tea set.

It only broke a little of Miss Jayne's china, and she was real nice about me teaching Emma to like doughnuts that much, but one of the customers got doused by a smidge of the coffee I spilled and told my mom. So Mom told me I couldn't work there anymore.

So I had to work even harder. See, I wanted to make enough money to buy Mom a present.

The present I wanted to get her was a beautiful, genuine ruby necklace that I saw advertised in the back of one of the magazines in Rainey Cecil's beauty shop. I stopped by Miss Rainey's a couple of times a day to sweep up the hair, and she'd give me some change out of her tip jar. Then I took the hair and sold it to Smokey Lincoln, the forest ranger, who sprinkled it on the edge of his garden to keep the deer from eating his plants. Forest rangers know stuff like that.

Anyway, this necklace had gold all around it and a real nice chain, and I just knew my mom would love it. So I saved all my odd-job money in a *Maxwell House* can that I kept under my bed. I wanted it to be a big surprise for her.

ǂ ǂ ǂ

The day in early August that I finally had enough money for the necklace was a big day. I planned to take the money and the order form to Rainey, who said she would write a check for the necklace and mail the order. That morning, after I got dressed, I took the money out of the coffee can and stuffed it in the pocket of my jeans.

At a little before nine o'clock that morning, my dad dropped off me and Mom at the church as usual and went on to work at the bank. As we were walking toward the door to the church office, we saw a man standing beside an old, beat-up pickup truck parked in front of the church.

I heard my mom sigh as the man came our way. She had told me that poor people passing through town would sometimes stop at the church for handouts. This man wore ripped and dirty overalls and plow shoes and looked like he hadn't shaved in a few days. He took off his ragged baseball cap and spoke to my mother. "Do you work at the church, Ma'am?"

Mom said that she did.

"I wonder if I could get a little help. I'm on the way to South Carolina with my family. My brother says there's a job for me there picking peaches, but I'm about to run out of gas and I don't have the money to buy another tank or to feed my kids another meal." He raised a skinny arm and pointed toward the church. "Do you think the preacher would help me out?"

Mom chewed her lip. "Mister, I gave the last penny of his discretionary fund to some folks in the same shape as you who came through yesterday." She got her wallet out of her pocketbook and took out a five dollar bill. I could see that she had no folding money left. "This is all I have. It should be enough to buy a loaf of bread and some peanut butter for your kids, but I can't help you out with gas. I'm sorry. I would if I could."

The man took the bill. "Bless you anyway, Ma'am."

We watched the man walk away in the direction of the convenience store, his head down like he was studying the pavement. Mom looked down at me. "Count your blessings every day, son. Count your blessings that you live in a town like Mossy Creek where your neighbors will give you the shirts off their backs and nobody goes hungry." She tousled my hair. "You run along now."

The neighbors might give you their shirts, but they also tell on you for every little thing you do. A kid can't sneeze in this town without some busy body telling his mom or dad.

For a second I wanted to run after the man and ask him if he would take me to South Carolina with him, where nobody knew me or my telephone number. Shoot, if I ran away I probably wouldn't even *need* a phone number.

My mom went in the church office and I walked over to the man's pickup. I could see a woman in the passenger seat, probably the man's wife, with her head propped on her hand, kind of weary like. I walked a little closer. The truck had sideboards, homemade out of lumber. Between two of the boards, I saw four pairs of eyes looking back at me. I walked closer still.

"Hey," I said.

"Hey," said the biggest pair of eyes. The smaller ones just stared.

I walked around to the rear of the truck where I could see them pretty clearly between the tailgate and the lowest board. They were sitting on top of a pile of pasteboard boxes and brown paper grocery bags full of clothing, pots, pans, and other house stuff.

"Where y'all headed after South Carolina?" I asked. The oldest and the youngest were girls. The two in the middle, boys. Each was dressed in cutoff jeans shorts and tee shirts. The clothes of the littlest, a redhead with a smudge of dirt across one cheek, looked worst of all. I figured once the clothes got passed down to her, they were pretty much done for.

"North," the older girl said. They all stared at me as if I was some creature the likes of which they'd never seen before. "My daddy said I might get to go to school this fall."

"Don't you go to school every year?" The girl was a little taller than me. I knew she had to be at least a third grader.

"Nah." She shrugged. "There's too much work to do. In the fall we pick apples. We're usually way up north by then."

I felt a little sick, thinking about my teachers and friends at Mossy Creek Elementary and all the fun we had. "I hope you get to go to school. You'd like it."

"I can already read some," she said. "My mom taught me. The other day I read the story about *Rapunzel*. Do you know it?"

I nodded and watched her pile some boxes higher in a heap. She climbed up on the pile and put an old work shirt on her head so the long sleeves looked like pigtails hanging down. "I like to pretend I'm in the tower waiting for my handsome prince to climb my hair and save me."

"I like to act out stories, too," I said. "Have you ever read *Heidi*?"

"Yeah, that's a good one. I liked how Heidi and her grandfather got to eat all the cheese they wanted because they had all those goats. I wish I had a goat."

Her littlest brother started to scramble up the stack of boxes, grabbed one sleeve of the shirt she held on top of her head, and caused her to fall off the pile. She brought him the rest of the way down with her in a heap. The other two children piled on, and the four of them broke into giggles.

By that time, their daddy had returned from the convenience store carrying a brown bag. His sad look turned into a smile as he heard his kids laughing. I stepped back so he could lower the rusty tailgate of the truck, where he carefully spread out the flattened paper sack and started making sandwiches with a loaf of white bread. He spread thick gobs of peanut butter onto the bread with his pocket knife. I secretly hoped he hadn't recently gutted a buzzard or anything like that with the knife, but it looked pretty clean to me.

He gave a sandwich to his wife and each of his kids. Then he made one more, for himself, I figured, but when he got through, he handed it out to me. I took it and thanked him. I asked him,'"What are you going to do now, mister?"

He looked up toward the church steeple. "We'll sit here a while, I reckon, and see what happens. The Lord will provide. He always does." With that, he fastened the tailgate and went to the cab of the truck to sit with his wife.

The kids were quiet as they ate their sandwiches. I couldn't help but wonder where their next meal was going to come from. Where the oldest girl's next book was going to come from. I thought and thought as I chewed my sandwich. When I was done I brushed the crumbs off my hands and dug the money out of my pocket.

It was the most money I had ever had in my life and it had taken all summer to earn. I looked up and saw that the littlest girl had finished her sandwich and grinned at me over the top of the tailgate. With her red braids, she looked like the drawing of *Pippi Longstocking* in one of the story books I'd read to the kids at the library.

I felt real sorry that these kids didn't have a home town. I probably knew all the other kids in Mossy Creek and even the names of most of their dogs and cats. Nobody was a stranger to me except people passing through. These kids would always be strangers. They'd never have a place to belong, never get a chance to put down roots like Miss Bingham's tomato plants. Instead, they'd be like dandelions, blowing in the wind and scattering who knew where. I felt guilty for ever wishing that I didn't live in Mossy Creek.

I went around to the driver's side of the cab where the man was finishing his sandwich. "I have some money, mister," I said, holding out the roll of bills. "I was going to buy my mama a present, but I want you to have it."

The man broke out into a wide grin, making him look younger than he had before. "Thank you, son. You're an angel of the Lord. I knew that God would provide." He shook my hand and his wife thanked me, too.

As he headed his truck toward the tanks at the convenience store, I waved goodbye to the kids and they waved back at me. I sat on the curb and rested my elbows on my knees, my chin in my hands. Now my mom wouldn't get the beautiful ruby necklace. So many times I had pictured her smiling face as she opened my present. Now that vision was gone.

"Was that wad of cash the money you worked so hard for this summer?" somebody said. I looked around. Miss Maggie Hart stood on the sidewalk behind me. She was carrying a big, two-level silver tray full of teeny tiny little glasses. She was in charge of washing the communion glasses, the ones they put the grape juice in.

"Yeah," I said with a sigh. "I was going to buy my mama a necklace for her birthday, but those folks needed it more than I do. I guess now I'll have to make a necklace out of macaroni and glitter like the ones I helped the little kids with during vacation bible school." I laughed a little.

"After I return this communion set I have to attend a meeting of the Mossy Creek City Council," Miss Hart said. "I want you to meet me at my shop at eleven. I've got a proposition for you."

I said okay, and she went in the church. I looked back down the sidewalk and saw some other church ladies heading my way. Snow Halfacre, who runs the nursing home, said, "What's wrong, young man? You look like you just lost your last friend."

That's pretty much how I felt too. I only shrugged.

"You know, the residents at the home miss you a lot. I've even heard they have a petition drive going to have you reinstated as a volunteer. I think we could manage that."

"Really?" I asked. It made me feel good to know my friends at the nursing home had stuck up for me.

Mrs. Beechum was right behind the nursing home lady.

"John Wesley, Bob hasn't bitten anybody since you taught him a lesson by biting *him*. Maybe you'd better come on back to the shop and take up your sweeping and dog walking again."

Sue Ora Salter Bigelow came up beside Mrs. Beechum and said, "Ingrid, do you mean to tell me that you had a boy-bites-dog story and you didn't even tell Katie Bell so she could write it up for the *Gazette*?" She shook her head and laughed.

That's when Miss Jayne came along, carrying her laptop computer. "Emma and my customers miss you, John Wesley. I'm going to call your mother and ask her permission for you to come back to work at my shop, too."

I thanked Miss Jayne, and she bent down and spoke close to my ear. "We all — your mom and dad included — understand that you haven't been quite yourself this summer. Sometimes when you suffer a loss like you did this spring when your grandpa died, it takes a while to get your head back on straight. I know all about that." She smiled sadly into the distance, and I knew she was remembering her husband who passed away before their baby was born.

As Miss Jayne, Miss Ingrid, and Miss Sue Ora made their way into the church, I ran around back to the cemetery and plopped down in the cool grass at Grandma and Grandpa's feet. "Those ladies made me feel so good I almost forgot about giving away the money," I told them. "I reckon it's not too bad living in a place like Mossy Creek after all."

I thought about the poor kids in the truck as I watched an ant drop the seed it was carrying and another ant come up to help him carry it. "I guess having your neighbors knowing all about my business isn't the worst thing in the world, Grandpa. They're only trying to make sure I grow up straight, like Miss Bingham's tomatoes."

A little later that morning, I waited for Miss Maggie on

the bench outside *Moonheart's Natural Living,* her herb shop. In a few minutes she came outside. Her hippie skirt twirled around her legs in lots of pretty colors. "That was a really nice thing you did for that family in the truck."

"You didn't tell her I gave them all my money, did you?" I asked. She shook her head. I sighed. "Now I don't know what I'm going to get my mom for her birthday next week."

"I do," Miss Maggie said. I followed her inside her shop.

Miss Maggie's shop smells the best of any shop in town, even better than Mrs. Beechum's bakery when Bob is under control. She sells lots of natural things, like special soaps, bath oils, and incense. Most of the stuff she sells is kind of girly, but I like to look at the rocks and crystals. Sometimes she lets me help her unpack boxes and pop the bubbles in the bubble wrap.

"I have a brand new line of jewelry, and I think that one item in particular would be a perfect gift for your mother." Miss Maggie opened a box she'd taken from under the counter and held up the most beautiful necklace I had ever seen. It had pink stones with silver beads here and there. At the center was a rosy pink heart.

"This stone is rose quartz. It's one of the stones of the heart chakra. It's all about understanding and love — the perfect gem for a mother."

I took the necklace and held it up to the light from a window. The stones caught the sun. I didn't know what a *chock-ra* was, but I knew it was the most wonderful necklace I'd ever seen. "It's great," I said. "But I don't have any money left. I can't afford it."

I tried to hand the necklace back to her, but Miss Maggie put her hand up gently and pushed it back toward me. "I have an idea. Down at the theater, the Mossy Creek players are going to put on a production of *The Sound Of Music,* and Anna Rose Lavender says we need an assistant to help my friend Tag Garner build and paint the sets. You can start now and continue to work after school until the sets are finished. I'll advance you the necklace as payment for your work. Do you think you're the man for the job?"

"Am I ever!" I said.

❦❦❦

I had no idea that the job at the theater would be so much fun. Miss Lavender, the director, and Mr. Garner taught me lots about carpentry and painting. When you think about it, what I was doing was a lot like what I do anyway for fun — creating make-believe places where I can pretend to be my favorite characters from books.

Miss Anna Rose even let me play one of the Von Trapp kids, and it was lots of fun. I'd never played pretend with grownups and costumes and all. I thought my friends would tease me for wearing make-up, but they didn't. In fact, Little Ida said she thought I was cute.

My mom loved the necklace. She says it is the *most fabulously gorgeous* necklace she has ever seen and she wears it all the time. Well, a lot of the time, anyway.

So I have to say that I had a pretty good summer. I learned how important roots are for plants and people. And I learned that Mossy Creek is the best place to plant them. I also learned that God works in mysterious ways, especially here in Mossy Creek.

I was pretty blue when I thought I'd lost my chance to give my mom a nice present that she would really like. But just like the man said, "The Lord will provide." The man called me his angel from the Lord, and I reckon Miss Maggie was mine. In Mossy Creek, we take turns.

Mossy Creek Gazette

215 Main Street • Mossy Creek, GA 30533

From the desk of Katie Bell

Lady Victoria Salter Stanhope
The Cliffs
Seaward Road
St. Ives, Cornwall, TR3 7PJ
United Kingdom

Dear Vick:

I debated not running John Wesley's story because it was so personal. I always ask permission from the parents in a case like this. His mom read the story and cried, then told me she'd be proud to see it in the newspaper. So I ran it last week, and the response was tremendous. That family John Wesley helped? Mayor Walker and Chief Royden assigned Sandy to track them down. She found them at a campground outside Charleston, South Carolina. Hope Bailey Stanton and her husband-to-be, Marle Settles, offered the husband and wife jobs and a home at the Sweet Hope Apple Orchards at Bailey Mill. At last report the family is happily ensconced in a cabin and the kids are in school at Mossy Creek Elementary. I love happy endings! So I'm in a good mood and now I'm off to interview Michael Conners about his secrets, er, I mean his, uhmmm, blessings.

In Mossy Creek, you learn right away that disputes are solved in two ways: the world's way and the Creekite way.

👣👣👣👣👣👣👣👣👣👣👣👣👣👣👣👣👣👣👣👣👣👣👣👣👣👣👣👣👣👣👣👣👣👣👣👣👣👣👣

Home Is Where The Sword Is

Chapter 4

All right, Katie. You want me to be honest with you for your *Blessings* column? Here goes.

The first time I saw a naked woman — I was all of six years old at the time — I thought I'd discovered one of the seven wonders of the world. Talk about blessings.

The woman, whose name I probably never knew, was in an old, folded-many-times *Playboy* centerfold Jerry McMillan and I had literally stumbled across in the basement of an abandoned tenement being renovated in our south Chicago neighborhood. I recall the cool, stuffy smell of moldering brick and the distant neighborhood sounds beyond the dusty windows — not to mention my thundering heart — as I stood mesmerized.

Looking at her made me sweat.

The years between then and now have blurred the specifics, but I remember thinking her smooth bare skin reminded me somehow of the angels in the stained glass windows of St. James church, or the statues overlooking the flock. An angel who'd flown out of her robes. A heavenly vision with red hair.

Even at the tender age of six, being a good Irish Catholic boy, I recognized a blasphemous thought when I had one. But knowing I'd probably end up in Hell's basement —

dragged kicking and fighting from my red-haired angel straight to the fire — couldn't make me look away. And, although gawking at a naked woman hadn't been my first ever transgression, now I see how it set my feet on the wayward path.

I kept that centerfold tucked under my mattress for two years. When my mother found it and showed it to my old man, the hell part caught up with my backside. My mum sent me straight to confession after my dad gave me a belting that made it doubly hard to kneel and face Father Harrigan through the grate. The punishment fit the crime, I suppose, since they were trying to save my immortal soul, but it also must've permanently set a pattern in my mind. *Naked redheads — bad.*

I've been drawn to red haired women ever since.

Therein lies the problem. Mossy Creek, my adopted hometown, is sadly lacking in Irish redheads. Now don't get me wrong, it's a fine place with many fine folks. There are also some feisty, good-looking, unattached women — from the Mayor, Ida Walker, who is a borderline redhead with auburn hair — to Regina-Regina, the best waitress any pub owner could hope to find. Not to mention Jane Reynolds at The Naked Bean down the street and newcomer Jasmine Beleau, who fits nicely into the *blasphemous angel* category. Blessing or curse, I escaped a bullet on that one though. If Ms. Beleau's hair had had even a whiff of red in it, I'd be a dead man.

So what's a connoisseur of fine, red-haired Irish girls caught in a desert of blondes and brunettes to do? Why, venture out onto the Internet, of course. And that's what I did this past spring. Charming strangers don't worry me a bit although my sainted mother often warned me that the harvest of my sins would catch up to me. This particular harvest was named Michelle DeSalvo.

Michelle DeSalvo? Yes, I know what you're thinkin' — nothing that sounded redheaded and Irish in *that* name. But she hailed from Chicago and actually knew where my brother had his restaurant on the eastside. After seeing her photograph and talking to her on the phone, I didn't even care that she might not be a *real* redhead. Plenty of time to discover that later. We set up a visit. I had two weeks to get ready.

First, I had to spruce up my place so it looked more like a home than an unfinished *This Old House* project. It was hard enough to explain to a city girl why I lived a hundred miles north of Atlanta in the Georgia mountains. And, to convince her that I didn't even own an ax. The blinkin' chamber of commerce couldn't have done a better job of selling Mossy Creek than this lonely Irishman. I did prevaricate a bit about how quaint and comfortable an old historical home could be. At least half a home. But the jury was still out on that one.

A few years ago, I bought old Mrs. Chesterfield's place at 224 Pine, barely a block from my pub, O'Day's, on the square. It seemed like a no-brainer. Annie Chesterfield's husband had passed away two years before, and she'd decided to leave the big old house where she'd spent her married life and move into an assisted-living apartment at Magnolia Manor, the local retirement home. After we signed the papers, she asked for a month or so to 'get rid of a few things' and to move. Giving her time seemed to be the least I could do since the selling price had been reasonable. So, I'd had the workmen who remodeled O'Day's frame in a loft apartment over the bar so I'd have a place to sleep until Mrs. Chesterfield cleared out.

A year went by.

Finally, on the anniversary of getting a deed in my name but no house, I paid Mrs. Chesterfield a visit. I was prepared

to do whatever it took to help her finish moving. *Finish* being the operative word here. Pacing up the walk I noticed
how much she'd let the yard go. Easy enough to fix — I could
hire a neighborhood kid to help get the grass and flower
beds in shape. The front steps were a little wobbly but again,
fixable. Annie Chesterfield greeted me graciously at the solid
oak door, then invited me inside the house I'd made mortgage payments on for a year. That's when I knew I was in
trouble. The large rooms looked exactly the same as when
I'd last seen them a year before. Every stick of furniture remained in place, every knickknack and curio retained its
original dust. There were no suitcases or boxes in sight. For
all I knew Mrs. Chesterfield could've been wearing the same
flowered house dress.

And, I could be caught in one of those *Star Trek* time
warps.

It shook me, I have to say. You know the antiquated tale
about how crazy people think everyone around them is crazy
and that they are perfectly sane? I took this as a reality check.
Was it me? Or this nice lady, who was insisting on making
me a cup of Oolong tea she'd purchased at The Naked Bean?

After the aforementioned tea, a half an hour of small
talk, and two helpings of chocolate-mint Girl Scout cookies,
I got the nerve up to ask when she thought she might be
moving. That's when the tearful confession started.

It's a well-known fact that Irishmen are suckers for tears.
We'd rather have a screamin' fight or punch each other in
the eye before voluntarily comforting a crying woman. As
Mrs. Chesterfield went on about how she'd tried to give away
her things but each time she set one close to the door she'd
think of a reason to keep it, I went to find the box of tissues
she kept on the kitchen counter. She boo-hooed about her
furnishings being the symbols of her life, after all, and she
just couldn't decide how to let them go. That news was bad

enough, but then she confessed she'd given the money she'd gotten from the sale of the house — *my* money, as it were — to her son to invest in Enron stock. We all know how that turned out.

Like I said, trouble. I had no clue what to do. So, after thanking her for the tea and assuring her that I'd figure something out, I went straight back to the pub, phoned up Mayor Walker and invited her for a free round of Jack Daniels. The mayor would know what was needed.

"You can't very well throw her in the street," Ida helpfully pointed out.

"Should I call her son?" I ventured. "Convince him to fix the mess he helped make?" I could think of several unsavory ways to get him in high gear. Most of them involved bruises.

Ida warmed the glass of bourbon between her capable hands and watched me. One on one with Ida Hamilton Walker was a unique and slightly intimidating experience. She was beautiful, she was older than me, she was rich, she was a tough businesswoman, and she wasn't above scheming to get what she wanted. If I didn't know better, I would think she was sizing me up for something. I fought the urge to squirm like a teenager. As a man, I couldn't tell whether I was being asked to dance, so to say, or being measured for a rail out of town.

Ida already had a dance partner in Del Jackson. That would be retired Lieutenant Colonel Del Jackson. I wasn't interested in stepping on his combat boots. I'd have to take my frustrations elsewhere. Also, I'd learned the hard way about mixing friendship with let's say, *physicality*. Bad feelings after a romantic flame-out had to be reserved for strangers, not for women who held the fate of your liquor license in their diamond-studded hands.

"I'll stop by and talk to Annie," Ida said. "We ought to be

able to work something out." She knocked back the remainder of her drink and aimed a 'not-to-worry' smile in my direction.

I let out the breath I'd been holding, nodded and offered a refill which she declined. As I watched her slide off the bar stool and move toward the front door, stopping to speak to a few of the regulars, I was reminded of that old saying, *Be Careful What You Wish For.*

We Irish have a love/hate relationship with wishes. We come from the home of the Leprechaun and the four leaf clover, yet never has a country had the distinction of having so many wishes *not* come true. The people are some of the friendliest on earth — except to their own countrymen. Well, and then there's the bad relationship with our neighbors on 'the island.' A mob of us had to come to America to fulfill our true potential. The land of the free and the brave. And in Mossy Creek — of the crazy.

I remembered the sentiments of my Irish heritage when I heard Ida's solution two days later.

"You get half the house," she said, as though: 1) it was all settled, and 2) it made any sort of sense.

Genuinely puzzled, I tried to clear the forest for the trees. "What do you mean, *half the house?* What am I supposed to do with *half* a house?"

"Live in it," she said. When I couldn't find a suitable reply, she went on, "Call Dan McNeil and send his carpenters over there to put up temporary walls and divide the space. Annie only needs one downstairs bedroom, the kitchen and bath. You get the rooms on the other side and the second floor since she can't navigate the stairs. It's the perfect solution. You don't need a kitchen. You eat most of your meals here at the pub."

I must have looked as flummoxed as I felt because she patted my hand. "I know you won't put an old lady out of her home. Think of this as a Do-It-Yourself experiment. Half a home is more than you've had in a year. I'm behind you one hundred percent."

"But —" I managed.

"No 'but.' It's settled." Ida waited, looking so serene I knew I didn't have a chance.

"That'll work." I said finally, without a clue how to make it happen.

❦❦❦

That brings us back to Michelle DeSalvo — my imported, faux, almost-Irish redhead, due to arrive in two weeks. I'd spent the last nine months working on my half of Annie Chesterfield's house, doing some of the labor myself and contracting out the rest. I also had Miss Annie make a list of things she needed fixed. I had to say, the whole house looked a lot better after replacing sagging gutters and wobbly stairs, cutting back overgrown shrubs and adding an updated coat of paint.

My suite of rooms had been patched and painted, the floors refinished, and the bathroom updated. I'd moved my lonely bachelor twin bed from the bar to the upstairs of my new home and the big screen TV with matching recliner into the living room. But that's as far as I'd gotten. Time was running out — I knew my chances of impressing Michelle would increase dramatically if I at least had a couch and some curtains on the windows.

As my mother would no doubt tell you, I knew better. I hadn't grown up in a house without furniture. But let's just say, beyond a bed I hadn't had the need to branch out into the other rooms. Until now. Even I recognized I had what Josie McClure, Mossy Creek's budding interior designer, called *a design emergency.*

But there was no way I was dialing 911 for Josie's pit

bull of a boss, Swee Purla. Even the persuasive Ida wasn't going to talk me into letting that woman put up gold, two-hundred dollar curtain rods with little flying angels on them. Turns out, Ida had a different kind of torture planned. She turned the cops loose on me. Specifically, Sandy Crane.

On Monday morning at ten o'clock (early for a bartender who closes at two a.m.) someone started banging on my private front door at Annie's. Since I sleep in the 'boof' — that's Irish for *buff*—I had to yell down, "Hold your horses!" before draggin' on a pair of sweat pants.

In Chicago, my apartment door had a double dead bolt and a peep hole for security reasons. Opening the door to strangers in the city could be hazardous to your health. In Mossy Creek, I rarely even locked the door and had no advance warning what I was about to face when, scratching a red mark on my bare belly from sleeping on rumpled sheets, I swung the door open.

Three women faced me from the other side. One curly-blond little dynamo in a police uniform. That would be Sandy. One sweet-faced, brown-haired failed beauty queen holding an armful of fabric samples. That would be young Josie McClure, who was engaged to Harry Rutherford. Their wedding was still a month away at the time. And then there was Jasmine Beleau, the aforementioned inspiration for all sorts of blasphemous thoughts.

After months of lonely bachelorhood, suddenly three sets of feminine eyes were staring at my naked chest. *Jaysus, Mary and Joseph.*

Sandy grinned but looked like she'd swallowed her walkie-talkie. Josie turned red from her fingertips to her matching hair. And Jasmine, well, all I could see was a slight narrowing of her wide green eyes as a kind of 'knowing' look crossed her features. Not embarrassed or particularly impressed, simply taking in the scenery. I didn't know whether

I wanted to hear her opinion of my manliness, but I was sure she had formed one.

Sandy recovered first. "Ida sent us. We came as soon as we heard," she said, still grinning.

"Heard what?" I managed before realizing I had to do something before Josie swallowed her tongue and Sandy arrested me for indecent exposure. "Hang on a sec. Be right back." I turned and took the stairs two at a time up to my alleged bedroom. After digging through the laundry for a T-shirt I pulled it over my head, smoothed out a few of the wrinkles, and ran a hand through my bed-head hair.

By the time I came back downstairs, my three visitors were in the center of my empty living room, holding a deep discussion.

"We can't have some out-of-towner looking down on us just because Michael —" one was whispering.

"Because Michael *what?*" I asked, a little out of sorts. I'd been up till four doing book work and I hadn't had any coffee yet. Before I could hurt everyone's feelings, another knock sounded on the door that separated my half of the house from Miss Annie's. Without waiting for an answer, the door opened, and Miss Annie herself tottered through it. Thank the saints she was carrying a cup of black coffee. She handed the coffee to me and I thanked her, but her attention zoomed right past the 'Good morning, Michael' part.

"What's all the excitement?" she asked Sandy.

"Mayor Walker sent us over to help Michael decorate his place," Sandy said. I swear on my sainted mother that Josie McClure then confirmed, "It's a design *emergency.*"

"Well," Miss Annie replied, "I have plenty of extra furniture if you need something." She gazed at me. "Michael? Do you remember that chest of drawers you moved out of this room? We could put it back."

I'd only had half a cup of coffee at this point and I wasn't certain I could say anything resembling a good mannered reply so I kept my mouth shut. That chest of drawers smelled like a mothball factory. And although I appreciated the coffee, I was already deciding to put new locks on all the doors, especially the one between Miss Annie's side and my own.

"Oh no, thank you, Miz Chesterfield," Sandy said. "Mayor Walker said we had to start new and do it fast." She put her hands on her utility belt — the one with the notepad where the gun should be — and pinned me with her curly-blond, Barney Fife stare. "Isn't that right, Michael?"

"Yes, Officer." I slugged back the rest of the coffee and handed the empty cup to Miss Annie. "Better get started," I said.

I'd had no idea what I was in for.

Between Josie looking in the vicinity of my feet every time I walked into a room and Sandy's non-stop list-making I thought I'd surely died and gone to Martha Stewart hell. But that was before I had to face Jasmine Beleau across my own rumpled twin bed and discuss new mattresses and sheets. It takes quite a lot to stun an Irishman but let me tell you, I found my Achilles heel. Watching a woman who makes your palms itch and other parts of you rise to the occasion sit on your bed to test the firmness struck me dumb.

"Sure . . ." was all I could manage.

One of her slender eyebrows arched and her amazing lips twitched into a smile. "I'll take care of your bedroom," she said, pushing to her feet. "Don't worry, your girlfriend'll love it."

The sound of Sandy clearing her throat behind me saved the day. "Uh, I've got to get back to the station. If I'm gone more than half-an-hour the chief starts to worry. He doesn't say so, but I can tell. The whole durned place falls apart without me there to run things." She looked down at her notepad. "I think we've got the essentials here. Don't you,

Jasmine?"

"We've made a good start," Jasmine answered.

I was hoping that meant I could shoo them downstairs and out the front door so I could catch my breath. Sandy did that for me, however. Once you put Sandy in the driver's seat you might as well take the bus. Personally, I was just happy that the chief had seen fit to hire her on the side of law and order. I shuddered to think how good a crook she would be if she put her mastermind to it.

"We'll be back day after tomorrow," she promised, and I had no reason to doubt her.

I determined that the best thing would be to leave my credit card and a key under the mat and let the trio of women have at it while I hid out at O'Day's. Hell, how bad could it be? It had to look better than empty walls and bare floors. That was before my rickety twin bed was delivered to the pub, however, with a bag of clean clothes and a note from Jasmine.

You can come back on Friday.

I took that to mean it would take most of the week to finish everything. As curious as I might be as to how they were spending my money, I decided to let nature or, ah, *femi-nature* take its course. The closest I came to spying was an occasional walk down Pine Street. On Wednesday I spotted Dan McNeil's truck parked outside my house and wondered if they'd decided to tear down my temporary walls and start over again — but I resisted the urge to find out. Friday would be soon enough to face my own version of *While You Were Out.*

❦❦❦

"That's the biggest bed I've ever seen."

Jasmine Beleau smiled. "It's a California king. Plenty of

room for —" her appraising gaze measured me from my running shoes to my hairline — "two people, or whatever." Her smile transformed into a challenging grin. "Why don't you stretch out and see how it feels?"

No way. I was about to swallow my tongue as it was. "I'm sure it'll feel . . . great." I wasn't lying or *lie-ing*. At that point I could only hope, though, that each time I slid between the Indian cotton, 380 thread count sheets, Jasmine Beleau's fallen-angel face didn't haunt my dreams. If we were talking baseball, she was so far out of my league we'd need an interpreter. My only defense was to change the subject, so I turned to check out the rest of the room.

"What's with the sword?" She'd transformed my empty utilitarian sleeping quarters into the black and white lair of a Samurai. A sleek black dresser had been placed so the large mirror would reflect the Japanese screen serving as a headboard for the aforementioned largest-bed-in-Mossy-Creek. The bed itself was covered with a mostly-white-but-with-big-blue-geometric-chrysanthemums comforter, flanked by matching lacquered night stands. From the woven mat on the floor to the dueling pillows situated on either side of a low table complete with glass enclosed sword, the only thing missing was a geisha. Pretty soon Ms. Beleau would have me speaking Japanese. At that moment I probably would have agreed to speak pig Latin, if she'd been the teacher.

"You don't like the sword?" Jasmine asked.

"I'm more the baseball bat type," I said, snapping out of it. If Katie Bell saw this room, the news would be all over Mossy Creek before you could say *Benihana*.

"Boys play with baseball bats, men play with swords."

Jaysus, Mary and Joseph. That pretty much shut me up. "Oh," I managed. "Let's go back downstairs," I said, trying to sound cool and casual.

Sandy and Josie were waiting at the bottom of the stairs. By the time I reached them, I was feeling a little less stressed and a lot more grateful. "You ladies have done a great job." I crossed the room to try out the leather sectional artfully arranged between my own big screen and the fireplace. My old recliner had been banished to a corner. Accordion blinds and sensible curtains covered the windows and an abstract painting in manly tones of charcoal, red, and black hung over the mantel.

Before I could sit, Sandy interrupted. "Come and see your kitchen."

"My kitchen?" Now I knew what Dan McNeil had been doing here — adding rooms. I made a mental note to sit down before I opened my next Visa bill.

"It's more like the galley of a ship," Josie said, looking saucy. I had to figure it had been her idea.

And a good idea it was, too. They had installed a granite-covered bar complete with sink and small refrigerator. A microwave was tucked beneath the counter along with my very own espresso coffee maker. Cabinets on the wall behind the bar held a wine rack complete with glasses.

"You girls are a wonder," I said, no blarney intended. I'd never have thought about putting in a mini-kitchen.

"This is all you'll need for entertaining and those midnight snack attacks," Josie added. Jasmine and Sandy both nodded their heads. "We filled your linen closet with new towels and updated the bathroom with a fresh shower curtain and rugs. Oh, and I'm supposed to tell you that Dan said it would only take half a day to install a deck and a hot tub out back. Said you could make it hot or cold as it suited your mood."

A hot tub? I'd never live that down. Since the ladies looked like they thought it a fine idea, I kept my misgivings to myself. "I'll think about it."

"One last thing," Jasmine said. She motioned for me to follow her out of the kitchen toward the front of the house. She stopped at the door that led to Miss Annie's side of the house. "I had Mr. McNeil install a lock in this door." She handed me a key. "We wouldn't want to give Mrs. Chesterfield heart failure, now would we?" She glanced at my chest, and all the sudden I felt naked as the day I'd first answered the front door. "By the way, I picked up a few things when I was down in Atlanta. I hung them in your closet."

I nodded in agreement, secretly wondering if she'd bought me some leather pants and silk shirts like those romantic pirates wore. Saints preserve me. "Looks like you've thought of everything."

Sandy joined us. "Yep, it's all up to you now."

I didn't want to think about what she actually meant by that. "I don't know how to thank you —"

"We're putting your name on a reference list for Josie here. You can repay her by recommending her for design work. You're gonna give Swee Purla a run for her money, right Josie?"

"You bet. She's a Scorpio-rat. Doesn't stand a chance against a Cancer-snake."

I had no clue what she was talking about and frankly, I didn't want to know. "What about you two?" I'd included Sandy but I was looking at Jasmine. I'd heard something about her being in the image consulting business. *Business* meant money. "What do I owe you?"

"I'm just doing my community service," Sandy declared.

Jasmine gave me that unreadable look she wore most of the time. "I'll think of something — not money — but something."

I'd almost rather have written her a check. That would have put me closer to even ground. I got the feeling she liked having me in her debt, however.

"Well," I opened the door for them. "You have this Irishman's eternal gratitude," I said. Mother would have been proud. Although I'm not sure if she'd understood why Miss Jasmine Beleau thought that statement was funny.

❦❦❦

In the next seven days I was tortured in one manner or another by what seemed like every single solitary soul in Mossy Creek. Thinking I could stay under the radar by bringing in an outsider had shifted from a better idea into a pipe dream. Dan McNeil had done his job well. Not the carpentry, the gossip. Suddenly my impending love life became the local pastime. Dan was placing odds and raking in bets on the outcome while Katie Bell took to visiting O'Day's each afternoon for a glass of root beer and a chat about my Love Shack.

She was determined to 'get the story,' and I was just as determined to keep quiet. Even Amos stopped by to give me a man-to-man pep talk. Made me wonder if he'd put some money on my machismo. By Thursday I'd started to worry that Katie Bell had hired a photographer to follow me around and look in my windows. Thank the lord for Josie's curtain expertise — at least I didn't have to worry about peeping *paparazzi*.

When Friday morning finally rolled around, I was a nervous wreck. Michelle's plane was due in Atlanta at two o'clock. I'd planned to take her to a nice early dinner in the ritzy Buckhead area before driving back to Mossy Creek. We had tickets to the Braves game on Saturday but getting through Friday night was the first priority. Freshly showered and shaved I stood in front of the closet in my socks and skivvies contemplating the new clothes Jasmine had picked out for me. I chose a pair of charcoal gray slacks and pulled them on. As I zipped them, fastened the waist and gazed into the mirror, I had to hand it to her. The pants were a perfect fit. On the other hand, I didn't even want to know how she could gauge a man's size without the benefit of a measuring tape.

I was pondering shirts when my newly installed door bell rang. I yanked the nearest one out of the closet and buttoned it securely on the way down the stairs.

Like a wishful mirage, when I opened door number one, Ms. Jasmine Beleau stood before me. She started to speak but stopped, her smile melting into a frown. She was staring at my shirt. "You're not going to wear *that*, are you?"

I looked down and realized I'd put on my league shirt from the Bigelow Sparkle Bowl-A-Rama. Talk about a geek.

I shook my head *No* but Jasmine grabbed a handful of the material just above my name and propelled me toward the stairs anyway. Faster than you could say *nakedidity*, my prized bowling/beer drinking shirt hit the floor and I stood half dressed while a beautiful woman flipped through the hangers left in my closet. She came up with a white dress shirt shot with pale gray stripes. "Turn around," she ordered, then held the shirt to help me into it. When her fingers brushed my bare shoulder, I felt like I had when I was six and stuck a fork in the wall socket to see what would happen. Blew four fuses and singed my hair the first time. This time I had the sense to keep my hands to myself. "There, that's much better," she said, not paying any attention to whatever stupid look I had on my face. She started to button the first button and I pulled away to a safe distance.

"I can do it," I said, sounding more aggravated than terrified, thank the saints. She didn't bat an eyelash as I buttoned then unzipped to tuck. Her clinical attitude was beginning to annoy me so I got straight to the point. "I'm not your boyfriend or your brother. So, why are you doing this?"

Her eyes sparkled with some private joke. "Let's just call it professional courtesy."

Something amazing happened just then. As the word 'professional' left her mouth a pink flush bloomed in her cheeks. If I didn't know better I would swear she blushed. Suddenly the room felt a lot smaller and that parking lot of a bed a lot bigger.

She cleared her throat. "I'd recommend you wear the shirt open at the throat," she said in a low voice. Her gaze followed her words. "You might also roll up the sleeves — makes a man seem more *accessible*."

I spread my arms to show off my new clothes. "Lady, if I were any more accessible I'd probably be in jail."

Her green gaze met mine and the blush deepened. "Take a jacket and a tie just in case. Good luck, Michael." Before I could even say thanks, she was closing the front door behind her.

I only hoped that my Michelle with the red hair was one of those uncomplicated types. Every man's dream date for the weekend — good food, good sex, a few laughs and a plane ticket home.

💖💖💖

Now I know that most of you are dying to find out exactly how my imported, red-haired fantasy turned out. But, as my mother always said, *A closed mouth is better than one with a size ten foot in it*. So, you'll have to wonder, just like the rest of Mossy Creek. Katie Bell settled for a short interview with the two of us over coffee at The Naked Bean. Dan McNeil paid or collected his bets based on the fact that Michelle was still smiling on Monday morning as we had breakfast at *Mama's All You Can Eat Café* before heading back to the airport in Atlanta. What was that song . . . *A Smile Is As Good As A Wink*?

I haven't seen hide nor beautiful hair of Jasmine Beleau. Perhaps that's for the best. I promised Michelle I'd come see her in Chicago — just for a visit, ya know. It would take more than one red-haired angel to drag me out of Mossy Creek. After all, here I have half a redecorated home. The possibilities are endless.

Mossy Creek Gazette

VOLUME IV, No. 2   MOSSY CREEK, GEORGIA

The Bell Ringer

The New Hot Couple in Town

by Katie Bell

This is your 'quaint' reporter with the latest gossip.

All of you know Mrs. Annie Chesterfield's house over on Pine. Well, it's been totally refurbished, thanks to Michael Conners, who shares the premises. Miss Annie explained when questioned by this reporter that her late husband, the Colonel, sent her word that he approved of a roommate for her, so long as there was no hanky panky. This reporter has to report that a trace of regret was present in her explanation. But there was no question of the twinkle in her eye when I asked her how she got her message from the Colonel.

At any rate, continuing with the *Gazette's* policy of printing all the news that's fit to print and some that isn't, I have managed to obtain a picture of the decorating of Michael's new digs. Contrary to what Miss Annie said, the bedroom is tasteful. The decorators in charge were Josie McClure and

Jasmine Beleau. The bad news is that so far Michael has refused to allow us to include his bedroom on the Christmas tour of homes scheduled for later this year.

Notice from the Mossy Creek Unitarian Church Concerning this week's Sunday Service

The minister is offering blessings ceremonies for Mossy Creek pets. Weather permitting, the ceremonies will be held on the town square on Wednesday evening at 6 o'clock. God welcomes all religions and species.

Note: All attending pets should be leashed, caged, or in a jar.

Mossy Creek Gazette

215 Main Street • Mossy Creek, GA 30533

From the desk of Katie Bell

Lady Victoria Salter Stanhope
The Cliffs
Seaward Road
St. Ives, Cornwall, TR3 7PJ
United Kingdom

Dear Vick:

What do you think about Michael and Jasmine? Hmmm, uh, me, too. I intend to keep a close eye on those two. *Very* close.

In the meantime, enjoy the enclosed story. What would a season in Mossy Creek be without at least one "tail" about a Creekite with four legs?

Katie Bell

In Mossy Creek, people always gets a second chance,
provided they learn some sense from the first one.

❦❦

Sugar & Missy Belle

Chapter 5

A person's name can be a blessing or a curse. If you're thinking Sugar is my nickname, you're wrong. Sugar is, in fact, my God-given name. Well, actually, it's my Mama-given name.

"I took one look at you and said, 'That's the sweetest thing I've ever seen. I'm callin' her Sugar. Sugar Jean Cole.'"

So, there you go. I'm a 22-year-old woman who's gone through life being called *Sugar*. And, for the most part, I've lived up to the name by being just the sweetest person you can imagine.

I was sweet when I got picked on at elementary school and later at Bigelow High. Being called "Sugar Cube" wasn't all that bad when you consider what poor Mutt Bottoms, the baby brother of Sandy and Boo Bottoms, probably had to put up with. It was bad enough to have the last name *Bottoms*, but you can't help what your last name is.

Hanging names like Mutt, Sandy, and Boo on those young-uns, though, was just wrong. But I doubt anybody picked on Mutt. He was a football star . . . a really handsome football star. I cut his picture out of my cousin's yearbook and kept it in my night stand for years. 'Course, he was four years older than me and never knew I existed. I was sweet about that, too.

I was sweet when I was sittin' home on Saturday nights because nobody wanted any of *Sugar's sugar.* Yeah, that's another little saying the creative high school crowd came up with.

I was extra sweet after graduation when I blossomed into a fairly pretty young woman that the boys finally took notice of. And I thought I had the world by the tail when that notice came from Bart Milford. He was all that, a bag of bar-becue potato chips, and a Coke. Make that a Coke with pea-nuts in it. I'm saying he was it.

I forgave every snotty thing he'd ever said about me as well as to my face when he asked me to go riding around town with him in his big black pickup truck with the tractor tires on it. That truck was so high up off the ground that Bart had to haul around a stepladder so I could get up into it. He could've used the stepladder himself, but his pride convinced him that it was a lot more manly to climb up the tires, grab hold of the steering wheel and swing inside like Tarzan.

Only once did I ever see Bart use the stepladder. That was the night he sampled Junior Higgins' daddy's homemade sour mash. His first attempt at the Tarzan leap had landed him flat on his back in the field near Junior's house. I had Junior get down the stepladder and haul Bart's butt into the passenger side of that truck so I could drive him home. That's when all of Bigelow County realized I was Bart Milford's girl. Bart hadn't ever let *anybody* drive his truck before. Now, I knew good and well there wasn't a lot of *let* involved, but I kept my mouth shut.

I liked being Bart Milford's girl, and I knew him well enough to realize how to keep on being Bart's girl. I'll have to hand it to Mama on that one — she was right about that buying the cow thing. With my milk locked tightly in my refrigerator every evening, Bart just kept coming back to see if he could pick the lock.

Bart had had his fill of the rest of the Bigelow girls and their milk — Oh, you thought I was from Mossy Creek? No, that came after . . . Well, you know how they say pride goeth before a fall; well, stupidity is oftentimes the trip wire.

I was so tickled to beat out my competition — the girls who'd given me hell my whole life — that I finally got Bart so anxious about that milk that he married me. Now here's where pride and stupidity go to a picnic. Pride told me that Bart was tee-totally in love with me, and stupidity told me he'd changed his roving ways. I should never have listened to those two, but I did. Nary a thought of challenging either one came to mind. At least, not then.

Me and Bart got married and bought a little house just outside Mossy Creek. Bart went to work at the candle factory, and I stayed home. I'd made an *A* in Home Economics, and I was busting at the seams to put my skills to use. We were happy. We drank a lot of milk. I thought everything was fine.

And then one evening, two years into the marriage, Bart brought Lu Ann Woods home with him from the candle factory. He packed him up a duffel bag, put the stepladder and Goofy, his redbone hound, into the back of the truck, and then he took off down the road with Lu Ann occupying my once-coveted passenger seat of Bart Milford's jacked up truck.

I'll tell you the truth. I didn't feel sweet at all standing there in the dust watching those two laugh as they sped off down our gravel driveway. But the real end of the *sweet little Sugar Doormat* story came about when Missy Belle came along.

That said, you're probably figuring Missy Belle to be another rival for Bart's attention. Well, you're wrong. Missy Belle was a gift from my cousin Rochelle.

Rochelle, God love her, has always reminded me of the Scarecrow in *The Wizard of Oz*. She's skinny, she can't do a thing with her hair, and you can't help wondering what she'd do if she had a brain. (If, by the way, you hear a Southern woman preface a comment with *God love him* or *Bless her heart*, lean in a little closer. You're fixing to hear somebody get slammed.)

Rochelle, being the kind-hearted genius that she is, could not bear for me to be "down there in that big ol' house all by yourself." Not wanting to be snotty, I didn't point out that four rooms did not really constitute a big ol' house; but I reckon everything is relative. Rochelle lived in a trailer with her husband, her mother, her two kids, a rabbit and a bird-dog.

I told Rochelle not to worry, that I'd be fine until Bart came back.

"Honey, he ain't comin' back. And, even if he does, he ain't worth havin'. Now Trudy just dropped a litter about four months ago, and we've not found a home for Missy Belle yet. Why don't you let me bring her over tomorrow?"

"Okay." Bird-dogs grow up to be big and loud, but they're some of the cutest puppies you'll ever see. Maybe by the time Missy Belle was grown, Bart would be home.

First thing the next morning, Rochelle showed up in her little red Toyota pickup. Grinning like the kid who'd got the first cookie at Bible school, she went to the back of the truck, lowered the tailgate and got my puppy out of a crate. At first glance it looked like a good-sized puppy, almost a foot high. 'Course, at four months a bird-dog puppy is tall enough to lick your knee without raising its head.

I squinted. "Is that a runt, Rochelle?"

"This here's Missy Belle. Do you wanna go say 'Hi' to your new mama, Missy Belle?"

Missy Belle didn't answer. Not that I really expected

her to, but she might've whimpered or barked or something.

Rochelle sat her down on the grass and turned her to face me. "There she is, Missy Belle."

Missy Belle took one look at me and said, "*Bleh.*"

My sentiments exactly. "Rochelle," I said, "either that's an awfully odd breed of dog, or it's a goat."

"That's right. Missy Belle's a pygmy goat."

Missy Belle had done dismissed my grass and was munching on my pansies.

"Hey!"

Missy Belle looked up at me . . . chewing . . . with pansy petals hanging out the corners of her mouth.

"What am I supposed to do with a goat?"

Rochelle shrugged. "Same as any other pet. Just love her." She smiled. "I'm glad you like her!"

With that, she got into her little truck and sped off down the driveway, leaving me saddled with a goat. And I called *her* the Scarecrow.

Taking my cue from Rochelle, I decided to talk the situation over with Missy Belle. "Hey," I said, taking her by her dainty pink collar and leading her away from the few bedraggled pansies I had left. "Let's sit down here on the porch and figure this out."

Missy Belle said, "*Bleh.*"

I picked her up and sat her on my lap.

"*Bleh, bleh, bleeeeehhhhh!*"

"Tell me about it."

She was right pretty. She was light gray with some white on top of her head and encircling her nose. The hair around her eyes was a charcoal color — almost black — and it made her look like she was wearing a *Lone Ranger* mask.

"I really don't have any place to keep a goat," I explained.

I waited for her to say *Bleh*, but she didn't. I looked down and saw that she'd settled her head in the crook of my arm. She was almost asleep. I stroked her head and neck. Maybe I could make room for Missy Belle. I mean, just how much trouble could one little goat get into?

❦ ❦ ❦

I awoke the next morning to the *clack, clack* of the little nanny goat *clippety clacking* back and forth across the front porch.

"*Bleh! Bleh!*" she called, protesting her confinement. I'd tied her to the oak tree in the front yard the night before. I'd used plenty of rope so she could still get onto the porch should she need shelter.

I got up, had a cup of coffee and half a stale doughnut — Missy Belle gladly ate the other half — and started walking the mile or so into Mossy Creek to get the things I needed for Missy Belle. She'd had *Cheerios* for dinner the night before, but I didn't want to make that a habit. Besides feed, I needed to go to Mossy Creek Hardware to get some chicken wire and metal fence posts. Plus I had to get some lumber and nails somewhere so I could make her some type of lean-to.

I hoped that the hardware store would deliver, as Bart had taken off in the only transportation we had. And I was hoping they'd let me get what I needed on credit. Bart didn't leave me with much money to begin with, but I wouldn't have put it past him to clean out our bank account on his way out of town with Lu Ann.

I could hear Missy Belle bleating until I was plumb near to Mossy Creek. I reckoned she wanted to go, too. But when you're trying to get credit somewhere, you don't just walk in with a goat on a leash. A little French poodle, maybe, but a goat? Never.

Before I got to the hardware store, I smelled coffee brewing at The Naked Bean. It smelled so good. I had a few dollars in my pocketbook and was still trying to get my mind around what I was going to say to the people at the hardware store, so I decided to think about it over one of those fancy lattes I'd seen 'em drink on *Friends*.

"Good morning," I said to Jayne Reynolds, the owner.

"How are you this morning?"

"I'm fine. Do you reckon the hardware store is open yet?"

"It should be. I'm sure it'll be open by the time you've finished your coffee. What can I get you?"

I didn't see any prices stuck up anywhere. "How much are your lattes?"

Jayne frowned. "You know, I'm running a special on those this morning — only fifty cents."

My head sure jerked around at that. "Well, I'll have one, then. I could even have two, if I like 'em!"

Jayne laughed. "I don't know about that. We don't want to get you *too* wired up!"

I laughed, too, as I dug in my change purse and handed her a dollar bill. I'd like to have told her to keep the change, but I didn't want it to seem like I was putting on airs. Besides, there was no telling if or when Bart would come home, and I didn't have a job yet. As Jayne gave me my change, I asked her if she knew of anybody looking to hire.

She pursed her lips.

"I think Win Allen might be hiring a waitress, and I believe I heard someone say Rob Walker at Hamilton's Department Store is looking for a sales clerk."

I took a crumpled *Piggly Wiggly* receipt out of my pocketbook and asked to borrow her pen. "Hamilton Department Store," I said, writing it down as I said it, "and —"

"And Bubba Rice Lunch and Catering," Jayne finished.

"Thanks."

She handed me my latte, and I sat down at a table. I

tasted the latte, and it was really good — a lot better than the instant coffee I had at home. I watched Jayne work and noticed how happy she looked. I knew she was a widow and that she was raising a baby boy all by herself. That had to be hard. But, at least, her husband was *dead*, not traipsing around with the likes of Lu Ann Woods.

My mama had depended on Daddy for as long as I could remember — all her life, I reckoned. It's how things were. When you got married and a man promised to take care of you, you took him at his word. You didn't figure on him leaving you with no car, no job, a house payment and a goat to support.

I was tracing the design of the tablecloth with my fingertip and didn't notice Jayne come by my table.

"Is your latte good?" she asked.

"Oh, yeah," I said. "If I find work up this way, I'll be sure to stop back in."

"Oh, don't worry. You'll find something."

"I hope so."

Before she could offer me any more encouragement, I heard the awfulest commotion that ever was. A woman was screaming, a dog was yipping, and something else that chilled my blood. *Bleeeehhhhh!*

"Oh, no," I whispered. I looked out the window just in time to see Missy Belle streak past The Naked Bean with a doughnut in her mouth. Then came a pretty, middle-aged woman with a Chihuahua in one arm. She shook her other fist while chasing Missy Belle down the street.

"I'm sorry," I told Jayne, as I hurried outside.

I ran smack dab into the angry woman with the Chihuahua.

"I'm really sorry," I said. "I take it the doughnut was yours?"

"Actually, the doughnut belonged to a customer. He'd

just bought it from me when that damned goat ran in and took it from him!"

I glanced up at the sign above her shop. *Beechum's Bakery.*

"Well, like I said, I'm sorry, Mrs. Beechum. I'll pay for any damage Missy Belle did."

"You're sure right you will."

Mutt Bottoms walked out of the bakery. Twenty-six years old to my twenty-two. Big and good-looking as ever, especially in the tailored khaki uniform of a Mossy Creek police officer. Great. Now, my humiliation was complete.

"Everything's all right, Miz Beechum," Mutt said. "No harm done." He nodded at me. "That your goat?"

"Yeah. Missy Belle."

"Did you see what direction she went in?"

"No." I shaded my eyes and looked down the street.

Suddenly, I heard a screech from behind the azaleas in the park. It sounded to me like the call of that common old-lady bird, the *White-Breasted Southern Big Hair.* We all took off across the street — me because I figured Missy Belle had caused it.

Mutt thought so, too. "That's Miz Abercrombie. Your goat must be in the flower beds."

Sure enough, Missy Belle had discovered a huge batch of pansies planted beside the gazebo. She'd even dropped her — or, rather, Mutt's — doughnut in favor of the pansies.

"I'm sorry." I muttered that phrase over and over like a stuck record. I made a grab for Missy Belle and wound up face down in the flowerbed.

"*Aaaaak!*" Old Mrs. Abercrombie sounded like she had something caught in her throat. "You . . . you . . . that goat . . . it . . . it . . . *aaaak!*"

I stood up and ran my hand over my face. "Yeah. Me and my goat. *Aaaak.*" I ran off in the direction Missy Belle had darted when I'd reached for her.

"Wait," Mutt called, as he steadied Mrs. Abercrombie and tried to take the deadly garden hoe she was waving.

But I had to catch Missy Belle. At that point, I didn't care if there was a single flower left standing. I hadn't asked for any of this. I hadn't asked for Bart Milford to leave me high and dry, and I hadn't asked for Rochelle to drop a homeless goat on my doorstep. I hadn't asked for Mutt Bottoms to witness my goat-chasin' humiliation.

You'd have thought O'Day's Pub would be closed that early in the morning, but danged if I didn't see Missy Belle's wagging tail go right through the pub's open front door. Come to find out, Win Allen was catering some big to-do that evening and was at O'Day's buying kegs of beer he'd need. By the time I got to O'Day's, Missy Belle had chewed a hole in a burlap sack of peanuts.

"Missy Belle, don't!" I cried.

Too late. Michael Conners, the pub's owner — one of the finest lookin' men in Mossy Creek, next to Mutt — came out of the back room along with Win Allen just in time to see Missy Belle hop up on a table and knock over a pitcher of beer. Beer went everywhere. There was no way I could get to Missy Belle without tromping on the peanuts that were strewn all over the floor, so I just tromped. Mr. Conners and Mr. Allen stood there gaping at me and Missy Belle.

Mutt rushed in behind me and had the forethought to sidestep the mess, but not before Ingrid Beechum's Chihuahua jumped out of her arms and right into a puddle of beer.

"Bob, don't!" she yelled, but he was already lappin' up beer with the gusto of an Atlanta Falcons fan drownin' his sorrow after another disappointin' football game.

I picked up my goat and leveled my gaze at Mr. Conners. "I'll take Missy Belle here on back home, and then I'll come back and clean up this mess. I don't have the money to pay for the damages, but I'll work for nothin' until we're square." I turned to Mutt. "Same goes for the flowers and whatever she did in the bakery."

"Excuse me for asking," Mr. Allen said, "but why in the world did you turn a goat loose in the middle of town?"

"I didn't turn her loose." Tears prickled in my eyes and my nose burned. "Best I can figure, she chewed through the rope I had her tied with and then she followed me here." By then, I was flat out crying and making an even bigger fool of myself than I had been to begin with.

"The reason I came to town in the first place was to get the stuff I'd need to build her a little pen."

Missy Belle started squirming in my arms, and I got scared she'd get down and I'd have her to catch all over again.

"I'll walk her home," I said, "and then I'll be back to make amends as best as I can."

"I'll give you and Missy Belle a ride in my patrol car," Mutt said.

"No, thanks. She'll just eat your upholstery."

I brushed past Mutt and Mrs. Beechum, and I started out Easy Mossy Creek Road toward home. I could feel the eyes of Mossy Creek boring into my back until I was plumb out of sight.

I was worn out by the time I carried Missy Belle all the way back home. I went inside and took Missy Belle into the bathroom. I sat her on the floor and started running her some bath water. I couldn't have a goat that smelled like a brewery. Besides, giving her a bath would give me time to figure out what to do with her long enough to bathe myself and then hightail it back over to Mossy Creek to clean up the messes she'd made.

I found out in a hurry that goats don't appreciate a nice warm bath. I didn't have time to think about anything but survival as I wrestled Missy Belle all over the bathroom.

"*Bleh! Bleh!*" She jumped out of the tub.

I caught her and got a head-butt to the chin for my trouble. I put her back into the tub and lathered her up with the dog shampoo Bart had used to wash Goofy.

"*Bleh! Bleeeehhhh! Bleeeehhhh!*"

The poor thing must've thought I was trying to drown her. She leapt out of the tub again and butted the door. Thank heavens I'd closed it, or I'd be chasing Missy Belle all over the house . . . and, frankly, I'd chased her plenty for one day. I decided I ought to try to calm her down a little before putting her back into the tub to rinse her off. I petted her head and tried to talk to her in a soothing voice.

She wasn't having any of that. "*Bleeeehhhh! Bleeeehhhh!*" She sounded like a little goat machine gun.

I sank back against the tub and closed my eyes. Could this day possibly get any worse?

Suddenly, someone pounded on the front door. I hoped like the dickens that it was Rochelle.

"Who is it?" I hollered.

"It's Officer Bottoms."

I sighed. It was just my luck that those people in Mossy Creek were gonna press charges. I managed to finagle my way out of the bathroom without letting Missy Belle out.

I wiped my sweaty palms on my pants and then realized that my clothes were sopping wet. I opened the door.

Not only was Mutt standing on the porch, it appeared that about half the residents of Mossy Creek were in my yard. They hadn't come to give me a summons! This was a lynching!

"Uh, wow," Mutt said. "Most people undress before they take a bath."

"I really was coming back," I said. "I was trying to . . . I haven't had time —"

"That's not why I'm here . . . why *we're* here." Mutt shifted from one foot to the other. "We heard about Bart and Lu Ann."

"Lu Ann's mama comes in and gets her hair done once a week," said Rainey Ann Cecil of the Goldilock's Salon. "She's awful disappointed in Lu Ann."

"We've come to help you fix a place for your goat," Orville Gene Simple said. "I brought the lumber. I'm pretty handy with wood, and I've had plenty of dealings with animals . . . mostly wild ones, but don't listen to any stories you hear about *that*."

Even *I'd* heard about Mr. Simple's run-in with the demonic beaver back before the Mossy Creek High School reunion.

"What's this gonna cost me?" I asked. "I don't have much money, and I've already got myself in more debt than I know how to repay."

"It won't cost you anything." Casey Blackshear rolled her wheelchair up to the porch. There was a box from Beechum's Bakery on her lap. "Ingrid sent you a coffee cake, and a couple of doughnuts for your goat." Casey looked around the yard. "Where is she?"

"In the bathroom. I was trying to give her a bath."

Every eye in the crowd widened, and somebody shouted, "We'd better get busy; and, Sugar, you'd better get that goat out of your bathroom!"

I hurried back to the bathroom. Missy Belle was lying beside the tub looking almost content. I sat down beside her and stroked her head.

I heard a tap on the bathroom door and turned to see Mayor Walker. It was like looking up to find the Queen of England in my toilet.

"M-M-Mrs. Walker . . . I mean, Mayor Walker, I —"

She smiled. "Call me Ida." She nodded at Missy Belle. "I

don't imagine you'll be able to rinse her off in that tub without a fight."

"No." I shook my head. "I'd rather not try that again. Do you have any ideas?"

"Let's just wipe her down with some towels for now." She took a towel off the shelf and ran warm water on it. "Try that."

I took the towel and gently patted Missy Belle's soapy back. She lay there complacently without so much as a *bleh*.

"She's a pretty little goat," Mayor Walker said.

"Thank you," I said. "Not just for the compliment but for everything." I bit my lip. "Why are you all doing this? You don't even know me. I'm a Bigelowan."

"Not anymore. You're a Creekite now." She smiled again. "Everybody in Mossy Creek has fallen on hard times at one time or another. All we ask is that you help out when you see a neighbor in need."

That day I learned the true meaning of community. I'd believed community meant gossip and whispers and backstabbing and pettiness. Now I knew that the true meaning of community was acceptance and caring and helping and giving back. It meant belonging, truly belonging for the first time in my life.

By the end of the day, Missy Belle had a fine pen and an even finer shed. The shed even had a feeding trough in it! I had a house full of friends and I got a waitress job with Win Allen. Those Home Economics classes would pay off after all.

I also got a lawyer — Mayor Walker's daughter-in-law, Teresa. She filed divorce papers for me against Bart on grounds of desertion. Once he got wind of that, he came back and tried to talk me out of it. He said he loved me and wanted me back, but I knew all he wanted was our house. I told him to take his dog, his truck, and his two-bit girlfriend and head on back down the road. I told him, "Me and Missy Belle have us a home now. We ain't goin' nowhere and don't want to."

Bart looked to start arguin', but about that time Mutt Bottoms rolled up in his patrol car. Just rolled up and stopped in my yard. Gave a little tip of his finger to me and Bart. Leveled a certain kind of look at Bart. That was all it took. Bart left.

Mutt nodded to me, then drove away.

Me and Missy Belle stood on the porch, watching him go. I smiled.

"*Bleh,*" Missy Belle said happily.

Who would have thought that a blessing could have four hooves?

Lady Victoria Salter Stanhope
The Cliffs
Seaward Road
St. Ives, Cornwall, TR3 7PJ
United Kingdom

Dear Vick:

Michael and Jasmine. Sugar and Mutt.
Wow! Turn on a fan, Vick, 'cause the
temperature is rising this fall!
Here's a little something sweet and
funny to change the pace and let us
catch our breath from the local
romances. Trisha Peavy Cecil is Rainey
Cecil's cousin-in-law. You know how
gregarious Rainey is — her Goldilocks
Hair, Nail, and Tanning Salon is a
gossip goldmine. But Trisha, being a
Cecil by marriage, not blood, is a
little less certain she wants to be
the center of attention in Mossy
Creek. Read on and see what I mean.

Katie

In Mossy Creek folks try to speak in soft words
'cause they know that someday they might have to eat them.

❦❦❦❦❦❦❦❦❦❦❦❦❦❦❦❦❦❦❦❦❦❦❦❦❦❦❦❦❦❦❦❦❦❦❦❦❦❦

Building Bridges

Chapter 6

People mark their lives by major events, either terrible or wonderful. Like when Elvis died, or when they won the Miss America Crown, or met Tom Cruise. Like those traumatic events, blessings can't be foreseen or planned. They have to take you by surprise.

The call came at seven in the morning. My husband Pruitt was on his way out the back door when the phone rang. Pruitt coaches at Bigelow High, and I work part-time for the county parks and recreation department. I rushed to reach the wall phone, and he hung in the open doorway waiting to hear if our early call was an emergency involving a student.

I heard the loud screeching of badly adjusted hearing aids, and then Miss Mazie Turnage was shouting at me. "It's my honor to inform you, Trisha Peavy Cecil, that you have been selected as the new standing member of the Mossy Creek Bridge Club."

I winced, held the phone away from my ear, and shouted effusive thanks. Grinning, Pruitt gave me a smack on the fanny and went on out the door.

Miss Mazie dropped the officious tone but continued to vibrate my head. "I wanted to get to you early 'cause I know your mama is fit to bust with the news herself." The

127

Mossy Creek Bridge Club has rules for everything under the sun, and the rare privilege of such announcements falls to club's most senior member. Miss Mazie is eighty-four and holding. To life that is. Arthritis keeps her from holding cards anymore.

I didn't get to do more than nod at her comment about Mother before she talked on, telling me how she missed my Grandma Peavy, who had died the year before and whose position in the club I would be filling, and how she hadn't seen Pruitt and my two kids in she didn't know when, and then she innocently delivered the sucker punch: "I'm so glad we're playing at your house. See you Thursday night, honey."

I hung up the phone and reached for one of Pruitt's brown paper lunch sacks. Visions of dust, dull hardwood, and fading drapes had me hyperventilating. I took a few deep pulls on the paper sack. Two days — forty-eight hours until Thursday — that's all I had. My first thought was to call Mother. My mother, Elizabeth Newcomb Peavy, is the one who nominated me to fill Grandma's place. She's been a member of the club for thirty-seven years, and I knew good and well she had to have known the new member would be expected to host the next meeting.

I actually picked up the phone before I remembered that Mother would be at my door by nine-thirty. Since she retired from teaching fifth grade at Mossy Creek Elementary, Tuesday is her day out. Besides, I couldn't accuse *her* of deception when I'd been helping Grandpa Peavy pull the wool over her eyes for nearly a year. Grandpa had been living next door in his gas station since Grandma died, a fact Mother wasn't aware of. I slumped against the counter and tried to decide whether I should clean the oven or put my head in it.

There wasn't a soul I could call on for commiserations. All my friends were on the list of nominees, and I was sure they'd think my selection was an inside job. Which it was, at least partly. I'm an above average bridge player, if I do say so myself; besides that, membership is a tradition in my family.

The club sits three tables, eight club members and four subs. According to the rules, there only has to be four members at each monthly meeting, but I had a sinking feeling all seven of the other members including Miss Mazie would be at my house on Thursday, and I didn't want to guess who the subs might be. My induction would mark four generations of family membership; the geriatric crowd would turn out to celebrate.

The thought of it had me flattening the paper sack to make a to-do list. I was looking for a pen when my skinny fifteen-year-old son, Jason, pushed through the swinging door from the hall.

While he depleted the family larder, I filled him in on my news.

"Cool." He dumped his loot on the table, eyeing my housecoat and bare feet as he sat down. "You ditching Gram Elizabeth or what?"

"No. I'm just not going to town today." I sat down across from him with pen and paper sack and began my list. I wasn't giving up four of my precious forty-eight hours to tool around town with Mother.

"What about Great-Grandpa Peavy?" Jason asked around a bagel. "You know he's expecting you."

"Don't talk with your mouth full, sugar." I glanced up. "Your Great-Grandpa is on his own. Is that your sister's earring?"

"Mine now." He twicked his left earlobe. "What if Gram Elizabeth finds out he's living in the gas station?"

"She won't," I assured him, although I admit his comment gave me pause. I didn't have time, though, to worry about my grandpa right then, or how Jason had acquired his sister's earring for that matter. "The bridge club is meeting here Thursday. *This* Thursday." I read aloud down my list, trying to infuse the magnitude of the situation into my voice, "I've got to clean, rake the leaves out of the front yard, cook —"

"Whoa, major eats."

"That's right." I smiled agreement and watched him shovel a tablespoon full of sugarcoated cereal into his gaunt cheeks (he got his daddy's metabolism). "And major work." I tore off the bottom of the list and handed it to him. "You get the garage and both porches."

He groaned.

"Ingrid Beechum is club secretary. She'll probably bring at least a dozen chocolate éclairs. If you'll put in a polite, five-minute appearance, I'll make sure you get two."

"Deal." He gave me a high five.

"And if you take off your sister's earring, put a belt in your pants and pull them up to your waist, I'll buy you a new Harley Davidson."

"Right." He chuckled, sounding exactly like Pruitt, and put his cereal bowl in the sink. "I still can't believe you're deserting Great-Grandpa Peavy," he said, then rammed another bagel into his mouth on his way out the back door.

"I expect you back here right after ball practice," I yelled after him. *Deserting?* He made it sound like I was turning my grandpa over to the Gestapo. My mother is a lot of things— meddling, overbearing, a socialite transplanted from the snooty world of Atlanta's most prestigious community, Buckhead — but her heart is in the right place.

She's been trying to elevate the mountaineer Peavys since she married Daddy and moved to Mossy Creek nearly forty years ago. Daddy died of cancer when I was in college, and I was the only child of an only child, so the Peavys available for elevation were then limited to me, Grandpa and Grandma. Grandma Hazel Peavy died last year; after that Mother concentrated on upgrading Grandpa Joe Peavy's social sophistication, but Grandpa, whose heart was also in the right place, treated her as he would if she were his daughter instead of his daughter-in-law. He ignored her efforts.

Hence, I was the only raw Peavy material she had left. Thus my dutiful Peavy participation in her Tuesday outings. Before doing the shops in town, we usually drove out Trailhead Road, a few miles west of Mossy Creek, to clean Grandpa's house. I tagged along to make sure she didn't become aware of his move into the gas station and throw a hissy fit. She went on and on about his tidy housekeeping opposed to what she called his *lack of personal hygiene.*

It was true he always smelled like motor oil and kept a grease rag hanging out of the hip pocket of his overalls, and never tied his right shoe because of a WWII injury that caused his foot to swell, and he chewed tobacco, and took his hound, Mercury, with him everywhere he went. But he was clean, and the kind of grandpa every kid dreamed of having — he rarely said *No.*

And that morning I was more concerned with making my bridge-hosting debut a success than with Grandpa's secret. My future in Creekite gossip circles, not to mention my relationship with Mother, depended on it. She was long on propriety, not to mention tradition. I had an honor to uphold.

I tore into cleaning my house and was clearing assorted sports junk from the broom closet when Mother arrived, dressed like she was going to church and gushing with congratulations. I jumped her immediately for not warning me about hosting the bridge club meeting.

She blamed it on me. "I spent six months putting together the club history and rule book. Don't tell me you didn't read it." I kept my mouth shut. I hadn't read it; I doubt anyone had, and I bet they didn't tell her either. She took out the apron she kept in one of my kitchen drawers, tied it around her waist and began helping Shelby, my thirteen-year-old, unload the dishwasher. "Now you go get showered. And wear something nice. I've planned a little celebration for lunch." She smiled coyly at me.

"I'm not going to town. I have too much to do." Jason's desertion had stuck in my mind, and I had dragged Shelby out of bed on a school holiday with the notion of sending her with Mother. Shel's a throwback to the Buckhead side of my family; she and Mother love to shop and socialize, and she'll do anything to get out of chores. "Take Shel with you. She'd love it. Right, Shel?"

"Sure. Eating and shopping — my middle names. How 'bout we go to the mall down in Bigelow, Gram?"

"Not today, honey. But you're welcome to join your mother and me in town. Then we'll go clean your great-grandpa's house. Do you good. I'll finish the breakfast dishes. You scoot upstairs with your mother and get dressed."

"This is a recording," I said. "*I'm not going.*" I threw my hands up. "I swear, Mother. Look at this place. How in the world do you think I can go sashaying around town all day when I'm going to have at least a dozen of Mossy Creek's most do-all, see-all, tell-all, white-glove-meticulous women in this house day after tomorrow!"

"Why, Trisha Peavy Cecil, you make it sound like ya'll're living in a pig pen. Your house is virtually spotless now, and I've —"

Shel cracked up, and so did I, after I got over the shock. There's never been a house that passed Mother's muster, especially not mine. She comes in my back door looking for messes to clean up, and usually finds them. And it's not just my house; she's embarrassingly dedicated to cleaning no matter *whose* house she's in. I also noticed she didn't deny that my housekeeping would be under scrutiny.

She looked injured. "I don't know what y'all think is so funny."

Shelby hugged her. "Gram, *spotless*? Get real. Jason lives here, remember? My brother, the Cecil slob?"

I pointed to a corner. "Mother, I can just *see* Mayor Walker shooting my dust bunnies."

"Well, I may have overstated it," Mother conceded, "but I'm ahead of you two. Trisha, I have your Grandmother Newcomb's dessert china out in the car, and you can use my silver tea service."

"Who will be here?" I asked.

"Everybody, of course. All eight members." Mother beamed. "This is a special occasion. We haven't inducted a new member in fifteen years." She turned to Shelby. "And the last time all eight members were together was years ago, when Michael Conners opened his pub. Imagine — liquor by the glass, in Mossy Creek! We had so many requests to sub, we wound up playing fifteen tables."

"Which brings us to the subs." I lifted an eyebrow.

"There'll only be four. There wasn't the least bit of controversy over your membership, honey."

I wanted to scream; instead I started gathering the junk I'd pulled out of the broom closet.

Mother said to Shelby, "Go on up and get ready, sugar. Your mother'll be right behind you."

To me she said, "Put that mess down. By Thursday night we'll have things so organized even Martha Stewart would be green with envy." She checked her watch. "But we've got to hurry. I told you I had something special planned. It's a little celebratory luncheon at the Hamilton Inn. My treat. I wanted to take you to Win Allen's place but Katie Bell said he's not open today."

"Why were you talking to Katie?" I asked sourly, as though I didn't already know that my election to the club, my celebratory luncheon, what we wore and what we ate would be in Katie's next column in the paper. I just wanted Mother to know I wasn't happy about it.

"I invited Katie and Jayne Reynolds and Maggie Hart, to join us. I thought we could go over all the arrangements with Jayne and Maggie and get that out of the way. Now don't give me that look. Jayne can provide the tea, and Maggie can make you some lovely herbal centerpieces for your tables. I know Katie will want to put a little something about you in her column, and I thought this way I could make sure she gets all the details right."

I dropped everything where I stood. A soccer ball bounced off the toe of Mother's leather pumps. And I didn't apologize. "For crying out loud, I can't ask Jayne to do the tea. She was on the nominee list."

"Well, of *course* she was on the list. Just goes to show how much we all think of Jayne. We think a lot of Maggie, too, but she didn't want to join fifteen years ago and she declined a nomination this time, too. Now *Katie* is another matter. She's never on the list. Her newspaper column doesn't make her a good candidate for standing membership. We can't have her reporting gossip that might be traced back to our games. How *gauche*."

I nodded and continued nodding as I stole upstairs to get dressed and make a few arrangements of my own. If Katie Bell was going to be printing every little detail, I didn't intend to come up short. I called the Goldilocks Salon and made an appointment to get the works that afternoon, and when I told Rainey why, she offered to come by late Thursday afternoon and do any touch ups I might need.

"Oh, Rainey, thank you!"

"Hon, I can't have my cousin's wife look anything less

134

than spectacular. I got a styling reputation to uphold."

Next I called Pruitt. He says I'm too non-confrontational and that when somebody steps on me I just lay real still. There's a lot of truth in that, especially when it comes to Mother. It's a Peavy trait. My daddy was that way, and Grandpa's that way, too. We don't lack courage; we're just not aggressive. But every once in a while, when the foot's lifted, we do take a plug out of the heel. And Pruitt owed me. He'd dipped into our savings to buy a new bass boat and spent the last two weekends fishing with Rainey and his other Cecil cousins. And I hadn't said a word.

I told him about me hosting bridge on Thursday night. "I want you to rake the yards, front and back. Plus plant fall pansies in the backyard flower beds. You'll have to go by Tom Anglin's nursery and pick up a couple of flats. And please try to get home in time to get them in the ground and watered-in tonight," I beseeched him. I didn't want it to look like we'd stuck things out for show.

"You're taking this way too seriously, honey," he said. "We're not going to turn that backyard into a botanical garden overnight. Lighten up. They'll all come in the front anyway, and probably go on half the night about your yellow mums along the porch."

"Never mind. Forget I asked." I meant to take a real plug out of him. "I'll rake the yard and plant pansies myself. Hmmm. . .better yet, I'll put the leaf bag on the John Deere and just mulch the leaves while I mow the yard. Don't worry about me running into anything. I'll get Jason to back your new boat into the garage before I start," I said. "If I have time."

Pruitt instantly became apologetic, pleading really.

I respond well to humility and he responds to anything sexual. So after a little forgiveness and encouragement from me, he even volunteered to take Thursday off to paint the porch furniture. I won't say what I used to bribe him, but you can bet it wasn't a Harley.

Procrastination is its own reward. I took so long upstairs that Mother decided we'd have to forgo cleaning Grandpa's house. Mother, Shel and I headed straight to town. I love the buildings around the square. Most of them have been there forever, but modern owners have transformed quite a few into tourist shops. Mossy Creek has as many of what Pruitt calls *artsy-fartsy little boutiques* as any ritzy Atlanta neighborhood.

We parked outside Hamilton's Department Store and Mother set off, intent on shopping our way around the square, but people kept stopping us on the sidewalk to congratulate me. And if we met someone we knew who didn't congratulate me, Mother assumed they hadn't heard about the elevation in my social status and spent fifteen minutes making them wish they had.

Bear in mind, this was a chilly day in autumn. We were shivering by time we got around the square to the inn. Jayne and Maggie were already seated. Maggie's ancient mother, Millicent, was with them, and I wasn't a bit surprised, considering the kind of day I was having.

Jayne was on her feet the minute she saw us. If she harbored any hard feelings about losing out to me in the selection process, it didn't show in the hug she gave me.

I squeezed a chair in between hers and Miss Millicent's, and amid a flurry of white napkins, Mother and Shel took their seats.

I said, glancing at Maggie and Jayne, "Bet y'all can't guess who's hosting bridge this Thursday."

Mother said, "I don't know why she's fussing. I told her we'd help."

"You can count on me, Trisha," Miss Millicent assured me. "I never miss important meetings. Y'all remember Christmas?" She smiled reminiscently. Maggie turned as white as her napkin, and I felt another anxiety attack coming on. Millicent, our resident kleptomaniac, attended the December meeting of the bridge club dressed as Santa and passed out a bag full of gifts, which poor Maggie spent two months returning to the rightful owners.

Jayne, bless her, launched into a discussion of English teas. Looking relieved, Maggie took up the conversation, and not to be deterred, Mother took out her to-do list. I settled back, ordered a bottle of celebratory wine (beats a paper sack every time), and let Mother have at it.

While she planned away, I sipped wine and watched Shel rescue various cutlery items from Miss Millicent's tote bag. Pruitt would have said I surrendered, but I hadn't, not really. I knew I could call Jayne and Maggie the next day and change any plans I didn't like.

When we finally stood up to leave I had a buzz, not enough to stagger, but enough to keep me glancing guiltily at Shelby. Thirteen-year-olds can be sensitive about their moms' behavior, so I was concentrating on not behaving like a drunk when Rosie Montgomery rushed up to us on the sidewalk outside the inn.

Rosie owns Mama's All You Can Eat Café across the square, so I launched into an apology for not having my celebratory lunch at Mama's.

She cut me off. "Congratulations and all that, Trisha, but I've only got a minute; the café's full. I just came over here to give you Joe's lunch and to see if he's sick or something." She held out a Styrofoam box.

"He's probably having tomato sandwiches drenched in mayonnaise," Mother deadpanned. Grandpa's eating habits (he had high cholesterol) and gardening practices were both sore spots with her. He raised vegetables in his front yard and sold them from plywood and sawhorse tables at the gas station. Vegetables, minnows, and Cokes (the only kind of soft drink he sells) were his moneymakers.

"Why would you think Grandpa's sick?" I asked Rosie.

"I just thought I'd check. I know y'all go over to his house on Tuesdays, and it's not like Joe to miss out on my short rib lunch special on Tuesdays. I worry about the way he's being living since your granny —"

"We'll stop by the gas station on our way out of town," I said, and took Mother by the elbow. "You take the plate, Shelby." I was already moving along the sidewalk. "Thanks," I added over my shoulder and tried to hustle Mother along before Rosie decided to elaborate on Grandpa's living arrangements.

"Slow down, Trisha." Mother freed her elbow but kept walking. "You're not hiding a thing I don't already know. *Short ribs*. Your grandfather might as well take his cholesterol *intravenously*, to save his money and his dentures." We'd reached Mother's little sedan. Shelby climbed into her cramped spot in back, between boxes of tablecloths and napkins and serving pieces — all the things Mother was sure I'd need for bridge. I tried to make myself comfortable for a short ride and long diatribe.

"Trisha, your grandfather's working himself into the poorhouse," Mother said as she drove. "Spends more keeping that station open than he brings in, and he's eating himself to death." Mother's one of those people in whom fear manifests itself as anger proportionally; the greater the fear, the madder she gets. I suspected there was a little guilt thrown in that day because we hadn't gone by Grandpa's first. Grandpa is set in his ways, but he does what he takes a notion to do, so I wasn't too worried about him. I was feeling too sorry for myself. My buzz had morphed into a rhythmic headache.

Besides, it wouldn't be unheard of for Grandpa to skip a meal; he looked like he'd skipped plenty, despite his high cholesterol. If you've ever seen those pictures of gaunt-faced farmers during the Depression, you've got an idea of what he looks like, except Grandpa wears an ancient Texaco cap with his overalls. His image perfectly suits his gas station. A trip back in time.

He has white tires outlining the station's front lawn like large sugar-coated donuts stuck in the ground. Grandpa painted and set up a few a year, from the time he came home from WWII until 1951, when he reached his property lines on either side. The hubcap-covered wooden fence behind the station — his contribution to Lady Bird Johnson's campaign to beautify American — he erected in the 1960s.

Grandma sowed all the wildflowers along the fence. She was inordinately proud of her little house and his station. Both she and Grandpa grew up dirt poor. When Grandpa came back from the war with a gimpy leg and a small pension, they built Peavy's Gas Station, the first full-service gas station in Mossy Creek.

It nearly killed them when Daddy, their only son, died. Grandpa still had the GTO he gave Daddy when he graduated from the University of Georgia. He kept the car in one of the station's grease bays; the other bay was where he kept everything he'd ever owned, and his rollaway bed. When the U-Pump Quick Stop opened up out on South Bigelow Road twelve years ago, Grandpa's business slacked off.

The gas station looked deserted when we pulled in. The sawhorse tables weren't out front — Grandpa sold pumpkins in the fall — and Grandpa wasn't sitting in his chair by the door.

"Oh, Lord," Mother said.

We scrambled out of the car, and Mercury came racing at us. He danced and jumped around barking, then darted to Grandpa's house next door.

"There he is." Mother pointed at the side porch, where Grandpa sat on the steps. He watched us until we were almost there and then dropped his head into his hands. "What in the world?" Mother ran to the steps. "Joe?" she said in a strident voice.

Grandpa lifted his sweat-beaded head; tears streamed down his grizzled cheeks. "I've gone crazy as a Bessie bug, Elizabeth."

Mother put a hand on his shoulder. "It's okay, Joe. Everything's going to be fine. Trisha, call 911. Shelby, get me a wet towel."

"Don't tell the whole county." Grandpa swiped at his face with his handkerchief. "I've lost my house keys. Lord, Lord. I woke up and didn't even know where I was, and I still don't know what day it is."

"Grandpa," I said gently. I sat down and put my arm around him. He looked pale and scared. Age spots, round and velvety, stood out against his neck and face. I hadn't noticed them until then; they reminded me of mold and I think I was more scared than he was. "It's Tuesday, Grandpa."

"It is?" He looked bewildered.

"Yes. We should have been here this morning—"

"Wouldn't'na made a bit of difference, T-girl. I woke up this'uh way. Didn't even know where I was," he repeated. "Locked myself out of the station, lost my keys." His voice broke and he put his face in his hands again.

"Can you stand up?" Mother asked.

"Hell fire, Elizabeth, I've lost my mind! Not my legs."

"Come on." Mother took one of his arms. "Shelby, you take his other side and let your mother go get my car."

"Ain't no sense in getting the car." Grandpa struggled

to his feet and steadied himself against the step railing. "I'm over it now. Just a bad spell; scared me is all."

"Grandpa, this is serious," I said. "You have to go to the hospital."

"No I don't. All I need is somewhere to lay down awhile."

"Joseph Willard Peavy," Mother said firmly, "you know good and well you've had something more than a spell — a seizure, or a stroke. God only knows. Now get in the car or we're calling the EMTs."

"A stroke?" He looked at Mother in surprise, then actually seemed to perk up. "I swear. I thought for sure I was havin' an old-timers attack."

"No, Joe, I think it's more likely you've had a sausage-gravy-induced stroke," Mother snapped, her fear exacerbated by his stubbornness. "*Get the car*," she said to me.

Grandpa hadn't had a stroke, but he had to spend a night at the hospital down in Bigelow. The spell scared him, though not as much as the threat of another night in the hospital. He and Mercury went to Mother's house. It was clear even to him that he couldn't go home alone. It wasn't as clear to him that he had to close the station, and he wouldn't hear any discussion of leaving the house he'd built for Grandma; never mind that he hadn't spent a night in it since she died.

While we waited for his test results, he came up with all kinds of schemes. The one he liked best was hiring help at the station and having Jason move in with him so he wouldn't be alone at night. You can imagine my teenage son's reaction to that: a learner's permit in his hip pocket, a vintage GTO with his name on it in the garage, and a Great-Grandpa who never said *No*.

One positive thing did come out of Grandpa's spell; it put my worries about bridge into perspective and diverted Mother's attention. After finding out Grandpa had been living in the station and I'd helped him keep the secret, she wasn't speaking to me.

Pruitt and the kids went at our house and yard as if Grandpa's reputation depended on it. We drove Grandpa over on Thursday to supervise the preparations. He needed something to take his mind off his troubles. So did I. I doubt anybody including Mother could have been more together than I was when the doorbell started ringing Thursday night.

Grandpa became our self-appointed *meeter-greeter* and planted himself in a freshly painted rocker on my front porch, where he could have a chew and spit tobacco juice on my mums. I ferried desserts to the dining room table. After helping get Miss Lorna Bingham and her wheelchair in the house, Pruitt and Jason took to the back porch as tour guides for anybody who wanted to watch Mercury hike his leg over my freshly planted pansies.

My mother-in-law, SuAnne Cecil, aligned herself with Mother as official spokespersons for Grandpa's health issues. Shelby stood by the huntboard, in charge of the silver tea service, with Jayne standing by in the kitchen ready to brew tea on command. Maggie drove Miss Millicent over and stayed to protect the tea service and help Jayne. And my neighbors decided we were having an open house and took the opportunity to drop in to see Grandpa and say hey to the ladies.

I wouldn't say the situation was out of control; people were enjoying themselves, as Katie Bell pointed out to me. I could just see her next column: *Trisha Cecil Hosts Bridge Club; Wild Party Erupts*. And it could have happened if Mayor Walker hadn't taken the situation in hand. Ida's our E.F. Hutton — when she speaks, Creekites listen. She called the meeting to order in my great room, and you'd have thought President Bush was holding a closed-door conference with his cabinet. Pruitt and Grandpa led the exodus, and within minutes we were playing bridge.

Luck of the draw put me at the table with Mother, Ingrid Beechum, and Violet Martin. Mother had suspended hostilities for the night; she'd have given up her girdle before letting people know she wasn't speaking to me or that she hadn't known about Grandpa's living arrangements all along. But she wasn't about to give up the opportunity to publicly voice her opinion of Grandpa's inability to operate a business.

"I know you're right, Elizabeth," Ingrid said, "but I don't know what we'll all do without Joe and that station."

"And just when was the last time you patronized that station?" Miss Violet demanded.

"It's the only place in town where you can still get real Cokes," Eleanor Abercrombie said from the adjacent table. Everybody agreed and launched into a discussion of the quality of Grandpa's Cokes. His old chest cooler used circulating water to cool and only six ounce glass bottles would fit in it.

"I've bought every pair of sunglasses I've ever owned from Joe," Lorna Bingham interjected.

Miss Violet harrumphed. "When was the last time any of y'all bought gas there, I repeat! Poor old Joe *passes* more gas than he pumps now days." Mother whacked my ankle beneath the table and I managed to keep a straight face. "As for those sunglasses, Lorna," Miss Violet continued, "that display card's been sitting on his counter since 1956. A pair of thirty-nine cent sunglasses every few years and Coca-Colas isn't gonna keep him open."

"Violet Rose Martin, don't go trying to make it our fault Joe's having to close," Ingrid said. "Joe took care of every car Charlie and I ever owned, and after Charlie died Joe was the only mechanic I trusted. But then Joe closed his garage. I had to find another mechanic."

Of course, then everyone in the room had to recount the times Grandpa had come to their motoring rescue. (Have I mentioned that every word said had to be repeated, usually by Eleanor Abercrombie, for the benefit of Miss Mazie?)

"I'll never forget the day Joe came home from the war," Alameda McPherson said. "He was the youngest of our boys to go and the last to come home. The Mossy Creek High School band marched him down Main Street and he had to make a speech. Y'all know how quiet he is, but he can be a ripper, too; he was when he was young."

The older members laughed, and Miss Lorna said, "It's a pity he's always been too bashful to ride in the Veterans Day parade. He was a real hero." At the mention of *hero*, the discussion turned to all of Mossy Creek's veterans, starting with the War of Northern Aggression, and wandering off on a tangent about a Creekite who became known as one of New York's most heroic firemen.

"God bless every one of those firemen and the city of New York," Alameda said.

"Say what you want to about big cities up North, but they know more about how to treat their heroes than we do ours."

"How can you say that?" Mother demanded; she was chairperson of the Veteran Day festivities. "There's not a veteran in town, in this county," she emphasized, "who isn't honored every year!"

"A flag or a white cross in their yard isn't what I meant. I'm not criticizing you, Elizabeth. I'm as guilty as any. I don't think I ever told Joe how much I appreciate what he sacrificed for our country, or, for that matter, how much I appreciate what's he done for our community. When we had that big ice storm back in seventy-two, him and Hazel fed and sheltered stranded Creekites for nearly a week, until the roads were cleared. And the last time I recall this town doing anything for them was when we gave them a bridal shower. Your grandmother organized that, Ida," Alameda said.

"I don't think Joe needs another bridal shower," Ida said, "but I do think you're right, Alameda. It's time we do something for Joe."

The words were no sooner out of the mayor's mouth than the group reached unanimous agreement; unfortunately, the dozen women had three dozen opinions about what that *something* ought to be.

We had finally reached the end of the first *rubber* — in bridge-playing terms — and, as is our custom, broke to eat before rotating for the second *rubber*. The discussion continued over plates filled with *just a pinch* and *little dabs*.

I was grateful because not wanting to miss anything, no one asked to see the new wallpaper upstairs or wandered off to inspect my kitchen. Jayne and Maggie rejoined us, and when Maggie suggested Creekites host a *Joe Peavy Day*, we quickly reached another unanimous agreement. Being mayor, Ida was charged with taking the matter up with the town council.

"Then consider it a done deal," she said.

"Grandpa will be eighty-three this fall. This is a great way to celebrate his birthday," I suggested as I leaned toward my partner, Pearl Quinlan, a frequent sub. I expected to spend the next *rubber* debating plans for Joe Peavy Day, and at first I was disappointed when the conversation returned to the past.

It was only natural, I guess, since some of the women there were at least as old as Grandpa. They had a lot to remember, good times and bad, and not all of them agreed on which was which. And, too, their age and infirmities keep them pretty isolated most of the time. I sat taking it all in and wishing I had a tape recorder.

The night was an eye-opener, literally; I couldn't sleep for thinking about the lives and trials of Grandpa's generation: the Depression; the tuberculosis epidemic and who had to go to the state sanitarium; polio; brothers, husbands and cousins who worked for the CCC building parks and roads; babies delivered at home, and too often buried at home. I couldn't get over it.

The elderly of Mossy Creek had past lives.

🌿🌿🌿

Grandpa agreed to stay at Mother's until he finished all the tests the doctors wanted to do, but he was chafing to go home, and I was so relieved to have the bridge night behind me that I decided to risk Mother having a conniption and took him and Mercury over to the gas station. We were supposed to be there just long enough to check on things, but Hank and Casey Blackshear dropped by (Hank's veterinary clinic is just down Trailhead Road from the station) and before they left, people from all over Mossy Creek were streaming in.

Win Allen and Michael Conners came by to get pumpkins. When they saw the sawhorse tables weren't set up and that Grandpa hadn't harvested the pumpkins from his garden yet, they took care of the harvesting then arranged the tables and staffed them. Within an hour all of Grandpa's autumn pumpkins were sold.

Grandpa is a humble man with a sense of humor drier than quartz, and I could tell he felt awkward and embarrassed by all the attention, but it was equally obvious he loved every minute of it, hobbling around faster than I'd seen him move in years, joking and grinning. He wore a path through the weeds to the wooden fence, where he located retired family hubcaps upon request, and there were plenty of requests.

I got into the spirit and cleaned the star-emblazoned glass balloons atop the old gas pumps, then started pumping gas. I was a good grease monkey; I'd worked at Grandpa's off and on since the sixth grade.

Sandy Crane drove up in her truck. She leaned out her window while I cleaned her windshield and said, "Trisha, I feel so bad. Most of us don't mind paying a few cents more for Mr. Peavy's gas — it's just that he won't let anybody pump their own, and he always has to check the oil and clean the windshield. Nobody wants to have him out cleaning their windows in all kinds of weather. So we try to leave him be."

I listened to similar comments all afternoon and repeated every one of them at supper that night, which had the desired effect. Pruitt and Jason took Grandpa to the station on Saturday and kept it open all day. On Monday, I took Jason and Grandpa to the station right after Jason's football practice. Tuesday was my turn again. Ida came by to say the city council was declaring the next Wednesday Joe Peavy Day.

"Damnation. I've never heard of anything so foolish in all my life," Grandpa muttered. He got up and hobbled off toward his empty pumpkin patch.

"He's thrilled," I said.

Jason, Shelby, and I continued to alternate afternoons at the station. Grandpa was in high cotton; Mother was having hissy fits. We knew nothing had really changed; Grandpa had to retire. But, being a Peavy, I didn't want to push the issue until we had to. Actually, I was hoping the doctor would tell him he couldn't continue to run a gas station at his age.

But that didn't happen. Mother and I took him to a neurologist in Bigelow the next week. All the tests were back: Grandpa was experiencing the onset of Parkinson's disease.

"My Uncle Early Peavy had it," Grandpa told the doctor. "Nearly shook hisself to death." He held out his hand. It trembled slightly as he closed it into a fist. "I don't get the shakes, unless I'm nervous, like now, and my head don't shake none."

"I'm sorry, Mr. Peavy, but you do have Parkinson's," the doctor reiterated. "The good news is that there are drugs you can take to minimize the effects and help control tremors." We left with prescriptions, brochures, and a fair prognosis, considering Grandpa's age. We didn't mention the station. We might have gotten the doctor to do our dirty work if we had, but the station was the last thing on our minds that day.

Grandpa stayed on at Mother's and we kept rotating days at the gas station. He didn't mention his condition. He did mention his Uncle Early, at least once an hour, and made sure we all knew Early hadn't let Parkinson's stop him from working a farm. We didn't say a word. The city council put Mother in charge of planning the details of Joe Peavy Day. She took it as validation of her Veterans Day efforts and threw herself into preparations.

Business at the station had slowed considerably, which was a good thing, otherwise Grandpa would never have sat still for hours talking to reporters. To Mother's consternation, Katie Bell and Sue Ora Salter Bigelow took over the job of publicity and managed to get everyone from the *Atlanta Journal-Constitution* to *Antique Roadshow* to do stories on Grandpa.

The AJC reporter wrote a huge feature story about Grandpa and his gas station. It came out in the *Leisure Living* section that Sunday, a two-page spread with pictures. The picture of the station was taken from the hill across the road, so people got a full view: Grandpa sitting in his chair by the entrance, the white tires, the sawhorse tables and old-fashioned gas pumps, the fence and hubcaps, the sweet little house next door.

"If that eyesore wasn't a landmark before, it is now," Mother said. Suddenly she wasn't happy to have all of north Georgia reading about what she called the *Peavy peculiarities*. "With everything going on in the world, I don't know why reporters think people want to read about an old gas station," she said.

I knew, but I was sure she didn't want an explanation and didn't want to hear that I'd decided the AJC reporter was my new hero. Mother was right about one thing, though; it seemed thousands of people had heard or read about Peavy's Gas Station. Grandpa wasn't just on the map; people were cutting a trail to his door.

WMOS Radio decided to do a live broadcast of Joe Peavy Day from the square; a documentary filmmaker came to talk with Grandpa about old Southern ways. A Mr. Hardy from the *Georgia Preservation Society* showed up. He said he'd been intrigued by the interior photographs of the station and wondered if Grandpa would mind if he looked around. Grandpa didn't mind; he was overwhelmed by it all.

It was obvious Mossy Creek was about to have another major media event, and anybody who hadn't jumped on the bandwagon took a running leap. Governor Ham Bigelow volunteered to officiate — no surprise there. Mother was bent on Grandpa leading the pledge to the flag and was working on getting ROTC students from North Georgia State College and University to act as honor guard and the chorus from Mt. Gilead Methodist to sing *God Bless America*. (She wanted them to sing *Dixie*, too, but didn't want to appear politically incorrect.) Joe Peavy Day was turning into the Fourth of July and Veterans Day rolled into one.

Strangers offered to buy the station and people in town wanted to know when Grandpa planned to close. He went from being overwhelmed to being depressed.

Joe Peavy Day dawned cool and clear. The smells of candy apples, boiling peanuts, and barbeque hung in the music-filled air. Several thousand people showed up to honor Grandpa. It was a proud day for all of Mossy Creek and especially the Peavys. Grandpa and Jason led the pledge to the flag together. Jason wore his Eagle Scout uniform (without his ear accessories, thank God). Pruitt and I were proud enough to burst.

The day was so full most of it became a blur. Mother and her committee outdid themselves.

The week following the celebrations, Mother went through something I can only describe as postpartum depression, and Grandpa's depression turned to defeatism. He didn't go to the station a single day and reconciled himself to living with Mother permanently. The day she took him over to the EMC office to have the utilities turned off at Grandma's little house, they both cried.

A few days later, Grandpa received a call from an archivist at the Smithsonian Institute (you got it, the one in Washington!). The man wanted to talk about the sixty-year horde of dusty trinkets stashed in the grease bay at the station. Then Mr. Hardy from the Georgia Preservation Society called again. He wanted to hold a meeting with us and the Smithsonian archivist and anyone else Grandpa wanted present.

Grandpa, Mother, Ida Walker, Ham Bigelow, and I met with the two men in the reading room at the Mossy Creek Library. The gist of the matter was, they wanted to inventory and archive the cards of key rings, sunglasses, breath fresheners, bottle openers, cans of old motor oil and all the other unsellable stock Grandpa had pitched aside through the years. And they wanted to keep the stuff *in context*, which meant at the station. They also wanted Grandpa to record an oral history of his life and the history of the gas station. If

Grandpa agreed, he could keep the station and they'd help get it registered as a historic site, which meant he might qualify for a grant to help maintain the old gas station as a museum. Talk about heaven sent.

Mother was speechless. Not me. I jumped in to suggest a whole collection of local oral histories and pointed out our treasure trove of elderly citizens. When the archivist started talking about national grants and federal funds, Ham Bigelow allowed the state would be more than happy to help in the production of such a worthy project. We were off and running.

Soon it will be my turn to host the bridge club again, but I'm not the least bit intimidated this time. I'm still the same non-confrontational chicken I've always been, but now I'm the chicken who's in charge of The Mossy Creek History Project, interviewing elderly bridge club members for their life stories.

And they don't mind my dust bunnies at all.

WMOS RADIO

"The Voice Of The Creek"

News Flash.

This is Bert Lyman, interrupting your afternoon of golden oldies featuring Little Jimmy Dickens and the Carter Family, the greatest hits of Andy Williams, and the best of Kathie Lee Gifford. WMOS is activating the first-ever *Willis the Cat Memorial Lost Pet Alert.* Named in honor of the late, great Mossy Creek police mascot, Willis the Cat. Here goes.

Willis the Cat Memorial Lost Pet Alert!

Be on the lookout for a yellow tomcat, *Otis.* Otis is missing, and his owners say there's a reward for his return. Otis is about twelve inches high, ten pounds, mustard colored with white feet and mustache. If you have any information, call or drop by the police station and tell Officer Sandy Crane. Do *not* bring Otis to the station if you find him. Sandy says the chief's parakeet, Tweedle Dee, could only tolerate one cat — Willis — and now that Willis has passed away Tweedle Dee is swearing off friendships with cats and any other animal that likes to eat birds.

Stay tuned for breaking news as we get it.

Sometimes, you can do a job a little too well.

👣👣👣👣👣👣👣👣👣👣👣👣👣👣👣👣👣👣👣👣👣👣👣👣👣👣👣👣👣👣👣👣👣

The Cat Nappers

Chapter 7

The sign taped to the lamppost read:

HAVE YOU SEEN OTIS?

My best friend, Patty English, and I put down our can of nails, hammers, and scraps of wood in order to stare up at the blurry, furry face in the black and white photocopy. He was ugly, like a cross between a sheepdog and Shrek, except we knew he couldn't be green. We were doing our best to remember this now-famous missing cat. After all, being kids, we knew most of the local pets by name or by reputation. Mostly the dogs. Some dogs like Mrs. Brill's golden retriever Sammy or Miz Beechum's little dog, Bob, were either naturally friendly or at least smaller than we were. Others, like Mr. Shaw's big rottweiler over on Pine Street, had made us detour around his little corner of the world more than once.

But cats . . . now *cats* were more likely to ignore us than not. They seemed to have their own business to attend to and as long as we didn't do mean things like tie cans to their tails or worse, they stayed out of the way. And, we returned the favor. Only a few had impressed us enough to remember them, like Miz Reynold's cat who hung out on the square in front of her store or Miz Caldwell's coon cat that was almost dog-size. But knowing what *this* cat, Otis, looked like could pay off. The rest of the sign offered a $20 reward for information.

"We must know something," Patty mumbled, tapping the flier with one dirty finger like Otis would speak to us if she got his attention. "We could use that money for the movies."

"Or to buy doughnuts from Beechum's," I added helpfully. Doughnuts were my new favorite things. Especially the chocolate-covered ones. Every time we bought two, Miz Beechum would put an extra in the bag for us to split.

"Forget doughnuts, Nancy Bainbridge, our fort needs a roof," Patty announced.

The fort. That's where we spent every Saturday afternoon — maybe Sunday if we could get away with it — along with Janie Hughes, Teedie Wertz and sometimes her little brother Raymond. We called him *Whammer* because whenever he hit a nail or kicked a can or sneezed, he yelled, "*Wham!*" He learned it from TV and nobody seemed to be able to make him stop.

Anyway, we were building our fort — our *secret* fort — in an empty lot halfway between Church Street where we lived and Mossy Creek Elementary. The lot wasn't really empty. Way back off the road was an old broken-down house that my mother called somebody's 'homeplace.' I wasn't sure how a homeplace was different than somebody's regular house except that it was old and empty, but I didn't ask her to explain. She'd already forbidden me to go anywhere near that house or — on the threat of having my backside tanned — going inside. Heck, there were plenty of places to hide and play without going *inside* the house. The yard had tall, bushy hedges — as tall as my daddy — that had taken over the front walk forming a natural tunnel, and the backyard was a jungle of bamboo so thick we could build a fort in the center of it and never be found if we didn't want to be. We called it *Sha-La-La Land*, like Frontierland at Disney World.

That's where we'd been hurrying to when the sign slowed us down.

"I bet we can find this ugly cat," Patty said. She looked around to see if anyone was watching, then tore the sign down and stuffed it into the pocket of her jeans. "Let's go get Teedie and Janie."

We picked up our tools and boards and trudged on toward Sha-La-La.

"Keep an eye out," Patty ordered as we passed fences and yards.

I did. We'd voted Patty our leader back when we'd first started to build. For one reason, she was almost a year older at ten than Janie and I — two years older than Teedie. And for another reason, she had nerve. She wasn't afraid of anything. Not right off, anyway. You had to convince her not to jump in the fire so you wouldn't be called upon to jump in after her.

"Hey, there's a yellow cat!" I pointed up ahead, eager to be the finder of the twenty-dollar Otis.

Patty dropped her board and pulled out the flier. "Not enough hair," she said. "Besides, it must belong to the people who live there, it's in their yard."

"Oh, okay," I said, disappointed. "At least I saw one."

Two more blocks of fast walking and casual searching brought us to the faint path leading through the weeds to our secret world. We stopped and pretended to rest as a car passed us. One of the rules of *Sha-La-La Land* was that you couldn't let anyone see how you got there.

"Okay, let's go," I said, after the car turned at the stop sign.

As quick as rabbits we hurried off the street and disappeared into the brush. Halfway down the path I stopped to break a branch of sweet shrub and stuck it in my top pocket.

I liked the way it smelled. Lots of it grew around the secret entrance to *Sha-La-La Land* perfuming the air like sweet apples and honey. I figured someone who'd lived in the old house must've planted it and like everything else, it got out of hand. My mother says a lot of the old plants do that — they take over when the people leave.

By the time we reached the leafy tunnel leading to the front door — or where the front door used to be — of the house I felt my usual shiver of excitement. I loved *Sha-La-La Land*. Every overgrown bush, every new, determined to spread, shoot of bamboo, every bird's nest and rabbit hole, and all the smells of old wood, rich dirt and autumn leaves. I loved it because it was secret and it was *ours*. We'd claimed the land when it looked like nobody else wanted it.

I didn't love the old 'homeplace' though. It's not like I thought it had ghosts in it, or anything. I'm too old to believe in ghosts. Just sometimes, starin' at the broken windows and the missing door made me feel like the house was starin' back. Grinning with no teeth like old Mister Rufus down at the hardware store. In the second place, ivy grew along the roof like tangled green hair and when the wind picked up it kinda whistled or sighed through the missing boards. My mother didn't have to threaten my backside to keep me clear of it. I didn't tell Patty and the others about being scared though. 'Cause, best friend or not, I was sure if Patty found out she'd have to march right across the rotten porch and through the hole that used to be a door and expect me to follow her step for step. As my grandma would say, "into the belly of the whale."

No thank you. I'd rather walk through fire or be a life-sized dog biscuit for Mr. Shaw's yard demon.

Teedie and Janie were waiting for us in the last sunny spot before the curtain of bamboo became a nearly solid wall. They'd brought their own assortment of tools and supplies. Janie had two plastic garbage bags, a ball of kite string, and a Tupperware bowl with no lid. Teedie had a rusty bucket with a frayed piece of rope tied to the handle, a pair of equally rusty pliers, and a flashlight with a cracked lens. Whammer was absent

In single file, we slipped through the small gap in the bamboo and followed Patty along the dim green tunnel too slender for any adults to get through. Above our heads the autumn-yellow bamboo swayed and creaked in the chilly breeze, but near the ground everything around us was still. Like walking through a box of giant chopsticks. When we reached *Sha-La-La Land* — the cleared center of our private world, we stacked our building supplies on the ground.

Patty looked over our contributions and announced, "We need more boards." She pulled the flier we'd swiped off the pole and showed it to Janie and Teedie. "And here's how we get 'em. If we find this cat, we could buy all the stuff we need."

"Let me see." Janie took the flier. She and Teedie stared at Otis's homely face. "Looks old. That cat must be from out of town. I don't remember ever seeing him before."

Teedie said, "That's why he's lost, silly."

"Otis could be a girl, ya know," I added.

The other three turned to stare at me for a moment. Then Teedie said, "So?"

I just shrugged. I'd run out of smart aleck replies so I moved on to brilliant ideas. "Since we don't have boards, let's go on a Otis hunt."

🐾 🐾 🐾

I'd heard people at church call Mossy Creek a "small" town. Actually, I'd heard Miz Purla say somethin' like small, *stubborn* town but I didn't really know what she was talkin' about. My mother said Miz Purla was always pitchin' a fit about one thing or another. First it was the famous Foo Club, because they wanted to set up a booth at the fall festival and give out buttons that said, *Until further notice, vote Heil, No*. I thought she'd been upset because they spelled the "H" word wrong. Then she stood in front of the Mayor's office and handed out fliers demanding that the *pur-petraitors* who burned down the old high school should be brought to justice. Whatever that meant. Half the kids in Mrs. Anderson's third grade class found out the fliers made great paper airplanes — we folded and flew them all over the square before Sandy down at the police station made us pick every single one of them up and throw them in the trash. She didn't seem mad though.

No matter. To us, the kids from Church Street, Mossy Creek was the whole world. Bigger than the bunch of us. We'd have to split up to search it proper.

Janie and Teedie went off toward the square while Patty and I hiked over toward East Mossy Creek Road. We cut down the alley behind the newspaper office, heading for the swimming hole behind Hamilton Inn. Patty had some notion that any lost cat would look for water. What better place to start a search than at the swimming hole? She'd decided. I didn't mention the rumor that cats didn't like water all that much. I followed the leader down a deer path.

"Pee-uw. What's that smell?" I asked, doing my best not to breathe.

"Somethin' dead." Patty answered, then picked up the pace.

Oh no, not Otis. What if that same hawk who tried to carry off Miz Beechum's Bob a couple of years ago came back for our twenty-dollar cat? "Do you remember if the poster said, *Dead or Alive*? Like in the movies?"

Patty stopped, propped her hands on her hips and

looked at me. "Why would anyone pay twenty dollars for a *dead* cat?"

She had me there. All I could do was shrug. I'd never understood that whole proper burial thing. Patty turned and continued down the path.

Once we reached the swimming hole the smell went away, so we weren't required to investigate further. We searched all around.

No Otis.

❦❦❦

The sun was hanging low over the mountains by the time we all met up back at *Sha-La-La*. Patty and I had found one cat that sort of resembled Otis but we weren't sure since he didn't look much like the picture. When Janie and Teedie came crashing through the bamboo, though, we could see they'd had better luck — each one was carrying a big yellow cat.

"That's him!" Patty said, holding the picture next to the bigger cat's face — one Teedie had found near the barber shop. "That's gotta be Otis! Says here, to call Sandy at the police station. Let's go get our money."

Teedie's arms tightened around Otis. She seemed reluctant to give him up. "*Our* money?" she asked, like she'd forgotten what the whole plan was about anyhow.

Patty frowned. "We said we'd use the money for the fort."

It only took a minute of facing possible suspension from *Sha-La-La* before Teedie remembered, "Oh all right. Here, you take him. I carried him all over town and he's heavy."

"What do we do with these other two?" I asked.

Patty, in the middle of taking possession of Otis, said, "We'll put 'em back."

"Back where?" Janie asked.

"Where you found them."

Janie looked at me — both of us holding squirming cats who'd lost all interest in us or our plans. "I don't remember *where* we found them — we just *found* them," Janie confessed.

"This one was in the bushes near the church," I volunteered.

The look on Patty's face changed slowly from aggravation to, as my mother would say, *revelation*. I should've run then. But since Patty was our chosen chief, I decided to be a good Indian.

"Well, these cats must be lost, too." She ran a hand over Otis's matted fur. "We'll go get our twenty dollars for this one and save the others until someone puts up another sign. We need a place to put 'em 'til then."

"My mother won't let me have a cat," Janie said. "My sister's allergic to 'em."

"I can't take two cats home," I said in a hurry. I couldn't lie worth a flip. I knew if I even *tried* to sneak our two extra cats into the garden shed behind our house my mother would get to the bottom of everything in nothin' flat. I would be the betrayer of *Sha-La-La*.

That's when Patty picked up the broken flashlight, turned toward the path and said, "Follow me."

Sooner than I wanted, I found myself facing the empty-eyed stare of the old house. "We'll keep them in there."

I don't know about Janie but I was ready to drop my furry contribution to the cat round-up and, twenty dollars or not, let it take its chances. The sun was already sinking below the top of Mount Colchik and shadows were filling every unfriendly place with darkness and dire possibilities.

"We'll be lucky to make it to the police station before sundown. I'll be in trouble if I'm not home soon." It was easier to blame my mother's rules than my fear for not wanting to go in the old house.

"Here, Teedie, stay here and hold Otis." After securing our paying customer in Teedie's lap, Patty waved me and Janie forward. "Let's get going, then." She set off through the tunnel lined with ever darkening air, expecting us to follow.

I didn't know whether I wanted to be first or last, then decided it was safer in the middle. I swallowed back any confessions of being a sissy and headed up the walk behind Patty. I could hear Janie's hesitant footsteps behind me.

Patty stopped halfway there to wait for us. "Come on, you guys!" she whispered fiercely. That was when I realized that Patty might not be as brave as she acted. It wasn't a particularly comforting thought.

In a triple knot of trepidation, we stepped up onto the creaking porch. The stairs had long since fallen in. I had a little trouble balancing my cat and keeping my knees from knocking. The dark open door stood before us.

Patty switched on the flashlight and the dim beam lit the front room. Without taking time to think, I imagine, she stepped inside and we followed.

The floor boards were littered with leaves and old newspapers. In the back corner of the room an old kitchen table and one chair had collapsed into a pile of rust and Formica. The place smelled like the attic at my grandma's old house — the nose-wrinkling smell of dust older than dirt, sun-baked wood, and families of mice.

"We need to find something with a door to close them up," Patty declared and headed for the short hallway that had only half a floor left.

"Be careful," I said and watched my own feet. I had the feeling that if I fell through the floor in this old place, I'd never get out. I'd be fertilizer for the sea of ivy, or worse.

Turned out there wasn't a door in the place. As a matter of fact, the last room at the end of the hall didn't even have a floor. Patty shined the light down into a hole at least six feet deep that had been dug out of the clay. It was a smaller version of my grandmother's cellar except there were no stairs — only hard clay with a few floor boards and leaves resting at the bottom.

"What do we do now?" I asked, wanting to get out of there as fast as my feet could move. Cat or no cat.

"Stay here while I go get the bucket and the rope."

Janie and I both spoke at once. "What?"

"Just stay here." Patty shoved the flashlight in my hand and headed for the front door.

As Patty's footsteps faded away, the wind picked up and the house squeaked and creaked. I kept the flashlight aimed at our feet to watch for snakes and silently vowed to vote Patty out of Sha-La-La if she'd left us there for a joke.

"Are you scared?" Janie whispered.

A popping sound of a branch or a few acorns dropping onto the roof made me jump and tighten my hold on the flashlight. Fear can be a great motivator for the truth.

"Yeah," I answered. "I wish she'd hurry up." Actually, I was beginning to wish the old house had a bathroom. I didn't want to wet my pants if we had to face a snake or worse. That's something that would be pretty hard to live down.

Then, the flashlight began to dim.

"Oh, great!" I said, and shook it. The light blinked and brightened slightly. I figured we had about two minutes of light left. It seemed like the shortest two minutes of my life because before I was ready, the light faded again.

"Here I come!" Patty called. I suppose she didn't want to scare us into jumping into the hole. She came through the door with the bucket and the plastic bowl in her hand.

She held the bucket out to me. "Here, put your cat in here."

I was glad to put down my burden — that would make it easier for me to run if the occasion called for us to *skeedaddle* as my grandpa used to say. Then I watched in amazement as Patty lowered the cat into the hole.

"We can keep them in here 'til we find a better place."

I didn't know what to say. Since I didn't have any better idea, and I wasn't required to lie to my mother, I nodded and kept quiet.

"We'll have to bring them food and water," Janie said as she deposited her cat into the bucket for the ride to the bottom.

I shined the flickering flashlight into the hole. The cats didn't seem alarmed by their new home. As a matter of fact, they looked relieved to be set free from our sweaty arms.

Patty smiled. "Now, let's get over to the police station and collect our first reward. It'll cost us a dollar, but I bet I can talk my older brother Davey into coming back with us to feed them. In case you two *scaredy* cats are afraid of the dark, that is."

I was so happy to be leaving I wasn't going to bring up the fact that she could come back by herself to feed them if she was so much braver than we were.

❦❦❦

We were the *he-roes* — I mean *her-roes* — of the day. When Sandy produced a cat cage for Mr. Otis and his owners showed up with our twenty dollar bill, we were suddenly famous. We even got to smile and pose with Otis, his owners, and our moola, for the front page of the *Mossy Creek Gazette*.

Patty's brother earned his dollar by going in the old house all alone to deliver water and two cans of cat food we'd bought with our reward. He grossed us out by telling us one of the cats had already caught a mouse on its own.

The next four days we took turns delivering cat food — two of us went at a time. Whammer, who'd come into our cat-wanted business late, tagged along whenever it was Teedie's turn to open the cat food. He was a nuisance, but the cats seemed to like him. The other team — the one *not* feeding the cats — was supposed to keep an eye out for the next wanted poster and pick up any other lost cats we found.

By the end of the week we had *ten* cats.

"How come nobody is looking for those cats?" Janie asked the following Saturday. We were gathered around our pile of sticks in the center of *Sha-La-La Land* pretending to have a campfire. Janie had come up with the idea when her dad installed what he called *fake logs* in their fireplace so they wouldn't have to tend a woodpile. We knew better than to start a real fire. We didn't go into the 'cat house' as we called it now except to feed them because they made so much noise when we showed up. All they had to hear was the pop and hiss of a can being opened and, oh, brother! We'd used most of our reward money to buy cat food, which was bad news for *Sha-La-La*. Besides, Patty said we needed our privacy to do some more plotting.

"Maybe we should go back down to the police station," Patty said, poking the fake fire with a stick. "Maybe they put the fliers up on that side of town first."

"What if these are Bigelow cats and nobody in Mossy Creek will take 'em?"

"They couldn't have walked all the way up here from Bigelow," Teedie said. "They can't even climb out of a bro-ken-down cellar."

"We could ask Sandy or Miz Katie Bell — they know all the news. Or, we could put up our own fliers."

That seemed to be the best we could come up with. We re-walked our original path of glory to the police station. Of course we had to stop at Mossy Creek Hardware and Gardening and buy Coca-Colas in the short bottles for our temporary reward. Whammer used his own nickel to buy a piece of bubble gum. That's when we saw the flier taped to the inside of the glass near the front door.

WANTED: CAT NAPPERS

There's been a sudden outbreak of missing cats. If you or anyone has information, please call Officer Crane at 678-555-MOSS or dial 911. A $50 reward has been offered for the capture of the perpetrators. The theft of a family pet is a misdemeanor which carries a $100 fine and five days in jail.

"What's a *per-pe* —"

Patty interrupted Whammer's painful sounding out of our doom. She ripped the flier down and headed out the door. Janie, Teedie, Whammer and I followed. My heart was doing it's own *boom, boom, boom*. But then, worse, old Mr. Rufus, who ran the livestock feed section for the store's owner, Mr. Anglin, was sittin' and rockin' in his usual spot near the bags of chicken feed and bales of hay. He grinned his toothless grin and said, "*Ew gurls know anythang 'bout them kets?*" On most days I couldn't understand a word he said because of his lack of teeth, but somehow today each word was as clear and cold as the water in Mossy Creek.

"No, sir," Patty, Janie, and Teedie said in unison. Whammer and me stayed quiet.

We ran all the way back to *Sha-La-La*.

"*What are we going to do?*" Janie wailed, while Patty paced the grass near the front door of the cat house.

"We'll just let 'em all go. Nobody'll know it was us," our fearless leader decided. "Let somebody else find 'em."

We took the flashlight from it's hidey-hole and hurried inside. The cats, as usual, set up a *rowwwl!* when they heard our footsteps. Patty and I worked on a way to charm each cat into the bucket for the trip to freedom — this involving our last half-can of cat food — while Whammer stooped down to yowl back at the prisoners. He always did this and I secretly wondered if the cats and Whammer might actually understand each other. As we fretted over the length of the rope, I saw one calico, who must've recognized Whammer's voice, leap toward him from the bottom to the top. She almost made it, at the last second snagging her claws into Whammer's tennis shoe. Whammer must have thought that was cool because he laughed and let out with his trademark, "Wham!" before turning to see if we'd all witnessed the cat on the flying Nike trapeze.

Less than a second later, the cat gave a squirm, part of the packed clay at the edge gave way and Whammer's feet went out from under him. He tumbled into the hole, scattering cats and kicking up red dust. The boards at the bottom broke his fall but for a moment we all stood stunned.

"*Wham*," he said weakly before Teedie set to wailin'.

"*Whaaaaaammer!*"

The cats, after initially scrambling out of the way, returned to sniff and stroke and rub all over him as though he was a kitten who needed their attention. Whammer's fearful look disappeared and he did his best to smile. "They like me," he said as he tried to pet each one in turn.

"We've got to get him out of there!" Teedie said. She kneeled at the side and reached down her hand. "Grab my hand, Whammer."

Reluctantly, he pushed the cats off him and did his best to stand on the broken boards beneath him.

That's when the boards shifted and he slipped up to his armpits into an even deeper part of the hole. There was no way he could reach his sister's hand.

"Here, catch!" Patty slung the bucket toward him and he managed to grab ahold of it, but when he did he pulled the rope out of Patty's fingers. Now the bucket, the rope and Whammer were all at the bottom of the hole.

Teedie started crying and I did the first thing I could think of. "I'm goin' to get my daddy!" I yelled and headed for the door. My dad had belonged to the Mossy Creek Volunteer Fire Department since I could remember. And one of the things he always said was — when there's trouble, get a fireman.

I ran so fast I tripped on the porch boards and fell with an *oof* onto the walk. My knees stung like fire but I got up and ran on. By the end of the tunnel I thought I heard someone yell but then again, maybe it was my imagination. I didn't want to think that it might have been Whammer being eaten by the cats. I ducked under some bushes and ran faster.

I popped out of the tall grass like a deer in hunting season with dogs on my trail. That's when I experienced the twin feelings of terror and relief. There was a Mossy Creek police car parked on the street at the beginning of our trail to *Sha-La-La*. The first thing I recognized beyond that was Patty's brother Davey, next to him was Officer Mutt Bottoms, Sandy's brother. And, standing next to Officer Mutt was Chief Royden. I didn't even care that I would surely go to jail. I started wailing as loud as Teedie. "Whammer fell! He's being eaten by cats!"

Let me tell you, that got their attention. I had to stop and bend over my stomach was hurting so bad but I still managed to point. "In the old house . . . in the back. . ."

They didn't wait for me. Both Officer Mutt and the chief set off through the bushes without regard to their pressed uniform pants and shiny shoes.

Davey hung back for a moment to torment me. "You're gonna go to jail for stealing cats. I told them the whole thing. I'm gonna get fifty dollars."

I didn't have enough spit in my mouth to speak, so I

watched him parade down the path toward the house in silence. I decided then that Davey was a mean boy; he didn't even seem to care that Whammer was being turned into cat food.

Unable to escape anyway, I followed everyone back to the scene of our crime.

"Are you hurt anywhere?" the chief called down. Whammer looked unhurt enough to me — still for once, and up to his armpits in worried, yowling cats.

"Unh-uh," he answered.

"Stay still," Amos told him. "We'll get you out of there."

Then Officer Mutt sneezed. The chief just looked at him. "Somebody has to go down there, Mutt," he said, and smiled. "I'm the chief. You're not."

Officer Mutt's eyes were turning red and watery. He handed the chief a flashlight and pulled out a handkerchief from his back pocket to blow his nose. He shoved it back in his pocket and sighed. "Allergic to cats," he said then sat down on the edge of the hole and slid down the side.

Man, I knew we were in deep trouble then because that red Georgia clay stuck to his backside like spitballs on a dry erase board. He sneezed again and I winced. When he stopped sneezing and saw what had happened to his clean uniform he was gonna make us stay in jail even longer.

He reached down, pulled Whammer out of the tangle of boards, then stooped down to look him over. The cats took this as a sign that they might get food or pets from this stranger and proceeded to rub and climb on Officer Mutt. He sneezed three times and I could have sworn the chief laughed. It was so quick though, and I was so worried about our immediate future I couldn't be sure. Officer Mutt lifted Whammer by his armpits and handed him to the chief.

The chief told Teedie to hold Whammer's hand, then he crossed his arms and looked down at Officer Mutt. Now the cats were trying to climb up his legs, making claw holes in his uniform pants.

"Looks like we found the Cat Nappers, and the cats," Chief Royden said.

Officer Mutt sneezed again and reached a hand toward the chief. After a small hesitation, the chief took it and pulled Officer Mutt out of the cat house. Tears were running down Officer Mutt's face. I wondered why he was so sad.

"I've got to get out of here," was all he said.

The chief nodded. "I guess it won't hurt the cats to stay here until we can get Hank Blackshear on the scene. He can probably identify them and track down the owners through the vet clinic's records."

But Officer Mutt didn't answer. He was already stepping out onto the porch and away from the house.

The chief looked at us then. "Ladies, come with me. And bring Raymond."

Uh-oh. It was true what our parents told us: The chief knew *everything* about the bad kids of Mossy Creek, even Whammer's real name.

🐾🐾🐾

We didn't go straight to jail like I thought we would. We did have to do something Sandy called *community service*, though. Whenever someone needed their dog walked or cat box cleaned, one of us would have to show up and do the job. In a way, we were even more famous than when we found Otis. Although, cleaning cat litter is not a job of the stars. Personally, I didn't care if I never saw another cat close up again.

I didn't get my backside warmed either — mainly because I told the truth, my mother informed me, and because I was running to get help for Whammer when I got caught, rather than running away. I *did* get grounded with no TV. But Daddy took me to watch the volunteer fire department burn down the old homeplace. They called it a practice burn, and my father was the officer in charge of it. He even got Wolfman Washington to bring over his bulldozer the next day and bury the ashes and flatten the old cellar so that no one would ever fall in it again. Or, use it for a life of crime.

Patty's brother Davey got his money though. And it was gonna take a long time for me to forgive him for being such a sissy tattle-tale. On the other hand, I'd been willing to sacrifice any reward in order to save Whammer, and finding that police car without having to run all the way into town was a good thing.

I swear, the older I get, the more complicated things look. Just when I thought we'd never see *Sha-La-La Land* again, my dad built us a brand new fort in our back yard — way up in an old Mulberry tree. It's waaaay better than *Sha-La-La* — it's got a roof, a door and during the summer all the mulberries we can eat. And it's all mine.

From the desk of Katie Bell

Lady Victoria Salter Stanhope
The Cliffs
Seaward Road
St. Ives, Cornwall, TR3 7PJ
United Kingdom

Dear Vick:

Here's a handful of clippings I call the "I remember my childhood summer club." It seems summertime in Mossy Creek has a magic effect on people. They never forget those lazy, flower-colored mountain days and watermelon-scented nights. The weather's been cold lately, with more rain. All the leaves are off the trees now, and Mount Colchik looks awfully forlorn outside our windows. I decided my readers needed all the warm memories of childhood blessings I could give them. Enjoy this trio of "good times back then" stories.

Katie

In Mossy Creek, you can't judge a book by its cover.
The richest man in the county is just as likely to be buried
in his overalls as a fine suit.

🐦🐦🐦🐦🐦🐦🐦🐦🐦🐦🐦🐦🐦🐦🐦🐦🐦🐦🐦🐦🐦🐦🐦🐦🐦🐦🐦🐦🐦🐦🐦🐦

The Pulleybones

Chapter 8

My daddy was a Baptist when my mama fell in love with him, and Baptist he remained. And though she'd loved him enough to marry him, there'd never been any question of Mama forsaking her church for his. Every Sunday of her life she took her place beside her mother and her two sisters on the third-row pew of Mossy Creek's Mt. Gilead Methodist Church. I went with her, of course. There'd never been any question about that either, not in Mama's mind. As for what was in my daddy's mind, he never said, but it was a condition of their marriage that any children would be Methodists.

Of course, from time to time some cousin or other from Daddy's side of the family suggested I ought to attend their church every other week. "The way I see it," they'd say, "it's only fair to let the child try 'em both, then when she's older, she can choose for herself."

Each time the suggestion was made, Mama just smiled and shook her head. "Polly goes with me."

"Don't seem right," the cousin would say. "Sounds down right prejudiced to me. Have you got something against the Baptists?"

"Me?" Mama'd say ever so sweetly. "Why, I haven't got

a prejudiced bone in my body. In fact, my views are quite catholic — that is to say, catholic with a little 'c.'"

I never was sure what that meant, except that it had something to do with a person seeing some good in every denomination. I do know, though, that it was having to stand behind that little "c" boast that forced Mama into letting me spend the last week of summer vacation with Yvonne Clay, my best friend in all the world.

Although Yvonne and I were best friends, we saw each other only at school, on account of I lived on the north side of town while she lived to the south, on the outskirts of Mossy Creek, in the country. In that summer of 1952, the distance between our homes was a significant consideration since most of the roads outside town were bumpy, dusty, unpaved dirt lanes. Mrs. Clay had invited me to come out to help celebrate Yvonne's ninth birthday, but Mama was having trouble agreeing to let me go. "If it was just for the day," she said, "there'd be no question. But an entire week? I don't know about that, Polly."

"But, Mama, you know Yvonne. She's real well behaved, and her mother is the sweetest person you'd ever want to meet."

"I know, honey, but you're not accustomed to being away at night. You might get homesick."

"I wouldn't. I promise."

"Besides," she added, as if presenting the clincher to my not going, "you'd miss church on Sunday."

"Oh, no, ma'am," I said, happy to reassure her on that point, "Yvonne goes to church every Sunday. I could just go with her."

"To the *Children of Jesus Tabernacle!*" Mama stared at me like I'd said I was fixing to run out to the mailbox buck naked. "Absolutely not!"

"'Scuse me for putting in my two cents' worth," Daddy

said, lowering his newspaper so he could look right at Mama, "but do you know something I don't know about the folks who go to the Tabernacle?"

"No, but —"

"Am I in the wrong house?" he said, "or aren't you the lady who professes to be so broad-minded? Er, catholic with a little 'c'?"

Mama's mouth got sort of puckery, like she'd bitten into a green persimmon, and she didn't say anything for a solid minute. To my surprise, my daddy started grinning like a cat who'd finally cornered the family canary. "What's the matter, Delilah? Something got your tongue?"

When she just kept on staring at him, Daddy chuckled. "It's just us Baptists and Methodists here, so feel free to continue with your list of reasons why Polly can't go to her friend's church. I'm especially fascinated to know why a Methodist —"

"You can go!" Mama said, surprising the dickens out of me. "I'm sure it will be very educational for you to see how other people worship." Immediately, she turned back to Daddy, and if looks could kill, poor Daddy would have met his Maker that instant. "As for you, Ralph Walter Varner, maybe you'd like to visit the Children of Jesus Tabernacle as well?"

"Me?" Daddy said, almost choking on his laughter. "The thought never crossed my mind. I'm Baptist with a big 'B' and proud of it. So until every last Child of Jesus brings his letter of membership over to First Baptist, guess they'll just have to make do with Polly."

Mama packed my suitcase like I was going to New York City, rather than a mere six miles on the other side of town, and at the last minute she agreed I could take the pretty pink bathing suit Grandmother Varner'd given me for my ninth birthday. "But don't you suggest swimming," Mama warned, "just in case it's against their religion or something."

I couldn't imagine anybody having something against swimming, but I said I would be on my best behavior the entire week. "I'll say 'Please' and 'Thank you,' and I won't take anything at the table until it's offered to me."

Naturally, I was much too excited to sleep that Sunday night, and by Monday afternoon, when Mrs. Clay drove up in her dark blue Ford truck, I was ready to begin what I was convinced would be the most exciting adventure of my life. In my mind, the coming week was destined to leave me with a memory I would treasure for all my days. I could just picture Yvonne and me skipping through a lovely green meadow, a picnic basket held between us, with her dog, Rollo, trailing happily behind us. I didn't have a dog, but I was certain I would like Rollo.

The first hint that things might not be as I had imagined them came when Mrs. Clay made a left turn onto a dirt road so rutted it bounced and tossed us until I thought surely my teeth would break. After about a quarter of a mile of this, she stopped the truck beside a small, country house. "Here we are," she said. "Welcome to our home, Polly."

Several weeks ago Daddy and I had seen an old movie on TV called *Kentucky* starring a lady named Loretta Young, and because Yvonne's house was on the edge of town, I had begun to imagine it a twin of the magnificent, white-fenced horse farm in the movie. Of course, I knew the grass in Georgia wasn't blue like that in Kentucky; even so, I wasn't prepared for the reality of the Clays' house.

This unpainted wooden structure, with its corrugated tin roof, was a far cry from a Kentucky horse farm. And the elderly lady who came out onto the sagging porch to wave to us, wearing a faded blue dress and men's leather boots, was no Loretta Young!

"That's my Grandma Wilson," Yvonne said. "We live with her and Grandpa. Oh, and my cousin is here too. His mother sent him out here for a few days, on account of she just had a new little baby girl."

Her cousin! I got a real queasy feeling in my stomach. Not Bobby Wilson! *Please*, I prayed, *don't let that be the cousin she means*. Bobby Wilson was a year ahead of us at Mossy Creek Elementary, and though there wasn't the least chance of my ever being double promoted, if there had been, I would have turned down the honor simply because I would have wound up in the same class as Bobby Wilson.

"Your cousin?" I said, the words little more than a whisper.

"Surely you know Bobby Wilson," Mrs. Clay said.

"Yes'um," I replied. And to myself I said, *All too well!*

"Don't worry," Yvonne whispered in my ear, "Bobby won't bother us. My grandpa told him he's not to pester us, and if he tries, I'll just tell on him. He'll behave."

I sure hoped so, but I had my doubts.

We climbed down from the truck, and while Mrs. Clay got my suitcase, Yvonne took my hand and led me around to the back of the house to show me the new baby pigs.

The back porch sagged even worse than the one on the front, and over to the right was a rusted iron water spigot, with a metal bucket hanging on its nozzle. The spigot dripped, so the ground for a good four feet around it had become a circle of oozing mud.

Pitted peaches were strewn all over the porch, lying on what I later learned were bleached flower sacks. The peaches were drying in the sun, and later they would be stored in jars and put up for use during the winter months.

Yvonne gave my hand a tug. "The sty is down this way," she said, though saying it was a waste of breath. My nose told me where the pigs were. To the right, about a hundred yards away, was a fenced area containing a pinkish-gray animal that resembled a tall, fat dog. While I batted a few dozen horseflies away from my face, four little piglets went running over to the mother and began nudging her belly and squealing. The big old fat pig just grunted and plopped down so the piglets could suckle. "Look at their little curly tails," Yvonne said. "Aren't they adorable?"

Good manners kept me from saying what I really thought, and since speaking would mean I would have to open my mouth, which was the last thing I wanted to do in all this stench and flies, I nodded and did a little grunting of my own.

"Uh huh," I muttered in my throat.

Mrs. Clay came to the back door and yelled for us to come to supper, so we left the pigs and walked back up to the house. After stepping around the mud surrounding the spigot, we reached the porch by way of a cement block that replaced the broken bottom stair. I just did whatever Yvonne did, it was the polite thing to do, but the more I saw, the more I began to wonder how I would ever stay here a whole week.

On the other side of the screen door was as old-timey a kitchen as I'd ever seen, and when I looked around the room, I marveled at what it had and what it didn't have. Among the furnishings was a round oak pedestal table, several mismatched cane-bottom chairs, an old wooden hutch, a sink, a kerosene stove, and a refrigerator so old I didn't recognize the brand name. Worst of all, empty mason jars covered every square inch of the faded linoleum floor.

There must have been a hundred of those jars!

I thought of the peaches drying on the porch, and I wondered if it would take all that many jars to hold them. As if in answer to my thoughts, Yvonne said, "Grandma's in the midst of canning. I'll have to help her some while you're here, but you're company, so you don't have to help if you don't want to."

I knew what my mama would expect me to reply, so I said, "Oh, I'll be happy to help if I can." It must have been the right answer because Yvonne gave me a hug, and her grandma, who'd just turned from the stove, gave me a grin so wide I saw where some of her back teeth were missing.

"Everybody sit down," the old woman said, motioning toward the pedestal table, which was practically groaning from all the food crowded in the middle. Circling a platter of fried chicken were bowls of mashed potatoes, boiled okra, crowder peas, stewed squash, and cabbage slaw. In addition, there were plates of sliced tomatoes and hot flaky biscuits. "I don't mind doing the cooking, but I get down right cranky if I can't eat while the food is still hot. Speaking of which, Yvonne, sugar, look in the pantry and get me the hot sauce."

While Yvonne went to a small curtained alcove of shelves, Mrs. Clay introduced me to her parents then showed me which chair was mine. "And you know my nephew, Bobby, of course."

Bobby made a face at me, then he yanked back his chair and sat down. Thank goodness his grandfather was between him and me. "You like hot sauce?" Mr. Wilson asked when Yvonne returned with a mason jar containing dozens of little green peppers covered over with liquid.

"No, sir. I don't care for any."

"To each his own," he said. "Me, I like a drop on my slaw."

Mr. Wilson was tall and gray-haired, just like my grandfather Varner, and though he wore overalls and heavy boots, where my grandfather wore a white shirt and tie every day of his life, he made me think of my grandfather. Hoping I hadn't insulted him, I said, "My grandfather pours pepper salts on his collards."

"Well, he wouldn't pour *my* pepper salts on anything," Mrs. Wilson said. "As my husband will tell you, when it comes to my pepper salts, one drop will inspire, two drops will set fire."

This was obviously a family joke, for all three of the grown-ups laughed.

After Mr. Wilson finished saying the blessing, he told Yvonne to pass me the platter of fried chicken. "Since you're the company, Polly, you may choose whichever piece you prefer."

For as long as I can remember, the pulleybone has been my favorite piece of chicken. I can eat a leg or a wing if I have to, but the sight of a crispy pulleybone makes my mouth water. "Thank you," I said, "I'll have the pulleybone if nobody minds."

When no one said a word, I took my fork and reached toward the platter. My hand was no more than an inch away when suddenly Bobby Wilson reached out and snatched the pulleybone right out from under my fork. I was still getting over the shock of that when he did something so disgusting I could hardly believe my eyes. He licked that piece of chicken on both sides, his vile tongue working as fast as a thirsty dog laps water from a bowl. Then, pretending to be surprised that everyone was staring at him, he said, "Oh, was that the only pulleybone? Here, you can have it."

"Boy," Mr. Wilson said, "get up from the table this minute, and don't come back 'til everybody's finished eating."

Bobby got up, and though he didn't make a sound, he looked straight at me. *Watch out*, his eyes said, *I've just gotten started.*

Mrs. Wilson tossed the pulleybone into the sink, and though she apologized for her grandson, the damage was already done. My stomach was doing flip flops like it might turn sick on me. Thank goodness I managed not to embarrass myself. Not then. The embarrassment came a couple of hours later.

After we ate slices of birthday cake with chocolate icing and pink candles, Yvonne and I went to her bedroom to cut out the paper dolls I'd brought her as my gift. I was maneuvering the scissors around a particularly difficult neckline when Yvonne said, "It'll be dark soon. If you need to pee, now'd be a good time to do it."

I must have looked as dumb as I felt, for she giggled. "It gets pretty dark here at night. Much too dark to go outside."

Outside? Was she teasing me? Dark or light, why would I want to go outside to pee? I found out soon enough. Yvonne swatted my arm like we were playing tag, then she ran from the bedroom, through the kitchen, and out onto the back porch. I followed, of course, but she's taller than me and has longer legs, so she always outruns me.

She was waiting for me on a footpath just beyond the dripping spigot. It was only when I joined her that I noticed a small wooden structure at the end of the path. Built of wood, the little building was about seven feet high and about three feet wide, and it was so dilapidated it looked like the first good gust of wind would send it flying all the way to Florida.

An outhouse! I swallowed a sob, though I felt my lip quiver. My daddy always called Mama and me a couple of *hothouse plants*, and I guessed it was the truth, because the only place Mama would let me sit down on the toilet seat was at the home of a relative.

In addition to my 'prissy ways' as Grandmother Varner calls them, I'm afraid of everything that crawls on its belly, and just about everything that walks on four feet, and I'd heard there were *Daddy Longlegs* spiders in outhouses. I shuddered just thinking of spiders.

Yvonne and I had been best friends since we were in first grade, and it was okay with her that I was a bit of a scaredy cat, and it was okay with me that she wasn't. Because she knew I was a hot house plant she usually took the lead. But not this time. "You can go first," she said, and though I knew she was being polite, this was one time I wished she'd be rude.

The door to the outhouse was held on by two rusted hinges, and there was no handle to open it, just a hole about the size of a fifty-cent piece to put your finger through. Naturally, I was reluctant to put my finger through that round hole, but I did it anyway on account of I was beginning to need to pee. I had opened the door no more than a couple of inches, with the hinges creaking in a spooky sort of way, when something brown and furry came running out. Before I could jump back, that furry thing dashed right over my foot, then disappeared into the tall weeds to the rear.

I don't know what sort of creature it was, but I screamed. When Yvonne heard me scream, she let out a yelp of her own and turned to run back to the house. I ran, too, and for the first time since I'd known her, I stayed ahead of her the entire way.

I wouldn't have made it through those next five days if it hadn't been for an old ceramic baby potty Mrs. Clay found in the attic. Even so, I hated having to use it, just like I hated everything else about being in the country. All I thought about was going home. If there were any lovely meadows for picnicking, I never saw them. As for Yvonne's dog, Rollo, that crazy old bloodhound did nothing but sleep half the day and chase chickens around the yard for the other half.

That was another horror I'd discovered about the country, that chickens are allowed to walk around loose!

Even so, I preferred the days to the nights. Yvonne didn't

have any trouble falling to sleep, but the crickets and the hooty owls were so loud they kept me awake most of the night. And it was so dark I couldn't see my hand in front of my face.

Most mornings we helped Mrs. Wilson with her canning. She was putting up soup mixtures, and by Saturday I'd gotten pretty good at peeling tomatoes. The tomatoes were allowed to sit in a pan of hot water for several seconds. After that the skin could be pulled off fairly easy. I'd been peeling for two days now, and I had the shriveled, pruney fingers to prove it, but at least that job was better than shucking corn. Corn, I'd discovered, had worms in it. Fat, green worms.

While I looked around me to make sure none of those loathsome creatures were crawling about, Mrs. Clay surprised me by suggesting that as soon as Yvonne and I finished what we were doing, we might like to go down to the creek for a swim. "I think you two have earned some play time. Never saw two such helpful little girls."

As soon as Yvonne and I washed our hands, we went to her bedroom and put on our bathing suits and sandals. "Let's go," I said, throwing a towel over my shoulder, "before your cousin hears us and tries to come along."

"He's gone off someplace," she said, "so we'll have the whole afternoon to ourselves."

Happy to hear it, I tagged her shoulder then ran for the door. "Last one in's a rotten egg."

"That'll be you!" Yvonne yelled, running after me.

We skipped all the way down an old dirt road with ditches on either side, and it was great to be alone, just her and me. The sun was shining, the birds were singing, and we were telling silly jokes and giggling.

It hadn't rained for several days, so the road was dry and powdery, and our footsteps kicked up the silt, making our feet and ankles as red as the Georgia clay. I didn't mind, though, for the creek was just ahead — I could smell the fresh, cool water. I couldn't see it yet, on account of it was down a hill and the hill was literally covered by thick, green kudzu vines, but I knew it was there.

When we reached the one spot where the kudzu didn't grow, we half walked, half slid down to the sandy creek bank. I laid my towel across a bush and sat down to take off my sandals. The sand was warm beneath my settee.

I had taken swimming lessons during the first weeks of the summer, but with the creek only a few inches deep, swimming was out of the question. Mostly all we did was wade and splash each other, but after a while we worked up the nerve to sit down in the icy water.

We were lying on our backs, spitting mouthfuls of water high into the air, when Bobby arrived. He just stood there on the bank watching us, and grinning like butter wouldn't melt in his mouth! I wouldn't have cared, except that he had that look in his eyes — the look I didn't trust. "Go away," I yelled.

He didn't go. Instead, he pointed to my new pink bathing suit then pinched his nose as if to say the suit stunk. "Hey, *Piano Legs*. Where'd you get that ugly rag? At a rummage sale?"

He laughed like that was the funniest joke in the world. He even pretended to fall down laughing. I secretly hoped he'd fall in a hole and come out in China, but I didn't give him the satisfaction of knowing I'd even heard his remark. "Just ignore him," Yvonne said.

"You know," he said after a while, "you girls are pretty brave. You sure wouldn't catch *me* in that creek."

"Don't ask him why," Yvonne whispered. "He'll just say something nasty."

I sat up to let the sun warm me, my back to Bobby.

"I wouldn't go in that creek," he yelled, "because I heard Grandpa say the thing was plumb full of cottonmouth water moccasins."

I froze, but Yvonne yelled,

"You're a liar, Bobby Wilson!"

"It's the pure-and-tee truth. I swear it on a stack of Bibles."

"Then you're a blasphemer as well as a liar," I said, "and you're probably going to hell! Besides, Mrs. Clay wouldn't let her own daughter go in a place full of cottonmouths."

He didn't answer right away, then he said, "Oh, my aunt doesn't know. Grandpa was telling it to Grandma."

I didn't believe him for a minute — at least I tried not to. Still, I'd have let a cottonmouth take a sun bath on my shoulder before I let Bobby see I was scared.

I made a big to-do of splashing Yvonne for a few more minutes, then I said, very casually, "I guess we'd better get back to the house now, it's getting close to supper time." She agreed so quickly I could tell she was as nervous as me to be out of there.

We slipped our feet into our sandals without bothering to buckle them and grabbed our towels. While we climbed the hill back up to the road, I had to bite my lips to keep from looking down at my feet for cottonmouth water moccasins!

We'd just reached the road when a big old June bug buzzed past my head, and I thought I would have a heart attack. I screamed, which made Yvonne scream, and her cousin doubled over, just laughing his fool head off.

After a time he ran on ahead of us. At first I thought it was good riddance, but that was before we rounded a bend in the road and saw Bobby standing perfectly still, looking down into the ditch on the left. "Come here, quick," he yelled. "I found a snake."

"You did not, Bobby Wilson, you're just lying again." I said it, but I didn't mean it. This time I believed him, mainly because he was standing still and not taking his eyes off the ditch.

We took our time getting to him. I didn't get close enough for him to push me into the ditch, which is something he would do, but I got close enough to see where he was looking. There was a snake!

It wasn't a very fat snake, but it was about two feet long, and it had blue-black skin that shown like a jewel in the sunshine. It lay perfectly still. "Is it asleep?" I whispered.

"If it is," Bobby said, "I'm fixing to wake it up."

The fool picked up a rock about the size of a plum, then threw that rock right at the snake's body. Thank goodness, nothing happened. Then he picked up a larger rock and threw it, hitting the creature smack on the head. Again, nothing happened.

"It's dead," Yvonne said. "Let's go."

I was willing, but Bobby stopped me by asking if I saw a big stick any place. "What are you going to do?" I asked, though I really didn't want to know.

"Grandpa says there's a snake that you can hit with a stick and it will break into pieces. Then, when you go back later, the pieces have grown back together again. I'm fixing to see if this is one of those snakes."

I believe Bobby Wilson is one of those children you hear about sometimes, the kind who get their brains injured while they're being born. When he started looking around for a big stick, Yvonne and I took off running. Somewhere along the way, I dropped my towel, but nothing would have tempted me to stop and pick it up.

At supper, all Bobby could talk about was how brave he'd been to kill that snake. Of course, I knew the snake was already dead, so I didn't pay him any mind. Not until later that night. Just as Yvonne and I were getting ready for bed, Bobby came to the door of our bedroom and said he thought he'd better tell me something. "For your own good."

"What?" I asked, suspicious of his concern.

"You know that snake I killed today?"

"You mean the dead one?"

"If you say so," he said.

Uh-oh. If Bobby didn't want to argue, it was only because he had something better in mind.

"What about it?" I asked.

"Well, I didn't tell you before, but I hit it with the stick, and it come apart, just like Grandpa said."

"So?"

"I took the tail away so the snake wouldn't be able to get itself back together again."

"So?" I asked again.

"I was just wondering how far a snake would travel to get its tail back."

"Well, don't look at me," I said. "I sure can't tell you."

"That's okay," he said. "You can just tell me in the morning."

Boys can be so stupid. "If I don't know the answer now, I won't know it any better in the morning."

He giggled. "Maybe you will. 'Cause I hid the snake's tail in your bedroom."

Yvonne said he was lying, and she went right to sleep. I wished I could!

I kept telling myself that Bobby just wanted to scare me so I would sit up all night worrying. Deep down in my soul, I knew that the only snake in this house was sleeping on the sofa in the living room. I knew it, and yet I lay there wide awake, staring into the inky darkness, scared beyond description.

That snake was blue-black; he'd be almost invisible in

the dark. All that night, every time a breeze blew across my arm, I would jump clear out of my skin. The only thing that kept me sane was imagining the various things I would do to Bobby Wilson once daylight came. Some time during that endless night, exhaustion must have claimed me, for I fell asleep. The next thing I knew, I heard the rooster crow.

By the time I got dressed, streaks of pink were lighting the dawn-gray sky. No one else was up, so I opened the back door carefully to keep it from creaking, then I hurried down the path. I didn't want to see a snake again, but I had to know for sure. I saw my towel lying in the road, so I knew I was near the spot.

I walked slowly and carefully toward the towel and beyond, then I looked over the side of the road into the ditch. That blue-black snake lay there just as it had yesterday, whole and unsevered. The two rocks Bobby had thrown were still there, but there was no sign of a stick of any kind.

That big liar! He hadn't even gone into the ditch to hit that snake. Probably scared to! All my dreams of retribution from last night came rushing back to me, but in the light of day none of them seemed cruel enough to serve for Bobby Wilson's punishment.

I didn't get a chance to speak to him until later, when Yvonne, her mama, and I were about to climb the front steps of the Children of Jesus Tabernacle. Bobby had ridden with his grandparents, and he came running up to us, a big old grin on his face. "How did you sleep?" he asked.

"Why, just fine, thank you. How did you sleep?"

"Like a log," he said, "but, then, I didn't sit up all night waiting to see if a snake came for its tail."

"Oh, that's right," I said, nonchalantly. "I forgot you asked me about that. I guess I was just too sleepy to care. When we get home, if you want to, you can go in the bedroom and see if the tail's still there."

Bobby didn't say a word, but to my surprise Mrs. Clay winked at me. "Come on, King Solomon," she said. "They're already singing the first hymn."

When we got home, Mrs. Wilson cooked a marvelous dinner. This time she fried two chickens, and though I didn't wish to ponder where those birds came from, the aroma that filled the kitchen was mouth-watering. "There'll be two pulleybones," she said, when she saw me looking at the big old white crockery platter, "and one of them is just for you."

I thanked her, though my mind was more concerned with retribution than food. Two *pulleybones.* Hmm.

Remembering how Bobby had grabbed the pulleybone the last time and licked it all over, I knew on the instant how I would get my revenge for the night of fear he had put me through. While Yvonne and her mama went to take off their Sunday clothes, I snitched both pulleybones, took them to the pantry, and set them next to Mrs. Wilson's jar of pepper salts.

"One drop will inspire," the lady had said of her pepper salts, "but two drops will set fire."

The little green peppers lay at the bottom of the jar, but the liquid came up to the half-way mark. I unscrewed the lid, set it aside, then speared one of the pulleybones with a fork and dipped it all the way down into the jar.

I held the chicken in the liquid for a full minute — no point in doing a thing half way. This was no Methodist sprinkle, but a good old Baptist dunking. When it was finished, I put the lid back on the jar and took it and the baptized pulleybone to the table, leaving the other piece of chicken in the pantry.

I pretended I had to push several bowls around to make room for the jar of pepper salts, and in the process I slipped the pulleybone back onto the platter with all the other fried chicken. I put it just on the edge where it wouldn't touch any other pieces, then I turned the platter so the pulleybone was in front of Bobby's plate.

"Come and get it," Mrs. Wilson yelled. "The food'll be gettin' cold, and y'all know I like my chicken while it's hot." I had to swallow my giggles.

Mr. Wilson said grace, and the moment he finished, Bobby snatched the lone pulleybone. Just like the last time, he started licking it like a dog.

In less time than it takes to blink, Bobby dropped the chicken on the table and jumped straight up, knocking his chair back in his haste. He gasped for air, then grabbed his water glass and poured the contents into his mouth. As soon as he emptied that glass, he flung it across the room and grabbed Mrs. Clay's ice tea.

Bobby was the only person moving; everyone else sat in stunned immobility, watching his strange behavior.

When he'd emptied his aunt's glass, he started to cough. It was magnificent coughing! Liquid oozed from every opening: his nose, his mouth, his eyes. I'm not sure, but I think some even dribbled out of his ears.

"The boy's havin' one of them fits!" Mrs. Wilson yelled, and she jumped up, threw her arm around his neck, and began forcing a spoon handle between his teeth.

"Help me, somebody, 'fore he bites his tongue off!"

Still coughing, Bobby grappled with his surprisingly strong grandmother. Finally breaking free of the old lady's iron hold, he made a beeline for the back porch. Everyone but me and Yvonne followed him outside.

I heard the spigot squeaking, and while I pictured Bobby on all fours in the mud, with his head underneath the running water, I got up and retrieved the unbaptized pulleybone from the pantry. When I returned to the table, I broke the pulleybone in half and gave Yvonne her choice.

We served ourselves liberal helpings of mashed potatoes, corn, and okra, then Yvonne and I bit into the crispy pulleybone at the same time. "*Umm*," she said.

"Double *umm*," I said, licking a bit of warm crust off my lips. "You know, your grandma was right. Chicken tastes a whole lot better when it's hot."

She must have guessed that I was responsible for Bobby's distress, for she was grinning from ear to ear.

"Polly Varner," she said, nodding at the pulleybone, "I thought you were a good, God-fearing Methodist."

I grinned back. Sometimes, blessings come from a complex mix of religion and food. "Oh, I am, except when it comes to paying off a debt. Then I'm what you might call catholic with a little 'c.'"

Mossy Creek Gazette

215 Main Street • Mossy Creek, GA 30533

From the desk of Katie Bell

Lady Victoria Salter Stanhope
The Cliffs
Seaward Road
St. Ives, Cornwall, TR3 7PJ
United Kingdom

Dear Vick:

Polly Varner is one of my favorite
people. I'm sure you can see why,
after reading that story from her
childhood. Not every Creekite
childhood is as nostalgic as Polly's,
but we do try to take care of our
young Creekites, and the community
always rallies to help children in
need. A few still manage to slip
between the cracks. But not for long.
I dare you to keep a dry eye when you
read the story I just got from one of
our Creekite teenagers (who's doing
very well now, I'm happy to report!)

Katie

You don't know who you are
until you realize who your friends are.

ᵛᵛᵛᵛᵛᵛᵛᵛᵛᵛᵛᵛᵛᵛᵛᵛᵛᵛᵛᵛᵛᵛᵛᵛᵛᵛᵛᵛᵛᵛᵛᵛᵛᵛᵛᵛᵛᵛ

The War of the Good Deeds

Chapter 9

Dear Katie Bell,

People keep tellin' me my childhood is the best part of my life. But there are parts that I would just as soon forget. My mama says us Creekites wear our superstitions like an old coat. And sometimes, a bad thing is a blessing.

My name is Shirley, and this story I'm sending you happened to me last summer when I was eleven. It started the day everybody later called the beginning of the *War of Good Deeds*. The day Mama later called *The End of Soap Sally*.

The day I almost caused my baby brother to die.

My family has lived just outside Mossy Creek all my life, but before three years ago I hardly knew anyone in town. What with all the gossip my daddy stirred, Mama said it was best we stick to ourselves. And when she looked at the town motto painted high up on Mayor Walker's corn silo, *Ain't Goin' Nowhere and Don't Want To*, she'd just break down and cry.

"We got to get out of Mossy Creek and start over," she'd say. "Some place where no one knows our shame. We'll be like gypsies stealing away in the night, off to some new adventure."

But I had keen Dumbo ears, that's what Daddy called 'em, and I'd heard Granny and Mama talking. Moving meant

192

the debt collectors were on our tails, that Daddy had lost his job cause he'd gone to *pitchin'* again. *Pitchin'* meant he'd gone on another long, drunken tear where he got mean and tore up things.

Then one day, Daddy took his pitchin' too far and drove his pick-up straight into a plate glass window down in a Unadila hair salon. "Thank god it happened way off somewhere else," Mama said, "so maybe nobody up here in the mountains will ever find out." I guess none of y'all ever did. You didn't report it in the paper. Mama was so depressed. See, after three months of being laid off, Daddy'd finally gotten a job delivering hair products but still couldn't give up his liquor. Or maybe he was high sniffing perm solutions. Anyways, he 'bout near killed a little old lady in pink rollers. The Unadila law locked him up for what Mama said would be a considerable time.

Hence, the reason Mama wanted to move from Mossy Creek. She thought maybe we could escape while Daddy couldn't follow us. But Granny's rheumatoid arthritis flared up, bless her heart, and she had to take to the wheelchair, so she sure couldn't go nowhere, even if she had wanted to, which she claimed she didn't.

Granny lived for her soap operas and had never missed an episode of *Days of Our Lives*. Every night, we lived for her to tell us more stories about the Bigelowan and Creekite feuds. Over pinto beans and a glass of sweet milk and cornbread, we heard one tale after another. Our bedtime story was her version of your gossip column. "I *swannee*," Granny would say. "Sometimes the goin's on between us and them Bigelowans is better than my soaps."

But seein' as how we lived in an old trailer out in Chinaberry and I hadn't gone to school the year before on account of bein' sick a lot, I hadn't kept up on any gossip about Creekites and Bigelowans. School was startin' again soon though, and Mama was already talkin' about getting me signed up for the free lunch program and headin' down to the Bigelow Wal-Mart to buy new undies. Undies was the only thing she didn't buy second hand.

Anyway, although I was eleven and hoped I'd get into college someday and be somebody, I didn't actually want to go to school. Kids might call me *white trash* and make fun of my thrift store clothes and my jailbird daddy. Sometimes I walked to the top of our rutted driveway and looked down on the road to town, judging from all angles to see if the woods between our trailer and the road had grown much since the fall before. Maybe this year the kids couldn't see our ratty old trailer from the school bus.

But nothin' was gonna keep me from school, Mama said.

Like later, when nothin' would keep me from tremblin' every time I walked past the old well in our front yard and thought of Soap Sally.

🌱🌱🌱

The day the *War of the Good Deeds* began, the *Truce*, the day my baby brother almost died — whatever you want to call it — was a Tuesday, the fifteenth day of August, right in the middle of the worst dog days I'd ever seen. Heat blazed the parched dirt and red clay while flies and mosquitoes fed on us for lunch and supper. Behind us, Mount Colchik loomed among her sister mountains like some big secret haven God had planted from the heavens, but she was too far to touch or give us any shade. It hadn't rained for going on a month, and whatever grass our pitiful yard once had was brown and so brittle it crackled like dead roach bugs when you walked on it.

"It's so danged hot you could fry an egg on the cement," Mama said. On the front porch, she loaded the metal tub full of tomatoes and dumped steaming water on them to soak. "Makes 'em easier to peel," she explained. "Then we'll can 'em for soup for the winter."

Being the oldest, I'd have the miserable job of peeling and canning, while my little sister, Annie Mae, waved away the flies that swarmed to suck on the tomato juice we splattered all over ourselves. She got paid a penny for every fly she killed and had almost a dollar saved in a mayonnaise jar. I got the same amount for every ten tomatoes I peeled. That didn't seem fair.

Anyway, Annie Mae and I were playing out beneath the shade of a big old cherry tree. Granny's heart couldn't take the heat, so she hovered inside by the trailer's window air conditioner, sipping sweet iced tea and watching her soaps on a little TV. I poured water into the dirt pile Annie Mae and I had dug with our hands. Annie Mae stirred the mess with a stick to make it thick for mud pies.

"Mama, why'd you tie those handkerchiefs in the cherry tree?" I asked. They waved at me from above like white flags floating against the blue sky.

"To scare off the blackbirds," Mama said. She wrapped a scarf around her head and gathered a bucket. "They'll make us a good cherry pie one day."

Annie Mae added dried berries to the mud, humming a nursery rhyme. "Four and twenty blackbirds, baked in a pie."

Billy Paul, who'd just joined the terrible-two crowd, screamed from the inside. Mama sighed, looking weary. "I do wish that baby boy would take a nap. I've got to go pick some peas for supper." The screened door slapped as she went inside. Mama lugged him out, propped on her hip, and sat him on the ground next to me. She put a bowl full of crushed vanilla wafers soaked in milk in front of him.

"Shirley, watch him long enough for me to go to the pea patch, will you?"

"But me and Annie Mae's busy."

"You're just making mud pies, child. Your granny can't keep up with him inside. I won't be gone more than a few minutes." She pointed to the old well house.

"Just make sure none of you young'uns go near the well," Mama warned. "Else Soap Sally will get you."

"I know. I know." I shivered as I imagined what Soap Sally must look like. I'd had nightmares ever since Granny had first told me about the old witch who lived in the well, dragging herself back and forth, hiding in the dark crevices. I could see long bony tendrils growing from her webbed fingers. She'd latch them just below the well edge, ready to grab us kids and drag us down to feast on for supper. I could hear her screeching, her cries like birds pecking the dead, and see her craggy mean face in my sleep, eyes hollow, fire seeping from her nose. She was as ancient as the hills and had been around since Cherokee times, Granny said. Her skin was wrinkly, her long scraggly hair filled with bugs, and her face was snow white from never seein' the light of day. And her rotten teeth were jagged from chewing children's bones.

I waited until Mama had yanked on gardening gloves and headed to the pea patch before I said anything. Then I shook a finger at Billy Paul. "You just better mind me, little brother, or I'll get a limb from the cherry tree and blister you."

It was the same threat Mama used on me and Annie Mae. Annie Mae's eyes bugged out but Billy Paul simply giggled. I was beginning to think he was an *idgit* baby. Nothing scared him. He was such a daredevil he'd climb on a table and walk right off. And even though he'd turned two, he wasn't talking much.

He stuck his chubby hands in the vanilla wafer soup, scooped up a fistful, then jammed it in his mouth like a greedy pig. No wonder he couldn't talk, he was too busy eatin' to learn.

Granny hollered from the inside.

"Heavens to Betsy, it must be time to change the channel for *Days*." Granny's crooked fingers had trouble with the buttons on the TV remote, and since her eyes had turned bad, she couldn't read the numbers.

"Don't move." I wagged that finger at Billy Paul and Annie Mae again. "I'll be right back."

I ran up the porch steps and hurried inside. Granny would be chomping her dentures if she missed even a minute. But I had to wash the mud off before I touched the TV. Then Granny needed her spit can for her daily dip of snuff. I grabbed it from the kitchen, and carried it to her.

"Thanks, child," Granny said. "You want to keep me company?"

I hated for Granny to sit by her lonesome, but I'd get the blisterin' of a lifetime if I left Billy Paul and Annie Mae out there alone. "Maybe when Mama gets back from pea pickin'."

The music for *Days of Our Lives* began and Granny dipped her snuff, then turned to watch. I hurried to the screen door, then froze in horror. Billy Paul's chubby little body was climbing up on the well.

"No!" I tore down the steps. Annie Mae was so busy patting mud she'd been payin' no mind. Billy Paul grabbed the flat part of the well top and dragged his body up. He had always been a climber.

"Stop it right now!" I shouted. "Get down, Billy Paul!"

Annie Mae turned, her brown eyes shinin' like copper pennies through her mud-covered face, and screamed like a banshee. I was running so fast I tripped down the steps and fell flat on the ground. My knees burned, gravel dug into my hands, and I tasted blood and dust. I looked up and saw Billy Paul on top of the well house, sprawled on his stomach. His butt was poked up in the air as he wiggled his legs. He was inching toward the hole, jiggling the rope that held the bucket, clanging it back and forth.

"Nooooo!" I jumped up and ran toward the well. My heart was pounding so loud I thought there might be a train coming through the mountain.

Just as I reached the well, I grabbed Billy Paul's holey tennis shoe, but it slid off in my hand and he toppled inside. The rope and bucket clattered, Billy Paul screeched, and then there was nothing.

🐾 🐾 🐾

The next few hours were a blur of screaming and crying. Me. Mama. Granny. Annie Mae. I even threw up twice.

The only one who was quiet was Billy Paul.

Deathly, deathly quiet.

"Lord help, lord help," Mama chanted. "My baby has got to be all right."

Sirens roared and Chief Royden arrived, catching Mama's hands between his to calm her. She was squalling so much she could barely squeak out the story. Smokey Lincoln, the forest ranger, arrived, then the mayor, Ida Hamilton Walker, zipped up in her sports car, her face worried. Granny rolled her chair to the trailer's front porch to stand guard. She gave me a lowdown on who everybody was and where they fit into Mossy Creek as they made an appearance.

The fire engine carrying the volunteer firefighters barreled up the graveled drive, spraying dirt and rocks, with more volunteers behind them. The *WMOS Media* van pulled up with fancy letters on the side, and Mr. Lyman jumped out with a video camera.

"Gracious, Bert Lyman's puttin' us on the cable TV," Granny whispered.

Chaos erupted as everyone raced to hear the story. I

had never seen so many people in all my life. Soon the whole world would all know that it was my fault my brother was at the bottom of the well.

I hugged my bloody knees to myself, wanting to die. Did Soap Sally have Billy Paul? Had she already sunk her claws into his chubby baby skin and finished him off? Would she eat him alive or did she have some cast iron oven down there to bake her catches?

The grown-ups congregated to access the situation, hovering to discuss the best possible way to rescue Billy Paul. They would need to send someone down inside the well, but the blustery men couldn't fit through the hole. A few minutes later, the Bigelow paramedics arrived with all kinds of equipment in case Billy Paul was still alive.

I threw up again, barely missing Granny's feet and hittin' the boxwoods instead.

"Let's just think positive," Granny said as I scrooched up beside her chair. She'd clutched Annie Mae in her lap and had a death grip on her, while I had a death grip on Granny's wheelchair. The soap opera had been long forgotten, and now *Judge Judy* was blaring to the trailer's empty kitchen. A cold wave of shock washed over me. Poor Billy Paul. He was just a little bitty thing; he didn't have a chance against the monsters in the dark well. And if Soap Sally hadn't got to him, there were snakes and rats and spiders and god knows what else. Trolls maybe . . .

Even more Creekites rolled up the drive. Some blue-haired ladies bringing casseroles and pies. The bakery lady, Ingrid Beechum, toted boxes of donuts into the house. A young woman named Jayne, who'd opened The Naked Bean coffee shop the fall before, brought tea and coffee and shortbread and set it up on our Shaker wood table. "People need caffeine and sugar," she said, "After all, this might take a while."

The sea of people was endless. Rainey Cecil, looking

like a young, red-haired Dolly Parton, roared up in her pink late-model pick-up truck with the *Goldilocks Hair, Nail and Tanning Salon* sign on the driver's door. Pearl Quinlan brought a sack of Bibles from her bookstore and passed them amongst the growing crowd. And of course Officer Crane, Chief Royden's right-hand woman, was running around relaying Chief Royden's orders to everybody in sight, and adding a few of her own — especially to Officer Mutt Bottoms, her brother. Besides the police, the firemen, and Mayor Walker, there was Mossy Creek councilman Egg Egbert on a cell phone calling for more help. One of the young firemen, Nail Delgado, came over and hunkered down in front of me and asked me in his New York Yankee accent if I was okay. Nail looked like Justin Timberlake. I had the biggest crush on him. I could only nod.

A bulldozer arrived on the back of a big flatbed. Wolfman Washington climbed down from the cab. I felt a momentary surge of comfort. Mr. Washington looked like a cross between James Earl Jones and God, if God wore overalls and a Braves cap. "What do you think, Ida, Amos?" he said to the mayor and police chief. "My advice is to board up the top of the well so when we yank off the concrete supports, dirt and debris won't fall down on the baby."

Everyone agreed, and got to work. Within a half hour our well house sat ten feet above the earth, cupped in the scoop of Mr. Washington's giant bulldozer. Then everyone stared down at the naked hole, frowning. An old, hand-dug well is wide enough for a grown man to fit inside. But our well had dried up a few years before, so Mama scraped up the money to have it drilled deeper. The well-digging company fitted the re-built shaft with concrete pipe. So now, instead of the wide, shallow well shaft they'd expected, the rescuers were dealing with a concrete-lined hole no more than eighteen inches across.

Billy Paul's soft, scared mewls echoed up from the

depths. Mama covered her face and sobbed. At least he was alive.

"All right," Chief Royden announced. "Let's get some more equipment in here and start digging a parallel shaft. We'll have to go down and tunnel across to the shaft."

I imagined the only ounce of light Billy Paul had being snuffed out, his air cut off. He must be so scared . . .

I ran to the chief. "Let me do it, I'll fit down the hole. You can drop me down there and I can grab Billy Paul."

"Shirley," Chief Royden said in a soft voice, "that's awfully brave, but it's too dangerous. We don't want anything to happen to you."

But I wasn't brave, I was the cause of all this. "Please," I begged. "Then leastways Billy Paul won't be alone till you can figure somethin' out." And maybe I could fight off Soap Sally. I was bigger. I had more meat on my bones. Maybe she'd eat me in place of Billy Paul.

"Get back and stay out of the way," Mama snapped. *You have done enough damage.*

She didn't say it, but I heard the words anyway and knew it was true. It was my fault Billy Paul had fallen in that dark hole. My fault he might die. My fault if Soap Sally ate him.

It should have been me down there instead.

❦ ❦ ❦

Governor Ham Bigelow was in the midst of a closed door meeting to discuss the possibility of his presidential candidacy when the telephone rang. He ignored it, letting his assistant take the call, but seconds later, the door opened.

"Excuse me, sir, it's your mother. Line one."

Ham glanced up and shrugged. "Unless it's an emergency, tell her I'll call her back."

"Err, it is sort of an emergency." The woman hesitated,

shifting back and forth. "She said you should turn on the TV. Said something's going on in Mossy Creek that you need to know about."

Oh, good Lord, what now? Was Aunt Ida shooting more official highway signs or staging yet another attempt to defame her own nephew in public? Ham gestured wildly toward his team of advisors. One of them grabbed a remote and punched up the volume on a large television encased in the office's elegantly paneled wall.

"This late breaking story, happening as we speak," Bert Lyman intoned. "A two-year-old child is trapped in an old well north of Mossy Creek. The mother is distraught, as you can see." The camera swung to a shot of a woman in jeans and a sweat-stained T-shirt, sobbing. "The local police department and fire department are doing everything they can to rescue the child. Local citizens have turned out in droves to offer support and help with efforts. Mayor! Mayor Walker! Have you got any comment?"

Ham's extremely charismatic Aunt Ida, looking slim and tanned in a sleeveless linen blouse and snug summer skirt, stepped into view. Ham groaned silently. If anybody ever started a magazine called *Hot Baby Boomer Babes*, Ida could be a cover model. Why couldn't she look dowdy and inconsequential, like a normal fifty-year-old? She leveled long-lashed green eyes at the camera, directing a laser beam of accusation right at Ham. "We're going to save this child," she said in a steely voice. "But I'd just like to point out that this child would be back in his mother's arms by now if we had better equipment for our local rescue unit. We don't have that equipment because *Governor Bigelow* vetoed the legislation to provide grants for rural volunteer fire departments. Of course, there'd be plenty of money for those grants if the governor hadn't pushed tax cuts that benefit only the corporate interests that donate money to his campaigns."

"Thank you, Mayor Walker." Bert Lyman, her sly conspirator, faced the camera. "We'll continue to bring you live coverage of this tragic drama in the mountain town where Governor Ham Bigelow's mother grew up —"

Ham drowned out the words with a stream of invectives that sent his staff scurrying to close the office doors. He got up and paced, invoking his aunt's name in unpleasant ways along with the reputation of every Hamilton relative of his in Mossy Creek, the outlying communities, and the entire length of Bigelow County.

The phone rang again. "Your mother again," a staffer whispered. Ham sighed and took the phone. Ardaleen Hamilton Bigelow's elegantly Southern, elegantly furious voice curled into his ear. "You *cannot* allow my sister to eviscerate you *again* in front of the voters. *Do* something."

"Just what do you have in mind, Mother?"

"Get yourself up there to those white-trash hinterlands my sister loves so much and rescue that child and get yourself on camera. Show people that *you're* in charge of this situation, not my sister!'"

"I'll take care of it, Mother." He gestured toward his staff. "Get me a helicopter."

"Good. I'll see that our family in Bigelow is aware of the situation and gets involved. No righteous bunch of Creekites are going to upstage *us*."

"Mother? You were sixteen years old when Aunt Ida was born. Couldn't you have dropped *her* down a well?"

His mother hissed. "I wish I had."

🐾 🐾 🐾

While men, women, and equipment worked feverishly to dig my brother out of the well, Chief Royden jogged up the trailer's steps, grabbed a glass of tea from the tray the women kept refilling, leaned down and smiled at me. "It's gonna be all right, Shirley. We'll get your brother out of there."

He was tall and handsome and reassuring. If Nail Delgado was Justin Timberlake, Chief Royden was George Clooney with dark hair. I had a crush on him, too.

Again, I could only nod.

Mr. Lincoln, the forest ranger, squatted down so I could see in his eyes. "I rescue kids all the time. Few weeks ago, I pulled some kid from a cave. Smelled like a skunk, but he was all right."

He tweaked my cheek and I tried for a smile but failed. My stomach had jumped up in my throat again. By now Soap Sally might be sharpening her fangs or finishing off the last of Billy Paul. What if they found him and there wasn't nothin' left?

In the yard, a truck pulled up and a man with a camera jumped out carrying a reporter's notepad and a camera bag.

"That's Jess Crane, from the *Gazette*," Granny said. "That's Sandy's husband."

A big van pulled up the drive. Dr. Blackshear, the veterinarian, helped his wife maneuver her wheelchair down a ramp. Then a bunch of girls unfolded from the seats and ran toward the porch, their matching purple shirts bobbing like a pack of grape popsicles.

Casey Blackshear rolled herself up to the edge of our porch along with them, and smiled at me. "Shirley, I think you can use some company. These are a few of the Lady Mustangs, the Mossy Creek champion softball team. Meet Rabbit, Boom Boom, Slick, and Killer."

Killer? I frowned. That ought to be *my* name.

Granny thanked Casey, then nodded to me to do the same. Even in crisis we had to mind our manners. I murmured, "Thank you, Miz Blackshear."

"Tell me something about yourself."

I went blank. After gulping for a minute I could only say, "Mama named me after Shirley Temple. Because I had curly hair when I was a baby."

"That's great," Casey said with a smile. "She was an old-time movie star and she grew up to be a foreign diplomat. You'll be someone important some day, too."

I hung my head in shame. Yeah, I'd be famous, I could see the headlines in the paper — *Jailbird's daughter, Shirley Stancil, the girl from Mossy Creek, who let her own little brother fall down a well and get eaten by a witch.*

Rabbit sidled up to me and squeezed my hand.

"I'm named after my grandmother. The mayor."

I glanced toward the beautiful Mayor Walker. "Her real name's Rabbit?"

Rabbit Walker hooted. "No. *Ida.* I'm Little Ida."

"Oh."

"If you join the Lady Mustangs and play softball, we'll give you a good nickname, too. It's fun. I'm one of the very best players. We got a real Mustang for a mascot. Sort of. He's a pony, but we call him a mustang."

I nodded, distracted. A fleet of big, fancy cars roared up the drive.

"Oh, hell," Rainey Cecil whispered to Chief Royden. "It's a caravan of Bigelows. I guess mah-jong night at the country club was canceled."

The governor's family came bearing fruitcakes, fried chicken, and casseroles, just like the Creekites. The Mossy Creek women stepped aside slowly, both groups eyeing each other as if they expected the other to start throwing food. Though sweat ran down my face, the chill felt like winter. In the yard, the Bigelow and Creekite men stared at each other like a pack of wild dogs ready to fight. Were they going to start fighting right in front of the reporters?

Then a deafening roar rent the air, and the trees around us suddenly wavered, dry leaves fluttering and flying.

"Good God almighty, what's that?" Mama shouted.

"A helicopter!" Boom Boom and Killer shouted.

"It's gonna land right here in the yard."

"Oh, my word," Granny whispered.

"It's the governor," Casey said.

Seconds later, a tall, middle-aged man in a suit wove through the bushes, and the cameras swung his way. The Creekites and the Bigelowans gathered on opposite sides of the yard just like someone had drawn a chalk line they couldn't cross. Mayor Walker tilted her head, then walked up and stared him in the face. "I believe we have this situation under control, Governor. We're here to rescue a child, not pose for the media."

The big man smiled, his white teeth gleaming in the fading afternoon sunlight. "I couldn't agree more, Aunt Ida." He waved a hand at a pair of men standing behind him. "I've brought two top engineers to take charge of the digging."

"Councilman Egbert is an engineer, and our digging is going just fine under his supervision."

The governor began to scowl. "Now look, Aunt Ida, don't hog the spotlight, all right? I'm here to provide inspiration and leadership —"

"Dung beetles provide more inspiration and leadership than you —"

"We've reached the shaft!" Mr. Washington yelled.

Everyone hurried over. The fire department rigged Nail Delgado with a harness and ropes to lower him into the parallel shaft. He disappeared from sight with a group of Creekite men struggling to lower him safely. The governor turned to his fellow Bigelowans. "Let's see if we can't all work together, just this once, and get this little boy out safely. I'm sure his mother wants to take him inside for supper before it gets dark." The governor scowled at Bert Lyman. "Do you think you can get some *positive* news about me on videotape?"

Mr. Lyman guffawed slyly. And so, for the first time in

history, or at least in the last few years, a peace treaty was called for the night. The Creekites and Bigelowans formed one team, lining up in a chain to hold the pulley rope that dropped Nail Delgado down to the tunnel that would lead him to my brother.

There were hundreds of us in the yard, all tight-lipped, holding hands and watching to see if Billy Paul came up alive. Pearl Quinlan led us all in a prayer.

Finally a flashlight waved back from inside the well, and Mama yelled down, her voice squeaking as Chief Royden held her on one side and Smokey Lincoln supported her on the other. "Did you find him, Nail? Is . . . my baby all right?"

A collective gasp of held breaths rattled through the quiet. Then I heard the sweetest words I've ever heard as Nail yelled up, "Yes, ma'am. I found him, and he's all right."

When they hauled Nail into sight, holding Billy Paul in his arms, everyone cheered. I nearly collapsed from relief. Mama threw herself at him and began to cry. Sobs broke out all over the place. There wasn't a dry eye.

I wanted to hug Billy Paul and tell him that I was sorry, that I'd never fuss at him or threaten to blister him again, that I'd play his stupid truck games and let him pull my hair. But I didn't deserve to get to hug him.

I ran down from the porch and went to the cherry tree, broke off the biggest limb I could find and carried it around to Mama. Then I pushed through the crowd.

"Here. "I held the stick out to her, trying not to shake like a cornstalk in the wind. "Go ahead and blister me. I deserve it. I almost let Soap Sally get him."

Mama stopped sobbing long enough to look down at me with big old tears in her eyes. A hush fell over the crowd, then Granny's voice screeched out. "Get me off this porch."

The men hoisted her wheelchair down to the ground and Granny rolled toward us, stopping right in front of Mama.

Mama's fingers were shaking as she reached for the stick. I stood up straighter, bracing myself for the *whoopin'* of my life.

"Don't, Ellen," Granny said. "It was my fault, not Shirley's. I ought to be able to change the TV myself." The awful helplessness of old age quivered in Granny's voice.

But I couldn't let my frail old granny take the blame. "No, it was my fault, Mama. I knew better than to leave Billy Paul alone." I looked down at my brother, searching for teeth and claw marks from Soap Sally. He looked so small. "I'm so sorry, Billy Paul. Did you see Soap Sally? Did she try to get you?" My voice cracked. "I could see her, Mama, big and hairy, her teeth sinking into Billy Paul's fat legs, crunching his bones —"

"Mercy," Mama said with a hefty sigh. "I ain't gonna punish you, Shirley. I reckon you suffered enough, just like the rest of us." She tossed the stick aside, then dragged me into her arms. Her body trembled against me as we both cried. "And sweet Jesus, honey, there ain't no such thing as Soap Sally. You must have been imagining such awful things. I'm sorry for that."

I was crying again, like a flood of water busting out. "There isn't any old hag in the well?"

She shushed me with a kiss. "No, big girl, we just told you that so you wouldn't go near the well. Granny told me that story when I was little. I thought it'd keep you kids safe."

"But I let Billy Paul get up there anyway." My chin bobbed up and down as I cried. "I shouldn't have left him alone."

She combed down my matted hair with her hands. "No, but it's my fault, too. I should have done something about that well a long time ago. You're just a half-grown girl, Shirley. You didn't mean for it to happen."

Maybe I was just a half-grown girl, or I had been when

the day began. But I didn't think I'd ever be that same girl again.

"Now, cover up that hole," Mama told the men. "Soap Sally is dead and gone. And we ain't never goin' through this again."

Suddenly, I looked around and realized everyone was smiling at me. And finally, I smiled back.

Maybe school would be all right this year. Maybe Creekite kids wouldn't call me a jailbird's daughter.

I looked out at all the people who'd come to help us. They'd all been so kind. *Ain't going nowhere, and don't want to.* I didn't ever want to leave Mossy Creek. Maybe Mama wouldn't either, not after that day.

The paramedics began checking Billy Paul out. Rabbit ran over and grabbed my hand. The rest of the Lady Mustangs tagged along. On Rabbit's other side, the mayor lifted her hand toward the sky. "I hope to shout," she said. Her favorite invocation. It was a kind of old-timey-sounding tribute to her grandmother, who had also been a staunch, rebellious Creekite named Ida, too. A way of connecting to the thread of memories and blessings that helped pull Creekites out of the holes they fell into or dug for themselves.

🌱🌱🌱

The *War of the Good Deeds* continued, at least for a little while, with my family at its heart. Both the Creekites and the Bigelowans adopted us. If a Creekite did one good deed for the Stancils, a Bigelowan tried to top it.

Creekites showed up out of nowhere and installed a new well with a sealed top. A Bigelowan painted the front porch. Wolfman Washington scraped our rutted driveway and coated it in a thick new layer of gravel. A Bigelow landscape company sowed the first lawn our trailer had ever had. The Mossy Creek Garden Club sent seed for the next year's garden. Hank and Casey Blackshear gave us a puppy complete with vaccinations, a free-spaying certificate, and a good, warm doghouse. A Bigelowan fenced in our front yard so the puppy could play on the new, enclosed lawn. Mayor Walker sent Mama down to Hamilton's Department Store where the mayor's son, Rob, personally escorted Mama on a buying spree for our whole family. The governor sent the head of state social services to visit us, and like magic we suddenly qualified for all sorts of medical and dental programs.

Mama filed for divorce with the free legal aide of Mayor Walker's daughter-in-law, Teresa Walker. Daddy didn't even contest it. We cried a little over him, then put him out of our lives. From then on he was a specter, no more real than Soap Sally.

"You've been too dumb and proud to accept help, before," Sandy Crane told Mama. Officer Crane had a way of puttin' things in her twangy little voice so that they were just facts, not a judgment. "Now you need to be proud enough to accept a hand up in the world." That made sense to Mama.

In the meantime, the *War of the Good Deeds* just plain got out of hand. Casseroles were spilling out of our freezer, sheet cakes and apple pies covered the counters, and poor Granny could barely watch her soaps for folks knocking on the door. But the straw that broke the camel's back was when a Creekite sent Billy Paul a fancy toy motorized car, and a Bigelowan sent Granny a VCR to tape her shows if she nodded off. Mama put her foot down and said she didn't cotton to any more charity. She could take care of her own, thankyou-very-much, and from then on, she did. She got in our old truck, went down to town, and started working the evening shift as a waitress at Mama's All You Can Eat Café. She left me in charge at home. She trusted me. I was so proud.

This past summer I joined the Lady Mustangs, and

pretty soon, thanks to my power with a bat, I earned the name Slugger. Truth be told, when they asked me where I learned to bat, I said, "I just practiced with a limb from a cherry tree."

Little Billy Paul's favorite pastime is throwing cherries for me to hit. He's forgotten about falling down the well, and Soap Sally is just a silly little story for telling at Halloween. I spend a lot of time playing with him, and laughing.

Sometimes, in Mossy Creek, a bad thing is a blessing.

Mossy Creek Gazette

215 Main Street • Mossy Creek, GA 30533

From the desk of Katie Bell

Lady Victoria Salter Stanhope
The Cliffs
Seaward Road
St. Ives, Cornwall, TR3 7PJ
United Kingdom

Dear Vick:

People ask me if we ever really do
have "bad things" happen in Mossy
Creek, as Shirley wrote. Yes, we do.
But we try to take care of them and
turn them into something good. If we
can't, we have a network of people who
quietly come to the rescue and do what
can be done, just as they did in the
case of Shirley and her baby brother,
Billy Paul. I don't always print the
sad details, unless it serves some
good purpose. I know that makes me
quaint in today's greedy, tell-all
media world, but, hey, I'm proud to be
different.

Katie

. . . feeling more than a little
quaint today.

In Mossy Creek we've learned to be patient.
The longer a thing is in coming, the sweeter it is.

❦❦❦❦❦❦❦❦❦❦❦❦❦❦❦❦❦❦❦❦❦❦❦❦❦❦❦❦❦❦❦❦

Crying for the Moon

Chapter 10

Some people are blessed to be born knowing their place in this world. Others gradually grow into the idea, like breaking in a new pair of shoes bought to last two seasons. Still others spend their entire lifetimes trying to find what was always right beneath their noses to begin with.

The summer I turned twelve was hotter than most and Mossy Creek's third year in a record-breaking dry spell. It was the first year I can remember that my mama's gardenias wilted on their stems, not able to suck enough moisture from the cracked red earth to give them what they needed to survive. I still remember those doomed flowers of that summer, especially because that was the same summer I met Vivien Leigh Bodine, as much of a fated and thirsty bloom as the gardenias.

We'd all heard of Vivien, of course, just not ever seen her up close. She'd been born in Mossy Creek, but she'd never been allowed to play with the rest of the children from town. Mama would just say that Vivien was a Bigelow, and members of the Bigelow family did not fit in well in Mossy Creek. Then she'd send me outside to play kick the can in the Royden's back yard. Amos's father, Battle, was the police chief then. Amos was just four or five years old.

What I knew about Vivien I'd found out at my open win-

213

dow listening to my parents talking on the front porch below. Even now, I can remember the hot sticky nights and my parents' soft voices, the tangy smell of my father's cigar and the clink of ice cubes in my mama's iced tea glass. I can see my father's discarded newspaper, fluttering like a moth on the floorboards of the porch, and picture my mother's hands stroking the back of his neck as they talked. I can attribute everything I ever learned about the facts of life from sitting at my window when I was supposed to be in bed.

Vivien's mother, Julia Bigelow, had *got herself in trouble*, as my mother put it back then, and had to marry Alton Bodine, a young banking executive who worked for the Bigelow family's financial businesses. Alton Bodine was not the father of her baby, but the wealthy Bigelow family forced her to marry him. Vivien's real father had been a well-known actor traveling through the South with the national touring company of a famous musical, although nobody ever acknowledged him.

At any rate, Julia Bigelow Bodine was the most beautiful woman any of us had ever seen, and it surprised no one when her husband doted on her and her daughter, even agreeing to spend the money to send Vivien to a private academy in Atlanta as soon as she was old enough to start school. She only returned home for weekends and holidays.

During that long, hot summer Alton Bodine died, and, as if released from a contract, Julia brought Vivien home from boarding school. Vivien returned to Mossy Creek and to a mother whose hopes and dreams seemed to be completely fixated on her only child.

Daddy sent me to the hardware store to get more hooks for Mama's hanging flower baskets. I was barefoot and wearing cut-offs made from my brother's old jeans. My tee-shirt was a size too big, but it was my lucky shirt and I was planning on pitching a softball game after supper.

I'd never thought to be embarrassed by how I looked until I came upon Vivien Leigh Bodine sitting in the shade of the hardware store, wearing a white linen dress, straw hat, and red patent leather shoes. She even had a red leather purse to match. I think it was that which made me stop in my tracks and stare. She was sucking on a lollipop — red, of course — and her cat-like green eyes were staring at me speculatively.

"Hey," I said. All she did was raise an eyebrow just like her namesake did in the movie at the part about Ashley's surprise birthday party. I almost burst out laughing.

"What's so funny?"

I snorted loudly. "You. You look like a candy cane."

She tried to look stern but I could tell she was trying not to laugh, too. "I do not. I look like a proper young lady. Which is more than I can say for *you*. You look like a boy."

"That's only because I'm playing softball tonight. I don't usually dress like this."

She gave me that eyebrow look again, and I could tell that she knew I was lying. She sucked on the lollipop for a long moment before delicately waving it at me. "What's your name?"

"Sammie Louise Pritchard."

"Sammie's a boy's name."

"It's short for Samantha. But everybody calls me Sammie because I can pitch a softball better than most boys."

"My mama says it's not nice to brag."

I shrugged. "I'm not braggin'. It's true. We're playing tonight at six-thirty if you wanna come see for yourself." I'm not sure why, but it was important for me to show this confectionery girl that I was more than I appeared.

She looked anxiously at the front door of the store. "I'll see if I can come. I've never been to a softball game before. Mama thinks it's a tacky sport because the players spit a lot. And they touch their privates in front of everybody."

"That's *baseball*. That's *boys*. I don't touch *my* privates in front of everybody!" I climbed the steps of the hardware store. "You're Vivien Bodine, aren't you?"

She looked away, her green eyes reflecting the relentless summer sky. "The one and only."

Her mother chose that moment to leave the store. Julia Bigelow Bodine looked beautiful but scary. I had enough sense in me to pretend I hadn't been talking with her daughter. Without a word, I held the door open for her and ducked inside, letting the door bang shut behind me.

I was surprised to hear the whoosh of the door as it flew open again. I turned to see Vivien running down an aisle toward me. She thrust her lollipop into my hand. "Thanks," she said, before turning in a whirl of white linen and red patent leather, and ran back the way she had come.

I stared at the lollipop for a long time, then put it in my mouth before I approached the counter. If there was ever a symbol of friendship, that was it. I knew then that Vivien Leigh Bodine and I were destined to be best friends.

❦❦❦

"Strike two!" Doug Elmore shouted from behind the home plate. Though he was only twelve, like me, Doug often refereed the girls' games. People said he already showed enough talent to play professional baseball when he got older. I'd been moon-eyed over Doug since the fifth grade, when he'd been the only one not to laugh when I'd given my book report in the front of the classroom with the side of my dress tucked into my panties.

I was winding up for my next pitch when I realized that an unusual quiet had settled on the field. I paused and glanced over at Doug, then followed his gaze toward the stands. Sitting on the bottom bench, her legs crossed neatly at the ankles, was Vivien Bodine, her fine blond hair swaying prettily under her large, straw hat. But instead of clutching a lollipop this time, she was pulling a drag from a cigarette.

As the rest of us waited, Doug strolled over to her with the confident swagger of a twelve-year-old boy. "You can't do that. You have to be eighteen to smoke, and the person who gave them to you could go to jail. Besides, it'll rot your lungs."

She did that eyebrow look at him and blew a puff of smoke in his face. I expected her to put him in his place. She surprised us all by saying, "You're pretty good-looking. But you ruin your first impression by being such a fussy-pants."

I could see the darkening red of Doug's face from where I stood on the pitcher's mound. I glanced around at the other players to see if anybody had plans to come to Doug's rescue, but they were all hang-jawed staring at a girl getting the best of him.

I felt as if I'd been hit square in the middle with a fast pitch. Doug started smiling at her, his expression almost dopey. When he sat down next to her, I thought I might puke right there on the pitcher's mound but all I could do was stand by hopelessly. I watched as she handed him her cigarette and he neatly and effectively squashed it under his high-top sneaker.

Then Vivien turned her attention back to the game. Cupping her hands around her mouth, she shouted, "Let 'er rip, Sammie!"

Reluctantly, Doug returned to his spot behind home plate and I wound up for my pitch. I never pitched a better game, before or since, but it did me no good. Every time I looked back at Doug, he was watching Miss Vivien Leigh Bodine. I learned my first lesson in heartbreak.

I guess Doug did, too, eventually. But his was a lot harder won than mine.

🐾🐾🐾

By the end of that long, hot summer, Vivien and I had become inseparable. We were more different than night and day, but I suppose we saw in each other that part of us that God forgot when he made us. Not that I ever felt the need to want to priss around in a dress. It was more about her being clever and funny and the way she could make people turn their heads without even opening her mouth. Mrs. Bodine called it *stage presence*. My mother called it *the ability to know who buttered her bread*. But whatever it was, I wanted to know how to do it. I was getting tired of having to climb onto a pitcher's mound to get people to notice me.

My life before she came into it had been like vanilla ice cream. Nice, but not too exciting. Vivien came and added the hot chocolate syrup, and I was unaware at the time that sometimes chocolate stains and nothing you can do can ever rub it out.

As for why Vivien wanted to hang around me, I didn't understand that until my mama explained it to me the week before school started.

Mama and I had been tying up her tomato plants when Vivien came by. She was wearing pink silk shantung pedal pushers with a matching top and looked like a strawberry sundae. I could tell even Mama was impressed by the way she slid her glasses down her nose to look more closely.

"Mother's having one of her headaches," Vivien said, "so I thought I'd stop by."

Mrs. Bodine's headaches happened at least three times a week. I knew from my window eavesdropping that the headaches were a result of too many nights spent with a bottle of gin. I felt kind of sorry for Mrs. Bodine. But her headaches meant that she wasn't paying any attention when Vivien escaped from her house and came over to mine.

My mother smiled and stood and put a gentle hand on Vivien. "I'll go get us some Cokes. I'll be right back."

Vivien watched my mother disappear inside the house, a strange, wistful look in her green eyes. She faced me again, the expression gone. "You need to start wearing a bra. Do you think your mother would take you to go get one?"

I looked down at my flat chest beneath the Braves tee-shirt I wore. If my mother bought me a bra, it would have been for encouragement purposes only. "What are you talking about? I don't need a stupid bra."

She acted as if she hadn't heard me. "Because if your mother takes you, maybe I could go along, too. I've started to develop a womanly figure, but Mother still pretends I'm six years old and won't get me one."

For the first time I noticed Vivien's chest. She normally wore loose fitting dresses that concealed everything, but today was different. She had breasts that were nearly the size of Mama's.

I thought of Doug looking at those unfettered breasts and knew we had to get her a bra. That's what friends were for. Maybe I could get one with padding.

When Mama returned with a tray of Cokes and cookies, she said, "I need to run into town and get a few things. Would you girls like to come with me?" Vivien and I shared a look. I suspect Mama had overheard our conversation through the open kitchen window. "Sure," I said.

Vivien just smiled and nodded. We went shopping for bras. That night at dinner, Vivien joined us. It had become a regular thing, with her mother having her headaches all the time. It was so expected that Mama had stopped calling to ask permission from Mrs. Bodine.

When we bowed our heads and said the blessing, Vivien

squeezed my hand tightly, and I looked up to see her gazing around the table at my family before bowing her head again. She seemed to be in as much awe of us as we were of her and it made me happy and sad at the same time. Even my brother, Hutch, who was two years older, seemed to be caught under Vivien's spell and I thought, not for the last time, that Vivien was a force to be reckoned with.

That night, as my mother tucked me into bed, she paused before turning off the light. "I can see that you and Vivien have become really close friends. And I'm glad. Truly I am. But . . ." Her voice trailed off as her eyes traveled to the high shelf above my bed that housed all my softball trophies. Her cool hand touched my forehead as she pushed my bangs aside. "I just want to make sure that, despite her influences, you'll always remember who you are."

"I know who I am, Mama. I'm Samantha Louise Pritchard."

"But who you are is more than just your name. You're who your parents are, and your grandparents. You're all the things we've taught you and all the things you've learned. Who you are is in your heart. It's the things you hold close — like your family. It's knowing where you come from. Knowing *that* is more important than where you're going."

I thought for a long moment, studying a framed poster of the Beatles on my wall. Pretty people got so much attention. "But what has this got to do with Vivien?"

"Everything, sweetie. She doesn't know who she is. She knows she's beautiful, and smart, but she doesn't know those other things. It's not her fault. It's mostly because of the way she's been raised and her mother . . . well, her mother seems as lost as poor Vivien. She and Vivien don't know what they want because their hearts are so empty. They try to fill their hearts up with what feels good for the moment. They're like children crying for the moon, but once they have it they don't know what to do with it. So then they put it on a shelf where it slowly fades until all its light is gone."

I frowned. "I thought you liked Vivien." My eyes stung from unshed tears.

"I do, sweetheart. It's just that I want you to be careful around her. She's got one of those personalities that can swallow a person whole. Just remember who you are." She leaned over and kissed my forehead and I smelled her Youth Dew perfume mixed with talcum powder. "Goodnight, Sammie."

She had already turned off my light and closed my door before I remembered to say goodnight. I was too busy thinking about what she said. It took me six years to figure out what she'd been talking about.

🐾🐾🐾

By the time Vivien and I reached high school, half the boys were madly in love with her and the other half were simply sideswiped with awe. She pulled me inside her inner realm where I could sit and be admired just for being in her light. She also came to every one of my softball games and headed up the loudest cheering sections along with my parents and brother.

She convinced me that the world outside Mossy Creek was flat and swore Creekites who moved out of town never came back. "They follow the creek to the edge and jump off," she deadpanned.

I always laughed at Vivien's put-downs about Mossy Creek and her claims that she was headed for the big time. She didn't date any of the local boys, since, according to her, they were only after future wives who would give them children who were as stupid as they were and live in the same dull town their parents had been raised in. There was always an edge to her voice, a longing I couldn't recognize.

But it wasn't until our senior year that Mama's words came back to haunt me.

Doug had apparently given up mooning for Vivien and had started dating me the summer between our junior and senior year. It was clear to everyone but me that I was just the runner-up, and that he still carried a large and flaming torch for Vivien. Looking back, I probably *did* know. But I had loved him for so long that it didn't matter.

Doug's father was pushing Doug's baseball talent. It seemed that I was the only one who saw that Doug was much more interested in biology and chemistry than throwing a curve ball.

Vivien never said anything, but I knew that she didn't approve of me dating Doug. She'd complain if I wasn't available for her because of him and made a point of being at my house when Doug would show up to take me out.

One night, I asked Doug to stay in the car while I went back to speak with Vivien.

"Why are you doing this? You had your chance to go out with him but you didn't want to. So let me be. You know this is what I want."

Her beautiful face was furious. "How do you know what you want? You've never been out of Mossy Creek! How do you know what else is out there to want?"

I studied her carefully for a long moment. "Because what I want is already here." I placed my hand over my heart. "I don't need to go anywhere else to find it."

The blood seemed to drain from her already pale cheeks and she stared at me while her green eyes snapped. "I thought you were different. But you're just like your mealy-mouthed mother and all the rest of the women here in this stupid town. You'll never be anybody or anything special. You deserve Doug because you're the kind of woman he'll want to marry down the line. Barefoot and pregnant in a little starter house with linoleum floors and Formica countertops. It makes me sick. It all makes me sick."

She stood there shaking like a leaf in the crisp autumn breeze and I stared at her for a long moment. Finally I just said, "Goodnight, Vivien," and went back to Doug's car.

I never told Doug about our conversation. Sometimes, looking back, I wonder if it would have made any difference at all.

When we returned from our date, Vivien was still sitting on my front porch, her bare arms limp beside her, her lips a pale blue in the light from the porch lamp. I refused to have sympathy for her. "Why are you still here?"

She looked at me with lifeless eyes. "I was waiting for Doug to take me home."

Doug walked up behind me. "Get in the car, Vivien. I'll be right there."

He took my arm and led me to my front door. "Tell your parents good night for me. I'll take her home before she dies of exposure."

"I could get Daddy . . ."

"No." The word was firm and non-negotiable.

He leaned down and kissed me on the cheek, but there was no warmth, only bitter chill. "I'll see you tomorrow."

I nodded and watched him walk toward the car before letting myself into the house.

🌱🌱🌱

Nobody knew where they'd gone until five days later when Doug and his car returned to Mossy Creek without Vivien. I never talked to Doug after that — about him and Vivien or anything else, for that matter. I learned what had happened through eavesdropping on my parents through my bedroom window.

My daddy's voice was thick and gruff, filled with cigar

smoke. "Mr. Elmore told me that Doug thought he and Vivien were eloping. That's why he helped her sneak into her mama's house and pack up her belongings. They drove all the way up to New York. Who would have thought that girl would do such a thing? And Doug, too."

"Oh, Lloyd," was all my mama could say. She'd seen enough of my weeping for the last three days to take away any sympathy for Vivien or Doug.

"They stayed in some flea-bitten motel room and Doug swears he tried to get Vivien to a justice of the peace, but she wanted to wait. On the second night she disappeared. He called the police and helped them search for two more days before driving back home."

There was a long pause before I could hear my mother speak. "It's best this way. I don't think she could ever have been happy here. It breaks my heart about Doug and Sammie, though. I don't know if she'll ever get over it."

I closed my window against the chill and went to bed. Mama was right. I never really did.

💗💗💗

Doug and I graduated with our class but that was about the only thing that turned out the way it was expected. I stopped playing softball and concentrated on my studies for the first time. Perhaps galled by Vivien's accusations, I went away to college in South Carolina and studied agriculture. I guess I surprised everybody, including myself, when I decided to return to Mossy Creek and help my daddy run his landscaping business. Even bought my own house, a fixer-upper across town from my parents. I proved the world outside Mossy Creek wasn't flat after all.

Doug left town, too, first for college and then medical school at Emory University down in Atlanta. Most people thought it was to get out from under the thumb of his daddy and his thwarted dreams of having a major league baseball player in the family, but I knew the reason was as much Vivien as anything else.

Vivien's mother never left her house anymore except when she'd receive a letter from Vivien — first from New York as she worked in the theater, and then Hollywood. Vivien got some small rolls in a few films and I went to see one of them. Vivien had five lines spread over two scenes. I wanted to say that she wasn't anything special, but she was. She looked beautiful up there on the screen, and she had an ease of movement that showed she was comfortable pretending to be other people. But she still had that hungry look in her eyes and I couldn't watch it. It was as if she were borrowing lines from somebody else's life. I left halfway through the film.

I didn't date much. Mama said I needed to move on with my life and I did by throwing myself into the landscape business. I knew what she meant but I just couldn't seem to find anybody worth moving on for.

And then Vivien came back to Mossy Creek.

As I was tending to the flowerpots on my front porch, I heard a car pull up in front of the house. When I turned, I saw a tall, willowy woman climb out of a rented sedan. She wore a large hat and sunglasses, but I knew who she was right away. Then behind her, a little boy of about four stepped out of the car.

He had white-blond hair and large green eyes and wore a child's suit and tie. But he didn't squirm or look uncomfortable. He just stared up at me with those eyes that were so much like his mother's.

Vivien paid the cabdriver and he drove away, leaving the two of them standing by the curb.

With the little boy's hand in hers she approached, stopping at the bottom step before removing her sunglasses. "Hello, Sammie. I'm back."

I put down my gardening gloves and spade and came down the stairs to stand next to her. She moved the boy in front of her. "This is my son, Joshua. Joshua, this is the nice lady I told you about. Miss Sammie."

He held out a small hand and I shook it, wondering why he was so still and solemn.

"Nice to meet you," I said and then looked up at his mother. "I didn't know you got married."

"I didn't." Her eyes met mine coolly.

"Welcome back, Vivien." I tried to keep the emotion out of my voice and for the most part, I succeeded. "How long will you be staying?"

I looked at her closely for the first time and saw how thin she was, saw the black circles under her eyes and the way her veins seemed to show under her translucent skin.

She sighed. "I was hoping we could stay with you for a while. Come on inside. We need to talk."

Unsteadily, she walked up the stairs toward the front door. I picked up the small suitcase that sat by the curb and followed.

We sat on opposite sides of the parlor sofa with Joshua perched in the middle. His feet barely reached the edge of the couch. Vivien's delicate brows knitted tightly together. "Is there some place Joshua can go so we can talk in private?"

I held out my hand to the little boy and led him into the kitchen where my new puppy, Maxwell, was napping in his crate. I sat Joshua at the table with a glass of milk and a plate of cookies and told him I would be back soon to let Maxwell out so the two of them could play.

When I returned to the parlor, Vivien lay against the back of the sofa with her eyes closed and her chest barely moving with each breath. She didn't open them until I had sat down.

She pulled some papers out of her bag along with a pen and laid them on the coffee table. "I'm looking for a home for Joshua."

I remembered the sweet face of the silent boy and felt my anger rise. "For how long?"

"For forever."

"He's not an old shoe to be discarded, Vivien. I don't think he particularly wants to be given away to a total stranger."

She closed her eyes again, her mouth set in a wan smile. "You're not a stranger to him. He's heard about you since he was born. He even has a picture of the two of us on his bedside table."

Part of my anger disappeared with the dust motes floating in the shaft of sunlight from the bay window. "Oh," I managed to say.

She looked down at her lap as she spread long, slender fingers over her lap. "I'm dying, Sammie. The doctors say I only have a couple of months left. I wanted to make sure Joshua was taken care of before . . . before."

I stared at her, almost at a loss for words. Finally, I said, "But why here? Why me?"

She shrugged and looked away. "Lots of reasons. Mostly because this is where I know he'll be taken care of the best. And I want him to have the kind of childhood I wasn't allowed to have." She took a deep breath and I heard the catch in her voice. "I want him to know his place in the world so that no matter how far he goes, he'll know where it is in his heart."

I knew that was as much of an apology as I would ever get from her, and I was all right with that. She leaned over and picked up the papers on the table.

"These are the adoption papers. My lawyers have already drawn them up and I've signed everything. He'll have a trust fund for college and enough to start a little nest egg. And money for you, too, to help with raising him. All it needs is your signature and he'll be legally yours."

"I don't know . . ." I stopped, my eyes clouding with tears.

"He's a wonderful kid, Sammie. I know you'll love him like he was yours." Her eyes swam before mine and I could hear the desperation in her voice. "He's the only thing I've got that's worth anything. And that's why I'm giving him to you."

We hugged each other tightly and I cried, grieving for the girl I had once loved but had never really known, and for the woman I would never know at all. Most of all I cried for Joshua, who would not remember the vibrant person his mother had once been.

When she pulled away, she said, "I'm so tired. Is it all right if I go lie down while you and Joshua get acquainted?"

"Sure." I led her to the sunny front guestroom and brought her suitcase. She was asleep before I left the room.

I checked on her twice — once before Joshua and I sat down for a dinner of tomato soup and grilled cheese sandwiches and once before I went to bed. She hadn't moved from her position on the quilt so I placed a blanket on her and left the room.

She stayed with me for two weeks. Each morning she'd awaken and dress as if she were going to a movie premiere, and she would have me parade her and Joshua around town. With her makeup and sunglasses, it was easy to disguise her illness. Even her own mother was fooled, although Mrs. Bodine now lived in a constant haze of alcohol and didn't notice much of anything anymore.

But when Vivien would come home after our excursions she'd collapse into bed, barely able to move with exhaustion.

While she slept, I'd take Joshua to my mother's or to the park. My heart opened to this beautiful little boy. On a Saturday, about two weeks after they'd arrived, I was in my mother's back garden with Joshua and we were cutting flowers to make a bouquet to bring back to Vivien.

As he leaned forward to smell a rose, I noticed a silver chain around his neck and tucked into the collar of his shirt.

I touched the chain. "What's this, Joshua?"

He looked at me with his mother's eyes as he pulled out the necklace. I recognized it immediately. It was one of those "best friends" necklaces with a heart split in the middle, and one friend keeps one half and the other friend keeps the other. I had given it to Vivien for her fourteenth birthday and my own half was somewhere in the bottom of my jewelry box. "Mommy gave it to me yesterday. She said that it was my turn to keep it."

I met my mother's eyes and knew she was thinking the same thing. Vivien was saying goodbye. I grabbed Joshua's hand and nearly ran the whole way home.

I left Joshua in the kitchen with Maxwell and raced up the stairs two at a time before throwing open Vivien's door. I felt nearly weak with relief when I spotted her under the quilt. I was about to leave quietly when she called my name. Walking over to the bed, I sat on the side and took her hand.

Her voice was so quiet I had to lean down close to her face to hear her. "Joshua loves you."

Her hand was cold in mine. "I love him, too. Not like that's hard to do, though."

She smiled weakly. "It's time for me to go, then."

I started to cry and she laughed. "I'm not dying yet. I meant to leave here. It wasn't my plan to have everyone see me deteriorate." She turned her head away but I could tell she was crying. "I want to be forever young and beautiful."

"You always will be, Vivien. I'll take care of you, you

know I will. Just don't leave. There's still time for us to be friends — and for Joshua. Give us that. Please."

She looked back at me and took my hand again. "I'll think about it." Then she closed her eyes and I left the room.

In the morning she was gone.

I raced to Joshua's room to see if he was still there and was relieved to see him curled up beneath the floral sheets, a nearly threadbare stuffed bunny on the floor by the side of the bed. I retrieved the animal to the arms of the sleeping boy and sat in the chair to wait for the sun to rise on my first day of motherhood.

🌺🌺🌺

Joshua and I planted a magnolia tree in the front yard in memory of his mother. It's one of the ways I tried to ground him and Vivien in Mossy Creek, to give them both something to hold on to, a place to always come home to. Sometimes, as the sun is setting through the young limbs of the tree, I can feel her presence there. It's like the restless tug of the wind, an impatient feeling of the need to move on. And then it calms and settles around us and I know that she is finally at peace.

Doug has now returned to Mossy Creek, too. He's setting up a medical practice near the big hospital down in Bigelow. Not a few of us wonder if he's back now to prove to us all that he was meant to be a doctor all along.

He stopped by my landscaping offices last week to buy some pansies for his yard.

He hadn't changed that much, no more than me, I guess. Mostly older and wiser by the creases around his eyes and the surprise he carefully hid when I introduced him to Joshua.

While he juggled the two flats of pansies, I suggested some bulbs, too, and by the time I had his truck loaded, we had a dinner date for later that evening. I'm in no rush, and he's got a lot of explaining to do, but I think I've earned the right to enjoy myself.

I think a lot about what Vivien said, about us all needing to know our place in the world. I was lucky to have been born knowing it while Doug needed to eventually grow into the idea. And Vivien gave it to Joshua as a gift of her love — full and ripe, like an autumn harvest. He will leave one day, but his heart will always have a place to hold on to. A place filled with people who love him and nurtured him. A place called Mossy Creek.

"The Voice Of The Creek"

Good morning, Mossy Creek! This is Honey Lyman, filling in for Bert, who has a cold with a touch of laryngitis, thanks to the rainy autumn weather. He sounds like Kermit the frog on helium.

Our niece came for a visit last weekend and brought her five-year-old daughter, Alice. When the child asked for some ice-water, my husband went to the kitchen, took out a glass and opened the freezer door to get ice cubes. When he filled the glass with water from the faucet, Alice refused it, saying. "I don't want that. I want the water that comes from the door."

It took us a while to figure out that she'd never seen a refrigerator *without* an ice maker and water dispenser. Bert laughed and took little Alice out on the porch to see the well built into the porch just outside the kitchen door. I'm not sure what Alice's mother is going to think when Alice refuses to drink any water that isn't drawn in a bucket.

Have you ever noticed how small towns attract famous people? I think I know why. We all know how to keep a secret; we learned it by protecting our own. Movie stars, sports figures and business tycoons move here and become ordinary folks for a time. I have a theory about that. We have real problems and real people to solve them. We believe in forgiveness but we don't tolerate excuses much. If a thing needs fixing, we fix it. But certain kinds of creativity seem to thrive on angst, angels and outlaws, and every now and again those creative people have to come home and have their spirits renewed. Maybe it's our Cherokee heritage. Maybe it's the creek. Maybe it's because we're family.

So come sit on our porch. We don't talk about religion here, though all our denominations really do get along. They may agree to disagree, but it doesn't stop them from getting married, moving out, leaving home or coming back.

We'll serve you some fried chicken, tell a few tall tales and sip lemonade made from cold mountain water purer than anything bottled in Switzerland. And we'll try not to talk about cantankerous topics like religion or politics. Much.

In Mossy Creek, the description of an annoying adversary
is fondly followed by "Bless her little ol' heart."

👑👑👑👑👑👑👑👑👑👑👑👑👑👑👑👑👑👑👑👑👑👑👑👑👑👑👑👑👑👑👑👑👑

The Look

Chapter 11

Some say being in the ministry is one of the most demanding callings a person can have. But I'd have to say
marriage is harder.

When I first heard the call, it was as if the heavens
opened and an almost audible voice told me I was to be a
pastor. I would lead God's flock. I would preach God's word.
The awesome responsibility sat heavily on me at the age of
nineteen. Still did. But it was nothing compared to being a
husband to Amelia.

No seminary training could have prepared me for the
ache that gnawed at me every time I heard her sobbing in
the shower. Every time she sniffed quietly in our bed at night.
She was disappointed in me. She thought I would get sent to
some huge church in Atlanta. And I guess I let her dream,
because it made me feel good to have her beaming with
pride at what she considered my many pastoral talents.

Even during those first three years in our first tiny
church, she seemed to consider it paying my dues. She still
saw me in a grand pulpit somewhere. Pipe organ. Massive
stained glass windows. Television ministry.

But the day we got the call that we were going to Mossy
Creek Mt. Gilead Methodist Church (and we had to get out a
map to try to figure out where in the world Mossy Creek

was), the light faded in her eyes.

My stomach tied in one big knot after that call came. I kept hoping she would give me *The Look* once again. The one that put me back at the top of the world — her world at least. But as we sat in our new parsonage with boxes all around, I couldn't quite see beyond her anguish. Or her disappointment.

🕯🕯🕯

The Saturday after we moved into the church parsonage, Amelia and I awakened to the sound of the doorbell. She bolted up in bed with a panic-stricken look on her face, swiped the hair out of her eyes and glanced at the clock. "Ten-thirty a.m. and the new minister and his wife are caught in bed. You answer it."

"They won't kick us out of town for sleeping in on Saturday."

By the time I had put one foot on the floor, she was in the bathroom with the water running. I yanked on a pair of gym shorts as the doorbell rang a second time. "Coming," I hollered in the general direction of the front door.

Amelia's soapy face peeked out of the bathroom. "Hurry! And get a shirt on, for heaven's sake." She slammed the bathroom door, then I heard her moan.

"Oh, this is terrible."

Pulling on my dirty tee shirt from the day before, I opened the door to a stranger.

The sleek, fortyish woman in slim tweeds gave me a quick once-over, but I had the distinct feeling she'd had enough time to register the minute details — lack of shoes, bed head, morning breath.

"I'm Mal Purla Rhett, church treasurer. Good morning, Reverend Phillips."

"Come on in, Ms. Rhett. Call me Mark."

"Oh, I couldn't do that. It would be inappropriate."

I could see we'd never be best friends.

She picked her way around boxes and perched on the edge of a worn velvet Queen Ann chair. The same chair Amelia and I decided must have been the original purchase for the parsonage.

"I thought I'd come fill you in on how I do the paychecks and pay the bills. And welcome you, of course," she said without a hint of welcome. Then she handed me a shiny gift bag with tissue paper sticking out and a big fancy bow. "I'm also president of the Mossy Creek Welcome Club."

"Thank you. That's real kind. If you'll give me just a minute, I'll run and let Amelia know you're here. "And *I can brush my teeth.*

"Fine."

I'm not one to worry so much about what everyone thinks of me (except Amelia, of course), but this woman made me nervous. Maybe it was the designer pantsuit on a Saturday morning. Or maybe it was the Jennifer Anniston hairdo and perfect makeup when I looked like something the dog had dragged in. Whatever it was had me hurrying to locate Amelia, who'd always been a natural hostess.

She bumped into the bedroom door as I flung it open.

"Help." I held up the frou-frou package. "The church treasurer is here bearing gifts."

With smoothed hair and a touch of lipstick, Amelia looked as if she'd been up for hours. "Go start the coffee. I'll entertain her while you make yourself presentable."

My calm, collected (at least on the surface) wife took the gift and glided down the hall. "Good morning. I'm Mark's wife, Amelia . . ."

By the time I managed to finish dressing in clean clothes, locate an extra mug out of one of the moving boxes and start the coffee, my normally unflappable wife sat across from the treasurer with a brittle smile on her face.

As I came in the room, Amelia said, "Mal was telling me about her idea for us to host an open house."

Mal. What a creepy name. I smiled. "Certainly."

Mal Purla Rhett eyed me. "I think it's a good way to meet the community. To establish your place here in Mossy Creek."

I sat next to Amelia on the couch and took hold of her hand. "Sounds like a great idea." As an afterthought, I glanced to see what she thought. She still had a smile on her face, but one I couldn't read. "Of course, only if that's what my wife wants to do."

"Of course," Mal said. "I can help with the decorating, if you'd like. My sister, Swee Purla, is one of the most success-ful interior designers in the South. She lives down in Bigelow, but I often assist with her projects. She and I have wanted to get hold of this parsonage for years, but the congregation has resisted." She sniffed. "Creekites tend to be obsessed with maintaining the historic status quo. Even when that *quo* is an embarrassment."

I looked around at the ragtag furniture and mismatched end tables. Probably an interior decorator's idea of hell. "It's a little worn, but we can make do."

Amelia laughed. "And we plan to start our family, any-way. You know how messy kids can be."

A family?

"How nice," Mal said. "No need to put too much into new furniture if little ones will be running around destroy-ing everything."

I raised my eyebrows first at our visitor, then at Amelia, wanting to tell them both that kids wouldn't be along any-time soon.

"So, Mal," I said as I leaned forward on the cushions. "When do I get paid?

My smile was meant to tease her into lightening up, but Mal Purla Rhett seemed to have only one mode. Uptight.

She pulled a computer printout from her brushed suede organizer. "I'll pay you twice a month. Out of the first check, I'll pay your electric bill. In the middle of the month, I'll pay your water and gas. I'll also pay the phone bill out of that check."

"*You* pay our bills?" I couldn't stop the incredulity in my voice. I'd never heard of such a thing.

"Yes, I pay anything that's in the name of the parsonage: water, gas, electric, phone, trash pickup. It's a policy we adopted years ago after a pastor let the bills slide. The church got a bad credit rating because of him."

I caught myself with my hand on my back pocket, protecting my credit cards. "I don't mind paying the parsonage bills myself, Mal. Amelia and I managed the parsonage at our previous church without any problems. You can check with the church treasurer. She'll vouch for us. I think the parsonage family should be trusted to take care of their own utilities."

"I'm sorry Reverend. It's non-negotiable. Church policy is church policy."

With my teeth on edge, I held my tongue and decided it wasn't a battle worth fighting. Maybe not handling the bills would end up being a blessing. I would have more time to enjoy small-town life. "I guess that'll work out okay. Will you forward us a copy of each statement, please?"

"Always do. They'll come with your paycheck." Mal Purla Rhett directed her gaze to Amelia. "I'll give the check and paperwork to you each time. In my experience, pastors' wives are far more competent than their husbands when it comes to managing business matters."

Amelia smiled. "Well, how about I get us all some coffee?"

And so started my relationship with Mal Purla Rhett, Evil Treasurer.

❦ ❦ ❦

By the time we'd been in Mossy Creek for about two months Amelia was fit to be tied. Our Creekite congregation adored me, except for Mal Rhett. And they had plenty for me to do. Even though Amelia knew that being a minister's wife meant sharing me with my flock, she'd never seen a flock so determined to keep the shepherd in the field. Luckily her socialite upbringing kept her from making an all-out attack on anyone in the church. Unfortunately, she took some of that anger out on me.

"So you have another meeting tonight?" Amelia asked, standing beside the dinner table. It was loaded with food.

"Yes, I always do on Mondays."

She turned away and stirred something on the stovetop. "It wasn't on the calendar. How am I supposed to keep up if you don't write it on our home calendar?"

Her voice was calm, but I could hear the tension. Besides, whenever she couldn't look at me, I knew she was really mad.

"I thought you'd know by now that Mondays are always taken."

"So are Tuesdays, Wednesdays and Thursdays . . . I thought I finally had an undisturbed evening to cook a nice meal. I'm happy to do my job as the minister's wife, but I'd like to practice the 'wife' part with you a little more often."

Now, I'm usually pretty hardheaded, but that was one time I knew I had to tread carefully. "I'm sorry. Can we talk about this later? I have about fifteen minutes before I leave. I barely have time to eat." I sat and grabbed the cloth napkin she'd folded into some sort of bird. She'd been hanging out with Josie McClure, Mossy Creek's origami-napkin queen.

"Fifteen minutes for a gourmet meal. *Fine.* I hope you choke on it." She rushed out of the room, tears running down her face.

I wasn't born yesterday. I knew this was about more than hurriedly eaten chicken *cordon bleu*. I followed my distraught wife and found her angled across our bed, the covers all bunched up as if she'd thrown herself there. Her sobs cinched the knot in my gut tighter.

"What is it, honey?"

"You're never here."

"I know. It's the nature of my job. You knew that when you married me."

"No I didn't. You were supposed to preach on Sundays and do weddings every now and then."

"And I'm going to be Bishop someday, too." I rubbed her ankle. "What's really bothering you?"

As she reached for a Kleenex on the bedside table and gave a totally useless dainty blow, I sat beside her. "Go on. Give it a real blow. Then tell me what's got you so upset."

She followed orders, then her pale face colored in embarrassment at the loud sound she'd made. She drew in a deep, quivering breath. "It's Mal Rhett."

I'd realized one rushed meal couldn't be the real issue, but the leap to Mal Rhett was a long one. "Honey, I may be slow to follow sometimes, but you've lost me on this one."

In a near whisper, she said, "She's been calling around. Comparing you to the old pastor."

"That's bound to happen when someone new comes in."

"No. She's asking questions. Apparently, she's been comparing our electric bill and water usage to the other family. She seems to think we're wasteful."

"Wasteful?"

"According to her, we're not good stewards of our natural resources."

"And the person who told you this is . . . ?"

"It's just the talk going around. I don't know where it originated."

"Don't people have better things to do than keep tabs on the new pastor's family?"

"This is a small town, Mark," she said as if that were a logical explanation.

"Why on earth would any of this matter to Mal Rhett? The utilities are all coming out of *our* paycheck. It's not like the church is paying."

With a pained look on her face — almost like shame — she glanced down at the wadded tissue in her hands. "I think it's my fault that she's being so nosy. The truth is, she doesn't trust me to manage the utilities."

My breath expanded my ribcage. I had the ridiculous urge to beat my chest like some kind of gorilla. How dare someone hurt Amelia? "Of *course* she likes you. *Everyone* likes you."

That seemed to give her strength. Or at least a little starch in her spine. "I got ugly with her the other day. She hasn't forgiven me."

"What could she possibly need to forgive you for?"

"Promise *you'll* forgive me once you hear what I've done?"

I wasn't so sure I liked the sound of that. A suspicious gleam in her eye gave me further pause. Hopefully my normally sweet-tempered wife hadn't shortened my tenure in Mossy Creek. I nodded.

"I called her a stingy, meddling, gossipmonger."

"*You what?*"

With what could almost be considered a smirk, Amelia said, "You heard me right."

"Not to her face."

"I'm afraid so. I couldn't let her talk about you behind our backs."

I laughed, and it rang loud in the tiny bedroom. *Stingy, meddling* was the truth. I couldn't fault Amelia for telling the truth. "Is *gossipmonger* even a real word?"

She swatted at my arm. "Quit trying to make light of it, because I haven't told you the worst yet."

"I don't even want to know."

"Oh, I think you'll appreciate the fact that she mistook an Italian proverb as Scripture."

"Which proverb?"

Amelia flopped back onto the pillow and grinned at the ceiling. "You know the one I have posted on the side of my computer monitor? '*He who sows thorns should not go bare-foot.*'"

"Mal Rhett thinks that's in the Bible?"

"She started flipping through the big Bible she keeps in her giant suede organizer. Honey, the woman's Bible has *an alligator skin cover.* I swear to you. Alligator skin. Anyway, I told her to let me know when she found that proverb and I walked away — head held high, I might add."

I ran a hand over my chin, trying to imagine the next time I would see Mal. Or worse, the next time Amelia would see her. "What a mess."

"I know. It's unforgivable. But I had just found out Mal called the former pastor and asked what temperature he had kept the thermostat set on."

I watched as she grabbed a bottle of hand lotion off the nightstand, pumped one squirt and rubbed her hands together, never once cracking a smile. "You're serious," I said.

"Of course I am. I don't think I could dream up something so off-the-wall to kid about."

We'd already noticed Mal passing our house slowly a few times in the evenings. Apparently, checking on our usage of electricity. It made me want to turn on every light in the house and let them burn all night, just to send her off the deep end.

Instead, somehow, I would have to smooth the feathers of that stingy, meddling gossipmonger, yet at the same time get her off our backs. I could deal with Mal, though. I figured every church had at least one of her type. But I refused to let her make Amelia's life miserable. Besides, if I wanted to spend my whole paycheck on kilowatts of energy, it was no business of hers.

"You'd think with a successful business, she'd have better things to do," I said. "Of course, I've heard the rumors of her sister cheating assistants out of decorating awards."

Maybe the Purla sisters are just all-around sneaks. Or maybe Mal only wanted to get credit for saving the environment.

"So what do you think we should do?" asked my overly-protective wife.

"We could always send you to tell her off again. Maybe you'd scare her out of town this time."

"I would love to. But I'm afraid we'd be packing our belongings before they're even all out of boxes. Then again, we could invite Mal over just to drive her crazy. When she visited that first time — what, two days after we'd moved in? — she had the nerve to say she was surprised — meaning *appalled* — that I hadn't finished the unpacking yet."

That got my blood boiling. "Maybe I really should send you. I might not be very polite."

"Let's give it some time. Surely she'll get tired of meddling."

"No, I'm more determined than ever to demand that we handle our own bills. I'll take it to the next finance committee meeting."

"Do you think they'll change church policy?"

"We won't know until we try."

"Then I want to go to the meeting, too. I want to be sure they know what that woman has been doing. How she has tried to ruin your good name in the community."

Amelia wanted to fit in, to make her place in society. It's what she'd grown up thinking was important. I wouldn't let Mal Rhett mess that up for her. "You come if you want to speak your mind." I smiled at my brave wife. "As long as you don't call her names. Or quote *proverbs* you saw on the wall of an Italian restaurant."

She crisscrossed her hand over her heart, but the wicked twinkle in her eye cancelled the solemn gesture. "On my honor, I'll behave."

I called the church to say I couldn't make the meeting that night. Amelia and I spent the rest of our rare evening at home in peace and quiet. As I was turning off the lights for the night, I happened to see Amelia's Bible open on the table. Two yellow-highlighted passages in *Matthew* popped out at me:

Therefore I tell you, do not worry about your life, what you will eat or what you will drink, or about your body, what you will wear. Is not life more than food, and the body more than clothing . . . and can any of you by worrying add a single hour to your span of life?

The thought of Amelia worrying about food and clothes made the ache in my stomach multiply tenfold. The fact that she'd had to find comfort in Scripture proved my worry that she was dissatisfied with our life. With the move to Mossy Creek.

With me.

At least I didn't hear any sobbing or sniffles in bed that night. I pulled her into my arms, and her breathing became deeper, more even. "You know," I whispered, "Mossy Creek is just another step up the ladder. Someday we'll be at that big church you dream of. And I'll make enough money to support a family. And you'll have some of the nice things you're used to."

She made a little laughing sound, half asleep, half awake. "And get rid of our purple and gold van?"

"You bet."

"And have five kids?" she mumbled.

"If we can afford that many."

"How about just one? Sooner. Not later."

The suggestion jolted me wide awake. "Once we're able to save a little money."

"You said that at the last church."

"And I only got a five-hundred dollar raise moving here. That won't even pay the obstetrician's fee."

"This is about more than just money, Mark."

"No, it's not. I'm simply not willing to add kids to the picture when we hardly make ends meet."

"We do fine. Please think about it."

Fine? She'd been relegated to driving a 1987 Dodge Colt Vista, for heaven's sake. Forget designer clothes and real jewelry.

I sighed and pulled her closer, tucking her head under my chin. "Okay, Amelia. I'll think about it. But I'm not going to change my mind anytime soon."

A few minutes later, she scooted to her side of the bed. "It's hot. We should turn down the thermostat."

Not long after, when she was so still I thought she was asleep, and the only sound was that of the whirring furnace, I heard a little sniff.

I'd failed her again. I hadn't protected her from Mal Purla Rhett's insults. And I still couldn't give her the quality things she was used to.

How could I ever live up to her ideals?

❦❦❦

I waited for the date of the finance meeting to roll around. Mal remained blessedly quiet. Life was good. Church attendance had increased, too. Regular members seemed surprised to see Foxer Atlas, who hadn't been to church since his wife Ellie died. I was also pleased to see Maggie Hart, since I'd heard the Unitarians were wooing her. Since Maggie was Mossy Creek's resident new-age flower child, I'd better darn well impress her with my sermons. So far, so good. And where Maggie went, Tag Garner could be found. I enjoyed seeing the middle-aged, ex-pro-linebacker-turned-sculptor sitting in the front pew, his graying hair pulled back in a thick ponytail, the blue streak making an artistically manful statement. Or something.

A few members complimented my preaching, but only with vague comments such as *appreciated the sermon,* or *enjoyed the message.* And who could figure out *I'll be digesting that one all this week*? Did that mean it was thought provoking? Or that it gave them indigestion?

Mayor Walker, a Baptist, came by after the service one Sunday. She said, "Tell me if I'm correct. Your theme was that God wants to save everyone, even those in hell. I'm not sure I totally agree, but you made your point well."

"Well now, Mayor, you're the type of listener who keeps a pastor on his toes. You got the theme exactly right. I appreciate you listening."

"I hear you and Amelia are going to have an open house. Excellent idea. That's always good PR."

The open house was a done deal. Amelia had made up her mind to follow Mal's advice. "Yes. I hope you can make it."

"I wouldn't miss it." She leaned in a little closer. "Just a word of advice. Make sure Amelia personally invites all the Mossy Creek Garden Club. Plus the Mossy Creek Social Society. Not just the ones who are members of your church.

Believe me, Amelia doesn't want to slight them."

"I'll be sure to tell her."

She waved as she walked away.

"Nice preaching today, Preacher," Amelia said from behind as she wrapped her arms around my waist.

I turned to face her. "You think so?"

She smiled and, for a second, gave me *The Look*. It was fleeting, but it was enough to hang my hopes on for the moment.

"Are you happy here?" I asked without thinking.

Her smile faltered, and I wished like anything I hadn't let the question slip.

"I'm learning to like it," she said diplomatically. "Once we get you-know-who's nose out of our business, I think we'll be okay."

"Not just okay. I want you *happy*."

"I'm still a little lonely. That'll take time."

"I just heard you announced an open house. That's a start. I know how you love to throw parties."

"Yes. I decided during Sunday School this morning."

"You need to make some personal friends, though. How about —"

"Just this morning I made a lunch date with someone. I have a feeling she's going to be that special friend that God always provides."

Considering I took Amelia from a lifetime lived in one house to a life of being uprooted every few years, Amelia was a trooper. But for the first time, I began to doubt the wisdom of becoming a pastor. What if Amelia wasn't cut out for this kind of life? What if making new friends each time we moved wasn't enough?

"Come on, let's go home," she said.

"Before I forget, the mayor says to invite all members of the garden club and social society to the open house."

"Are you sure? I've heard some of those women aren't real crazy about your *liberal* preaching." Her eyes sparkled, teasing me like old times.

"Maybe I'll convert them before then."

There it was again. The *Look.* "You probably could."

As long as she looked at me that way, I imagined I could do anything.

❦ ❦ ❦

Before we knew it, the day of the open house had arrived. Amelia was in the kitchen taking hors d'oeuvres out of the oven, and I was putting the vacuum cleaner back in the closet as the doorbell rang.

Amelia appeared in the doorway from the kitchen and smoothed her dress. She was so beautiful it still took my breath away. Sometimes I wondered how she could look twice at a working-class boy like me. I'd grown up in a small house in suburban Atlanta with a dad who did factory work. He and my mom worked hard to send me to college and seminary. They loved me and were proud of me.

Amelia was from an old-money Nashville family who lived alongside country-music stars in one of those mansions in the Bellemeade area. Her family was society-conscious and about had a fit when she took me home to meet them. But she stood up to her mother and daddy and married me anyway.

With her long dark hair and chocolate brown eyes, she looked exactly like her mother. But the likeness stopped there. Amelia was warm and loving. She was funny, sensitive, generous.

The doorbell rang again.

She smiled at me.

"Do you think we should answer it? Or should we ignore them and eat all the food ourselves?"

"I didn't do all this work for nothing."

She kissed my cheek, then wiped the lipstick off. "Thank you for helping me. I couldn't have done it without you."

With a warm buzz flowing through me, I answered the door. When what to my wondering eyes should appear, but Mal Purla Rhett and five of the most humorless matrons in town.

I resisted the urge to slam the door in Mal's face. After the things she'd said, I couldn't believe she had the gall to come to our party.

Poor Amelia. Why did these six have to be the first to show up?

For my wife's sake, I bit my tongue. "Welcome, ladies. Come in."

Mal nodded her greeting. "Reverend." Then she headed straight toward Amelia. I almost followed, but the first woman, a skinny blue-hair who wore a silver cross lapel pin, came in and grabbed my hand.

"I haven't met you yet, Pastor. I'm Adele Clearwater," she said in a grating voice. "And these are some of the members of the Mossy Creek Social Society. In case you haven't heard, the society is a non-denominational prayer group and political action committee. We consider it our calling to support issues of ethics and morality in Mossy Creek. Most of us are also charter members of the Mossy Creek Garden Club. We believe people reap what they sow."

As each old lady marched past and introduced herself, I asked where she attended church. A couple of the ladies belonged to Mt. Gilead. Then I realized Adele Clearwater hadn't mentioned *her* home church.

"Ms. Clearwater, you didn't mention where you're a member."

The room quieted, except for Amelia, who was chatting with an ancient red-haired gnome named Eustene Oscar.

Adele harrumphed. Or maybe she was just clearing her throat. "I see you haven't looked at the roll of Mt. Gilead since you got here."

"No, I'm sorry. I haven't had a chance."

"Well, I'm officially a member. But I've been going to the First Baptist Church of Mossy Creek for forty-five years."

There was a story there somewhere, but since everyone looked uncomfortable with the topic, I decided to let it drop for now. "You ladies help yourselves to refreshments in the kitchen. Have a look around and see what Amelia's done with the parsonage."

As I was about to close the door, Foxer Atlas walked slowly up the front path, leaning heavily on a cane. "Hello, Mr. Atlas. Come on in."

I helped him through the door. He thanked me, then froze with his eyes on Amelia. A wistful smile tugged at his craggy skin. "Your wife reminds me of my Janey about fifty years ago."

I gazed at the target of his admiration. "She's so beautiful, inside and out. I still can't believe she married me."

With a dreamy expression, he seemed a million miles away. Or maybe just fifty years away. "*Every living thing becomes beautiful when it's loved.* Janey always said that."

"Yes. I'm sure she was right." Amelia laughed at something Eustene said. "I do know that my wife is loved."

Foxer put his hand on my arm. "I'm glad. She's a brave soul. If she can survive this roomful of biddies, she'll do okay in Mossy Creek."

❧❧❧

Eventually, the house was as packed as a church on Easter Sunday. It seemed everyone decided to show up during the first hour — the mayor and police chief included.

Having insisted on using her grandmother's cut glass punch bowl set instead of paper or plastic, Amelia had already had to run to the kitchen to wash a load of punch cups.

When I caught up with her in the kitchen, she was beaming, rosy-cheeked from the heat of the oven — the only warm place in the house. "Oh, Mark, it's going so well."

"The food looks fantastic, honey. Everyone's having a good time."

"You-know-who hasn't made a peep," she whispered.

"Did you ask if she's been doing a lot of Bible reading lately?"

She laughed. "Stop. You won't believe it. She even grudgingly complimented me on the artwork I hung yesterday. And the Adele brigade seem pleased."

Her face glowed with pride. She hadn't seemed so happy since we moved. "It's all your doing," I said. "You're a success."

"Thank you." With a quick peck on my cheek, she was off to refill the punch bowl.

The living room was freezing. Guests were shivering and rubbing heir hands. I headed to the hallway to turn up the heat.

And there stood Mal Purla Rhett, Superintendent of the Thermostat, staring at the darn thing. As she started to jot something on the screen of her Palm Pilot, I reached past her and turned the lever up to seventy-five degrees just to aggravate her. Then I said, "We can talk right here, or we can go out back where we won't make a scene."

She huffed. "Why would our talking make a scene?" But her face was flushed, and her eyes darted around as guilt washed over her features. Everything about her demeanor shouted *caught in the act.*

"Last chance to go out to the back porch where you won't be publicly embarrassed."

She stuffed the electronic notepad into her alligator purse, then viciously snapped it closed. "I was just making a note of the brand name on the furnace."

"I'll be happy to jot down all the information for you."

"No, thank you. I got everything I need."

"And why would you need that information?"

As if she'd just chomped down on a lemon, her lips formed a sour little sun. "It's for some research I'm doing."

"Would that research have anything to do with my electric bill?"

"Why, uh, well . . . yes, it would." She ratcheted her chin up a notch. "I called the EMC and found out that if you keep your thermostat set at sixty degrees through the fall months, then the monthly bills shouldn't be more than —"

"*You what?*" I roared.

I admit my voice tends to carry, even when I'm not in the pulpit. When everyone nearby turned toward us, I hesitated. But it was time for the showdown. No waiting until the finance committee meeting.

Mal's forehead glistened with a sheen of perspiration. She clutched her alligator purse tighter and said, "I'm only doing research. I was afraid something was wrong with your thermostat."

"I assure you that nothing is wrong with it other than the fact *that you don't like where we're setting it.*"

"You don't need to get so upset about it. It's part of my job."

"Monitoring our bills is *not* part of your job."

"I'm the church treasurer."

"Yes, you are. And you're supposed to monitor the church's bills, which you do well. But you're not my keeper. And I won't have you upsetting my wife by spreading nasty comments about how we spend our own money."

With her face gleaming like a waxed and buffed red

apple, she sputtered, "I did no such thing."

"Then why did you call former Pastor Hickman to see how he kept his thermostat set?"

She didn't have an answer for that. She sputtered. I charged ahead. "I want you to know that at the next finance committee meeting I'm asking them to turn the bill-paying over to Amelia and me. It's *our* business what we spend on utilities. And I *insist* that you apologize for embarrassing my wife."

For the first time, I noticed the silence around us, not to mention the crowd of gawkers. Adele Clearwater had her head craned like a small, hyper-alert hen. Amos Royden chewed a smile on his lower lip but stood posed as if ready to intervene in an assault. I could see the headlines now: *Pastor Arrested for Terrorizing Church Treasurer over Thermostat.*

I sighed. "Look, everyone. I'm sorry about airing my dirty laundry here at the party."

"That's okay, Pastor," Foxer Atlas said. "It's nice when a man'll stand up for his wife." Then he glared at Mal. "Girl, you should be *ashamed* of yourself, terrorizing the pastor's wife."

"I'm merely doing my job." With a loud huff — huffing must be a regular part of her vocabulary — Mal pushed her way through the crowd, chin held high, and marched right out the front door.

Someone started clapping. I looked around until I found the source. A sweet-faced young woman, Geena Quill, who'd been done out the decorating award by Swee Purla, grinned. "Ms. Rhett is a lot like her sister. She needs to be put in her place. Thanks from one of the Purla victims."

The mayor walked up to me. Her expression was neutral, her voice, formal. But her green eyes twinkled. "I'm glad you have God on your side. You've just dissed a Purla sister.

In public. You're going to need all the help you can get." She smiled. "I'll attend the finance committee meeting. Even though I'm a Baptist, I have some clout. You'll be fine."

Conversations resumed; guests mingled back to the family room and kitchen. A sense of relief, and even pride, stole its way through me, easing the constant pain in my gut. Only one person to locate now. Now that I had defended her, maybe I would see *The Look* on her face once again.

I searched until I found her leaning over dirty punch cups in the sink, scrubbing at a smudge of lipstick on one.

"Honey?"

Her hair hung down over her face. "I can't believe you just did that," she whispered, then her shoulders began to shake.

My heart crashed to my feet. "Oh, honey, I'm sorry. I know this party means a lot to you. But everything will be okay now. She'll leave us alone. And she still owes you that apology."

I pushed her hair behind her ear and discovered her laughing. "I thought you were *crying*, you rascal."

"I'm still mortified."

"Look at the bright side. You don't have to worry about making a scene at the finance committee meeting. I've already done it." Once she made eye contact, I winked at her.

After setting the freshly-scrubbed punch cup back into the soapy water, she turned to face me and stifled a laugh as she glanced around the room. "I think you took care of making a scene quite well. Thank you for taking up for me. You're my hero."

My puffed up ego carried me through the rest of the afternoon.

❧❧❧

All in all, we had about 150 people drop in for the open

house. And all 150 talked about *The Incident* to every person who came by too late to witness it personally. The story was passed along like that old game called *Telephone Line*. By the time the last guests left, I heard Buck Looney tell Hank Blackshear that I had yanked the thermostat off the wall and stuffed it in Mal Rhett's alligator pocketbook. I hoped that version would stop circulating when visitors noticed the thermostat still hung intact in the hallway.

As Amelia headed to bed that night, she picked up her worn leather Bible. I found her on the bed sitting in her nightshirt, face scrubbed clean of makeup, hair pulled back in a headband, with the open Bible on her lap.

I could see the yellow highlighted sections.

"What are you studying, Amelia?"

"Matthew."

And I knew exactly which verses.

"Therefore I tell you . . ." she began to read. ". . . do not worry about your life, what you will eat or what you will drink, or about your body, what you will wear. Is not life more than food, and the body more than clothing . . ."

I'd embarrassed her in front of a house full of people. In front of leading members of our congregation. Even though they seemed to find it amusing — and even admirable — I hadn't exactly demonstrated my qualifications to be a spiritual leader.

I sat down beside her on the bed. "I'm sorry. I know you're worried about me losing my job. About us getting by. But they can't up and fire me. At worst, they can ask that I be moved somewhere else. And if that happens, then so be it. I just don't want you feeling bad about the life we have."

She reached for me and started to speak.

"Wait," I said. "I want to say what's been on my mind since we moved." I ran my finger over the tissue-thin pages of the chapter in Matthew. "I know you're disappointed in me. You had no idea, when you fell in love, that I'd earn so little money. Believe me when I say I never imagined how little I would earn, either. But I'd hoped I could make it up to you in other ways. I had hoped —" My throat stopped working. A big lump of pride clamped it closed.

"Oh, Mark —"

"I had hoped that our love would be enough. That *I* would be enough." My eyes stung, and I had to blink. As she set the Bible aside and climbed into my lap, I said, "I borrowed your Bible and found these verses you've highlighted. About not worrying. About trusting God for all that you need. I guess you needed to reassure yourself because I —"

She put her fingertips over my mouth. "That verse was for *you*. You worry all the time. I was claiming it while I prayed for *you*."

Love poured out of the look she gave me. *The Look.* I basked in it, yet couldn't grasp it. How had we gone from my apologizing about failing her to her praying for me not to worry about failing her? "You know, sometimes you just leave me standing in the dust behind you," I said. "Tell me what's inside you. Make me understand why you sob in the shower. Why you cry in bed at night."

"You heard?"

"I know you need more."

"No, I don't. I don't need anything but you. You're the one who's needed more."

"I'm still here in the dust."

She smiled and put her hand on my chest, right over my heart. "I wanted you from the moment I first heard your laugh. It didn't matter what your dad did for a living. It didn't matter what *you* were going to do for a living. I wanted a man with the kind of joy in life that you had. I wanted a man who was firm in his convictions, a good man."

"Have I changed? Is that why you're not happy now?"

"You don't trust God to take care of us anymore. You're

trying to do it yourself."

I let that sink in for a minute. Could she be right? "I thought you wanted more . . . things. A better car. Clothes that don't come from Wal-Mart."

"The only reason I cry is because I want you back. The *old* you." She clasped her hands in front of her and looked down, almost nervous. "And I want us to start our family."

"But we don't have enough saved to —"

"Stop right there. Think about how God has provided for us before. How paychecks seemed to stretch and stretch until we couldn't figure out how it happened, but we somehow made it through until the next one."

"But a *baby?*"

"A big, loud, loving family is what I want more than anything. With you as the dad."

She really wanted to have a baby with me. Something that would tie us together forever. "There'd be no backing out once we have a baby."

"Is that what you're afraid of? That I'll leave you?"

"You could do a lot better."

"You know, a kind older man told me something tonight at the party," she said as she placed her soft palms on my cheeks. "*Every living thing becomes beautiful when it's loved.*' And you're about the most beautiful thing I've ever seen."

The Look. She was giving me *The Look.* And it didn't appear to be going anywhere anytime soon.

As she kissed me, the knot in my gut finally let go for good.

The furnace kicked on. It was a fine, cozy autumn night.

A perfect night for starting that family.

Blessings.

Mossy Creek Gazette

215 Main Street • Mossy Creek, GA 30533

From the desk of Katie Bell

Lady Victoria Salter Stanhope
The Cliffs
Seaward Road
St. Ives, Cornwall, TR3 7PJ
United Kingdom

Dear Vick:

These are the only two interviews I did that made me cry. Imagine. A tough, professionally *quaint* award winner like me. Crying and smiling at the same time. Don't tell the newspaper awards committee. I'm not just quaint. I'm sentimental, too.

Katie

In Mossy Creek, men learn pretty quick that there are two ways to argue with a woman, and neither one works.

🌷🌷🌷🌷🌷🌷🌷🌷🌷🌷🌷🌷🌷🌷🌷🌷🌷🌷🌷🌷🌷🌷🌷🌷🌷🌷🌷🌷🌷🌷🌷🌷🌷🌷🌷🌷🌷🌷

House of Straw

Chapter 12

When Isaac walked into the kitchen for breakfast, it was like seeing a stranger walk into the room and click a lock behind him. Nothing seemed quite real between us anymore.

He sat down at the table, but instead of eating, he picked up the *Mossy Creek Gazette*. Day was barely breaking on our farm just outside town, in the Lookover community. The only sounds were a bird singing, coffee trickling as I filled Isaac's cup, and his newspaper rattling. Like a shield, he kept his paper in front of him and felt for his cup. I said nothing. Neither did Isaac. Mostly, it had been that way for a couple of months now.

Enough, I thought, as I set the coffeepot back on the stove. *We're in this situation together.* "Would you put that paper down a minute?"

He didn't answer or move.

"Look at me."

Not looking up, he pushed his plate away and his chair back.

About to explode, I banged on a pot.

He put the paper down, an irritated look on his face.

I jabbed a finger at him. "Cut me out if you want, but I took you for better or worse, and I'm not leaving."

"Nancy, I've fought and I've lost. This farm is gone.

259

I know it. You know it."

"You had nothing to do with the weather over the summer or the price of corn," I countered. He had no comment this time. "I have a stake in this place too, you know . . . and in our marriage and any children we might have."

Isaac glared. His face was set, his mouth clamped, and his eyes fixed. Looking at him, I shriveled a little. "There won't be any children . . . at least not here."

Though they shouldn't have, his words came as a shock. I crossed my arms and faced him. "Are you saying that if there were, you wouldn't want them?"

"Stop putting words in my mouth. I said, there won't *be* any." He glanced at the broom straw I kept in a crockery jug in the corner. "Like a house of straw, our life has fallen down around us."

I couldn't give up. "What about the pumpkin crop? Won't that tide us over?"

"It will be too late."

"Other farmers around here lost their crops over the summer, and they didn't give up." Trembling, I went around the table to comfort him. When he lifted up his eyes, the pain of failure flickered there.

He put up his hands. "Nancy, talk is useless. Hugging is useless. Even if we do make a crop, it'll come in too late."

"Isaac, don't give up. Not yet."

He rubbed his hands over his face as if he were hearing the same song, second verse.

"Your family made it through wars and hard times and didn't resort to moonshine like some of the neighbors. We'll make it."

"Don't spout your positive thinking at me. Lot of good that does." He reached for a piece of toast. "Isn't that right, Nancy?" His brow lifted, waiting. I hungered to put my arms around him, to give him comfort, but I knew it was useless.

He'd push me away again. With that piece of toast in hand, he hurried out. The door slammed behind him.

I watched as he walked past the kitchen window on the way to the barn. Then I turned away. If I'd let him handle his pain in his own way, he wouldn't be working all morning doing heavy farm work with no breakfast.

His words about not wanting children rang in my ears. Sighing, feeling useless and forgotten, like someone unwanted, I swallowed hard and tried to stop the tears that ran down my throat and seeped from my eyes. He didn't mean it. He loved me, but he felt he'd failed me as well as family who'd gone before us. We'd made it through other hard times. There had to be a way now. Puzzled as to how to end this stalemate, I sipped my coffee.

Still flushed with maudlin thoughts, I stared at that sink and cabinet stacked with dirty dishes and thought of the laundry room piled with dirty clothes. I used to keep a spotless house until our finances went downhill and I'd started sewing to help pay the bills.

The old farmhouse had a long hall. Isaac had put a wall and a door in the hall, leading to a backroom where my big, commercial sewing machine and worktables shared space with bolts of fine fabric. I made good part-time money sewing custom drapes and bedspreads for Swee Purla's interior design business down in Bigelow. Just not good enough.

Weary from finishing a king-sized duvet cover late the night before, I blinked my tired eyes and looked over the list of what was yet to do. If I worked hard, I could finish the duvet's matching pillow shams and bedskirt today. Isaac hardly seemed to notice anymore what I did or where I was anyway, as long as he had a meal on time. I set to work. The time flew by. I stopped in late morning to make Isaac a thermos of hot tea.

Carrying the tea to the fields seemed to take the cobwebs from my brain and free the tension from my neck. As I walked across acres of terraced land covered in green vines and fat orange pumpkins, I felt proud. Surely this crop would be our salvation. As my mother used to say, "It's not over 'til it's over."

Isaac, his jacket thrown aside and flannel shirt open, carefully stacked harvested pumpkins inside a large wooden crate layered with hay. He'd forklift the crate along with several others onto our creaking flatbed truck, then drive the load down to the farmer's market in Bigelow.

Oh, how I loved to watch him work with his shirt open or off, then come up behind him to slide my hands over that tanned muscled chest and feel his heart beat faster at my touch. That welcoming smile on his face always made my own heart beat faster. But this time he made no effort to smile or even look up. Hugging the hurt to myself, I handed him his thermos, deliberately touching his hands with the tips of my fingers.

"Thanks," he said, and backed away.

How desperately I needed his comfort and he, mine, but my energies were wasted against his granite stand. I tried to ignore my need, had to ignore it for now if we were going to save our farm.

Isaac took a swallow, then wiped the dampness from his mouth as if nothing had changed between us. "What are we having for lunch?"

"Roast beef sandwiches," I mumbled.

"Again?" He wiped the perspiration from his forehead. "If I'm going to work out here all day, the least you could do is *cook*."

This wasn't the Isaac I'd married. "Eat it or do without," I said. We were supposed to be in this together, but he didn't seem to see it that way. My life was hard, too. My sewing money paid for groceries and the electric bill.

Struggling against discouragement, against the realization that there was no safety from life, I turned away and headed back to the house, stopping by the mailbox. There was a handful of junk mail and one very serious-looking letter from the Bank of Bigelow. Trembling, I opened it and read, "Payments on your line of credit are four months past-due. Please remit *immediately*."

Fighting my way through the fear that Isaac might be right about us losing the farm, I knew I couldn't handle this alone. I thought of my Aunt Emma. Maybe she'd help.

🐾🐾🐾

Impatiently, I waited for my aunt to pick up her phone. The answering machine came on. After telling my quandary to a cold digital recording device, I hung up. There was nothing to do now but get back to sewing. Wasting time wouldn't help matters.

The fine, heavy fabric felt soft to the touch. It was even the perfect color for Isaac's and my bedroom, a swirl of sage-green shades that would make our bed look like a soft spring field. Swee Purla had designed the custom bedding and matching drapes for her client, Sue Ora Salter Bigelow, a longtime Creekite, who I considered a friend. Sue Ora's husband, John, was president of the Bank of Bigelow. Sue Ora could buy whatever she fancied. I wondered if she'd insisted that Swee Purla assign me this sewing job to help me out.

Not wanting to get maudlin, I put down my sewing, changed from jeans into slacks and a sweater, and pulled my blond hair up in a twist. I couldn't wait for Aunt Emma to call me back. Maybe if I explained the situation to one of John Bigelow's loan officers, the bank would give us an extension.

"Nothing ventured, nothing gained." I told myself.

Even though it was only a thirty-minute drive, the trip

to Bigelow had never seemed so long. Now that cataract surgery had restored his eyesight, Ed Brady crept down South Bigelow Road in front of me, his rusted green pick-up rattling, blocking my passing on the numerous curves. Gripping the wheel of my dusty sedan, I thought about tapping his bumper so he'd go faster than forty.

The subdivisions and strip shopping centers of Bigelow finally came into view. I headed downtown to the bank. Isaac had given up, but I couldn't.

A receptionist ushered me to an office off the main lobby. The office door opened. A plump little guy smoothed his tie and grinned at me. "Nancy. Come on in."

"Mickey, hi," I acknowledged. Mickey Trent and I had been classmates at Bigelow County High.

"What can I do for you, Nancy?"

"I'm here about the past-due notice on my line of credit." I tried to look composed, but my fingers felt damp and my heart thumped hard against my rib cage.

"And?" He shifted some papers in an open folder, then studied the screen of his computer monitor.

"Isaac and I have a great pumpkin crop — the best in years, but it's going to be late."

He eyed me as if he were thinking about something, making some decision. I hoped it was in our favor. I went on quickly, "We can catch up on the back payments if you'll give us another three weeks."

Mickey's expression fell. "I'm sorry, but your credit rating is so bad that I can't give you and Isaac any extension."

"*What?*" I rose and leaned against his desk. "Mickey, we used the farm as collateral on that loan. If you foreclose, we'll lose everything."

"I'm sorry, Nancy. I really am."

His answer floored me. "You mean to tell me a family who has banked with this institution for several generations can't get a three-week extension? Are you telling me John Bigelow would allow his family's bank to take a farm away from his own wife's neighbors?"

Mickey looked miserable. "I really *am* sorry."

"I want to speak to John Bigelow."

"I'm afraid he isn't here this week. Nancy, there are a lot of pressures in modern banking. This is still a privately held financial institution owned entirely by the Bigelow family, and John tries to cut his customers some slack. But he has to compete with national banking conglomerates. If you want me to see if I can get a message to him —"

"Just tell him he'll get his money from me, one way or another. Good day."

Isaac was still working in the fields when I got back to the farm. I paced the kitchen, trying to think. I heard a car pull into our yard. It was probably Swee Purla coming to pick up Sue Ora's order.

But when I ran to the front door, Aunt Emma stood there, every bottled-blond hair in place, her nails light pink, her embroidered turquoise sweatsuit immaculate. Emma grabbed my hands reassuringly as I led her to the kitchen. "Nancy, I've found in my long years that life seems to have a rhythm. Sometimes it goes our way. Others it doesn't."

Remembering Isaac's words from this morning, I added dully, "Like a house of straw."

"Well, yes, but there are other factors."

She didn't say what other factors. I supposed she'd tell me later.

"I have to fix lunch," I said. I sliced a roast into thick slabs, put mustard and mayonnaise onto some bread, then lettuce and onion and sliced tomatoes. Emma watched in silence. The grandfather clock in the hall chimed noon. Isaac walked in. "Hi, Emma." His welcome sounded flat.

"Could I ask the blessing?" Emma asked. Isaac nodded.

I was surprised. He hadn't wanted to say it lately. Afterward, as we sat at the kitchen table, she carried on a conversation, told about other family members, little incidents that brought a laugh, but nothing about the message I'd left on her answering machine.

Isaac finished and pushed back his chair. "Where's the mail?"

I hesitated, not wanting to handle his reaction when he saw the bank's letter, not with Aunt Emma here. "It's in the basket on the hall table."

In less than a minute the backdoor slammed and his pickup roared off. I feared what he'd do. I bent my head to the kitchen table and sobbed. Aunt Emma patted my hand. "Honey, I waited until Isaac left to ask you just how bad things are. I guess they're worse than I thought."

"Aunt Emma, this time the bank means business."

"I know you're desperate, but I can't help financially right now."

I felt my heart sink. Aunt Emma had been our last hope. "Thank you, anyway, for coming."

"I have a story to tell you and I want you to listen."

"A story?" What in the world could a story do to save us?

"If you get something from it, fine. If you don't, there's nothing lost."

I settled back to listen.

"Years ago, when I was a young married woman, your uncle Sam and I found ourselves getting close to the day when we'd have to pay our rent. I'd canned and dried and preserved until I almost couldn't stay on my feet. My hair was limp and dishes were everywhere, but I prided myself on helping Sam. I'd see that we didn't starve even if we had nothing else. We had a little shoe store downstairs from our apartment, but people weren't buying much. Sam became more and more despondent and let the store look disheveled.

"Then one day, this fancy lady came by in her big car with her driver and asked to see 'the lady of the shop,' which was me, of course. I wondered why a woman like her would want to see me. I didn't run the shop. I didn't make the living. But I invited her upstairs and served her lemonade.

"The woman looked around at our living room. I was embarrassed at the dust on the furniture, at the rug needing the sweeper. Her perfume wafted over the room. My dear, I was embarrassed, to say the *least*, but I didn't let on. 'I have a story to tell you,' she said. I listened, wondering what she could possibly tell me that would make a difference in mine and Sam's situation. This is what she said.

"'Years ago, when my husband and I were starting out, life was hard, and somehow I sensed that whether or not we made it might be up to me. When things looked down, I'd spruce up the house extra-special, hunt flowers out of the yard, put them all over the house, ask people to visit, and make what food we had look great on the plate. We'd have good fun, good conversation, good music, and my husband's spirits seemed to rise. His renewed spirit seemed to rub off on those around him and his business prospered. Looking at your little shop, my dear, I'm suggesting that you take the same approach.'

"The stranger thanked me for the lemonade, went downstairs, bought a dozen pairs of shoes from Sam, then went on her way."

I sat there staring at my aunt. Even though the story must have worked for Aunt Emma, I couldn't see how it could help Isaac and me. Besides, I didn't have time to try it. I thanked Aunt Emma and she left. I cried some more. Then I cleaned up the kitchen, cut some autumn mums out of a bed outside, and set them in a vase on the kitchen table.

Isaac pulled up in the yard a short time later. He looked downcast when he walked in. "Why didn't you tell me you'd been to the bank?"

"There wasn't time."

He stopped, glanced at the mums dully, then back at me. "Flowers?"

"Positive thinking."

He sighed and walked out.

Thoughts of losing this place sapped my energy, too, but I couldn't give up. I went back to sewing. That night we ate dinner in silence. The about-to-be loss was killing us. We went to bed lying beside each other, but miles apart in every way that counted.

When Isaac came in from the field the next evening, the kitchen was shining. A tempting meal sat on the table amidst the fresh mums and candles. I had on make-up and perfume. "What's the occasion?"

"No occasion. Just you and me."

Saying nothing, he continued to glance around as if he couldn't believe the change, his gaze stopping on the candles gleaming and flickering, reflecting off the stemware. "I'll wash up," he said.

He seemed to take an unusually long time. I felt uneasy. Isaac came back, having showered and shaved. I served our favorite meal, straight out of the Southern soul-food memories of our childhood: pork chops, rice and gravy, turnip greens, and corn bread.

"Dessert?" I asked when he'd finished, not wanting to ruin the mood.

"You had time for dessert, too?"

"Yes, apple cobbler. I have a bushel of Sweet Hope apples from over at the Bailey orchards."

"Bring it on," he said. He cleaned his dessert dish. "Want to sit on the porch?" he added at last. "It's a beautiful night."

"It's a little cool, isn't it?"

"Not if we wrap up in your mother's quilt."

"Sure."

We sat in the old swing, both of us barely pushing it, looking out at the quarter moon and a scattering of stars above the mountains, taking in the stillness. I thought of past Daniels couples who'd sat in this same swing and had gone through their ups and downs on starry nights like this. I took a chance and leaned against him. He put an arm around me.

"So, what do you think, Isaac? About our chances?"

"We'll just *keep on keeping on* 'til the bank puts us out."

I smiled. Together we could survive anywhere.

In the bedroom, I put on a plum-colored teddy with spaghetti straps. I pulled back the covers and uncovered the fresh sheets. Isaac took one look at me and lit the candle I'd placed on the dresser.

A few days later, John Bigelow came by from the bank. I saw his car through the window as he opened the door. When that door closed, I trembled. Each step the man made was one closer to the end of this family farm. This was it, the day he'd tell us it was time to foreclose on the loan.

Though my fingers curled and uncurled in fists at the thought of what he'd come to tell me, I met him in the yard with a smile. "Hi, John. I'm glad you came to deliver the bad news yourself. Isaac and I appreciate it."

He winced. "Nancy, I'll come right to the point. As head of the bank, I've had to take into consideration the fact that you've been late on other loans."

I thought, *here it comes, the final notice.* "Look, John, I know it's not like the old days when the Bank of Bigelow did business on a handshake and let local farmers trade a load of vegetables for a mortgage payment. I understand."

He frowned. "No, you don't. I *want* the banking business to be like the old days. If I can't take a chance on good people like you and Isaac, then I don't deserve to be part of a community where people care about each other." He paused. "Besides," he said wryly, "if I don't give you a break, my wife will publish my picture in the *Gazette* with a head-line that says, *Local Publisher Estranged from Evil Bigelow Husband Again.*"

After a stunned moment, I burst out laughing. Then I hugged him and ran to the pumpkin field to tell Isaac.

❦❦❦

"Aunt Emma."

"Are you calling me to tell me good news?"

"It worked."

"Oh?"

"I'd been expecting Isaac to make all the changes, but it finally dawned on me that the only person I could change was myself. I had to *act as if* everything was going to be all right. That's what you were trying to tell me. That's what faith is all about, and being thankful for our blessings in the meantime."

"But what about your finances?"

"You won't believe this, but John Bigelow himself came out and talked to us." I told her the rest of the story.

"I'm so proud, my dear. I only ask one thing. That you pass my story on to others when you see the need."

"I promise."

After the phone call, I prepared a picnic lunch. I had plans for that hunk of a husband of mine. We still had other hurdles: gathering the pumpkins and getting them sold on time and one other issue, which I hadn't revealed. Isaac could handle the first, but the last . . .?

With the lunch and a quilt in the trunk of my car, I drove out to the fields. Isaac was busy repairing the tractor. I opened the car door. "Get in," I said.

He grinned. "I have work to do."

"It can wait, and it will."

He got in. I drove to a special place by a tiny creek at the edge of the woods. Autumn leaves drifted down on us. When I spread the quilt Isaac arched a brow.

"It's the middle of the day."

"Humor me."

He looked suspicious. "You're not softening me up for bad news, are you?" I flopped down on the quilt. He stretched out beside me, took my face between his hands, and eased his lips temptingly close to mine. Smiling he said, "Now tell me, or do I have to try other ways to get you to talk?"

I pressed my hands against his chest and looked up into his eyes. "We're going to have a baby."

He was silent for a long moment, then tears filled his eyes. He took my hand in his rough one and kissed it.

"So it's all right?" I asked softly.

"After the way I've acted lately, I'm just glad you still want to have a baby with me." He pulled me close. Very gently, he touched his lips to mine. "Thank you."

I grinned and silently gave thanks, too, for all our blessings.

Mossy Creek Gazette

VOLUME IV, No. 3   MOSSY CREEK, GEORGIA

The Bell Ringer

Birds & Babies

by Katie Bell

Tweedle Dee, Chief Royden's parakeet, will make a special guest appearance this week on "Cooking with Bubba Rice" on WMOS Cable. We've been assured that Tweedle Dee is not on the menu.

Hannah Longstreet announces the Mossy Creek Literary Society will host Casey Blackshear, who'll read stories at the weekly children's hour. I'm sworn to secrecy, but you heard it here, first: Casey and her husband, Dr. Hank Blackshear, DVM, have some very exciting news to announce.

In Mossy Creek, a family is where the love is,
no matter where the family starts.

👣👣👣👣👣👣👣👣👣👣👣👣👣👣👣👣👣👣👣👣👣👣👣👣👣👣👣👣👣👣👣👣👣👣👣

Lucky Girl

Chapter 13

When I was growing up with my doctor father, I never expected to be the wife of a country veterinarian. I was training for the Olympics as a softball player. But that didn't happen.

Instead, I'm in a wheelchair and there are many things I can't do. I'm Hank's part-time receptionist and bill collector. Even that isn't working. I end up reducing the bill. He doesn't complain. He's accepted our lot in life. I haven't. Hank tells me not to worry, but I know he's impatient with me because I'm not the determined person I once was. Since I helped our softball team beat Bigelow in the co-ed league, I've not strapped on my braces again. But when puppies or kittens are being delivered, Hank always calls.

Hank's Tree and Walker Hound, Belle, delivered her second litter of fat little hounds, now two weeks old and climbing over each other to find the freest flowing nipples. Their liver-colored speckles aren't there yet, but they will be by the time they're ready to be sold. Laying her head in my hand, Belle stretches out, allowing her babies more access to the dinner table. I think back a year ago to her first litter and feel an ache scissor through me. I was jealous of Belle for having babies when I couldn't.

Hank and I have been married for over four years and I

stopped taking birth control pills almost that long ago. I could live with not being able to walk but even though I'm paralyzed from the waist down, I never gave up on living a normal life. Not having children was a big void Hank and I wanted to fill.

"If it's meant to happen, babe, it will," Hank always said, as if it didn't matter. But he did care and so did I. That's why he gave in and went to the fertility specialists down in Atlanta. Neither of us wanted to confide our dilemma to my father. Dr. Chance Champion might keep secrets, but we didn't want to take a chance on his staff. It turns out that the specialists down in Atlanta couldn't give us answers. We ought to have children, but we don't seem to be able. We might blame my medical condition for that but the doctors didn't.

"We could adopt," Hank would say, unable to conceal the tightness in his voice.

"We could," I always agreed, but the possibility floated around in the air and never settled anywhere. Every time a four-footed patient whelped I felt the joy of new birth and the pain of having it withheld from us.

❦ ❦ ❦

It's almost lunch time today and Hank's heading over to Chinaberry to check a mule named Mason who conveniently becomes lame every year when it's time to pull the wheel that grinds the sorghum cane to make syrup at the annual Mossy Creek Harvest Festival. Hank's dad could probably have told the farmer the mule was faking but it took every reference book in the university library for Hank to realize that a mule needs a psychological approach rather than a medical one. Hank finally had a heart-to-heart talk with Mason and offered him a bribe. A half pint of moonshine at the end of the day in return for a split work session of two hours each. Hank mixed the moonshine in what he calls Mason's vitamin mixture and directed Mason's owner to administer the treatment.

"But be careful," Hank warned the farmer. "Don't let Mason anywhere around O'Day's Pub. He might decide to join happy hour."

My husband might have started out to be a veterinary surgeon in a research hospital, but James Herriott has nothing on him now. And, to his credit, he actually thinks it's fun, treating every kind of animal in north Georgia. That, or he's fooling me. With a final word of congratulations to Mama Belle and her new pups, I wheeled myself back to the clinic's front desk and checked my e-mail. I had a lot of free time so that, other than volunteering at the library and working with the girls' softball team, I'd become a secret chat room lurker, particularly those dealing with adoption. My first stop was the site dealing with the adoption of Chinese babies, mostly girls.

On the message board proud parents extolled the virtues of their round-faced, black-eyed little girls. After waiting for years, they told stories about being denied American children because they were single parents, too old to qualify, or there weren't enough babies to go around. These Chinese children didn't care and since there are more than 300,000 little girls abandoned every year, the Chinese government was happy to make adoption easy.

My heart went out to them and I wondered what Hank would say when I told him that I've contacted an agency, CCAI, Chinese Children Adoption International, for information.

Later that afternoon I drove my specially equipped van into the library parking area and operated all the levers and lifts to get my electric scooter and me to the pavement. I gave a wave to Dan McNeil, our local fix-it man, as I worked the throttle that gives my machine the juice to head up the ramp he built for me. There's even a sign naming the ramp the Casey Blackshear Bridge. So far, there aren't many other handicapped people in Mossy Creek, but there will be for our population is growing and our retirees are getting older.

Hannah Longstreet, the librarian, met me at the door with a smile. "You've got a crowd. What story are you reading today, Casey?"

Until this morning, I hadn't been sure. "*A Mother for Choco*," I said, driving my chair to the circle of children already waiting. From the carrying box Hank had attached to my scooter, I pulled out a soft-stuffed doll sporting shiny, black hair and big black eyes. "Good morning, children. This doll's name is *Ming*. Do you know where she came from?"

"Maggie Hart's store?" one child said.

"As a matter of fact, she did," I answered. "But I mean what *country*? We're Americans. But some of our ancestors are from other places. The original surveyors who laid out Mossy Creek came from England. Where did Ming's family live?"

A sea of confused faces finally brought an answer from Hannah. "China," she said.

"How do you think a little Chinese girl would feel coming to Mossy Creek to live with people who weren't like her?"

"She'd be sad," one child said.

It was time for my story.

"Not necessarily. Listen to the story of Choco, a little bird who lived all alone. He wished he had a mother. He went to look for her. Choco was just a baby; he didn't know he was a bird when he came upon a giraffe. Choco asked if the giraffe was his mother, the giraffe said, "No, I don't have wings like you." A walrus said, "No, you don't have striped feet," and the penguin said, "You don't have round cheeks." Choco was very sad. He was all alone and nobody wanted him. Until he came to the bear who listened to Choco's story. The mother bear took Choco home to meet her other children. Choco was surprised to find Hippy Hippopotamus, Ally Alligator and Piggy Pig. All the children rushed out to welcome their new brother. It didn't matter. They were all different."

Half the children wanted to check out the book, and the other half wanted to take the doll home for the week. When the youngsters had gone Hannah suggested that we get cups of hot tea at The Naked Bean, then sit in the gazebo in the middle of the square. Once settled, she gave me a puzzled look. "Now what was that all about? And don't tell me you were just reading a story. I saw the tears in the corner of your eyes."

I told her about the fertility clinic and that they'd found no reason why I hadn't gotten pregnant. "Normal adoption can take years and I'll be on the bottom of the list because I'm in a wheelchair. We . . . I've been thinking about alternatives."

"Alternatives?"

"Chinese babies." There, I'd finally said it. The rest came out in a rush. "Hank doesn't know anything about my idea but I've sent for information. You have to meet the same home study requirements that American adoptions require. There are mountains and mountains of paperwork to be filled out and notarized. The agency is in Colorado. They set everything up. A team goes with you to walk you through the process and get you back home with the baby. It's expensive but we can afford it. What do you think?"

"I think this is the first time in a long time I've seen you excited."

"Then you'll go with me?"

"To China?

"Yes. I'll pay your way," I promised.

"What about Hank?"

"He . . . he might not be able to get away. It's all right. It's not uncommon for friends, grandparents or other relatives to accompany the mother."

Hannah didn't look too sure, but she finally said, "I'll go if Hank can't."

And so it was decided. Fair-haired Hank and Casey Blackshear would take in an abandoned black-haired, black-eyed child. Just like Choco, the little girl would join the motherless group I had already collected. Now all I had to do was find a way to convince Hank.

As it turned out, by the time I got home Hank already knew. He was sitting at the kitchen table reading the CCAI folder and my correspondence when I came in. He knew I was there but for a long time he didn't look up from the tablet he held in his hand. Then, he said, "I see you've been busy. When were you going to share this with me?"

There was no smile, no recriminations, only a hurt expression. I overlooked the mud on my clean floor and the unmistakable odor of the pig pen emanating from Hank's boots and drove my scooter as close to the table as possible. "I was waiting for the right time. I didn't know what you'd say."

"When have I ever refused you, Casey?"

"When I wanted us to elope. Then after our automobile accident when I told you to go on to Angel Memorial to do your residency and leave me in the hospital. Then when I wanted you to sell your father's clinic. Hank, I know this adoption is a wild idea. I . . . I sent for the details. Just forget about it."

"Casey, I can't say that this excites me. Maybe when I have had time to get used to the idea I'll feel differently. But I love you and I want a child as much as you. So, get over here, and look at this."

I swallowed hard and took the paper he was holding out. He'd drawn an extension onto our house labeling it baby's room. Everything penciled in was child height — which coincidentally was perfect for me. He smiled. "What do you think? It's either this or use one of the inside kennels. And I don't know how to make them wheelchair accessible."

"Oh, Hank. Are you sure? I mean it's going to be expensive. I have to go to China to get her and she'll be different and . . ."

"*We'll* have to go to China," he said, cupping my cheeks in his big rough hands. "We never had a honeymoon, did we? I don't think I would have chosen China, but why not? And why on earth would you ever think we'd be ordinary? I'm a trained small animal surgeon knee-deep in the mud while I'm learning how to deal with large animals, and you're an Olympic athlete in a wheelchair who coaches a softball team. I'll start on the nursery and you start on the paper-work."

🐾🐾🐾

A small picture came of our daughter. Her face was covered with blotches, said to be chicken pox, and she was crying. Her name was *Li Hai Kui*. The agency said that she belonged to us, if we would accept her. How could we not? She was the most beautiful thing I'd ever seen. I looked at her and remembered Ellie Brady's philosophy in asking her husband, Ed, to bring her an 'ugly' Christmas tree each year. She said something that many of us in Mossy Creek took to heart: "Everything is beautiful when it's loved."

I didn't know how the town would feel about our plan but Hank was determined to involve them. "It takes a village to raise a child," he said. The baby girl's picture was published in the *Gazette*. Before Li Hai Kui Blackshear ever arrived, her family name, *Li* became her first name, and she'd been adopted by the entire town. O'Day's Pub had the official calendar which marked off the days until Li came home.

❦❦❦

We disembarked from a 747 in Hong Kong where we'd spend the night, then take a smaller plane to the airport in a city named *Guangzhou*. I was grateful that Hank had arranged for a friend to fill in at the clinic, though I knew it meant a drop in our income. Getting me around China would have been impossible were it not for a couple of men in our group who insisted on hoisting my motorized wheelchair when there were no ramps. The adoption agency arranges for several sets of parents to travel to China together. I was afraid Hank still had reservations about our adopting a Chinese baby, and I loved him even more for being with me.

While the other fourteen mothers, fathers, friends, grandparents and children in our group went out to eat that night, Hank took me to our hotel and ordered dinner brought to our room. We ate at a small table near the window and looked out at the most colorful panorama of people, lights and signs either of us had ever seen. I was too tired and too excited to sleep.

If New York was America's 'town that never sleeps,' Hong Kong had to be China's. I thought about Mossy Creek and our peaceful life there and wondered what had ever made me think I could do this. Now, over 7,000 miles from Mossy Creek, the small town that nurtured all who came, I allowed myself to acknowledge my fear. Could *I do this? Could I be a good mother to a tiny stranger?*

The next morning, a small silver plane with propellers that Hank swore operated on wind-up power took us to *Guangzhou*. We were then driven to a hotel near Li's orphanage. Our child would be delivered to our room where we would exchange the clothing she was wearing with what we'd brought. A final acceptance would be verbalized and we'd be responsible for a child we'd never seen before.

Nerves shortened my temper and I snapped at Hank. He didn't respond. Instead, as we waited he turned on the television and found a local news station with subtitles. He watched for a moment, then turned it off. The news in Chinese just didn't work.

"How can you be so calm?" I asked.

"You're jumpy enough for both of us," he said.

My heart seemed to twist. I'd pushed him into this. He didn't want to be here. He didn't want this child. A tightness welled up in my throat and I fought to breathe. Even after our automobile accident, when I learned that I'd never walk again, I'd never felt such pain.

The phone rang. One of our Chinese guides. "The babies have arrived. You must stay in your room. Your baby will be brought to you."

In the silence I heard the elevator open and a child crying. The sound of footsteps in the hallway paused and moved on. A door opened and the excited voices of the couple next door filtered out into the silence. One by one, the girls were delivered. Hank pulled the camera from his knapsack and waited by the door.

Finally, the footsteps stopped outside our room. There was a knock. I waited as Hank opened the door. This stalwart of strength on which I'd built this dream seemed frozen. Finally, I wheeled myself to the door and pushed him aside. A tiny wizard of a woman, identified as a nanny, looked at me and down at my motorized vehicle with shock in her eyes. She turned back to the man behind her. He nodded. Even I could recognize the reluctance with which she stepped inside and held out the pink bundle she was holding. I took it, searching for the baby within.

Every inch of the baby was covered except her small round face, which squinched up as she let out a wail of displeasure. I heard the click of the camera. Hank was making pictures.

"You must give back the clothing," the official explained as if I didn't know. "They will use it over and over again for the children they are giving to the new parents. You will have this afternoon with the baby, then we start on the paperwork. In the meantime, if you need me, we'll be in the business office downstairs. Do you understand?"

"Oh, yes!" I held the squirming child in one arm and guided my wheelchair to the bed. I hadn't counted on a fight with our new daughter, but she had no intention of making it easy on me. If I bonded with her, it would be up to me. So far, Hank hadn't moved. Finally I managed to remove the snow suit bunny outfit she was wearing, pulling back the hood to discover a mass of thick black hair. By the time I'd uncovered her totally, she had held her breath until she was a shade of pink somewhere between a tomato and a half-ripe watermelon.

"Hank? Could you help me, please? Hank!"

Finally, he walked toward us. Looming over the child, he whispered her name. Even now, I can't describe the sudden calm that swept over the room. Li stopped crying. She looked up at him and held out our arms. "BaBa?" she said, hiccuping as she repeated the word *daddy* in Chinese.

From that moment on, Hank was *BaBa* and she belonged to him, whether he wanted her to or not. Li let it be known right away that I would be tolerated so long as I kept my distance. "Don't worry, Casey," Hank said, allowing a rare weariness to creep into his voice. "She'll adjust."

I said yes, but I didn't believe him. For the next two weeks we visited one government office after another. Our papers were examined and accepted. Gifts were exchanged and Li was issued a birth certificate. We promised that we would never abandon the child we'd already come to love. Hank looked very unconcerned when the Chinese doctor gave her less of an examination than he would have given a new pup and pronounced her "*Well baby.*"

Hank said all the right things, joined in the conversations with the other American fathers and grandfathers discussing their worries and their plans, but in the night I'd hear him wake and walk to the window. He either paced or stood in the solitude like a sentry waiting for the sound of the approaching enemy.

Had I pushed him into something he was having second thoughts about? Was I being fair to this child I'd already taken into my heart? What if I couldn't keep up with her? What would she think when she was old enough to know that one day I could be her responsibility just as she would soon be mine? I didn't dare ask Hank, and I felt the constant pressure of the obsession of my longing.

Car seats adjust. Interest rates adjust. But my Chinese daughter showed no signs of doing so. As independent as I was in Mossy Creek, operating on my own in China was a different thing. Hong Kong might have been wealthy enough to provide handicapped access, but in *Guangzhou* the sidewalks were uneven and many of the shops were simply holes in the wall with the door opening off the steps leading to the next level.

Hank suddenly had two dependent children instead of one. Finally Hank put away the stroller and transferred Li to a *Snuggly* which attached her to his chest and satisfied her totally. It was *me* who cried, but I didn't let the others know. I pretended that everything was fine.

Li had no intention of doing that. She cried and refused everything but the rice formula she'd been accustomed to,

fought the clothing I'd brought for her. That I could understand for I'd badly misjudged her size. We used our bonding
time to shop for food and souvenirs that we would put away
for her as memories as an adult. The local shop women al-
ternated between admonishing us for not bundling up our
child in the layers the local children wore and patting Li on
the head as they murmured, *lucky girl.*

It was me who couldn't sleep then. *Me* who swung herself into her chair and rolled herself to the window where I
watched the movement and sound of the traffic die for the
night. Me who cried silently at the sight of Hank's big hand
stretched through the slats of the crib furnished by the hotel so that our daughter could touch him. I was jealous. I
hurt. But I kept it to myself, telling Hank that it would change
when we got home. The literature had warned us about this,
so I tried not to let it bother me.

A week later we were back in Mossy Creek but nothing
changed. Li cried for Hank every time he left the room. I fed
her, changed her, sang to her. I talked to her. I showed her
every musical toy and stuffed animal we'd bought. Eventually she'd stop crying, but I could tell she was simply waiting.

Finally Hannah came to visit, bringing her six-year-old
daughter, Rachel. Rachel had always looked on me as her
second mama and when *she* was rebuffed by Li, she crawled
up into my lap and stared at this strange cold child who was
nothing like Choco, the bird who'd been looking for his
mother.

"What's wrong with her?" Rachel asked.

"She's just afraid," Hannah answered. "She doesn't understand English. We're all strangers. We have to be patient."

It was then that I realized it was up to me. I couldn't
force Li to love me, but I could make her *want* to. If she
wouldn't let me show her my love, I'd show her that some-

one else would take it.

"Rachel, Hank's Tree and Walker Hound, Belle, has a new litter of puppies in the kennel. Do you want to see them?"

Eagerly she agreed. With a nod, Hannah watched her daughter, Rachel, and me head for the clinic. Rachel chattered all the way down the sidewalk, laughing at the antics of Ed Brady's hound, Possum, who'd come to visit. Inside the kennel, Hank had set up a play area for his boarders. Belle and the puppies were sleeping on a mat in the middle. In no time, Rachel was sitting inside with the pups crawling all over her. And I was inside the play area in my chair.

In the house behind me, I heard Li began to cry, but I didn't respond as I'd done for the three weeks. It hurt, but I stayed with Rachel. Soon, I heard footsteps and Hannah's voice. "Look, Li. Puppies. Do you want to play with the puppies, Li?"

Hannah was answered by a loud wail. Hannah didn't respond and neither did I. If Li wanted to join us, it was up to her. Rachel picked up one of the babies and held it out to Li. When Li made no move to respond, Rachel shrugged and offered it to me. I took the pup and arranged him in my lap, where he rolled over on his back and closed his eyes.

Rachel laughed and started singing her own version of *Old McDonald Had a Farm*.

Except it became Doctor Hank's farm and the animal became a dog. By the second chorus of *with a woof, woof here and a woof, woof there*, I sensed movement. Hannah stepped inside the play area, lowering Li to the floor near my wheelchair. The pull of the puppies and perhaps a tinge of jealousy finally reached Li. I held out my arms and she tottered to me.

I was overjoyed. Tears streamed down my cheeks. Li sat on my lap. The pup licked her cheek and she looked up at me and laughed.

"Come, Rachel," Hannah said. "We have to get back to town."

"No, don't go," I panicked.

"You can do this, Casey. You went around the world to get your baby and you'll manage. Mighty Casey won't strike out."

"But . . . but suppose she gets away from me. She's already walking."

"Just pretend she's Possum," Hannah said, snapping the hook of a leash into the clip on Li's suspenders and handing the handle to me.

"Look, Li," I said. "Babies."

Suddenly Toes, the clinic cat, so named because he had only two toes on one foot, hopped onto the rail and into the pen. He jumped up on my knees, sniffed Li's face, then rubbed against her. Finally, the cat jumped back over the rail and headed to the house, stopping to turn back and meow. Belle gave him a lazy look, eyed the open door to the pen and lumbered to her feet. I started to call her back then, thought better of it and fell in line.

Toes marched down the walk between the clinic and the house, leading his procession, me in the wheelchair holding Li and two of the pups, Belle and the other three babies through the kitchen and into the bedroom. Once there, Toes jumped into Li's crib and turned back to me with a curt meow. I didn't have to speak cat to know he was asking me what I was waiting for. I let down the side of the crib and lifted Li inside, then piled the pups around her. Belle stood watching. But that wasn't enough. Toes continued to call. It was obvious there was no room for me and Belle in the crib. I backed my chair away and pulled the baby bed from the wall. From behind, I pushed the crib toward our bed until they touched.

I wheeled my chair close but neither Li nor Toes was having any part of that. I had to get on the bed. Finally, I loosened the braces on my legs and moved my feet to the floor. With awkward movements, I managed to stand and throw myself to the bed where Li, Toes and the pups were tumbling against the pillows. Belle lay down with a deep sigh, content to let the cat look after her litter.

My mind went back to that day at the library when I read the story of the baby bird looking for a mother. Choco found his place with outsiders, just as the pups were accepted by a cat. Li, the pups, the cat and I were laughing so loudly that we didn't hear the outside door open.

"Casey?"

At the sound of Hank's voice, Li turned and laughed. "*BeBe?*"

Hank sat on the bed beside me. "No," he said, shook his head and pulled Li between us. He put Li's hand over his heart. "*BaBa.*" He put her hand over my heart. "*Ma,*" he said. And finally, he took Li's hand and my hand and laid them on *her* heart. "*Li.*"

Then he let go. Li touched Hank. Hank watched, not responding until a puppy crawled into my lap and licked my chin. Li smiled and copied the pup, then whispered shyly, "BaMa."

That was the beginning. Between Belle, Possum, Toes and the litter of pups which we still have, I've learned to use my crutches and my braces. But I still prefer the chair when dealing with Li. I've started a new exercise regime. I'm going to have to learn to cope, either that or hitch my children up to a buggy and let them pull me along. Hank doesn't know it yet but we're going back to China. This time, the shopkeepers may pat Li on the head, but I'll know that I'm the *lucky girl.*

Some blessings will turn you every which way but loose.

🌿🌿🌿🌿🌿🌿🌿🌿🌿🌿🌿🌿🌿🌿🌿🌿🌿🌿🌿🌿🌿🌿🌿🌿🌿🌿🌿🌿🌿🌿🌿🌿🌿🌿

Amos & Ida Have a Moment

Chapter 14

Being the son of Battle Royden meant I'd spent most of my life between *a rock and a hard case*. By turns he was a law enforcement legend, a good ol' boy, a philanderer, an unrepentant practical joker, trustworthy (outside marriage), forgiving (if you weren't his son or on the wrong side of his badge that day), and predictable. In life and in death. That's why I carried a battered green umbrella as I trekked out to Battle's grave for another of my dutiful-son visits. The temperature was chilly; there wasn't a cloud in the sky, but before today's visit was done, I'd need the umbrella. Always did.

The consistently ill-timed rain during my visits to my parents' graves felt a lot like one of Battle's little practical jokes, except that I liked rain. Always had. I couldn't quite see Battle providing rain as reward. That just wasn't his style.

Well, son, they say death changes a person.

I heard Battle's voice so clearly I almost laughed aloud. I'd forgotten he could be genuinely funny and completely pragmatic in the same sentence. Bits and pieces of *Battle wisdom* kept floating through my mind these days as I followed in his footsteps as chief. I found myself wishing we'd had the time to forgive each other. For what I wasn't sure.

But since I didn't have a therapist, I didn't have to dwell on that little revelation. Dwelling would mean I'd have to consider whether I'd been as much to blame as my father for our strained relationship. Why on earth would I want to dwell? Nope. Better to let sleeping dogs lie.

Besides, I had places to go, a parakeet to feed, and law breakers to catch. Even without the threat of rain, I had a full day and a fair-sized hike up the hillside to the old Baptist cemetery. Most of the founding families of Mossy Creek had kinfolk planted there. You'd be hard pressed to find a plastic flower or fancy stone angel.

Below was a smorgasbord of slick granite, fake flowers and statues, but not here on the big hill. The big hill took death seriously. Big hill families believed in the legacy you left behind, not in monuments. If you went far enough into the woods you'd find headstones that had long since lost their lettering. Some aren't much more than a round-cornered brick sunk into the ground next to a tree you knew good-an'-well hadn't been there when the grave was dug.

I didn't go into the woods. I stopped beside the familiar graves just inside the boundary of the big hill, beside two rose granite stones with crisp lettering, and wondered what my parents thought of their legacy. Silence suddenly surrounded me. I wasn't sure how one part of a cemetery could be quieter than another, but the old part was. A quiet so loud you could hear it.

Momma had always preferred the quiet. So why she had married a man who filled a room and boomed his sentences was something of a mystery. Battle's voice had been a lot like a distant roll of thunder. He'd ask Momma to pass the salt, and you could hear him from the other end of the house.

SARA ELIZABETH ROYDEN	BATTLE SAMUEL ROYDEN
BELOVED WIFE AND MOTHER	MOSSY CREEK'S FINEST

Funny how Momma's epitaph was private and Battle's was public. Fitting, though. Momma belonged to us and

Battle belonged to everyone else — a true public servant, like Mayor Ida Hamilton Walker. Although Ida somehow managed to hold her family closer than the town. Certainly closer than Battle had.

The second and closer grumble of thunder jolted me out of my thoughts because it came accompanied by a fe-male voice. "Neither rain nor sleet nor snow nor dark of night shall stay our police chief from his appointed rounds."

The mayor was smiling at her own humor when I turned around. I'd been so wrapped up in the past, I hadn't heard her. That bothered me. I usually had special radar for the woman, but she'd slipped past today. Seemed mighty pleased about it, too. Ida is never scarier than when she's pleased. Makes for an interesting working relationship.

"Afternoon, Ida."

"Afternoon, Amos."

She looked like she'd just come from a bout of garden-ing — plain red sweater, her jeans faintly grass-stained at the knees, her auburn hair pulled back in a haphazard fash-ion as if she didn't mind offering up her face to the scrutiny of the world. Lots of people in Mossy Creek envied Ida's strong sense of self. Women mostly envied the fact that a woman with a long-grown child could still wear a real bath-ing suit in public if she chose. The men mostly envied the power and influence Ida seemed to accumulate naturally.

Me . . . I enjoy the whole package. Not that I've told her, not in so many words. She is the mayor, my boss, an older woman and dating someone else. Any one reason was more than enough to make a man pause before saying something stupid. Hell, Ida'd give any man with half a brain pause just because she's Ida.

Today, even scruffy, she managed to look like a woman who could take on the world. That always set off some warn-ing lights in the back of my mind. I had personal experience with the crusading side of Ida's personality. I'd had to arrest her once or twice for taking on the world without a permit. Not that she held it against me. Ida enjoys a good argument now and then. She hates to lose, but she doesn't expect to win them all either. She's fair-minded.

And closed-mouthed. We'd fallen into the habit of trying to out-wait each other in conversation. Ida was just beginning to realize I wasn't the tame town chief, but she wasn't sure how she felt about that. So, we waited. She carried a cluster of flowers in her hand — red and sort of fluffy. I didn't recognize the variety, but I knew for whom the tribute was intended. Jeb. The husband she'd lost years ago. Even in death, he was a lucky man.

I nodded toward the flowers and spoke first. "Special occasion?"

She hesitated a moment too long and looked a bit too *caught.* "Not . . . really."

My cop intuition kicked in, and when that happens my eyebrow lifts all on its own. I can't control it. My eyebrow lifts. So, I stared. Ida caved.

"All right, I can see I've got about as much chance of skirting the truth with you as I did with Battle. What is it about you Royden men?" She adjusted the flowers gently, holding them up for a better inspection. "This is a peace offering. Anytime Jeb wanted to get around me about something, he always brought flowers."

"Flowers never hurt."

Ida smiled, memories obviously tugging at her. "That was his philosophy. So anytime I'd like his blessing, I bring flowers."

Blessing?

I gritted my teeth and stared again. Staring is more polite than swearing. *Jeb Walker's blessing?* My mind immediately focused on Del Jackson, the man the whole town watched at Ida's side on a regular basis. The man I thought she'd been casually dating. My competition. And Ida wanted Jeb's blessing.

An invisible Battle snorted with disgust. *Your competition? Not hardly. Boy, you never got in the game.* I did my level best to keep my features completely immobile and my jaw firmly clamped. As usual, Battle's advice was a day late and a dollar short. The fact that he was probably right irritated me, but what I was supposed to have done about Ida was beyond me. I'm not quite sure of the proper etiquette for seducing your boss while she's dating another man.

That uncertainty wouldn't have been a problem for Battle. He ever let etiquette get in his way when he saw a woman he wanted.

"Amos? You okay?"

"What? Oh, yeah. Just great." I lied well. Battle would be proud of that at least. "Flowers made me remember Sandy's birthday. Day after next. She loves those." I had no idea what *those* were.

"Come on by the house early that day and cut some out of the side flower bed before the frost gets them."

"Will do." They were red. Surely I could figure it out when I got there without having to ask. How many red flowers could she have in one bed?

We stood there for a moment, not much else to say unless one of us was willing to step over that line we'd drawn between us, the one that kept us safe from mistakes but didn't rule out the possibility. If she'd sounded at all uncertain about asking for Jeb's blessing I would have at least stepped on that line. But she hadn't, and I didn't.

Thunder rumbled closer. I checked the sky and offered the umbrella to her. She still had the trip to the graveside to make. "If I sprint, I can beat the rain to the car."

"Thank you. I'll take it. I'm not proud." At my inelegant

snort, she snatched the umbrella and amended, "At least not when it comes to umbrellas."

I wisely said nothing and headed for the Jeep.

❦ ❦ ❦

Almost.

I almost had them. My messages. Sandy, our dispatch and newest fully accredited officer on the Mossy Creek police department, waved the pink slips at me as I came in the station's front door. I swung instantly toward her, toward the counter that divides the public area from the dispatch and office sections. As soon as I extended my hand, she impaled the messages on one of those deadly spikes.

"Nothing worth your time, Chief." She gave her badge a little cuff-shine. I'm not sure she was even aware of the proud motion or my urge to choke her.

"Opal called to see if we'd heard anything on those Hispanic kids she's taken in. I've told her a dozen times, we'd call her the instant we heard anything. I swear, it's like she doesn't trust us."

I shook my head. For once I had an explanation before Sandy. "I think she's calling because the boy's asking."

Sandy's mouth rounded. "Oh. You mean he hasn't figured out yet that no one's going to be able to trace his grandmother in Mexico."

"Right. Soon enough, he'll figure it out. The calls will stop."

"Okay. Makes sense. Next — Dwight called and said that if Ida was too busy to come to the council meeting then he was just calling it off. Seemed a bit put out."

I'd already started turning away, but that announcement swung me right back to her. Like a bird dog on point. Dwight Truman lived for his position as the chairman of the council. "Dwight is blowing off a council meeting? It's budget time.

293

He loves budget. Especially when he gets to pick apart *my* budget requests. Tonight's my turn. I planned to spend the whole afternoon going over those numbers."

"I know." She smiled like someone offering a gift. "Now you're saved. You can thank Miss Ida. It's because of the bike the town gave him."

Sometimes you just had to give your head a good shake to clear out the jumble and start over when talking to Sandy. "Ida can't make the meeting and Dwight's ticked off. But he really canceled because of the bike?"

Sandy nodded and settled down behind her desk with a dangerously full, brown bag lunch. "That's right."

I edged toward my office, never taking my eye off the brown bag. Since she'd been promoted to officer, Jess — her husband the writer — thought it a good idea to pack her a lunch and include a poem each day. Sometimes he sent two. Poems, that is. He heard that officers who have loved ones take fewer chances in dangerous situations.

Jess didn't want Sandy forgetting she had a loved one.

No one who'd been a victim of those lunches could forget that Sandy had a loved one. You see, Sandy's so proud of Jess, she wants to share the poems. Out loud. The boys and I try to get out of range before Sandy remembers to share. To say we scatter like doves in a belfry at Sunday noon is only a slight exaggeration.

Jess is a really bad poet and blind to the fact we don't have much bonafide danger in Mossy Creek to threaten Sandy. And he's completely off base about our love of haiku. We have none.

Gentle stream awaits
Hopeful spirit flying free
When next we shop there

Trust me. That's at least as good as anything Jess has actually written. We've learned to run or keep mirrored sunglasses handy so Sandy can't see us roll our eyes. We wouldn't want to hurt her feelings when she's so proud of him.

I froze as she opened the bag, but then she looked up, completely oblivious to the terror her lunch inspired. "Dwight's got a bike race coming up. He's supposed to have a decent chance, too. He's been training for weeks now."

"Training?"

"With weights and everything apparently. Katie Bell says several women of the town have been stunned to realize that the wiry but buff biker on the trails is our very own Dwight."

Wiry but buff? I was stunned, too. And maybe just a bit nauseous at the thought of unnaturally pale Dwight riding shirtless. An unwanted image formed — all ears, elbows, reflective white skin, and three chest hairs. "He's blowing off the council meeting to train for a bike race."

"Right." She reached into her bag and I realized I was suddenly rooting for a poem — to take my mind off buff Dwight. All she came up with was a peach. "Oh, yeah. Two more things, Chief. Tweedle's out in your office and Jayne dropped by the sandwich you ordered."

"What?" Poem and Dwight were both forgotten in a heartbeat. "You left a defenseless sandwich in my office with Attila-the-parakeet?"

What might have been a grin creased Sandy's mouth as she sank teeth in her peach. I didn't wait to be sure. I sprinted for my office, slowing down only long enough to ease the door open. I didn't want a repeat of the day Tweedle exited my office for the wide-open spaces of Sandy's domain. You do not know embarrassment until you find a sign in the window of your police station that says, "Come back tomorrow. The chief will have caught Tweedle by then."

Sometimes I wished Sandy wasn't so helpful.

I made my entrance into my office without incident and closed the door behind me. Tweedle walked back and forth on the edge of my desk as if debating his opening remarks. Not an apology, I was sure, despite the fact that the wrapping of my BLT was shredded, the bread chewed, bacon crumbled, and the lettuce meticulously extracted.

"That was not your sandwich."

He gave me several annoyed chirps as if to say, "What's mine is mine and what's yours is ours. And where have you been all morning?" Then he flew to my shoulder and pecked at my earlobe. His previous owner was female. Tweedle remained convinced I was playing *hide the earring* and refused to give up the hunt. At least that was my story and I was sticking with it. Otherwise, I'd have to admit that my 'keet greeted me with little ear nibble-kisses.

I mean, I have my manly pride. Or I did.

My macho image took a blow over the whole "Dog Incident." All I did was take care of a homeless dog and then, after I'd gotten attached, gave that same dog to a troubled boy I'd pulled out of a bad situation and who needed Dog more than me. Simple logic really. But not to the women in town.

Lord! Old women sighed indulgently and patted my arm when they saw me in the grocery store. Told me I was "a good man." The teenage girls batted their eyes and that was worse.

I blamed Patty Campbell, surrogate sister and wife of my best friend. They'd taken in Clay — the troubled boy — as a foster child, and I'm sure she told everyone in town the story of Dog's transfer. Clay and Dog live with Patty and Mac and their two Labradors now. The boy's adoption is only a formality. I've become "Uncle Amos" and "a good man."

As if I didn't have enough trouble with women before.

And then I'd inherited the town's most famous avian

citizen. Everyone loved Tweedle, fabled hero of Laurie Grey's story time at The Naked Bean. Everyone had loved Laurie,, too. She'd come to Mossy Creek to quietly fade away, but Mossy Creek wouldn't have it. They couldn't stop illness from finally claiming Laurie's life, but they damned sure put a stop to the fading. Laurie and her bird became full-blown Creekite characters.

Tweedle nuzzled again. This time running his beak through my hair. "Stop that."

I reached a hand up for a new perch. He hopped on. Bringing him to the office was good for his spirits since he had people around most of the day, but not so good for my work schedule. Birds were demanding little critters. I looked at him and made a deal. "I'll put on that Celtic CD your momma made for you if you let me alone long enough to check the budget. Deal?"

Cht cht cht.

He flew onto the CD player. As soon as I hit play, he began gently poking at the speaker with his beak until the oddly soothing sounds of the Irish whistle spilled out in the office. I cleaned up the mess that was my sandwich, settled down to my budget and hardly noticed Tweedle again until an hour later when he began to play tug of war with my pen.

Have you ever tried staring down a 'keet practically hand-raised by a human and who has no fear? It doesn't work. He'd firmly transferred his affection from Laurie to me. I was his person. He need have no fear. Except when it came to cleaning and lining his cage. Tweedle didn't trust me one bit about that. Not anymore. I put the Sunday comics in once. The ones with the pretty pictures all in color.

While I was peeling a shrieking Tweedle off the roof of his cage, I realized that birds don't like color comics. They don't like anything on their newsprint except . . . news. And plenty of it. No two-color ads. Not even faint bits of red showing through from the other side.

Everything about Tweedle was trial and error. Laurie did not leave an owner's manual. Probably on purpose. That girl had an odd sense of humor at times. Like teaching Tweedle to say, "Who's a pretty cop?" before she died.

The intercom crackled. "Chief? Win Allen's on the phone."

Tweedle hated the intercom. He ruffled and did a *cht cht cht* scold at it for all he was worth. That bird can achieve some volume. To settle him, I gave Tweedle the pen and grabbed the receiver. "Hello, Win. What can I do for you?"

"I need a favor."

"Shoot."

Before he could answer, the most godawful racket roared through the connection. A couple of shouts, clattering, the sound of a flapping blanket. Then silence and then one more loud crash.

"Win! Win! You there? You all right? What's happening?"

Someone scrambled for the phone and hollered. "Yeah! I think so. Geez, Amos. I think that Clifford the Idiot Clown just blew up a kiddie science experiment."

"Clifford the Idiot Clown?"

"Look. I'll explain later. If you can drop by the WMOS studio before you go home, I'd appreciate it. Right now I gotta go sort this out. If he put so much as a dent or a scorch in the Bubba Rice kitchen set I'm going to pull off his stupid red nose and feed it to Bert Lyman with some fava beans."

Click.

I hung up the phone and told Tweedle, "Looks like trouble in River City. The budget's about done anyway. I'd better make sure Win doesn't do anything stupid to Clifford the Idiot Clown. Whoever Clifford is. And I'm sure that feeding your station manager a clown's nose is bound to have unpleasant job-related consequences." I deposited Tweedle back in his cage and headed for the door after asking Sandy to be sure Tweedle was settled for the night when she left.

❧ ❧ ❧

WMOS wasn't impressive. Bert Lyman ran the station with his wife, Honey, and some jumbled-together equipment in a renovated barn. Nevertheless, Mossy Creek was proud to have its own radio and cable station. There was already talk of syndicating Win Allen's alter-ego — Bubba Rice. His down-home-redneck-real-men-do-cook show was getting great reviews, and more importantly — steady advertisers.

I parked the Jeep along the edge of the gravel circle out front and wandered up to a door set in an obviously new addition to the barn. Before opening the door, I read the warning sign and double-checked the red light hanging off the roof. If the light was on that meant visitors should stop and wait before coming in. The light was off, so I hauled open the door.

Honey must have seen me from her office door. She came out into a tiny reception area to greet me, wearing what could only be described as guerilla fashion. She was either so far ahead of the curve that mere mortals couldn't understand her chic or so far behind the curve that she'd never catch up. Head to toe, she was encased in brown. Brown hair, brown eye makeup, brown earrings, sweater, pants, shoes, nail polish. She was a wall of brown.

"Amos! Oh! I guess I should call you Chief, seeing as how you're in uniform."

"Amos'll do just fine, Honey. I'm here to see Win."

She looked stricken. "Not with bad news I hope. He's threatened to quit once today already. He and Clifford aren't hitting it off."

I smiled. "I heard something about that. I was hoping to get here before any bodily damage was done."

"Oh, in that case, you go right on out through that door. Knock some sense into Win. He's convinced the clown's out to get his time slot."

I couldn't help laughing. "Paranoid, is he?"

"Well . . . no. The clown is out to get his time slot."

That made me laugh harder. Honey grinned as well. "See? It's a problem." She waved me on and went back into her office, which looked more like a sound and control room now that I could see into the space.

I was still chuckling when I wandered into the taping area. Equipment was strung everywhere, connected by ropes of electrical cords. Various modular show sets were on rolling platforms and pushed against the walls. An obnoxiously bright green stage was front and center at the moment. Yellow and blue circles made random splashes against the backdrop. A table with a charred black hole in it sat off to one side. Beside the table a pink and purple clown practiced juggling apples while spinning a hoop on his foot. One sleeve had a telltale char mark.

Win wandered over to stand beside me. He caught my expression and then looked back to the stage. "I know. It's a travesty. They'll let anyone with a few cans of paint, a box of matches, and three apples be a clown these days. No standards whatsoever."

I swiveled, amused at Win's viewpoint. "As opposed to the standards for cooking show hosts? I hear all you need to get a cooking show is to have one of those funny hats."

"Bubba Rice wouldn't be caught dead in one of those hats."

"I've seen your show. There isn't much Bubba Rice wouldn't do if it got a laugh and kept the advertisers happy."

Win didn't argue. "True. I'm a slave to my art form, which brings me to my favor."

I stopped him with upraised hands and tried to appear

serious. "Fair warning, Win. I can't look the other way when you kill the clown. Celebrities don't get special treatment in this town. I'll have to take you in just like Ida."

He huffed a laugh and pulled me further away from the practicing clown. "If you help me out now it won't come to that. Listen, Bert is all bent out of shape about that new kiddie-entertainment park someone's putting in over near Bailey Mill."

"Entertainment park?" My eyebrows hit my hairline before they stopped rising. "Does everyone in town know everything before I do?"

"It's been real hush-hush from what I heard. Land deal was supposed to close today. Katie Bell bird-dogged it out and gave the news to Bert." Win kicked a cable out of his way and reset his feet. "That's the only reason I know any of this. Bert's acting like someone's done this on purpose to ruin his plans to dominate children's programming. If the kids are all over there racing go-carts and putt-putting, no one will be home to watch WMOS Super Saturdays. No viewers means no advertisers."

"Bert sees all that advertising going over to Bigelow."

"Yep."

I never ceased to be amazed at the grandiose plans of some Creekites. "Bert actually thinks he can build programming that'll beat Bigelow stations? Forget that. Doesn't the man know that every major network devotes Saturday mornings to kids? Hasn't he heard of the Cartoon Channel?"

Win shrugged. "What can I tell you? He's not actually delusional, but he does see himself building an entertainment empire. This developer is well financed and raining on his parade. According to Katie, they're set to level the biggest tree tomorrow and start prepping the site. In Bert's mind, the park is the fly in the ointment. Not Bigelow or the networks. Bert's reacting to the threat he sees."

"Poor Bert."

"Poor Bert nothin'! Save the pity for me. I'm the one who's going to lose in all this mess. My Saturday ten a.m. time slot is prime time around here. Never mind that I've spent weeks building that time slot. Or that we have actual advertisers for the show. Bert wants me to jazz it up somehow or the clown gets the slot."

I couldn't resist. I'm an evil person. "Maybe you could cook in a clown suit? And I've seen you set things on fire."

Win's withering look spoke volumes about his appreciation of my joke. "No. And if you're through having fun at my expense?" He waited; I dialed down the grin and nodded for him to continue. "Okay, then I've got an idea. That's why I need the favor. I'm thinking if I get a celebrity to host with me that more kids may watch. I can even throw in a kids-in-the-kitchen recipe every now and then." He looked at me speculatively. "The key is the celebrity."

"Whoa, Win. Stop right there. I know I'm a pretty visible guy and popular with the kids, but I'm no celebrity. I don't —"

"Not you, Amos. Geez! Tweedle. What do you think?"

"Tweedle!"

"Tweedle."

I didn't *want* to be a celebrity on a cooking show, but that was beside the point. Everyone likes to be asked. Win didn't notice the fact that I was underwhelmed and recovering from being dumped in favor of a feathered nitwit. He patiently waited for me to tell him what I thought.

I thought I might wring my bird's neck.

"Amos, it's a natural. Kids have loved that bird since Laurie Grey's story time at The Naked Bean. We tape several shows at once. It's not like you'd have to drag him over here all the time. The beauty of this is that the bird won't talk much, so I'd still have control of my show." He beamed.

"No worries about the co-host taking over."

I snorted. "The bird can talk a blue streak when he wants — mostly inappropriate phrases or his name — and you have no idea how easily Tweedle can take over. He's like Sherman's march to the sea. But it's your funeral. Let me think about it, and I'll give you a call."

Win rubbed his hands together, confident he had a *bird in the hand* and moving on to his next plan. That's when I decided the clown had better watch his back.

🐾🐾🐾

A mile down the road from the station, I pulled to the side of the road and slammed on my brakes. Then I slammed the flat of my hand against the steering wheel. A horrible suspicion had taken shape suddenly, nurtured by the day's experiences.

"Oh, Ida. You are a first-class piece of work."

I shook my head, trying to do the math and make it add up to anything but Ida Hamilton Walker thumbing her nose at injustice. I couldn't. And I couldn't ignore my suspicion either.

I keyed my radio. "Sandy, this is Amos. You still there? Over."

"Amos, this is base. I'm here. Jess's working late. Over."

"I need a location for Wolfman Washington. And a cell number if he's got one. Over."

"Wolfman? What'd he do?"

"Nothing yet."

But I was willing to bet money that if Ida had gotten her infamous Foo Club together for another job that Wolfman would be right in the thick of it. Wolfman was part of the crew who removed (stole) the Governor's fancy new town welcome sign with its progressive, politically-correct, campaign-appropriate slogan.

Governor Ham Bigelow had family connections in Mossy Creek — embarrassing connections to his way of thinking, so he thought the new sign would "spruce us up for company." Ida's nephew might be Governor and he might be eyeing a run for the White House, but she was not amused. Neither was the town.

We liked our town slogan just fine — *Ain't going nowhere and don't want to.* We liked the fact that it was painted on a silo. We didn't want a new sign. When Ham wouldn't back down, Ida dealt with the problem directly.

Unfortunately, she was too direct. She got a shotgun and calmly blew his sign to kingdom come. I arrested her. Court-ordered, anger-management class simply gave her the opportunity to band together with other like-minded individuals and pad her criminal resume. The Foo Club was born, and Colonel Del Jackson walked into Ida's life.

Ham's replacement sign didn't fare well either. That was the stolen one.

The radio crackled. Sandy gave me Wolfman's number. I dialed. To my surprise, Wolfman answered.

No, Ida hadn't called him yesterday or today. No, he wasn't planning anything with Ida. No, he wouldn't tell me if he was.

I didn't really expect him to. All I wanted was a chance to hear his voice. Most people don't answer the phone if they're skulking around, about to make trouble. Plus most people can't fake bewildered with any degree of believability. Wolfman was out of the loop. He didn't have the faintest idea what I was talking about, and he was ticked.

The Foo Club might be Ida's, but Del Jackson and Wolfman were her lieutenants. Wolfman didn't know. So far so good. Oh, Ida was still planning trouble, but maybe . . . just maybe, she was acting alone this time. So I risked one more call to Sandy.

"Sandy, this is Amos. Over."

"Go, Chief. Over."

"Is Del Jackson in town?"

Silence answered me for several seconds, until Sandy replied. "No, sir. Over."

I'd have given a week's pay to see her face as she tried to work out what was going on. She wouldn't. Oh, she'd come up with the Foo Club, but she couldn't work it any further than that. I doubted anyone but me knew that Ida had gone to Jeb's grave to ask his blessing.

Not for Del.

For a small act of civil disobedience.

The first realization relieved me. The second had me reaching for Tums and doing the math one last time.

Ida asking for Jeb's blessing. Ida blowing off a council meeting. Someone developing a meadow in Bailey Mill. The developer needing to bulldoze a big tree to level the site. The Sitting Tree was in Bailey Mill. Jeb Walker kissed Ida the first time under that tree.

I knew that because one night a long time ago, I'd headed for the Sitting Tree to drown my sorrows of lost grid iron glory in a purloined six-pack and found a young widow, holding on to memories and trying to come to grips with raising a young boy alone.

Ida wasn't about to let the Sitting Tree go softly into that good night. Which meant I had to go talk a woman down from a tree.

🍂🍂🍂

I hate being right. Ida's empty car sat near the road. She hadn't tried to drive it up to the tree. I parked behind her and grabbed the leather backpack from the seat beside me. Night wasn't full dark yet; it was getting there. Cooling down. The rain had taken a lot of heat out of the day.

About halfway to the tree, I thought I saw someone scurrying around the base. I heard clinking.

Within hailing distance, I announced myself. "Settle down, Ida. It's Amos."

Clank.

"Of course it is!" Frustration rolled down the slope with her words. The lady wasn't happy.

I liked that. After the morning's wake-up call in the cemetery, I'd decided that the days of our polite, subtle conversations were gone. It was time to get off the bench and in the game. I was about to put the Sunday comics in Ida's cage and ruffle her feathers.

When I stopped about ten feet away, she said, "I thought you'd be in uniform."

"Not my jurisdiction." I'd stopped by the house on the way to grab my favorite old pair of jeans, boots, and a denim jacket. I expected the night to be long and cold; I wanted to at least be comfortable. "I thought you'd be in the tree. Or at least attached to it."

"I wasn't expecting you so soon." She gestured to the motley collection of chains intended to loop around her waist and the tree. "I haven't quite got this figured out yet. And speaking of that! How on earth did you figure it out so fast?"

"You pay me to figure things out, Ida. I'm the chief, remember?"

"I'm beginning to regret that."

"You have not yet begun to regret that. Sit down, Ida."

She sputtered for a minute, but when I ignored her and grabbed a patch of ground, she sat down as well, about six inches away, eyeing the backpack as I unslung it from my shoulder.

"Want a beer?"

"Love one."

"Thought you might. Civil disobedience is thirsty work. But you'd better make it last. I only brought two."

I popped a top and handed it over, then grabbed one myself. Ida fiddled with the aluminum ring on the lid, twisting it off. Having it gave her something to do. She flipped the ring end over end. "If this isn't your jurisdiction, why are you here?"

"You're here."

The ring stopped flipping. I smiled into my beer and said nothing.

"You're not going to try and talk me out of this?"

"Not at the moment."

"Good." Then she added, "Well, that's settled."

It wasn't, but I let it go and changed the subject. "This morning why'd you think I was slogging through my appointed rounds?"

That made her laugh. She pulled her legs up to her chest and rested her arms on her knees, one hand dangling the still nearly full can. She had on jogging pants and a long sleeved sweatshirt from the reunion — complete with gypsy image and the words, *Fergit hell!*

"I think you and Battle still haven't settled your issues. Until then the cemetery's always going to be a chore. Something you have to do because you don't know how not to do it."

"That obvious?"

"Probably not to everyone."

"Well, that's comforting."

"Hey, I'm a full-service mayor. We aim to please."

"I hear Dwight's none too pleased at the moment."

Ida shrugged. "He'll forget it all when he wins his race. If I didn't say it out loud before, you were right. We weren't giving Dwight a chance or appreciating that someone has to be Dwight, ask the hard questions, push us."

"You're welcome." I didn't know I was smug until the back of her hand connected with my biceps.

"Do not sound righteous! I do not need another Jiminy Cricket chirping at me. Jeb's already got that job."

"Does he approve of this?" I didn't need to explain. *This* was the big tree looming over us and the yards of chain in front of us.

She patted the tree. "Most definitely. Too many memories here. For the whole town. In Memphis, everyone has a story of how they met Elvis or has a cousin who met Elvis. In Mossy Creek everyone has a story about this old lady. Chopping her down would be criminal."

"I thought maybe this was a little more personal. That for once this was for Ida and not the town."

Even through the dark, I knew the moment she remembered I was probably one of only a few people in Mossy Creek who'd ever seen her cry. She went still. "Oh."

"Yeah. Oh. Ida, if the tree goes, your life is still here. It doesn't disappear with the tree. You don't have to stop being that Ida."

When she didn't answer, I figured I might as well confess something. It was only fair. "You know something else? This morning I thought you were asking Jeb's blessing on Del." I drained the rest of my beer. "I didn't like that."

That startled her. Or maybe made her more wary. "Why?"

I looked at her sideways. "Ida, I think it's time we stopped pretending that you're the mayor and I'm the chief. Or that that's all we are."

A speechless Ida Hamilton Walker is a sight to behold. I don't know that I could make out terror in the dark, but I do think Ida was shaking in her boots. I'd put some cards on the table and crossed that line. Now she was going to have to hold or fold.

I took the beer can from her and drained the last bit onto the ground before putting both cans in my pack, fishing out my flashlight, and heaving myself up. "If you ask me,

Ida, you've got some thinking to do and this tree's an excellent place to do it."

Three steps away and I heard her say, "I asked Jeb about Del a long time ago."

Without turning, I asked, "What'd he say?"

"Nothing."

I didn't react outwardly, but my heart hit one hard beat. I turned around and tried to sound sincere. "Too bad for Del. Seemed like such a good fit, too. Good man. Right age."

"Bingo." Ida thought that would settle everything. Poor woman. I'd come prepared.

I took a second to sling the pack more comfortably over my shoulder. "I heard something interesting on CNN Health News the other day." She saw the trap yawning in front of her. "They say forty-five's the new thirty. Let me see . . ." I pretended to do math in my head. "That'd put you at just about the right age for me."

Without waiting for an answer I walked away, but over my shoulder I told her, "I'll be back tomorrow morning, Ida. And if you're still here protecting that tree, we're going to have that talk. So you'd best decide if you want to hang on to the past enough to risk looking at the future."

🌿🌿🌿

I didn't expect Ida to be there the next morning.

I hate it when I'm right.

She wasn't there, but she certainly hadn't abandoned the tree. Oh, no. Not Ida. Her cohorts in crime surrounded the tree, and judging from their positions, I'd say the Foo Club was chained to it as well. Nail Delgado flashed me a peace sign. Wolfman waved. And the girl between them pointed to her sign. "Free the Sitting Tree."

I suspected they would.

Mossy Creek Gazette

215 Main Street • Mossy Creek, GA 30533

From the desk of Katie Bell

Lady Victoria Salter Stanhope
The Cliffs
Seaward Road
St. Ives, Cornwall, TR3 7PJ
United Kingdom

Dear Vick:

See what I mean about crying and smiling at the same time? All in all, it's been a good autumn, and I consider my *Blessings Of Mossy Creek* columns a success. Maybe I'll ask Sue Ora to nominate them for next year's newspaper awards.

As for me, it's time to settle in for the holidays and the winter ahead. But don't you worry — I'm not resting on my award-winning laurels. I'm already on the trail of some old melodramas and the new ones, too. In the meantime, you didn't think I'd forget to send you some more of Win Allen's *Bubba Rice* recipes, did you? After all, what would a long, cold winter be like without a taste of Mossy Creek to keep the world warm?

Until next time,

Katie

Bubba's Pork Tenderloin

A lesson in the manly Southern art of barbeque technique . Okay, you've all heard my rants about the fact that pork is barbeque, everything else is just grilled, right? The key here is *low* temperature over a charcoal grill. You can use a gas grill. Just don't tell me about it, okay?

Ingredients:

2 pounds pork tenderloin

1 cup apple cider vinegar

2 tbsp. extra virgin olive oil

2 tbsp. fresh lemon juice (orange juice works well, too)

1 tsp. lemon pepper

1 tsp. garlic powder

1 tsp. finely chopped fresh cilantro

Dipping sauce

1/2 cup soy sauce	1 tbsp. sugar
1/2 cup chopped red onion	1/2 tbsp. red wine vinegar
2 cloves garlic, minced	2 tbsp. fresh lemon juice
1 tsp. fresh ginger root, minced	

Preparation:

Mix the apple cider vinegar, olive oil, lemon juice, cilantro, lemon pepper and garlic powder and pour over the pork tenderloins in a large plastic freezer bag and seal. Marinate for the hour that it takes your charcoal fire to get ready for cooking (around 275 degrees). Place the tenderloins on the grill. Do not put them directly over the coals for the first hour. Turn after 30 minutes, and again 30 minutes later. After the second turn, place the tenderloins over the coals. Turn again after 15 minutes and cook for another 15 minutes, then remove. Total cooking time should be around 90 minutes. About 15 minutes after removing the tenderloins from the grill, slice into medallions about 1/2" inch thick.

Dipping sauce preparation:

Combine the ingredients in a blender or food processor and puree for 30 seconds. Refrigerate until ready to serve. Pour about half the sauce over the tenderloin slices and save the rest for dipping.

Serves 4

Dressed-up Mashed Potatoes

A fun variation on the twice-baked potato . . .

Ingredients:

6 large red potatoes	6 strips of bacon
8 ounces of fresh sour cream	4 tbsp. butter
1 bunch of green onions	

Preparation:

Peel and slice the potatoes and boil until fork tender, then drain well. Fry the bacon until crisp and save the drippings. Chop the green onions and sauté in the bacon drippings. Mash the potatoes, then add the remaining ingredients and blend well. Once blended, I usually use a hand mixer to smooth it out (I know that some of you consider it a sacrilege to use a mixer on mashed potatoes, but it gives it a much better consistency, so get over it, okay?). Spoon the mixture into a large casserole dish and bake uncovered at 350 degrees for 20 minutes.   Serves 6

Bubba's Dump Cake

Okay, I know there's at least ten different punch lines to that one, but really . . .

Ingredients:

One 24.5 ounce can of cling peaches in heavy syrup

1/2 cup blueberries

1/2 cup chopped pecans

1 package yellow cake mix (you pick the brand)

1/2 cup butter, melted

Preparation:

In a 9 x 13 inch pan, mix the peaches and the blueberries. Sprinkle the dry cake mix over the fruit, then stir lightly. Sprinkle with chopped pecans, then drizzle the top with the melted butter. Bake at 350 degrees for 35-40 minutes or until golden brown on top.

Now, aren't you ashamed for what you were thinking when you heard the name?   Serves 12

Mossy Creek Summer Salad

A nice, cool treat for a summer meal . . . and easy, too.

Ingredients:
2 cucumbers
2 ripe avocados
1 medium sized red onion
8 ounces Newman's Own Family Recipe Italian dressing

Preparation:
Peel and slice the cucumbers. Halve, pit, peel and dice the avocados. Thin slice and quarter the onion. Combine all the prepared ingredients into a large salad bowl and toss with the Newman's Own dressing. Take my advice on this one . . . don't try substituting your store brand dressing for the Newman's Own. It just won't be the same salad without it.

Some hints on preparation . . .
Here's a neat trick on how to pit an avocado. Slice the avocado lengthwise and twist the two halves to separate. Take the half that has the pit and place it in on a cutting board. Using a heavy knife, make a light chopping motion into the pit, then turn the knife blade (clockwise, counter clockwise, it really doesn't matter). The pit will turn with the knife blade and come out easily. Much easier than trying to scoop that sucker out with a spoon, huh?

Serves 6-8

The Mossy Creek Storytelling Club

(In order of appearance)

Martha Shields .... Harry Rutherford

Berta Platas .... Argelia Rodriguez, Ezekial Straley

Susan Goggins .... John Wesley McCready

Virginia Ellis .... Michael Conners, Jasmine Beleau
Nancy Bainbridge, Patty English

Gayle Trent ....Sugar Jean Cole

Lillian Richey .... Trisha Peavy Cecil

Martha Kirkland .... Polly Varner

Rita Herron .... Shirley Stancil

Karen White .... Sammie Louise Pritchard

Missy Tippens .... Mark and Amelia Phillips

Chloe Mitchell .... Isaac and Nancy Daniel

Sandra Chastain .... Katie Bell
Hank, Casey & Li Hai Kui Blackshear

Debra Dixon .... Amos Royden

Coming soon from BelleBooks...

All God's Creatures

by Carolyn McSparren

The story of a Memphis Cotton Carnival Princess who gave up her debutante throne to become a large animal veterinarian.

Mother's reaction to my announcement that I was changing my name and planning to become a veterinarian was typical.

"Don't be ridiculous, Margaret," she said. "Nice girls do not become veterinarians. And Maggie sounds like an Irish washerwoman."

In my previous attempts to break out of the mold she kept trying to force me into, I had meekly gone back to being a nice obedient daughter and relinquished my goals.

Not this time. Mother took to sighing deeply and casting her eyes to heaven every time I mentioned anything about Dr. Parmenter or vet school.

She even enlisted a couple of her Junior League buddies to 'counsel' me.

I never answered back or argued. I simply smiled and signed up for more chemistry classes. Now, that really infuriated her.

By the end of that August I had endured summer courses in biology and chemistry in un-air-conditioned classrooms, and nearly died of asphyxiation. The straight A's kept Mother's disapproval at bay, but only barely. She had retrenched, and was now suggesting that I become a nurse. Then I could marry a doctor.

Dr. Parmenter never questioned me about my plans, although I was up to working four afternoons a week and all day Saturday for him. I had also graduated to doing most of his anesthesia and was learning how to stitch up wounds on old innertubes.

One hot afternoon as he finished neutering a tabby cat, he looked over those glasses at me and asked, "Well, do you really want to do it?"

I nodded. I knew what he was talking about although we had never actually discussed my becoming a veterinarian.

"They won't like it," he said, and clipped the last suture.

"If you mean my parents, they already don't like it."

He pulled off his gloves, balled them up and tossed them overhanded like a basketball into the waste receptacle in the corner. "Goal." Then he turned to me and sighed. "Assuming you get into vet school, and that's a mighty tall assumption, your professors won't like it, your colleagues won't like it, and if you should graduate, a great many potential clients won't like it."

These days more than half the graduating veterinarians in this country are women. I truly think that when the men discovered the pay was lousy, the hours and conditions frequently frightful, and nobody appreciated them, they fled to more lucrative pastures like people medicine and left the field open for the girls. They have dashed through joyfully.

But not then. There were women vets, of course, but more up north than in the mid-south. Tennessee didn't yet have its own vet school, so that meant I'd have to vie for a place at Auburn or Alabama or Mississippi State. Against all their native good ole boys.

"Why should they care?" I asked. Because I spent twelve years in a girls' school environment, I had never worried about competition with males, and Southwestern at that time demanded good brains from both genders that attended.

He lifted one scrawny hip onto the edge of the examining table and clicked off the reasons on his fingers.

"Your professors will not wish to waste their time teaching you as you will undoubtedly get married, quit the profession and raise babies."

I snorted.

"Your male colleagues will dislike you because you are taking a place that should have gone to a man. Your female colleagues will resent you because they wish to be queen bees. Finally, your potential clients will think you're incapable of being as good a vet as a man, particularly if you should decide to treat large animals as well as small."

"So I'm doomed?"

He shook his head. "Indeed not. I saw the lust in your eyes five minutes after you walked into my surgery with your pup. I have since discovered you have an excellent brain, good manual dexterity, a complete lack of fear of animals— which will get you into trouble one day if you don't watch it—and a considerable amount of brawn for a woman. If you continue to be serious and to make the grade both in school and here, then when the time comes, I will get you into Mississippi State."

"Right. You and what army, Dr. Parmenter?"

"I, Miss Maggie, am an army." With that he turned around and walked out.

He was, too.

I have never known exactly how he cajoled and browbeat Mississippi State. I suspect there was an element of blackmail. He's the reason I can add D. V. M. to my name. I can never repay him.

But every life I save, every cripple I mend, even the animals in pain that I release from suffering, are tiny installments on the debt.

The Mossy Creek Hometown Series

Welcome to Mossy Creek, where you'll find a friendly face at every window and a heartfelt story behind every door.

Award-winning authors Deborah Smith, Sandra Chastain, Debra Dixon, Virginia Ellis, Nancy Knight and Donna Ball (*Sweet Tea And Jesus Shoes*) now blend their unique voices in a collective novel about the South, the first in a series set in the fictional mountain town of Mossy Creek, Georgia.

So welcome to Mossy Creek, the town that insists it "Ain't goin' nowhere, and don't want to." Welcome Home.

MOSSY CREEK

The first book in the series introduces a mayor who sees breaking the law as her civic duty and a by-the-books police chief trying to live up to his father's legend. We've got a bittersweet feud at the coffee shop and heartwarming battles on the softball field. We've got a world-weary Santa with a poignant dream and a flying Chihuahua with a streak of bad luck. You'll meet Millicent, who believes in stealing joy, and the outrageous patrons of O'Day's Pub, who believe there's no such thing as an honest game of darts. You'll want to tune your radio to the Bereavement Report and prop your feet up at Mama's All You Can Eat Café. While you're there, say hello to our local gossip columnist, Katie Bell. She'll make you feel like one of the family and tell you a story that will make you laugh — or smile through your tears.

"A sweeter, smoother-edged American South beckons! Conjures up the comfortable if ornery charms of a legendary culture."
—Publishers Weekly

Deborah Smith   Sandra Chastain
Donna Ball   Debra Dixon
Nancy Knight   Virginia Ellis

REUNION AT MOSSY CREEK

Deborah Smith Sandra Chastain Debra Dixon
Virginia Ellis Martha Shields Nancy Knight
Carolyn McSparren Sharon Sala Dee Sterling
Carmen Greene

This time around they've got the added drama of the big town reunion commemorating the twenty-year-old mystery of the late, great Mossy Creek High School, which burned to the ground amid quirky rumors and dark secrets.

In the meantime, sassy 100-year-old Creekite Eula Mae Whit is convinced Williard Scott has put a death curse on her, and Mossy Creek Police Chief Amos Royden is still fighting his reputation as the town's most eligible bachelor. Then there's the new bad girl in town, Jasmine, and more adventures from the old bad girl in town, Mayor Ida Hamilton. And last but not least, Bob the flying Chihuahua finds himself stalked by an amorous lady poodle.

SUMMER IN MOSSY CREEK

It's a typical summer in the good-hearted mountain town of Mossy Creek, Georgia, where love, laughter and friendship make nostalgia a way of life. Creekites are always ready for a sultry romance, a funny feud or a sincere celebration, and this summer is no different. Get ready for a comical battle over pickled beets and a spy mission to recover hijacked chow-chow peppers. Meet an unforgettable parakeet named Tweedle Dee and a lovable dog named Dog. Watch Amos and Ida sidestep the usual rumors and follow Katie Bell's usual snooping. In the meantime, old-timer Opal Suggs and her long-dead sisters share a lesson on living, and apple farmer Hope Bailey faces poignant choices when an old flame returns to claim her.